Praise for

C.E. MURPHY

and The Walker Papers series:

Urban Shaman

"A swift pace, a good mystery, a likeable protagonist,
magic, danger—*Urban Shaman* has them in spades."
—Jim Butcher, bestselling author of The Dresden Files series

Thunderbird Falls

"Fans of Jim Butcher's Dresden Files novels and the works
of urban fantasists Charles de Lint and Tanya Huff should
enjoy this fantasy/mystery's cosmic elements. A good choice."
—Library Journal

Coyote Dreams

"Tightly written and paced, [*Coyote Dreams*] has a
compelling, interesting protagonist, whose struggles and
successes will captivate new and old readers alike."
—RT Book Reviews

Walking Dead

"Murphy's fourth Walker Papers offering is another gripping,
well-written tale of what must be the world's most reluctant—
and stubborn—shaman."
—RT Book Reviews

Demon Hunts

"Murphy carefully crafts her scenes
and I felt every gust of wind through the crispy frosted trees....
I am heartily looking forward to further volumes."
—The Discriminating Fangirl

Spirit Dances

"An original and addictive urban fantasy!"
—Romancing the Darkside

C.E. MURPHY

RAVEN CALLS

LUNA™

LUNA™

RAVEN CALLS

ISBN-13: 978-0-373-80343-9

This one's for my Mom, Rosie Murphy,
because it's the rest of the story

CHAPTER ONE

Sunday, March 19, 9:53 a.m.

The werewolf bite on my forearm itched.

Itching was wrong. It wasn't old enough to itch. It should hurt like the dickens, because I'd obtained it maybe six hours earlier. Instead it itched like it was a two-week-old injury, well on the way to healing.

Only I was quite sure it wasn't healing. For one thing, I kept peeking at it, and it was still a big nasty slashy bite that oozed blood when the bandages were loosened. For another thing, my stock in trade was healing. Fourteen months, two weeks and three days ago—but who was counting?—I had been stabbed through the chest. A smart-ass coyote—kinda my spirit guide—had given me a choice between dying or becoming a shaman. Even for someone with no use for the esoteric, like I'd been, it hadn't been much of a choice. So now, nearly fifteen months on, a bite on my forearm was something I really should be able to deal with.

And it wasn't that I hadn't tried healing it, because I had. Magic slid off like oil and water, or possibly more like oil and gashed flesh, if oil slid off gashed flesh, which I assumed it did but didn't want to actually find out. Either way, the magic wasn't working. Normally that would be a bad sign, but my talent had taken both a beating and a boosting in the past twenty-four hours, and wasn't behaving. It reacted explosively when I tried using it, and I didn't want to explode my arm. So I was getting on a plane with absolutely no notice and flying to Ireland, because I'd had a vision of the woman who had turned werewolves from slavering beasties 100% of the time into part-time monsters, and in my vision, she'd been in Ireland. I figured if anybody could keep me human, it had to be the woman who'd bound the wolves to the moon's cycle.

That's what I was telling myself, anyway, because it was slightly better than a full-on panic attack in the middle of the Seattle-Tacoma Airport. A day earlier I hadn't believed werewolves existed. Now I was petrified that come the next full moon—which was tonight, the second of three—I would get all hairy and toothy. It was a dire possibility even without adding international air travel to the mix, which, who was I kidding, was possibly the worst idea I'd ever had. Turning into a werewolf was potentially bad enough. Doing it mid-flight presumably meant a plane full of handy victims, although I might get lucky and have an air marshal on board so it would just be me who got dead.

My life was a mess, if I considered that lucky. But I had this rash idea that because I'd be missing moonrise all the way around the globe, the magic shouldn't trigger. And I could always lock myself in the bathroom if I thought I was about to get bestial. Locking myself in the bathroom wasn't that bad an idea anyway. I was afraid of flying, and bathrooms didn't have windows. That automatically made them less scary than the body of the plane. Either way, it wasn't just the werewolf cure that had me wandering the duty-free shops at SeaTac. The *other* vision I'd had, the one of a sneering warrior woman, had made my healing magic respond as if a gauntlet had been thrown down. It felt like fishhooks in my belly, hauling me east. I was going to Ireland whether I liked it or not.

My personal opinion leaned heavily toward *or not*. There were places I'd rather be and things I'd rather be doing. Specifically, those things were Captain Michael Morrison of the Seattle Police Department, who up to about three hours earlier had been my boss. I'd quit, he'd kissed me and the more I thought about him, the more I wanted to tear out of the airport, jump in a cab and race back into his arms. The fishhooks pulling at my gut, though, weren't about to let that happen. Their horrible prickle and tug had become familiar enough over the past year that I knew it meant something serious coming down the line, as if finding a cure for a werewolf's bite wasn't serious enough. Whatever awaited me in Ireland, I was not especially looking forward to it. So I was trying to distract myself by shopping, which wasn't my favorite pastime in the best of circumstances. Still, I'd wandered the international terminal twice already. The shops hadn't changed displays since my first pass, but the second time through I laid eyes on something I neither needed at all, nor was I sure I could live without.

A not-helpful part of my brain whispered that I had a credit card. I mean, I was American. I didn't think I'd be allowed to keep my citizenship if I didn't have at least one rectangle of plastic money. But it was reserved for emergencies, like buying a plane ticket to Ireland on no notice.

An ankle-length white leather coat did not in any way qualify as an emergency.

I stood there staring at it through the shop window. The shoulders were subtly padded, just enough to give the mannequin a really square silhouette. It had a Chinese-style high collar and leather-covered white buttons offset from the center straight down the length of the entire coat. It nipped in at the waist tightly enough to look pinned, but nobody would pin leather of that quality. There had to be a discreet belt on the back. Its skirts fell in wide loose folds, and looked like they would flare with wonderful drama.

No normal person would wear a coat like that. A movie star might. A *tall* movie star. A tall, leggy movie star with really good sunglasses and enough confidence to shift the earth with her smile alone.

I stepped back from the window. Light caught just so, letting me see my reflection.

Nobody could argue that, at a smidge under six feet in height, I wasn't tall and leggy. I had cool sunglasses, although I wasn't wearing them. And that coat might instill enough confidence in the wearer that she could do anything.

Five minutes later I was eighteen hundred dollars poorer, but so pleased with myself I slept the whole flight to Ireland without once worrying about the plane falling out of the sky.

Monday, March 20, 6:28 a.m.

I wasn't a werewolf when I woke up. Fuzzy logic said I'd left the States on Sunday morning, flown all day and arrived in Ireland early Monday morning, thus having skipped the night of the full moon entirely and saving myself from shifting into a monster of yore. That was *very* fuzzy logic, but then, the whole not being a werewolf thing supported it. Besides, who was I to say an ancient curse *wouldn't* work that way, when magic by its very definition defied the laws of physics. I left the plane grateful to not be furry and, aware of the advantages of having been born in Ireland, slipped through customs on the European Union passport holders side.

The insistent ball of magic within me wanted me to head west, but Irish roads were legendarily convoluted. I needed a car, a map and a cup of coffee before I struck off into the sunset. Never mind that sun*rise* was in about half an hour, so I had many hours to wait before I could strike off into its sister darkness.

For a woman who'd slept the entire ten-hour flight across a continent and an ocean, I was certainly running on at the brain. I stopped just outside the arrivals area and scrubbed both hands over my face hard, trying to waken some degree of native intelligence.

"Hey, doll," said a familiar voice. "Can I give you a lift?"

I left my hands where they were, covering my face, for a good long minute while I tried to understand how that voice— the voice of my best friend, a seventy-four-year-old Seattle cab driver—could possibly be addressing me in the Dublin International Airport. Last I'd known, Gary Muldoon had been in California for the St. Patrick's Day weekend, partying with old Army buddies in a yearly event he refused to give details on. Since it was now the twentieth of March and the weekend in question had just ended, my information was pretty up-to-date. It was therefore impossible in every way for Gary to be here. It had to be somebody else. Satisfied with my reasoning, I lowered my fingers enough to peer over them.

Gary leaned against a pillar, arms folded across his still-broad chest, and gave me a wink and a grin that from a man thirty years younger would set my heart aflutter.

I rubbed my eyes again and squinted. Gary's grin got wider. He looked like a devilish old movie star in a set scene, and like he knew damned good and well his presence was the culminating factor. After about thirty seconds' more silence, I said, "Sure," and wished I'd been suave enough to just say that in the first place. And then because I wasn't suave at all, I squeaked, "What the hell are you doing here?!" in disbelieving delight.

Gary threw his head back and laughed out loud. He had suspiciously good teeth for a man his age who used to smoke. I suspected dentures, but had never been rude enough to ask. Then he stepped forward and swept me up in a bear hug, which put paid to any thoughts of his teeth as I grunted happily and repeated, "No, seriously, what the hell?"

"Mike called me. Told me to, and I quote, get my old ass on the next flight to Dublin and try to catch up to Joanne goddamned Walker, who's gone off again and needs somebody to keep her from doing anything stupid, end quote. So I got on the next flight outta L.A. Got in ten minutes ago. What's going on?"

I pulled my head back far enough to look up at him. "Mike? Mike who? You mean *Morrison?* Morrison called you? Morrison sent you to Ireland after me? Morrison, my boss? That Morrison?"

"That's the one." Gary set me back, hands on my shoulders, as his grin faded. "'Cept I hear he ain't the boss anymore."

"Not the boss of me, anyway." I wrinkled my nose. "I'm not six, really."

"What happened, doll?" Real concern was in my big friend's gray eyes. I'd gotten into Gary's cab over a year ago, on the very morning my shamanic powers had been violently awakened. He'd been at my side, backing me up, ever since. Gary was the sort of person I wanted to grow old to be: vital, fascinated by the world and always up for an adventure. At twenty-six, when I'd met him, I'd been none of those things. At pushing twenty-eight I was just getting on the bandwagon. I couldn't have a better role model.

"It's okay, I quit. I mean, I didn't get fired. Everything's cool. I just…" It turned out I had other things to not think about besides a werewolf bite. The enormity of what I'd done—quit my detective job on the police force with no notice and with no prospects for other employment in the future—hit me, a mere twelve hours after the fact. Or a full day, counting elapsed travel time. Either way, I felt myself go colorless and the insistent pit of magic in my belly turned to just a boring old pit of sickness for a moment.

Gary put a hand under one of my elbows and crooked a smile. "Don't worry, Joanie. I can always get you a job at Tripoli Cabs."

If Gary was calling me Joanie, I looked even worse than I suddenly felt. Usually he went with Jo, a nickname I'd never liked until he used it. Still, rough laughter bubbled up from somewhere beneath the ook in my tummy. "Petite would never forgive me if I took to driving another car most of the day."

"You better not tell her 'bout your plans to get a winter vehicle, then."

"She'd understand," I said unconvincingly. "Classic Mustangs aren't meant to weather the winters Seattle's been having lately. She's got no clearance. I'll just get her a boyfriend. A 1936 Dodge pickup. In red."

"They got no clearance, either, darlin'," Gary said with the confidence of a man who'd been there and done that, never mind that he'd been only four years old in 1936. "'Sides, you get that sweet young thing an old fella like a '36 Dodge and you'll start giving me ideas."

Laughter won again, this time because half the people I knew were convinced I had a Thing going on with Gary. Even Morrison thought so, despite it being fairly clear that I was hopelessly, idiotically, madly in love with him. "Petite's older than I am," I pointed out, like it made a difference.

"And I'm older than a '36 Dodge. You all right, Joanie?"

"Stop that. It makes me think I'm falling apart."

"Are you?"

"A w—" I nearly swallowed my tongue. I hadn't even told Morrison a werewolf had bitten me, and there I was about to confess all to Gary. It wasn't that I didn't feel like sharing. Mostly I just figured they couldn't do anything about it, so there was no point in worrying them. I said, "A wee little bit," instead, in honor of being in Ireland, where one adjective was never enough if three would do. "It's been a really long day. Weekend. You missed a lot."

Childish dismay splashed across Gary's face. "One weekend, Jo! I went to California for one weekend, and you had to have adventures without me?"

"You have no idea. I can shapeshift now," I said almost idly. The weird thing was, learning to shapeshift really did come low on the totem pole of what had gone on the past three days. No wonder I'd slept so hard on the plane. I was pretty sure the last time I'd napped had been in the shower a couple of days earlier.

Gary's eyes bugged and he pointed imperiously to the door. "We gotta get out of here so you can show me."

A tug in my gut wiped away the last of my job-related nausea. My boiling-over magic thought getting out of there was an excellent idea. We made mad rushes for different car rental agencies, eyeing each other to see whose line moved more quickly. I beat Gary to a counter by thirty seconds, and he came to loom over me as I filled out paperwork. "Second driver?" the woman asked, and Gary muttered, "Don't you dare think I ain't doin' some of the driving, Jo."

I obediently put him down as the second driver. He snagged the keys out from under my fingertips and in retaliation I grabbed his carry-on suitcase as well as my own. He looked ever so slightly smug and I suspected I had gotten the raw end of the deal, but he flashed me another one of his legendary grins. "Hey, Jo?"

I muttered, "What?" about as graciously as an angry alligator, and the big lug of an old man earned a lifetime's forgiveness with two words as we headed out the door:

"Nice coat."

CHAPTER TWO

The last time I'd been in Ireland—also the first time, over-looking the detail of having been born here, which I didn't remember—I'd had none of the phenomenal cosmic powers I was now endowed with. Part of me wanted to trigger the Sight and look into the depths of history and magic the island was legendary for.

The much smarter part of me didn't want to, since I'd stolen the keys back and was driving. The Sight had been whiting out and blinding me for the past twenty-four hours. Driving blind seemed like a spectacularly bad idea. So instead of calling up the mystical mojo, I filled Gary in on the weekend's details while we worked our way through Dublin traffic, which was negligible compared to Seattle. By the time I got to the were-wolves, we'd left the capital city behind, and Gary kept saying, "Werewolves," in audible disappointment. "Werewolves. I'm never around for the good stuff."

"Says the man who left an annual shindig to fly last-minute to Ireland."

"I couldn't risk missin' something else, now, could I?" Gary peered out the window. In theory there were green rolling hills out there. In reality, there were concrete walls fifteen feet high that blocked off the countryside. "Where we goin', anyway?"

"The Hill of Tara." I knew almost as much about Irish history as I'd known about shamanism a year ago, which was to say nothing, but even I'd heard of Tara. I scowled at the road, trying to remember if I'd gotten that far in what I'd told Gary. "It's in County Meath, which is sort of the wrong way, more north than west, and I keep feeling like I need to go west. But I had a vision last night. Or the night before. Saturday night. Anyway, I saw a hill in the vision, so Tara seems like a good place to start."

"What with bein' a hill and all," Gary agreed solemnly.

I said, "Exactly," even though I knew perfectly well I was being mocked. Gary laughed and I gave him a dirty look. "Besides, starting with a known cultural and spiritual center probably isn't a bad idea, even if it's the wrong one. Did I tell you about the woman wearing my mother's necklace?"

Gary arched his bushy eyebrows, which I took as a no, and I asked, "You ever get the feeling your life is a string festooned with bells and tied to hundreds of others you don't know anything about? And that sometimes somebody pulls their string, and your bells ring?"

Gary looked at me a long moment before rather gently saying, "Yes and no, darlin'. We all get that feeling from time to time. Difference is, with you, it could be real."

"But Coyote said I was a new soul. Mixed up fresh." I wasn't sure I'd ever mentioned that to Gary. Or to anybody else, for that matter. There were, according to my mentor, old souls and new souls. Mostly people were old souls, with all the baggage and all the wisdom from previous incarnations resting somewhere in the hind brain, there to draw on or drown in. I was something of a rarity, mixed up fresh and new by Somebody or Something responsible for those aspects of the universe. The positive side of being a new soul was a lack of baggage and the potential for great power. The negative side was the corresponding lack of accumulated wisdom with which to wield that power. I'd certainly demonstrated that lack time and again the past fifteen months.

Either I'd mentioned the whole new-soul thing to Gary, or he thought it didn't matter, because he snorted. "So what if you are? New soul don't mean no ties. You still got parents, right? Grandparents? Cousins? And friends or lovers can tug your strings, too. No man's an island, Jo."

That was not the first time Gary had gone philosophical on me, nor was it the first time I was surprised by it. Properly chastened, I swallowed and continued my original line of thought: "The woman with my mother's necklace rang my be…" That sentence could not end anywhere happy. Gary guffawed and I grinned despite myself. "You know what I mean."

"I know Mike's gonna be real disappointed if some woman's ringing your bells, darlin'."

"When did you start calling him Mike?"

"After the zombies," Gary said with aplomb.

I cast a glance heavenward and nearly missed our exit. Gary grabbed his door's armrest as I yanked us into the right—which was to say, correct, which in on Irish roads meant left—lane, and muttered, "After the zombies. Of course. Normal people don't say things like that, Gary."

"Normal people don't fight zombies."

That line of conversation wasn't going to end anywhere

happy, either. I let out an explosive breath and tried again. "The woman in my mother's necklace had some kind of pull with me. Maybe it was just that she looked all sneery and challenging, but there was some kind of connection. I have to find out who she was."

Gary, cautiously, said, "It wasn't your mother, was it?"

"No. She kind of looked like her, dark hair, pale skin, but no. My mother was sort of restrained and prim. She liked Altoids. This woman was more of a kick ass and take names type." Only it had turned out my mother was exactly that kind of person, too. I just hadn't known it until after she died.

I hadn't known much of anything about my mother until after she died, except that she'd flown to America and left me with my father when I was six months old. I hadn't seen her again until I was twenty-six. That kind of thing leaves a mark. In my case, it was an entirely unjustified mark, as Mother had been trying to protect me from a bad guy bigger and nastier than I ever wanted to deal with. But again, I hadn't known that until after she died. Nothing like a little "I was trying to save your life" to take the wind out of sails puffed up with childish abandonment issues. I wished I'd had the opportunity to tell her I finally understood.

But that was spilt milk, and I was getting better about not crying over it. I turned down the road leading to Tara and Gary frowned as a tour bus taking up two-thirds of the road came the other direction. "You sure this is the right way?"

"Yeah. Only in Ireland do they put cultural heritage monuments at the end of one-track roads." I couldn't decide if I liked the idea or not. It certainly gave the impression the heritage site had been there forever, which was true. On the other hand, I had to hold my breath as I pulled over to let the bus pass, for fear we'd be broadsided if I didn't. Gary let his breath out in a rush when the bigger vehicle rambled by, and we grinned sheepishly at each other as I pulled forward again. "Glad it's not just me. At least we're not on a mountainside with roads this narrow. The landscape kind of reminds me of North Carolina."

"Never been out there," Gary said. "I kept getting stuck in St. Louis. Annie and I used to go to the jazz festival."

"Did you play?" Gary's wife had died before I met him, but he'd mentioned once or twice that he'd been an itinerant sax player for a few years after the Korean War, while Annie, a nurse, had brought home the bacon.

"Nah. Left that to the guys who were really good." Gary leaned into the window as we went up the hill leading to the, er, Hill, and frowned. "Thought there'd be more cars."

"Me, too." The parking lot—small and graveled and graced at one end by gift shops and at the other by a switchback path—was completely empty of vehicles besides our own. I got out of the car and turned in a slow circle, taking in the view—there was a tower in the distance, soft with misty air— and finally came back to Gary, who stood on the other side of our car with a befuddled expression. "You remember that night at the Seattle Center?"

"You mean the night somebody stuffed a broadsword through me? Nah. Why would I?"

"Remember how quiet it was?" The parking garage had been empty. There'd been no late-night tourists wandering, nobody from the monorail hurrying one way or the other, no joggers making their way across the closed grounds.

Gary, very firmly, said, "Jo, no matter how much I love you, I ain't gettin' stuck with another sword."

"Don't worry. I've got mine now." I patted my hip like I wore a sword there, which of course I didn't, because I lived in the early twenty-first century, not the early seventeenth.

Not that as a woman I'd have been able to carry a sword in the seventeenth century anyway, but that wasn't the point. The point was I had an honest-to-God magic sword that I'd taken off an ancient Celtic god, and I'd spent a good chunk of the past fifteen months learning how to use it properly. If anybody tried skewering Gary—or me, for that matter—I had defenses.

"Your sword's in Seattle."

I put on my very best mysterious magic user voice: "A detail which is nothing to one such as I." Gary snorted and I laughed, then waved at the path. "Come on, if we've got the place to ourselves we might as well take advantage of it. Busloads of tourists will probably show up any minute."

Gary fell in behind me dubiously. "You really think so?"

"No. I think something's conspiring to keep the place quiet awhile, and that we'll probably regret finding out why. But I'm trying to keep a positive mind-set." The path up to Tara was foot-worn but not paved. Nothing suggested "tourist attraction" except for the gift shops, and even they weren't particularly in-your-face about it. Gary and I kept pace with one another, both stealing glimpses at each other from the corners of our eyes like we expected something to jump out at us but if the other was cool, we weren't going to show our nerves. After the third or fourth time we caught gazes, Gary actually giggled, which was unnerving in itself. Six-foot-one former linebackers in their seventies weren't supposed to giggle.

A woman said, "There'll be nothing to worry about," out of nowhere, and we both shrieked like little girls. I regained my equilibrium first. Gary, after all, had already been giggling, which was bad enough with me as an audience, never mind with a complete stranger looking on. We turned together, though, to find a lovely woman of indeterminate age smiling at us. She wore a white eyelet-lace sundress with gold scarves wrapped around her hips and shoulders, and sandals on her feet. On most people I would call it a hippy-dippy look, but somehow she imbued it with more elegance than that. Her hair was the color of sunrise shot with clouds. She wasn't young, even if I couldn't tell how old she was.

"You'll be Siobhán Walkingstick," she said to me.

Hairs stood up on my arms. The bite itched, and I rubbed it surreptitiously, resulting in a wave of *oh god, scratching feels so good I may never be able to stop* that sometimes happens. I wondered suddenly if that was why dogs would go *thumpa-thumpa-thump* with a hind leg when a human got a good itchy spot, and then I wondered if, as a werewolf, I would do the same thing.

I stopped scratching and muttered, "People don't normally use that name for me. Who're you?"

"Am I wrong to think until very recently it wouldn't have been you at all?"

Another chill ran over me. I made fists to keep from scratching again. "…you're not wrong." The name she'd used, *Siobhán Walkingstick,* was technically the one I'd been born to. Siobhán Grainne MacNamarra Walkingstick. Dad had taken one look at that mess and nicknamed me Joanne. I'd dropped the Walkingstick myself, taking Walker as my mostly official last name when I graduated high school. Joanne Walker and Siobhán Walkingstick had almost nothing in common, at least not up until the past year. More specifically, up until two nights earlier, when I'd been reborn under a rattlesnake shapeshifter's guidance. That had a lot to do with why my powers were out-of-control wonky. Joanne had had a handle on her skill set. Siobhán apparently resided in another league. And I was going to have to stop thinking of them as separate or I'd become a headcase in no time flat.

"But you'll prefer *Joanne*," the woman said with a nod, then looked to Gary. "And you come with a companion."

Gary, who was rarely gruff, said, "Muldoon. Gary Muldoon," gruffly, and she inclined her head toward him.

"Are you here of your own free will, Mr. Muldoon? Will you be traveling the roads Joanne travels, walking beside her, or will you stand aside and let her pass where she must go alone?"

"I'm here, ain't I?"

The woman smiled. "So you are. Now there're two ways to approach the Hill. You might go the way everyone does, and see what they all see. Perhaps more," she added, giving me a significant look. "Perhaps not."

I was pretty sure I would See more than most people, assuming the Sight didn't knock me for another loop. I was equally sure strange women didn't show up to make portentous comments if they expected me to take the path more traveled by. It hadn't passed me by that she'd failed to say who she was, but I'd lay long odds she wouldn't even if I asked her again, so I just said, "What's the other way?" like a good little stage player.

She gestured to the rise of green grass behind her. "Pass through the Hall of Kings, and hear what secrets they might share with you."

"I didn't even know there *was* a Hall of Kings. I thought Tara was…" For once I shut up before I made a total fool of myself. Truth was, I hadn't really thought much at all about what Tara was or wasn't. I figured it was mystical. Druidic. Stuff like that. I hadn't considered that ordinary mortals might have passed this way, too, not that kings were exactly ordinary.

The woman's mouth quirked, which was nicer than her outright laughing at me. "Tara is where the ancient kings were crowned, Joanne. *Temair na Rí,* Hill of the Kings. Here they wedded Méabh to become *ard rí,* the high kings."

"What, all of them? Liberal sorts, weren't they?" That time my mouth should have shut up before it did.

The woman gave me a sort of weary look, the kind mothers bestow on precocious but irritating children. "Symbolically, Joanne. Symbolically. Méabh was—"

"No, wait, I know this one! She was a high queen, right? Kind of a warrior princess?"

There was a certain expression I tended to engender in people more mystically apt than I. It started under the eyes with a slight tensing of fine skin, and went both up and down, making lips thinner and foreheads wrinklier. As a rule, I interpreted it as the pain of one whose cherished childhood dreams have just been spat upon, and it always made me feel guilty. The woman got that expression, suggesting that "warrior princess" was not how she thought of Méabh, but it was too late. I couldn't take the words back. I put on a pathetic hangdog smile of apology instead, and the look faded into resignation, which was generally how people ended up responding to me. At length she said, "Something like that. Queen of Connacht and of Ulster, descended from or perhaps incarnated of the Morrígan herself, and any man who would be king of Ireland needed the blessing of the trifold goddess."

"I thought that was Brigid," I said nervously. Brigid was the only deity I knew anything about—well, besides Cernunnos, but I had a close personal relationship with him—and what I knew about her fit in a nutshell. "Trifold goddess" was stamped on the nutshell, in fact, and that was the sum total of my knowledge.

A little of the dismay left the woman's face. Apparently I'd gotten *something* right. "Brigid would be the Morrígan's other face, perhaps. The coin turned upward instead of down.

Maiden, mother, crone, to the Morrígan's warrior, witch and death."

I swallowed. "Right. Um. We're not going to meet her, are we?"

The woman stepped aside with another smile, gesturing us up the hill. "There'll be one way and one way only to find out."

Gary was halfway up the hill before the woman finished speaking. I jolted after him, vaguely ashamed that even now, he was more enthusiastic for my adventures than I was. I caught his shoulder as he reached the low crest and tugged him back. "Hey, hang on a second, wait up."

He glanced at me with elevated bushy eyebrows, and I found myself mimicking the woman's gesture, waving at the low stretch of land beyond our hill. Annoyed that I'd done so, I glanced back to glower at her, but she was gone. I stared down the deserted pathway a moment, then passed a hand over my eyes and said, "Hang on a sec," again.

"I'm hangin', doll. What's up?"

"Obviously there's something down there for us to see. I'm just thinking it might be helpful if you could...See."

"I see just fine," Gary said in mild offense. "I wear reading glasses, but who doesn't?"

"No, not see. See. With a capital ess. With the Sight. Like I do."

Gary looked down his nose at me. It wasn't very far down—he was only a couple inches taller than I—but it was far enough. "Last I checked you were the one with the magic mojo, Jo." A glitter came into his gray eyes and I pointed a warning finger at him.

"You are not calling me Mojojo. Ever. I refuse it as a nick-name."

The glitter turned into a grin. "Sure...Jo."

I turned my pointy finger from him toward the green below us. "Do you or do you not want a chance to See what we're facing?"

"'Course I do!"

"Then no Mojojojo." I bit my tongue on getting carried away with the jojos, then exhaled. "Okay. I know this works because I've done it with Morrison and Billy." Billy, my police detective partner—former partner, which he didn't even know yet. He was going to kill me. Anyway, Billy was an adept himself, able to speak with the recently dead, but Morrison had the magical aptitude of a turnip. If I could make the Sight ritual work on him, I had no doubt it would work on Gary. "But I've only done it while stationary, which is no help."

Gary's eyebrows shot up, dancing with mad glee. I threatened to whack his shoulder and he laughed out loud, which made me laugh. "You're good for me," I informed him. "I laugh more when you're around."

"You need some laughter in your life, darlin'. Speakin' of which, how's things with Mike now that he ain't the boss?"

"Of all the awkward segues. I'll let you know. Stop distracting me."

"From what? You don't look like you're doing much."

"I'm trying to think!" Which wasn't my strong point even when I hadn't flown all night. I walked a few steps away, squinting at Tara. I'd never awakened second Sight in someone when I wasn't already using it. Quite certain it wasn't the best idea I'd ever had, I held my breath and triggered the Sight.

Time revved up a Roto-Rooter and tunneled through a thousand years of history.

CHAPTER THREE

The landscape changed. Hills reshaped, stone walls rose where none currently stood and in the distance a double row of wooden henges spread out in an unbelievably large circle, containing vastly more area than I expected. I could see modern-day shadows of the new highway cutting through what had once been sacred land, its effect so significant as to mar the world even in retrospect. Mist-softened sunlight caught a hollow between the sets of henges where it had been dug out, and dug deep, to create a true barrier around Tara.

I was accustomed to Looking at Seattle, which wasn't an old city even by the U.S.'s standards. The Native American settlements there had been so thoroughly bulldozed over that they left depressingly little mark on the modern city. I probably *could* See them if I needed to, but so far I hadn't had to.

Tara, despite the highway, despite its long-ago abandonment as a spiritual center, despite the tourists that tromped through it daily, *roared* with ancient power. Everything within the henge barrier shone brilliant, healing blue, with spikes of yellow that spoke of a warrior heritage. Where they blended, they became adamant green, a color I'd long since associated with the protective, stolid quality of buildings that knew their business as shelters for those within. My vision shifted and shimmered, trying to accommodate the changes Tara had seen. Changes that were still living within the sacred earth: what had gone on here left its mark, year after year, until years turned into centuries and centuries to millennia.

Only one thing remained the same. A white standing stone poked up impudently, barely altered by time. There was *life* within that stone, more life than the usual shaman-recognized spirit which infested all things. Everything had purpose, but most inanimate objects were rooted and calm and patient.

The standing stone screamed with impatience, a hair-raising shriek that echoed under my skin. I was used to the Sight showing me things beyond the ordinary. It had never before given me the ability to listen in on something that I was certain reached out of this world. I wondered if that was part of the upgrade to the shiny new Siobhán Walkingstick package, or if I'd simply never faced an inanimate object old enough to have a voice of its own.

"What *is* that?" I had the impression I was walking, an impression confirmed when Gary's hand closed around my biceps and stopped me from going any farther.

"Hold up, doll. Don't forget about me."

"Right." I turned away from the standing stone, though its voice still shrieked against the small bones in my ears.

Something uncomfortable happened in Gary's expression as I faced him. His voice dropped half an octave on one syllable: "Jo?"

"Yeah?"

"You look…" He circled one hand, and stopped, still discomfited. I waited for further explanation, which was not forthcoming. After a few seconds my eyebrows went up and I shrugged one shoulder. There was hardly any point in being magically adept if I couldn't use it to figure out what was bugging my friends, so I stepped out of my body to take a look at me.

Gary was right. I looked "…" and my noncorporeal self made a hand circle just like he had.

I would not have recognized me, eighteen months earlier. Not on the levels that mattered. The height, yes; the spiky short black hair, sure. The slightly too-generous nose with its scattering of freckles: those things remained the same. But my eyes, to hear me tell it, were hazel, while the woman I was looking at had eyes of blaze-gold. A thin scar cut across her right cheekbone, breaking a few of those freckles apart, and she wore cuff earrings—a stylized raven on one ear, a rattlesnake on the other—which I'd never done. Nor did the me of a year and a half ago wear a silver choker necklace or the copper bracelet that barely glinted under the new leather coat, though I would have at least recognized the bracelet. My father had given it to me when I left for college. The necklace had been a gift from my dying mother, barely two weeks before I became a shaman. I didn't need to see the last of my talismans, a Purple Heart medal given to me by Gary, to know it was there: it lay over my own heart, pinned discreetly inside my shirt. I would probably die of embarrassment if Gary ever found that out.

I'd thought earlier I needed great sunglasses to really work that coat. Now I thought I needed them to hide my spooky eyes, which were the most visible change in me. Not everyone would be able to see the silver-blue psychic and physical shields wrapping around me so smoothly they looked like liquid silk, but those who could—people like my mentor, Coyote—would respect their strength. Actually, Coyote would just be astonished I'd finally gotten them so integrated that they were intact even though I wasn't consciously thinking about them, and annoyed it had taken a werewolf bite to force me into that mental space. That wasn't the point.

The point was, I looked *confident*. I had presence beyond what my height conferred. *That,* above all, was the element Joanie Walker, cop shop mechanic, wouldn't have known what to do with if she'd seen her future self reflected in the mirror. And that, apparently, was what Gary saw, too.

I said, "Ah," rather softly as I stepped back into my body. My Sight was still on full bore, and Gary's aura was its usual deep solid mercury-silver, reminding me of the old V8 engine I'd initially thought of him as being. His unease glimmered around the edges, lighter shades of silver, but it was turning to something else: a brighter white, like pride was overtaking discomfort.

"Lookit you, Joanie," he breathed. "All growed up."

I grinned, stepping forward to put my hand on top of his head. "Let's not be hasty. Stand on my feet." Unlike anybody else I knew, Gary didn't argue, ask why or prevaricate. He just stepped on my feet with his full weight, evidently unconcerned that he might crush my toes. Fortunately, I was wearing some of my favorite leather stompy boots which had lots of internal structure, and my toes were perfectly safe as I chanted, "This man I hold dear, let him See clear, let that vision hold sway til the end of the day."

A poet I was not. Fortunately, I didn't have to be Tennyson in order to trigger the power. The other times I'd done this, I'd felt nothing in particular, though Billy and Morrison had both reacted instantly and gratifyingly. This time, though, I was asking a whole lot more of the magic: it wasn't supposed to become independent. The spell I'd read about only worked if the caster and the castee remained standing the way Gary and I were, which would be no use at all if we had to explore ancient Tara. But shamanism was based on the precept of *change:* in theory, if I could imagine it, I could do it. I wasn't about to stop Italy from rotating while the rest of the world continued on, but in theory, I could.

Giving Gary the Sight until sundown was, by comparison, small potatoes. He already believed in not only the arcane in general, but specifically in my talent, so there was no resistance as the coil of magic within me built up and spilled out in a distinct, feel-able wave. My brighter silver-blue coated his mercury, then faded inside it, wriggling and adjusting to a different set of eyes. It left behind a sheen of blue on his aura, and only as that faded did Gary let out a long, slow whistle. "God almighty, Jo."

"Just Jo." I released him slowly, feeling the magic linking us stretch, then settle comfortably. "How's that?"

"Incredible." His voice softened with awe. "You can see like this and you *don't* all the time?"

"It's too much." I turned back to Tara, cold swimming over me as the stone screamed again. "I'm afraid if I always look at this world, I'll lose sight of the real one. I've been afraid of that since the beginning."

"I think there ain't much more real than this."

I smiled at him, then did a double take. Gary's eyes, usually gray, were as solid silver as his aura. I chortled and hugged him, inordinately pleased. He grunted, a sound intended to mask his own pleasure, and made a question with his eyebrows that I answered cheerfully: "Your eyes are silver. You're the only one who's ever held his own when I set this spell on him. Everybody else's have gone gold, like mine."

"Old dog's got a lot of tricks, darlin'." Gary did not look old, not one little bit at all. Not to my normal sight, and not to the Sight. Part of it was his totem spirit, a tortoise whose steady ways had gotten us out of major trouble at least once. I could See it now, surrounding him comfortably, always there if its strength needed to be drawn on.

But mostly it was his *joie de vivre*. Nobody who loved life and new experiences that much was ever going to get old, not really. Wiser and eventually dead, maybe, but not old. This time I said what I'd so often thought: "You're my hero, you know that, Gary? I want to grow up into somebody like you."

Color stained his cheeks, which I hadn't thought possible. "You're doin' just fine, doll. C'mon. We better go see what there is to see." He offered his hand. I slipped mine into it, and we walked together into the Hall of Kings.

The stone's cry went mute as the Hall's ephemeral walls surrounded us. I slowed, straining to hear it, and Gary stuck a finger in his ear. "What was that? I didn't even hear it until it quit."

"I don't really kn... Do you hear *that?*" Whispers rattled around the hall, bouncing off my skin. Drowning out the stone, maybe, except they were whispers and the stone had screamed. There was probably some old adage about a whisper being louder than a scream, but I couldn't come up with it off the top of my head.

Gary swallowed audibly. "What's weird is I can understand 'em, doll. Pretty sure that ain't English they're speaking."

"It's not." My mother had spoken in Irish a few times in the months we'd walked side by side without ever getting to know one another. It had sounded more or less like the whispers did, but somewhere in my mind the words twisted from a language I didn't know into one I did. "It's like with Cernunnos. Remember how you only understood him when he wanted you to? There's magic afoot."

The half-spooked expression faded from Gary's face. "I can't believe you just said that."

I grinned. "That's why I said it. All right, let me listen." Why I thought me listening would do any more good than Gary listening, I didn't know. Of course, if he was quiet then we could both listen, which was probably twice as good as just me listening. Which I couldn't do when I was running on at the brain, *again*. In the past, my brain babbling at such length had meant there was something it either didn't want to think about—which things numbered in the dozens right now—or it was working out some extreme cleverness that would at any moment leap out and surprise me.

Much to my dismay, nothing leapt out. The whispers, though, became clearer: men, all of them men, which in a hall called *of Kings* probably made sense. Some were bitter, claiming unrighteous loss of kingship; others were pure and joyful with their duties. Hints of decay spread through all of them like a warning that their histories and legends, that those stories were being lost to time.

Less lost than some, though. At least Tara remained and was recognized as an important site. There were so many places in the world completely lost, or barely rediscovered, that for a moment, standing in the heart of memory broke my heart.

Ice touched the back of my neck and I turned without thinking. A tall and slender man, almond-eyed and pale-skinned, stood behind me. He wore leather and wool and metal, and a crown of silver over fair hair, and there was nothing even remotely human about him.

I wasn't sure how I knew that. He had none of the telltale marks that non-human people in legend had: his ears were round, his eyes, while not Western-European-shaped, were hardly so tilted as to be inhuman, and his build was no more slender than that of a slim mortal man. But he wasn't human, and with my usual flair, I said, "What *are* you?" only realizing afterward that that was probably unforgivably rude.

"The *ard rí,*" he said in a tone which suggested I'd been unforgivably rude. "What are *you?*"

"*Gwyld.*" I was a bit startled the word came out of my mouth, but Cernunnos—and a woman who had died hours after I'd met her—had both used the word for me. It was, as best I could tell, an old Irish word for shaman or magic-maker, and it apparently meant something to this high king, because surprise filtered through his gaze.

"I thought I knew all the *connected* at Tara."

Delighted, I chewed on *connected* as a new term for magic users. I liked it more than *adepts,* and wondered why it had fallen out of use. Then again, maybe it hadn't in Ireland. It wasn't like I'd grilled my mother on the subject.

While I chewed, the high king looked me over, his expression growing incrementally more dour. "What," he finally asked, "are you wearing, *gwyld?*"

I said, "The fashion of my century," then kicked myself in the ankle for setting up a question that had to be answered.

Except instead of looking like he needed answers, his shoulders relaxed and he let out a soft sigh. "And which of us is displaced? The Tara I see before me wavers and trembles in my sight. Have you called me forward, *gwyld,* or have I called you back?"

I scrunched my face. "Joanne. My name's Joanne, not *'gwyld.'* And I think I'm the one displaced. Who...when...are you?"

"My name is Lugh," he said, "and today is the day I die."

CHAPTER FOUR

"Gosh," I said brightly, "good thing I didn't show up tomorrow." Then I wanted to kick myself, but I'd done that once already during this conversation. I didn't want Lugh to think I had a nervous twitch.

Much better he should think I was an unbelievable idiot with a terrible sense of humor and no manners instead. I puffed my cheeks and stared at the wavering walls a moment before trying for a more human and humane response. "I mean, how awful, are you sure?"

Judging from his expression, I had not much improved my original comment. "The dark of winter is upon us, *gwyld*. My wife and mistress must be assuaged to bring back the light."

"Has anybody suggested marriage counseling?" There was something wrong with me. I was usually mouthy, but not *this* much of a jackass. I took a moment for introspection and determined the cause of my behavior was probably the unmitigated terror sluicing through my veins. I'd meant to give Gary the Sight, not throw myself back through time. I had no clue how I'd done it or, more important, how to get home again. Lugh was attractive, but not worth staying displaced in time for. Especially since he was going to die soon. I held up a finger, asking for his patience, and knelt to curl myself up in a little ball, forehead against the grass.

Grass and stone: once upon a time there'd been a floor in this hall. In my time it was gone, but whenever we were now, it was present, but had modern-day grass growing up through it. That suggested I was still tethered in some fashion to my own era, which was reassuring. Some of the impulse to lash out faded, and I took a deep cleansing breath of green-scented air.

My leather coat creaked as I sat back on my heels. "I'm sorry. I wasn't expecting to step out of time and it's making me act like a jerk. I'm not usually quite this bad."

"The connected are often unusual." The way he said the last word implied he really meant "unforgivable assholes," but he was offering rope to hang myself with.

I took it, though I stayed kneeling. One knelt before royalty, after all. Also, equilibrium restoring itself or not, my legs felt shaky and I didn't want to test them. "Who's your wife? I thought stories about druids doing human sacrifices were just that. Stories. Also, dark of winter? Really? It's the spring equinox when I am. Or just past. Close enough, anyway."

He opened his mouth to answer two times while I rambled on, then stood there with a moderately patient glare until I fell silent. "I am wed to the Morrígan, and dark of winter or a balance of light, the quartered sun days are powerful. They do not have to be the same to draw us together. How is it that I, only a king, knows what a *gwyld* does not?"

"My training's been spotty." I got to my feet, feeling no need to add that the spottiness was entirely my own doing. "Wait, the Morrígan? The death goddess? That Morrígan?"

"The one and same," Gary said at my elbow.

I nearly jumped out of my skin, having sort of forgotten about him. Lugh, though, exhaled unmistakable relief, and nodded to the big guy standing behind me. "I see from your garb you are with the *gwyld*. Her teacher, perhaps?"

Gary said "No" and I said "Yes" at the same time, leaving the high king to look as though he'd rather be having teeth pulled than this conversation. I said, "You are, too," over my shoulder, and pleasure ran through Gary's aura.

Auras. I looked back at Lugh.

His was all wrong. Not like a human aura and not much like the blaze of light and power that was a god, either. He was more connected to the earth than that, his aura reflecting the health of the land around him. *That* was what had triggered the assumption he wasn't human. At the moment his aura lay sallow against his skin, dark of winter indeed. I could See the same quietness, even exhaustion, spreading through Tara to the countryside beyond. "Does this happen every year? I mean, no offense, but she must go through a lot of high kings this way."

"She comes and goes as the years call her," Lugh said patiently. "We kings rule in her name and with her blessing until the land hungers for us, and then she returns to claim us for it. *Gwyld,* why have you come here?"

My mouth, as it all too often did, skipped over consulting with my brain and blurted, "Maybe to save your life."

Hope flashed across Lugh's face and died again so quickly that I wasn't sure I'd seen it. There was certainly no trace of it in his voice as he said, "A generous proposal, but not one

I think you can manage. Not unless a high king called Lugh still reigns over Eire in your time, *gwyld*."

Dismay crashed through me, but Gary stepped in. "Hard to say. Legend says all your kind went underground thousands of years ago. Could be anybody on the throne. Lugh's part of the mythology here, though. Sun god, I think, so maybe not. What?" he demanded when I gaped at him. "Look, it ain't native knowledge, doll. I been reading up the past year, just like you have. Guess we've been covering different territory. Anyway, aincha ever heard of fairy mounds? 'Swhere the fair folk go to ground. Everybody knows that."

"No, I've never heard of fairy mounds! I swear to God, did I miss a college course? Life Lessons 103: How to Recognize Magic?" My hands waved in the air like demented puppets. "And I thought I was doing so much better!"

"You are."

That was not reassuring. I stuffed my hands in my coat pockets, shoulders hunched defensively high as I shuffled to face Lugh again.

He didn't look any more reassured than I felt. I sighed and scrubbed my hands through my hair, which needed to be washed. "So this Morrígan. Is she really a goddess? I've never met a goddess."

"*The* Morrígan," Lugh said, a bit severely. "She was one of us once, long ago. She has left us since, and rides the night sky with her ravens and her bloody blades."

"Ra…" The woman in my vision had been accompanied by ravens. I swallowed and gestured to indicate a height equal to my own. "Is she about yay tall, with hip-length black hair and a death's head face? Blue robes? Badass tattoos? Necklace like this one?" I stuck my thumb under my necklace, bringing it to Lugh's attention.

He focused on it momentarily. "All but the last, yes."

I tried to focus on the necklace, too—difficult, when it was a choker and didn't pass my chin when tugged forward—then muttered, "She's the reason I'm here. I mean, in Ireland. Not here—here, whenever this is. Hey!" I let go of the necklace, suddenly hopeful. "Maybe I really do get to save you! Maybe that's why she called me!" Of course, the call had felt like more of a gauntlet across the face than a request for a rescue mission, but maybe that didn't matter.

Or maybe it did. Lugh shook his head. "She is not known for her kindness. I think she wouldn't call you to rewrite my fate."

"Well, I'm here now. I think I'll give it a shot, if you don't mind."

Complexity crossed Lugh's face and he looked to Gary. "You are her teacher. In my time the connected say fate is not to be toyed with. Is it not so in your time?"

Gary's bushy eyebrows shot up. "Forgive me for sayin' so, your majesty, but what the hell's the point in being *connected* if you don't mess with fate? Rightin' wrongs, fighting the good fight, setting kids named Arthur on the path to be king? That's what the connected *do*."

Now Lugh shot a surreptitious glance at me. "Arthur?"

"After your time. Don't worry about it. What do your adepts do?"

He tipped his head curiously, then smiled. "Adepts. A suitable word. They maintain balance. Between justice and injustice, between life and death, between light and dark. What do you do?"

"That," I admitted, "only less portentously. I hope. My version involves getting my ass kicked a lot, and screwing around with fate. I don't know what else to call getting a kid turned into a sorcerer's vessel." There were a whole bunch of other threads I'd tugged in my year as a shaman, but that one continued to upset me.

"Your world," Lugh said after a long, long time, "must be badly out of balance."

"You have no idea."

He drew himself up, suddenly regal. "Then you must see what a world *in* balance looks like, *gwyld*. Perhaps that is why you're here. Come." He turned and walked away and I made to follow him.

Gary hissed, "Jo," despite my name having not a sibilant in sight. "Jo, hang on."

I hung, letting Lugh stride down the Hall of Kings without us. "What's wrong?"

His eyes popped. "We're standin' in the middle of a million-year-old hall that's just a bunch of green hills in our time, talkin' to an elf king, and you gotta ask what's *wrong?* What'd you do to us, Jo? This ain't what the Sight's like, is it?"

"Oh. No. Not normally. I mean, no—wait. What do you see?"

"I see Tara, Jo. Tara the way it musta been a million years ago. It's…" Gary, who was never at a loss for words, trailed off as he gazed around. "There's swords on the walls. Lot of 'em don't look like they've ever been used. They've got carvings below them, faces. Except they don't look like carvings, more like they just lifted right out of the stone itself. All the kings, I guess. Makes you feel like you're walkin' through history." He paused, then said in a more normal tone, "You know what I mean."

I grinned. "Yeah. I don't see that, not as clearly. I've got overlap going from our time. I don't see the faces."

"Too bad. They're somethin', Jo." He refocused on me. "So

what the hell'd you do? You said your rhyme, then disappeared for a minute, and then everything changed to this and the elf king."

I stared at him. "How'd you know he wasn't human?"

Gary did his plate tectonics shrug. "Pretty sure the human high kings of Ireland married Maeve, not the Morrígan. That and the mythology said Lugh was one of the *sí*. It stood to reason."

My hands started doing the Muppet thing again. "What the hell's a shee? No, never mind, forget it, just tell me how it *stood to reason* that some random guy in the annals of history wasn't human? How it *stood to reason* that—"

Gary gave me a level look. "Sweetheart, in the fifteen months I've known you, I been stabbed by a demigod, ridden with the Wild Hunt, fought a wendigo, been witched into a heart attack an' killed a couple zombies. What part of that would make a guy think there *weren't* any elves prancin' about somewhere in the world?"

I stared at him again. Pushed my glasses up. Stared some more. Then, in my very best academic tone, I said, "Oh. Well, when you put it like that, yeah, okay. I don't know how we got here, Gary. And what do you mean, I disappeared?"

"Poof," he said with a demonstrative puff of his fingers. "Gone. Had me worried for a minute, but then I got sucked back through time, too."

"I can still See our time," I said nervously. "I don't like that I went poof. That can't be a good sign."

He whacked my shoulder in a way that could, if I was liberal with my definition, be construed as a pat. "Roll with it, doll."

"Right. Because I don't know how to get us home, so what choice do I have."

Gary beamed and patted my shoulder again. This time I

didn't stagger from it. "That's my girl. You're getting the hang of this *carpe diem* stuff."

"I have a good teacher. I think I also have an impatient elf king up there." Indeed, Lugh stood framed by the hall's far doorway, looking for all the world like a graceful marble statue. A graceful, impatient marble statue, though I'd never encountered a statue which exuded impatience. It made me wonder if there was a Museum of Statues of Unusual Expression somewhere in the world. There should be, if there wasn't.

Lugh's statuesque pose relaxed as we caught up to him. Gary caught his breath—his own breath, not Lugh's—and even I, who still saw my era overlying ancient Tara, said, "Wow."

The screaming white stone stood a few hundred yards away in a straight shot from the hall's exit. I could See another version of it about a hundred yards off to the right; it had been moved in comparatively modern times, but the sheer solidity of its long-term presence beyond the hall made its modern-day location a mere shadow. Beyond it, the henges rose up with banners snapping, making the barrier around Tara that much more impressive.

Everything within the henges was focused on the screaming stone, which shone with gathered energy. It was capped with rich green magic at the moment, power waiting to be released. I wanted to yank the cap off to see if the energy shot upward like a spotlight directed at the sky. I kind of thought it would. That it would shoot up, crash into the cloud layer and rain back down over the entirety of Ireland in an island-size distribution of goodwill, serenity and balance.

Except Ireland didn't exactly have a history of goodwill, serenity and balance. I frowned at the screaming stone like that was its fault, but Lugh brushed the thought away with a dramatic sweep of his hand. "Here lies the heart of our civilization. The collected spirit of the *aos sí,* where at midsummer those who would rule pass through the hall and come to the *Lia Fáil,* the Stone of Destiny. The stone cries out for all of Ireland to hear when a worthy man lays hand on it. The Morrígan comes to wed him, and we kneel before our new king."

"You get a lot of people eager for that job when they know the wedding bed ends up with a sacrificial knife through it?" My analogy sucked, but Lugh got the point. So to speak.

"It is an honor and a duty to be tested," he said stiffly, and just to teach me a lesson, struck off across the hills while he spoke. I chased after as he replaced stiffness with haughtiness that I was sure covered uncertainty. "All creatures must die. What better reason than for your people?"

Wrongness twitched up my spine again, just like it had when I'd contemplated Ireland's emotional balance. "See, now, I get you're elves or whatever, but if I've learned one thing being a shaman it's that blood sacrifice is just not cool. It leads to all kinds of bad moj—" I broke off and glared over my shoulder at Gary, who had no problem keeping pace as we approached the *Lia Fáil.* He widened his eyes and mimed zipping his lips: no MojoJo from him. Satisfied, I finished, "Bad mojo. I can't see that undergoing a 180-degree reversal, even over the course of a jillion years. Also," I said, glancing around, "if there's going to be a sacrifice here, shouldn't there be a bloodthirsty crowd gathering?"

"It is a private affair," Lugh said, still uptight and arrogant about it.

I snorted, then gaped as the penny dropped. "Oh, shit. You mean you didn't know this would happen when you signed on, don't you. Oh, crap. This cannot be good. This can't be good at all. Sacrifices are bad enough. Secret sacrifices, that, no, just no. I put my foot down. That's enough of this bullshit. Where is she? I'm going to have a word with this chick."

Lugh, wordlessly, pointed skyward. I whipped around, arms akimbo.

The woman who stalked out of the sky was my mother.

CHAPTER FIVE

It wasn't really, not after a second shocked look. But that first one was a blow to the gut, sharp enough to make me breathless and sick. I took a woozy step backward and clung to the standing stone like an ingénue while I took stock of the Morrígan.

She was actually far more beautiful than my mother, but there was a definite similarity. More than just the long jet-black hair and light-colored eyes: they had a ferocity I didn't think I shared. In my mother, that ferocity came out in the way she chewed Altoids.

In the Morrígan, it was more in the way she charged down out of the sky with a blazing sword in one hand and a trio of shrieking ravens flapping around her shoulders. Lugh, the damned fool, stepped between me and her and flung his arms wide, making himself an easily skewerable target.

Gary muttered, "Elves ain't too bright," as he lumbered by

me and tackled Lugh to the ground just as the Morrígan swung her sword at him.

It slammed into the Stone of Destiny so hard that *something,* either the stone or the sword, should have shattered. Neither did, but the clang nearly broke me into a billion pieces. Chills dashed up my spine, down my arms, back up again and took up residence at the base of my neck, where they did a tap dance. Lugh gave a little grunt that made a nice counterbeat to the tapping. Gary rolled off him as the Morrígan squalled in pure outraged astonishment. The ravens took their distance from her and she landed on the ground in a cinematic rush of blue robes and black hair. It was very John Woo. All we needed was a flock of doves.

The Morrígan came to her feet in a surge of power and grace and began stalking toward Gary. "You dare deny me my sacrifice?"

He sat up and jerked a thumb my way. "Not me, doll. Her."

I waved and produced my best perky smile. "Hi."

The Morrígan gave me a dismissive look, then looked again more carefully. "You bear my lord's mark."

"I do?" I glanced at myself, half expecting the sign of the cross or some other inappropriately modern religious marker to have cropped up on my skin. Then I clapped my hand at my throat, where the necklace's pendant had a quartered cross. "Oh! This?"

"No." She flicked a finger and the sleeve of my new $1800 leather coat ripped apart to expose the bandaged werewolf bite. My vision washed out, leaving nothing in the world but my ruined sleeve. Static filled my ears, mostly drowning out her, "*That.* What does a sister in blood wish with my sacrifice?"

It hadn't split on the seam. The leather was damaged. It couldn't be fixed, and there was no earthly way I was going to get an exchange on an item damaged by supernatural beings. I lifted my gaze inch by incremental inch to fix the laserlike focus of consumer fury on the Morrígan.

Gary mumbled, "Uh-oh," and got out of the way.

"First," I said in the lowest, deadliest voice I had at my disposal, "fix my coat. Then we'll discuss what I want with your sacrifice."

To my utter astonishment, she arched an eyebrow, shrugged and flicked her finger again. My coat put itself back together, not a hint of damage done to it. The wind sailed right out of my rage and despite myself I said, "That was kind of cool. How'd you do it?"

"Will it and it is so. The Master gives us such gifts. You must be new to your mark, if you haven't yet learned that. Now." Her eyebrows arched again. "My sacrifice?"

"Oh yeah. You can't have him." I smiled at her, all pleasant resolution. Amazing what a little thing like an undamaged coat sleeve did for my humor. Then her answer began trickling toward comprehension, and cold slid down my spine. "Um. Mark of the Master? You mean your boss is the same… Shit. Shit, shit, shit shit shit." It didn't take very many repetitions for that to become an absurd-sounding word. I said it one more time for good measure, turned around, kicked the Stone of Destiny and turned back.

This time, though, I had a sword in my hand. My silver rapier, taken off a god and usually resident beneath my bed. It had at least two feet of reach on the Morrígan's short sword. I hoped like hell that was enough to make up for what I suspected were her vastly superior fighting skills.

She looked wonderfully nonplussed by the new addition to my accessories. It was all I could do to not dance a jig. The blade was part of my psychic armor, so I'd been pretty sure I could pull it from halfway across the world. The Morrígan's astonishment was just a terrific bonus. Gary gave a triumphant "Hah!"

Lugh, as astounded as the Morrígan, said, "No *gwyld* I know carries a sword," and then it was on.

She was fast. *God,* she was fast, and had obviously been using a sword forever, whereas I'd started learning barely a year ago. Her first flurry came down like an avalanche, short blade cutting the air so quickly it made the whipping sounds children usually add to swordplay. I couldn't see it, not even with the Sight running at full bore. Instead I watched her shoulders, her hips, her feet and somewhere at the back of my mind all the training Phoebe had pounded into me did its job. The rapier was where it needed to be time and again, preventing the Morrígan from skewering me.

My arms were already getting numb, and she'd been hitting me for only about half a minute. I hadn't come close to an offensive measure. I was going to earn Lugh a whopping fifteen seconds of life if I didn't do something else fast.

Do something else fast. That was the key. I whispered, *Rattler? I need your gift of speed,* silently, and a slithering, sibilant personality came to life within me.

We ssstrike, he agreed, but he sounded weary. As well he should: barely a day ago he'd stripped me right down to the core in order to make sure I survived getting smashed by a truck. It had taken a lot out of both of us, even if spirit animals didn't technically have *a lot* to be taken out of. He was less of a sketch of light in my mind than usual, but adrenaline pumped through my veins, lending me the swiftness of a striking snake.

The Morrígan was astonished again when my rapier came up and not just blocked, but tangled and threw her short sword to the side. Not away: her loose, strong grip was too much for that, but I made an opening with the parry, and for the first time pressed the fight. She dropped back, not retreating, but distancing herself so she could get a better look at me. I'd apparently suddenly become worthy. That wasn't exactly the accolade I wanted, but it was better than having my head handed to me. I took a step toward her, but just one. I had the screaming stone at my back and wanted to keep it there. Her mouth flattened, recognition of what I was doing, and for an instant her gaze went beyond me, to Gary and Lugh.

I knew I shouldn't look. I knew it, and I couldn't help it. Just one quick glance over my shoulder, to make sure they were all right.

When I looked back, ravens tried to eat my face.

I shrieked, dropped my sword and flailed at the damned birds. Beaks and talons caught my hands, my hair, my arms, my cheeks, scoring vicious digs and slashes. Healing magic sluiced through me, keeping blood from spattering, but I didn't know how to fight a flock of birds.

We ssstrike, Rattler said in audible irritation, and my left hand snapped out to seize one of the ravens by its throat.

The snaky impulse was to squeeze and crack its fragile bones. Somehow I didn't, though I felt the play of muscle in my arm and saw it enter my hand. It stopped just before my fingers spasmed shut. The raven, with no evident concern for its mortality, twisted its head and bit the tender flesh between the thumb and forefinger.

The other two ravens beat wings backward, taking themselves just out of my range of attack. Taking themselves out of *their* range of attack, too, for which I was grateful. Bird in one hand, I knelt to scoop up my sword, then leveled it at the Morrígan, who once more looked astonished. And furious, but she held still, which led me to a rapid conclusion. "Your power's tied up in the birds. What happens if one dies? You can't fly out of here on their wings the way you just arrived, that's for damned sure. Quite a letdown to walk where you once flew, eh? What else, Morrígan? What else do you lose if you lose a bird?"

Truth was, I hadn't stopped myself from killing the raven because I thought it might be a bargaining chip. I hadn't killed it because Raven was my other spirit animal, and I thought he might take issue with me obliterating one of his brethren. But the Morrígan didn't have to know that. I was pretty pleased with myself.

Right up until she snarled, "Less than if I lose the sacrifice," and with another twitch of her fingers, broke the bird's neck.

Don't ever try to tell me animals don't mourn. The remaining ravens made god-awful sounds, noises that I would call shrieks of horror in humans, and renewed their attack. On me, not on the damned Morrígan, even though she was the actual criminal here. I dropped the dead raven and swung wide with my rapier, cutting an errant feather as it fell. For half a breath I was impressed with the sword's sharpness, and then I was back to facing three opponents as the Morrígan took the fight to me again.

Rattler's power surged through me, lending me the speed to meet hers. I already had the strength, thanks to having spent most of a lifetime working on cars. I did not, however, have a duo of infuriated ravens on my side, and the birds were rapidly tipping the odds in her favor. I blurted, "Raven?" out loud and a pleased *kak kak KAK!* ricocheted through my mind as Raven exploded from the back of my head.

That's what it felt like, anyway, and from the Morrígan's expression that might have been what it looked like. Unlike

Rattler, Raven wasn't worn to a nub. Just the opposite, in fact. *He* hadn't scraped me off a highway after I'd been hit by a truck, but he *had* partaken in the following spirit dance. It had brought Rattler and me from exhausted to functioning, and had taken the already-lively spirit bird from functioning to exuberant. This was his first chance since then to burn off some of that energy. He came swinging around my head in a sparkling display of brilliance and smacked the nearest normal raven with his wing.

Nominally normal, anyway. I wasn't sure how normal any bird that helped fly a full-grown woman through the sky was, but it was black and glossy and looked like it belonged to the real world, whereas my Raven was made of fireworks. My Raven was also about two and a half feet long with a nearly five-foot wingspan, which made him gigantic in raven terms. The Morrígan's were merely ordinary in comparison.

And they were totally unprepared to be buffeted by those great long wings. He'd hit me with them any number of times. It hurt. Apparently the Morrígan's raven thought so, too, because it squawked in outrage and left off whacking me to claw at Raven. He did a lovely wing-tip pivot practically on top of my head and crashed into the other raven, then shot skyward with two black streaks of cawing anger chasing him. I said, "*Thank* you!" and got down to the serious business of having my ass handed to me.

I mean, really. I had strength, I had speed, but not in a hundred years would I have skill like the Morrígan's. Hell, she even *looked* tougher than me, though I had a brief vision of how Gary probably saw us—her decked out in blue robes with long flying black hair, me with my short-cropped 'do and flowing white leather coat—and I decided we probably both looked pretty badass. Her more than me, though, because she was obviously the one taking her opponent apart bit by bit with her swordplay.

I parried like hell and tried every trick Phoebe'd taught me, plus a few I'd made up myself. I ducked. I jumped. I threw grass in her face. I kicked and almost got my foot cut off for my troubles. My left forearm throbbed worse with every passing moment, and the Morrígan smiled every time I fumbled on that side, like she knew exactly where my weakness was and only had to wait for me to give in.

Well, I was nothing if not stubborn. I might be bleeding, cursed with a dark mark and about to turn into a werewolf, but I wasn't going to give the beautiful bitch the satisfaction of my failure. I retreated until I had the Stone of Destiny against my spine. Lugh and Gary weren't there anymore, which I hoped was good.

What I really wanted was a minute to stop and think. What I got was a merry chase around the Stone, which was small enough to hug and therefore not really much use as an object to hide behind. Still, I ran around it, the Morrígan on my heels, while I tried to put it all together. It was obvious Lugh was fundamentally wrong about his Ireland being a place of balance and peace if the Morrígan recognized a werewolf bite as her master's mark. I'd watched the werewolves being birthed from the mouth of a black hellhole. I knew their master, at least in passing. He was not one of the good guys.

In fact, he'd been trying to kill me since before I was born. My mother had thwarted him and sent me to America to keep me safe, but I'd regained his attention when my shamanic powers reawakened last year. If the Morrígan, mistress of death and war and doom, was under his command, then—

Then I tripped on the toes of my stompy boots, which were

not meant for running circles in, and did a nosedive into the soft earth of ancient Tara.

Lugh, the goddamned fool, came up out of nowhere and took the blow that would have ended my life.

CHAPTER SIX

Blood spattered me, the Stone, the green grass, everything, but I couldn't even cry out. My voice was lodged in my throat, held there by horror. The Morrígan howled a mixture of delight and anger. She'd gotten her sacrifice, if not her target. Lugh slid off her sword and dropped to the earth. For an instant even the ravens ceased fighting and we all stared at the king's prone form.

Then he dragged a shallow, shuddering breath, and hope seared me. I jammed my rapier upward, scoring the first blood I'd actually taken from the Morrígan, but not doing enough damage to take her down for the count. She shrieked and whirled, sword lifted to impale me.

Gary, hero of the revolution, bashed her on the back of the head with a rock.

There was something about watching the mighty fall ignominiously. Goddesses weren't supposed to be taken down with a stone any more than Goliaths were. It lacked respect, and if I'd learned anything, it was that power demanded respect.

With that in mind, I bellowed, "Hot damn, you go, Gary!" dropped my sword and scrambled across the Morrígan's unconscious body to get at Lugh.

Blood bubbled at his lips, a fine deadly froth. I was pretty sure that meant she'd gotten him in the lung. That should bode ill for him, but I'd healed myself from a punctured lung once. Healing somebody else couldn't be that hard, especially since he knew of and accepted the power shamans wielded. Nothing like a willing victim to ease things along. I reached for the healing magic within me, flexing it for the first time since I'd arrived in Lugh's era.

The Stone of Destiny stopped screaming.

It had gotten to where I didn't notice it anymore, so the cessation was very loud. My head jerked up and I scanned for danger, but the Morrígan was still out and there was no one else at Tara but me, Gary and the ghosts of sacrifices past.

One of which went *pop!* like a soap bubble. Disappeared like he'd been erased entirely, and a glimmer of brilliant emerald-green power filled the space his voice had been in.

Familiar power. The power of a teenage demigod, granddaughter to the Wild Hunt. Suzanne Quinley, who had, at Halloween, unraveled a thread of history, and wiped a man from existence.

A man who had been birthed from a legendary cauldron that raised the dead as zombies, bound to do the bidding of the living. The Master had made it. Somebody had bound it so it could do relatively little evil. And I had—with some help—destroyed it.

If an ancient king of Tara had been one of the unfortunates caught within the cauldron's magic, there was more than a little bad magic going on here. It was like the entire history of the world was corrupt, although as soon as I thought it I didn't know why I was surprised. Corruption was kind of civilization's story of humanity, from Adam and Eve all the way down the line.

That didn't mean I had to like it. It certainly didn't mean that in the here and now, thousands of years before my own time, I had to sit back and let him have his way. There was no point in having great power if I didn't sling it around a little bit. Lugh, *ard rí* of the *aos sí*—I bet that sounded much cooler if I said it all in Irish instead of pidgining it together—did not have to die today. Determined, I pulled my magic into line and turned it on the dying king.

And slammed headlong into Suzanne's power, lush and green and implacable. My own silver-blue talent shorted out in a fizzle of sparks, gathered itself again and buzzed against Suzanne's, searching for a way in.

I hit reverberations instead, shockwaves that came from the none-too-distant past. No matter how I tried to slither by, they caught me in their wake and tossed me back to the beginning. I had mad skills, but they didn't add up to godlike power. Despite this accidental traipse into the past, I also didn't make a habit of jumping around through time, and the more I pushed for a way through, the more I had the impression I was simply on the wrong side of time to change anything in the here and now. To heal Lugh, I needed to step even further back, back to before Suzy's rewrite, and work my way forward. Too much had already changed. The old needed to be fixed before the new could be altered.

Not very hopefully, I said, "Rattler? Raven?" but while my guides were still awake within me, they gave no clarifying power surge in response. Shapeshifting, dealing with the dead:

they could handle those things. Time travel was evidently a whole 'nother kettle of fish.

For the first time since I'd gotten a handle on my shamanic powers, I let the magic go without having healed someone I genuinely wanted to see live. Lugh dragged another blood-bubbly breath and my face crumpled. Failure *sucked*. "I'm sorry. Something's already happened here, Lugh. Time's been changed, and I can't change it again to heal you. Do you…"

Of course he wouldn't remember. I didn't even really have to ask. Suzanne had wiped out Lugh's predecessor so thoroughly that he'd never existed at all. Someone else had played his role instead, a thought which dropped through me like a lead balloon.

Time had been rewritten. The Morrígan had accepted the Master as, well, her master. I was willing to put money on that not being a coincidence. "Lugh, ah, God, I'm sorry, but how long have the sacrifices been going on? How long have the high kings been marrying the Morrígan?"

"Al…ways. Since…Haw-hee…was slain…by the Morrígan."

That was about as useful to me as a hole in the head, since I had not a clue what a Hawhee was, but this was not a good time to go into it. I nodded and clutched Lugh's hand, feeling once more like the useless ingénue. "I'm so sorry. I am so sorry, Lugh. It wasn't supposed to happen this way."

He smiled, faint bloody expression. "It was supposed to happen…*exactly*…this way."

Great. I'd just gotten an *I told you so* from a dying king. I was trying to figure out how to respond to that when his hand spasmed around mine and determined fear came into his eyes. He surged up half an inch, which under the circumstances was a heroic effort, and whispered, "Warn…Nooda…!"

I had no more idea what a Nooda was than a Hawhee,

but I nodded a vigorous, wordless promise, and Lugh, reassured, collapsed silently into death.

Gary stopped to pick up the Morrígan's sword and throw it several yards away, then came to kneel by me. We sat together silently for what seemed like a long time, but eventually I said, "Who's Hawhee?" with no expectation of an answer.

"I'm guessin' a king," Gary said, which was equal parts obvious and helpful. "Nuada's one. They called him Nuada of the Silver Hand 'cause his got— Ah, hell, that's who Hawhee was. It ain't spelled like it sounds. It's spelled..." He frowned, clearly calling the name up in memory, then rattled off, "E-o-c-h-a-i-d-h, Eochaidh, yeah. He's the guy who cut off Nuada's hand."

I'd heard of Nuada. He'd made my necklace. It was just, "I thought it was pronounced New-AH-da."

"Yeah, well, I thought Eochaidh was pronounced Ee-ock-chaye-d-hhh." He aspirated the last sound like an old wheezing dog and I coughed on his behalf. Gary closed Lugh's eyes, then cautiously asked, "What happened, Jo? I kinda saw you start to do your thing and then bounce right off a green granite cliff face."

I blinked up from the dead king in surprise. "You saw that? I mean, you Saw it? Wow. That was..." I trailed off and stared at Lugh again. "That was repercussions. That was Suzanne Quinley, Gary. That was her in the zombie fight. You know the one she obliterated? He came from here. Not quite now, but somewhen around now. Time had to be rewritten around the space he wasn't anymore." The language was not well suited to referring to events that had been made to not-happen. I wet my lips and kept going as best I could. "Maybe he was supposed to be Eochaidh's successor. Maybe he was meant to defeat the Morrígan, or to really marry her, but maybe instead the Master slipped in where he was supposed to be and made her a goddess instead."

We both looked over at where she still lay sprawled across the grass, a bit of blood leaking through her hair. I said, "Only she isn't, you know. She's more than Lugh was, but she's not like Cernunnos. She's just very, very powerful."

"So're you."

Somehow that made me feel a little better. I said, "Anyway," more softly. "Anyway, so this whole era, which I guess means the whole timeline going forward, is all screwed up because of Suzy wiping that zombie out. I couldn't heal Lugh because there was already too much interference. Something big already got changed. It wouldn't let me change even more."

Gary's gray eyes were big as a lemur's. "Are you gonna rewrite the whole history of the world, darlin'?"

"It doesn't work that way." I sounded very sure of myself, but I had, to a much smaller degree, already been there and done that. "Time tidies things up. The best I can do is close the loop, but I have to do it from our end of time. I can't set the fix in motion back here."

"But you can if we get home?"

"I can try."

"Damn," Gary said in a low voice. "I mean, *damn,* Jo."

A smile tugged at the corner of my mouth. "Yeah, well, don't get too impressed. I haven't pulled it off yet. And I still don't even know how we ended up here, much less how to get us home, never mind how to find Nuada, and I can't go home without trying to warn him."

Gary's expression went funny and he nodded over my shoulder. "We could ask her."

Alarm crashed into the pit of my stomach and I tried scrabbling for my sword and leaping to my feet at the same time. Neither was wildly successful. I ended up lurching in a half circle with fingertips full of grass.

Fortunately, the woman coming up behind us was unarmed except by radiant beauty. I stole a glance at the unconscious Morrígan and the dead king. They were both still inhumanly attractive. I knew plenty of good-looking people, but these guys made the best of them look like ugly stepsisters. I glanced at the new arrival again, then shot a look at Gary, whose eyebrows had risen. He nodded, and we both gaped at the woman.

She was youthful now when she hadn't been minutes ago, in the future. She wore a robe identical to the Morrígan's, only hers was white bound with gold rather than blue with black. She, too, had tattoos banding her upper arms, but in red, not blue. Her hair was coppery and her eyes green, and she had the same kind of gently overflowing aura that had helped tip me off to Lugh's alienness. Like the Morrígan, she exuded power. Also like the Morrígan, it wasn't honest-to-God deity-level power. I knew who she was before she spoke.

"Welcome to Tara, Siobhán Walkingstick. I am Brigid."

Score one for me. With my usual politeness, I said, "Couldn't you have told me all this from the other end of time?" instead of "Hello."

Surprised amusement shot her eyebrows toward her hairline. "I'm sure I wouldn't know what you mean."

I squinted. "Yeah, I'm sure not." Well, maybe she didn't. Not right now, anyway. I was going to have a talking-to with her, though, when we got back home. "Never mind. Doesn't matter. Hello, Brigid. Nice to meet you. I've heard a lot about you."

"Have you, now." She kept sounding amused, which was

better than the Morrígan's snide superiority. "And what is it you've heard?"

"That you're her opposite," I said with a thumb-jerk toward the Morrígan, "and…" Okay, maybe I hadn't heard all that much about her after all. I knew who she was. That was really about it, but for me, that was a lot. "And you're one of the good guys?"

Brigid's eyes grew more serious. "Death is not an aspect of evil, little sh—"

"Joanne." I really hated being called "little shaman." It was bad enough from Cernunnos, a certified god. I was not going to take it from people who were somewhere between human and sublime on the divinity scale.

Her eyebrow quirked. "Siobhán."

"For God's sake, what is this, a haggle? My name's Joanne. Use it or don't, but lay off with the insulting diminutives. And I know death isn't inherently evil, but I'm not so sure there's not something fundamentally wrong about war, 'cause, you know, basic rule of thumb: killing people is bad. So don't try to tell me *she's* one of the good guys—" I did the thumb-jerk again "—or that you don't represent basically everything she's not. Life, liberty, the pursuit of happiness." That was probably an unforgivably American way of phrasing it, but it got the point across.

Brigid made a face that indicated I had won a free pass for this round. I let out an explosive breath, tried to reel my temper back in and snapped, "So what do you want from me?"

So much for reeled-in tempers. Brigid smiled indulgently, like I was an ill-mannered five-year-old she wouldn't have to deal with for very long. Probably that should've chastised me, but it only irritated me all the more. I turned to Gary and made a series of exasperated faces, trying to work myself into a better mood as Brigid said, "It's your help I'm needing, *gwyld*. There's a thing that's been made in the near-distant past, and I can sense its touch on you."

I clutched my left forearm, then bit back a hiss. Gnashy dog bites were not meant to be seized. It hurt. While I waited for the pain to fade, Brigid said, "Not that mark. This is the touch of death and life reborn, visited upon you thrice."

I said, "Thrice, who says thrice," under my breath and tried to count up the number of times I'd been through the life-and-near-death cycle in the past year or so. I stopped when I got to five, satisfied that Brigid didn't know what she was talking about. Then I wondered if individual instances mattered or if it was a per-adventure count, in which case she might be on the money with three. There was the whole mess with Cernunnos and Herne that started all this, the dive into the cauldron and Saturday night's exhaustive rebirthing scene. I didn't think I'd been grievously injured the other thirty-seven or so times I'd figured I was about to die, so they probably didn't add to the tally. "All right, okay, thrice. So what does that mean? Why does three times matter if you need my help?"

"There's power in threes." It sounded as if she was having a hard time not adding "You idiot" to that statement, but after a moment she managed to go on without saying it. "Bran's cauldron has left its mark on you."

"Less mark than I left on it," I muttered.

Brigid laughed. "And it's that which makes me need your help. I can sense its history on you, *gwyld*. I can sense that for most of its existence it has done little harm."

I stared at her. "Little harm? Are you serious? That thing seduces the living. Invites them to crawl inside so it can suck their life out and turn them into zombies bidden to do the command of—" Bidden. Who says bidden? I turned my stare at the sky, as if answers or excuses for my word choices lay there. They didn't.

"How many…*zombies*…were within the cauldron, Joanne Walker?"

"I don't know, ten or so. Not very many."

"Ten men," Brigid murmured, "including Bres, he who was once *ard rí* of this land and is now taken from time, have died for the Morrígan and her master."

My jaw flapped open. "Wait. Bres? He's the guy who came undone? You remember him? How?"

"The world cannot abide imbalance. When my sister became death's warrior, a similar and opposite path was offered to me. We remember that which has been changed, and your presence here gives me hope that the cauldron might yet be bound."

"It can be. I mean, it was. Oh!" God, I was slow. "You're the one who did it! Somebody broke the bindings, but not until just last year. I knew something powerful had set them—"

Brigid's face froze momentarily, offense taken at some*thing* rather than some*one*. She let it go, though, as I rattled on. "I've been dying to meet whoever did it. Not actually dying. I do enough of that. But it didn't feel like human magic, and I was right!" I wanted to dance a jig, by gum, though doing so over the bodies of a dead man and an unconscious powermonger seemed ever so slightly inappropriate. "How did you do it? How will you do it?"

"How did you destroy it?"

The impulse to jig faded. An innocent soul had sacrificed herself to make sure the cauldron was destroyed. Much more subdued, I said, "With help."

"Then it is with help that I'll bind it."

I genuinely didn't get she meant *me* until she held out her hand in invitation.

"…is this why you threw me back to this end of time? I mean, you've been here before, right? You knew this was going to happen when you met us at Tara in the future. Seriously, couldn't you have just *said* something back then? Future then?"

Her eyebrows rose. "I meant what I said, Joanne Walker. I wouldn't know what you're talking about. You're the one unstuck in time, the one who passes through many points at once. I travel through time day by day, as most living creatures do. If you have met me again, it awaits me in my future even if it resides in your past."

I liked the idea of Brigid being responsible for our time traveling a lot more than I liked being responsible for it myself, so it took me a minute to get over that. Actually, it more like took me a moment to even approach it. Getting over it was still on the agenda. Gary, meantime, hissed, "That was *her?*"

He'd picked up the sword I'd dropped and had taken to

standing guard over the Morrígan, but that didn't mean he wasn't listening. I gave a big sloppy frustrated shrug. "I think so. Or an avatar. Do you use avatars? Never mind, it doesn't matter. How am I supposed to help? I don't know any binding spells."

I gave that a mental once-over to make sure it was true, then startled. It wasn't: I'd encountered a binding spell in my first hours as a shaman. It called on gods and elements and things, and it probably wasn't a safe bet to rely on me to cast it. Wisdom being the better part of valor, I said nothing about it.

Turned out it didn't matter, as Brigid said, "The binding will be tied to you. Now that I know you have the power and the will to destroy it, the binding need only last until the cauldron comes into your presence."

I stared at her. Began to speak. Held up a finger to stop both myself and her from saying anything. Turned around. Walked away. Stared fiercely at the southern horizon. There was a tower there, about a mile away, just like in my time. I glared at the tower until I trusted myself not to shriek like a harpy, then gathered myself to face Brigid again.

"I don't know why you'd set a binding that can be broken when the damned cauldron enters my vicinity, like, my *city*, rather than my actual physical presence, but that's what happens. People *die* because of that, Brigid. I get that closed time loops are tidy and all—" and, hoo boy, was I developing a hate-on for them "—but we're talking about people's lives here."

"I would not set such a spell," she said both serenely and alliteratively, "but the years are long between now and then, are they not? Even the most powerful of magics may slip, over so much time. And how many would die, Siobhán Walkingstick, if I did not make the magic at all?"

Using logic to derail my head of steam was a lousy trick. I

muttered, "Well, at least promise to tighten up the wards every few centuries so the bindings can only be broken if I'm *there*. Or better yet, so only I can break them. Without murdering poor Jason Chen." It didn't work that way. I knew it didn't, because it hadn't. I doubted we'd get back to our time and discover history had retrofitted itself and that Jason had gotten to take his sisters trick-or-treating after all. For one intense, searing moment I wished like hell it *did* work that way, but time, life and Grandfather Sky were not that kind. If I ever got to meet the makers of the world I had a word or two I wanted to say to them.

Brigid promised, "I'll do my best," and I nodded, knowing it wouldn't be enough. Then I followed her gaze as it went to Lugh. She murmured, "My sister must take her sacrifice so we might find the cauldron to bind it," apologetically.

It wasn't physically possible for my head to spin, but it tried. A headache sprang up for its efforts, and while I was struggling to find something politic to say, Gary growled, "You gotta be kidding, lady. All this and you don't even know where the damned thing is?"

Brigid stiffened. "It would be a great prize for my sister's master. They would not leave it somewhere easy to find."

"It's in the cave." I sighed as Gary and Brigid both raised their eyebrows at me. "The one the werewolves came from. Somewhere to the west of here, near a…" I waved my hands. "Near another hill."

"Ireland," Brigid said dryly, "is full of hills."

I glowered. "A built-up one. Somebody made a huge pile of rocks on top of a gigantic flat hill."

"*Cnoc na rí,*" Brigid said every bit as dryly as before. "We would call it a mountain, Joanne Walker. The mountain of kings. You speak of the cairns atop it."

"I don't know what *Knocknaree* is," I said, approximating her pronunciation as best I could, "but it's a marker for the cave, and if you know where it is, we should probably haul ass that direction and bind the damned cauldron so Gary and I can go home."

Gary squeaked, "That might be a problem, doll," and when I looked over, the Morrígan had my sword at his throat.

I had shot somebody four mornings ago. It was not something I was proud of and not something I wanted to repeat. Ever. Except I'd have dropped the Morrígan in a heartbeat, if I'd had my gun. I doubted it would change the whole history of the world. Someone else similar would just replace her. But I didn't have my gun, and later I would probably think that was good, because digging modern-day shell casings out of a millennia-old Tara hillside would really throw archaeologists for a loop.

Right now, though, my fingers clenched like I was squeezing a trigger, and the Morrígan gave me a tight, nasty smile. "Don't think of it, *gwyld*. You may draw a blade from the air, but not while it resides in *my* hand."

She was right, too. I could almost feel the hilt in my hand, but there was a trembling resistance, too, like a magnet not quite strong enough to pull its counterpart toward it. But the Morrígan's magic—or grip—was stronger, and the harder I tried calling it to me, the redder a scratch on Gary's throat became.

I stopped trying. The sword relaxed, giving Gary room to swallow. In fact, his whole big self relaxed. Sagged, some might even say. He had both hands on the Morrígan's arm, classic knife-at-throat pose, but he wasn't going to be able to pull her away without slitting his own gullet. His head fell forward, shoulders caved as best they could to protect his throat in a moment of defeat. His spirit animal's presence was agitated, not something I'd ever imagined a tortoise could be. But even tortoises had vulnerable throats.

I was trying to figure out what to do when Gary threw his head back and smashed the Morrígan's nose.

Roughly one million awful things happened at once.

Cartilage crunched. The Morrígan bellowed with pain. She even dropped the sword, but blood was already pouring from Gary's throat: he'd cut it himself with the sheer violence of his action.

The Morrígan dropped him, too, and staggered back with both hands clapped to her nose. Blood ran down her forearms toward her elbows. Normally I would mock a warrior woman who couldn't take the pain of a little broken nose, but Gary was bleeding, and besides, I'd broken my nose when I was a kid. It hurt like a motherfucker.

Gary's hands went to his throat, such a familiar cinematic response that it could have been funny if it wasn't a real person a few seconds from bleeding to death. He dropped to the earth with lumbering grace as I charged forward, vision turning silver-blue with fear and fury.

In the center of that brilliance, the Morrígan crouched over Lugh's body. She glanced up, saw me coming and splayed one hand open with much the same gesture she'd used to ruin my coat. Power exploded out, black wrath laced with blue.

Brigid, inexplicably, stood between me and the burst of power. Her shields flared, white and gold, but the blast of black magic still hit hard enough that her torso bowed with the impact. She fell gracefully, never in my way as I ran for Gary.

An ugly sound of frustration erupted from the back of the

Morrígan's throat, but she didn't try again. Her ravens came to her, one on each shoulder. She sneered at me, then dissipated in a whirl of blue mist.

The sleeve of my coat turned to shredded leather again as she disappeared.

I hit the bloodstained grass on my knees, both hands covering Gary's at his throat. There was no careful visualization, no rebuilding of vessels, veins, muscle, tendons, skin one by very quick one. No delving into the garden of Gary's soul to find the heart of him and the idea of how he thought he should be. I didn't need to, for two reasons. One, I'd tried healing a cut throat once before. It hadn't worked, but the concept was familiar.

Two, and much more important, he and I both had total faith in my ability to heal him. That was all it took, really. A rush of magic and suddenly all the blood was on our hands, on our clothes, on the ground, without any more pumping free of his body.

I sat back on my heels, my own heart pumping at about a zillion miles an hour. As far as I could tell, the entire incident, from the moment the Morrígan put the rapier to Gary's throat all the way through to his healing, had taken about ten seconds. Ten very exciting, heavily punctuated seconds, but ten seconds.

Gary, hands now exploring his throat to make sure I hadn't missed anything, croaked, "What took you so long, doll?"

I couldn't help it. I laughed. It was high-pitched and hysterical, not amused, but I did laugh, and he gave me one of the sexy old coot grins that had all my friends convinced he was my sugar daddy. I waved a bloody hand, said, "Oh, you know, I could tell she hadn't hit the jugular, I had all the time in the world," then burst into tears and fell over on him. "What were you *thinking?!*"

He put his arm around me, mouth on top of my head. "Figured I knew a girl who could fix me up in no time flat if I did somethin' crazy to break the status quo. You were never gonna risk it."

"Of course I wasn't! Jesus, Gary!" I wanted to punch him, but punching a guy who'd just had his throat cut seemed low. I sniffled into his shoulder instead.

He chuckled against my hair, then drew a deep breath. "Thanks, sweetheart."

I wrapped my arm over his ribs and hugged him as hard as I could. "I'd say 'anytime,' except if you ever do something like that again I'll kill you myself."

"Nah, you wouldn't. Who'd go on all these crazy adventures with you then?"

"Billy. Morrison, the poor bastard. Random strangers getting swept up in my wake. Ha—" The last sound wasn't a word, just an inhaled breath that Gary rumbled a laugh over.

"Yeah yeah yeah. Look, I hate to break our quality time up, Jo, but wasn't there a bad guy here a minute ago?"

We both pushed up on our elbows. The Morrígan's disappearing act had left no trace of where she'd gone. Brigid, though, sat against the bloodstained *Lia Fáil,* one hand pressed to her chest. I whispered, "Shit," and scrambled to her on hands and knees, then stopped with my hands hovering above her, half-afraid to touch her, totally afraid to try healing her after the disaster with Lugh. "Jesus, are you okay?"

"Well enough." Her voice was faint, and her overflowing aura weak. I bit my lower lip, waking healing power, but she shook her head. "Not in this time and place, I fear. My sister's strength is the greater here. Do not expose yourself to her any more than you must."

"You look like you could use some must."

She smiled, but it faded. "Do not concern yourself with me. Concern yourself instead with my sister. I had meant to follow her to her master's lair, to the cauldron's seat—"

"But instead you took one for the team. Um, thanks for that. I think you might have saved my life there. That was a *lot* of power she threw at me."

"Yes. Her success would have been unparalleled, had she taken your life so far out of your time. I could not allow that, even—" She sighed and I finished for her:

"Even if it meant losing her and the cauldron? I dunno, Bridge. Magic's damned hard to track. Unless you're better at it than I am."

Brigid shook her head. I nodded and glanced at the sky. Raven had been up there somewhere, fighting with the Morrígan's ravens. "I don't suppose you know where they all went, do you?" I asked him, and he flew down out of the sunlight to whack me on the head with a wing. "Yeah, sorry, I didn't think so. Next time I'll try not to lose the bad guy. You did a good job kicking her ravens' asses, though. Shiny food in your future."

Raven cawed with pleasure and faded away. Gary came to crouch beside me looking big-eyed and happy as a kid in a candy store. "I saw him, Jo. Your raven. I saw him."

I smiled, then leaned over to hug him again, hard. "Welcome to having the Sight, Mr. Muldoon. All right, let's head for Knocknaree so we can kill that bitch. Look what she did to my *coat*."

Gary grinned a little. "You're gonna kill her over a coat, Jo?"

For some reason it wasn't as funny as it should be. I shook

my head. "I'm going to kill her for cutting your throat. The coat was just petty."

"Good to know I'm loved."

"You are," I said, still solemn. "You are." Then in a rush of delight, I smacked his shoulder. "Dude! Dude, you totally busted her nose, you know that, right? How many people get to say they head-butted a goddess?"

Gary chortled, then tried to disguise his pleasure by saying, "Thought you said she wasn't a goddess."

"Oh, ffssht. Close enough for government work. Okay, Knockna…" We were several thousand years in the past. There were no itty bitty Irish cars to drive on the itty bitty Irish roads. In fact, I bet there weren't even many itty bitty roads to drive on. "…just where is this Knocknaree place?"

"In the West." Brigid sounded like Galadriel, except I was pretty sure she only meant the west of Ireland, not some far-off land of everlasting peace and calm.

From our perspective, however, the difference was negligible. Ireland wasn't a big island, but a couple hundred miles was a long way when you were traveling on foot. I exhaled noisily. "I don't suppose we can go home, drive over and meet you there in a few thousand years, huh? You oughta be able to make it there by then."

"I think not," a brand-new voice said, and Brigid faded away.

CHAPTER EIGHT

I refused to flinch. It took every last bit of willpower, but I refused to flinch. Instead, with all the panache at my command—which wasn't much—I said, "I'm getting tired of mysterious voices and people disappearing," to Gary before I allowed myself to look around.

The air had changed quality: mist sparkled more, like bits of ice rode on it, and my breath steamed as another of the annoyingly beautiful, slightly inhuman *aos sí* came up on us. This one looked like he'd been dipped in silver from his hair to his boots. I'd never seen genuinely silver hair before; even Cernunnos's was really brown and ashy. This guy's actually shone like the metal. My gaze fell to his left hand.

It *was* silver, the knuckles gleaming and flexing like molten metal as they moved. I stared at it, mesmerized, then shook myself. "You'd be Nuada, then." I gave myself bonus points for pronouncing it correctly. He didn't have to know I'd only just learned how.

"I would be. And you would be…" He was silent a long time, then cleared his throat uncertainly. "You would be my bride? The Morrígan?"

My jaw fell open and my eyes went googly while Gary had a good laugh. While it was nice to know having his throat cut hadn't changed his laughter, it was also clear Nuada wasn't keen on being the butt of a joke. I elbowed Gary, who manned up and stopped laughing as I said, "No, my name's Joanne. The Morrígan's stepped out for a bite to eat."

Gary snorted laughter again. I elbowed him harder, to no avail. "Look, no, sorry. She just took off with Lugh, and Brigid disapp—"

"Lugh?" Nuada's eyebrows made a heavy silver line across his forehead. "Lugh is half a year gone. How else might I be here, ready to wed the Morrígan?"

"What?" I'd thought the days of me saying "What?" all the time were past. Apparently not. "No, he just died not ten min—"

"Died?"

Oh yeah. The *aos sí* weren't hip to the actual goings-on with the Morrígan. I started to cast my gaze heavenward, as if to gather strength for an explanation, but it got only about as high as the horizon before Nuada's sword was at my throat. He repeated, *"Died?"* and it didn't take a super genius to grasp that I was up next on the list of dead people.

Panic was clearly the right response. Panic, some flailing, a frantic explanation; all the sorts of things I'd done before. They'd gotten old, though. This time I just sighed and said, "The Morrígan killed him, your royal nitwitness, not me."

His sword poked half an inch closer, which was enough to part the skin on my throat.

Or it would have been, if I hadn't *finally* learned the habit Coyote had been trying to hammer into me my entire shamanic career: shields up, Captain. Shields up at all times.

Nuada's sword rubbed against the glimmer of power layering my body, and didn't so much as leave a scratch. The Morrígan hadn't drawn blood, either. I had the damned werewolf to thank for that: *she* had driven home what Coyote had failed to. Unfortunately, she'd only done so after she'd bitten me. There was an argument for better late than never, but I probably wasn't the person to be making it.

The silver-handed elf king's forehead wrinkled ever so slightly. He pushed a little harder and the sword, rather than sticking in my gullet, began sliding sideways. Chagrined, he pulled it back into place, but stopped leaning into it. "What are you?"

"A shaman. *Gwyld*. You might as well put the sword away. It's not going to do you any good. What do you mean, six months have passed?" The landscape looked the same. No particular hint of winter. Of course, I neither had any idea what an Irish winter thousands of years in the past looked like, nor any call in judging what time was or wasn't doing. I was already millennia out of my league, after all. Six months here or there probably didn't count for much, and the air *was* colder.

"What do *you* mean, dead?"

"It ain't nice to go around interrogatin' people by holdin' swords at their throats," Gary rumbled.

Nuada looked at him. Looked at me. I could just about see the wheels turning: if the young woman could hold a sword attack off with the power of her mind, what could the old guy with several decades more experience do?

Judiciously, and with the expression of a cat who meant to fall off the wall, Nuada put his sword away. Then he spread his hands, palms up, in a gesture of conciliation and goodwill. "I would hear your tale."

"Yeah, I just bet you would." Snark would get me nowhere. I raspberried a long breath out, inhaled again and put on my best perky tour guide voice. "The Morrígan's been murdering your high kings for at least the last ten or so. I would strongly suggest not marrying her, if I was you. Were you. Was? Were. If I were you." I didn't care if it was right. It sounded better.

"Jo," Gary muttered, "shut up."

I said, "He asked," with the pitch and tone of an insulted child, then kicked myself in the ankle. It was a good thing I already had an Indian name, or my Indian name would be Kicks Self In The Ankle. "Nuada," I said with every ounce of patience at my disposal, "your bride to be is one of the bad guys. I have literally traveled through time to tell you this, a statement which I expect is supported by my outlandish clothing. I would beg of you, your majesty, to *listen to me*."

The poor guy recognized the patience in my voice, but not that it was directed at myself. Nobody could be as exasperating as I was. I suddenly felt sorry for Morrison. And for Nuada, who drew himself up with offense, because who wouldn't when some weirdly dressed chick from the future condescended at you.

"I'm sorry," I said before he had time to launch into a tirade. "Really. It's me I'm disgusted with, not you. I'm having a hard time with the explaining. Time travel sucks." Lightning struck—metaphorically, thank God; that was not the sort of phrase I should use lightly—and I shoved a thumb under my necklace, bringing it to his attention. "Look! Wait! Look at this!"

If nothing else, my increasingly bizarre antics caught him off guard, giving me time to unfasten the choker before he decided to berate my bad manners. The necklace gleamed as I handed it over, misty light catching the triskelions and the quartered circle that was its pendant.

Nuada took it with his silver hand, which wasn't articulated or in any other fashion prosthetic-like, aside, of course, from it being silver. It moved and flexed like flesh, and I fancied I could even see blood vessels beneath the surface as he turned the necklace up to examine it. "This is my work," he said eventually. "I would know it anywhere. And yet I have never made such a piece in all my years."

"And this?" I put my hand out and called my sword. It zinged across the ten or so feet of intervening space and slapped into my palm like it and I were magnetized.

Nuada's eyebrows shot up, though his words suggested he was more impressed by the sword itself than the zooming across space: "I've never seen a blade such as that. What is it?"

"It's called a rapier. They come into fashion in about…" I had a vague idea rapiers were sixteeth-century weapons, but I had no idea when that was in relation to us. "In a few thousand years."

"It's beautiful." He opened his hand in request and I put the sword into it, watching his attention flit between rapier and necklace. "Both mine," he said. "Both not yet forged. For whom do I make such pieces of art? A far-flung *gwyld?*"

"I think you make the necklace for the Morrígan. The sword belongs—belonged—to Cernunnos. I took it."

His gaze snapped to mine. "You took a blade from the god of the Wild Hunt?"

"It's a long story."

"This is not the sword I made for that god."

For a statement, it sounded remarkably like a demand. I nodded and made a space of about four feet between my hands. "You made him one about this long. Narrower at the hilt and broader at the point. It's beautiful, too, but it's brutal. It's for killing things. This one's more elegant. It's for killing things, too, obviously, but you can imagine it's for...toying with them, too. He asked for it, when they came into style, and after he lost it to me you wouldn't make him another." I wet my lips. "That happens in the future. Don't tell him I told you you didn't make him another, because I'm pretty sure that'd end up being my fault somehow and he and I already have a lot of water under the bridge to get over."

Nuada squinted. So did I. Gary just groaned. "You gotta learn to control your mouth sometimes, Jo."

"What fun would that be?"

"Can you call him here?" Nuada asked, ever so softly. "I am inclined to believe you, unborn *gwyld,* but I would like to hear it from Cernunnos, as well."

My heart jumped at the idea. If it was midwinter, Cernunnos rode our world with the Hunt at his back. I might be able to call him to a center of power like Tara. "He and I don't meet for thousands of years."

Nuada gave me a familiar look, the one suggesting I was the slow kid in the class. "Do you imagine one such as he is bound by time?"

"..." I shuffled my arguments away without even voicing them. Cernunnos had never mentioned meeting me in the distant past. On the other hand, it wasn't like our first encounters had been old home night at the bar. Having silenced my own objections, I glanced around Tara.

"It's too big." It wasn't, and I knew it. The tower to the south—southwest, really—was matched at the other three lesser compass points, too, though none of those had survived into my time. I could feel power lines dragging through all four of them, centering in Tara. Centering where we stood, really, at the *Lia Fáil,* the Stone of Destiny. Some idiot had moved it, in my time. Not very far, a couple hundred yards, maybe, but it was no longer dead at the center of a vast quartered circle.

I knelt, one hand on the blood-spattered stone and one in the cool green grass, and my last thought for a few minutes was that maybe it had been a wise man, not a fool, who had moved the Stone from its original resting place.

Tara required only a nudge to awaken. Just a touch of magic seeking out the power circle. I was astonished, in fact, that it hadn't roared to life when I'd healed Gary, but perhaps that had been internal enough not to draw the site's attention. Now, though, with my power seeking to build a sanctuary and to gain a god's attention, Tara came to the fore. I was little more than a conduit for a land so steeped in magic that it had its own will. No wonder the Master wanted this place under his thrall: with Tara's power at his command he could alter events in an ever-growing circle from this epicenter.

Magic shot up from the *Lia Fáil,* hit some distant invisible ceiling and spilled down evenly to set the four towers alight. The faintest gray taint ran through it all. Gray, not black; the Master's hold wasn't that strong, not here, not yet, despite the sacrifices. This was still a place given over to what was good in humanity, and if I had anything to say about it, it would remain that way.

I glanced up at the midwinter sun and whispered the closest thing to a prayer I'd ever spoken. A plea to a god to come and visit me, so I could prove myself to a skeptical elf king and perhaps alter the course of events back to how they always should have been. It was possible he would; these were the first days of his greatest power, the time from the solstice through to the twelfth night after Christmas. He rode across the world now, collecting souls, and would soon retreat to the world he had been born of, Tir na nOg, there to rest until Halloween welcomed him back to our world. He had ridden to others when they'd asked, in the past.

I was still somehow surprised when the sky split open and he came to me.

Even knowing what to expect, he was overwhelming. The changes were coming on him, earlier than they had in my time. A thickness to his shoulders and neck, preparing to bear the weight of horns beginning to distort his temples. His eyes were light-flecked, wild and alien: this was a being who belonged to the universe, and the universe to him. He went beyond time as I understood it, a raw piece of star stuff made into a beautiful, inhuman form full of lust and energy and anger.

His host was smaller than I'd seen it before. The gray-bearded king was missing, as was the archer who had shot Petite's gas tank full of holes. The boy Rider was with him, though, which gave me a shock. It shouldn't have, since we were centuries, maybe millennia, before Herne and his spells, but I'd never seen the boy looking quite so comfortable at his father's side. That child bound Cernunnos to time, but not, it seemed, to linear time. For a moment I wondered if magic was just physics nobody understood, but that was philosophy beyond my scope.

Particularly when Cernunnos himself was before me, taking up all the air in Tara. I loved Morrison, but something about the horned god just hit me on a primal level.

Probably the fact that he was a primal creature. Nuada, silver and beautiful as he was, looked like a bad knockoff beside the ancient god. Cernunnos swung down from his stallion, the beast that made me think of unicorns, if unicorns were depicted as savage, brilliant, vicious warmongers of devastating power instead of light fluffy balls of purity and rainbows.

"Little *gwyld,*" Cernunnos said, dry as a southwestern desert. "Siobhán Walkingstick. Joanne Walker. Thou has—"

Cernunnos rarely spoke English. Mostly, magic translated what he meant. In this particular case, I knew there were underlying words, a language I didn't actually know, but what I *heard* was an incredibly idiomatic, "Thou hast a lot of nerve, Joanne Walker."

That put the world back under my feet. I laughed and turned my palms up apologetically. "I know. Sorry. Hello, Cernunnos. It's been a while." It hadn't really. Not from my direction. But from another direction it had been a few thousand years, and I figured that counted for more. I turned to Nuada, hands still spread. "Is this convincing enough?"

Nuada looked a bit pale around the edges. "It is."

"A point?" Cernunnos asked in disbelief. "Thou hast—"

"I asked you not to do that. The theeing and the thouing." I found it disconcerting and peculiarly attractive, which added to the disconcertment.

Cernunnos snapped his teeth at me, but for the second time in our relationship, complied with my linguistic preferences. "You've brought me here to make a point, Siobhán Walkingstick?"

"More like to prove I am who I say I am so he won't marry the Morrígan and end up in that damned cauldron like the rest of them. Apparently elves need a lot of convincing," I added a bit sourly, because really, I felt like the whole being out of time and having magic items created by the silversmith should count for enough. On the other hand, though I would have never believed I'd end up thinking this, any day that involved a chat with the horned god was a pretty good one, so I wasn't going to complain too much.

"She speaks truly," Cernunnos said, just in case Nuada hadn't picked up on that. He nodded stiffly, and Cernunnos looked back at me, wickedness in his emerald eyes. "Ride with me. Let us go to Cnoc na rí and battle the beast who so nearly drains my spirit so many eons hence. Let us render the gift you gave me then unnecessary."

His memory really *did* work in both directions. A shiver spilled over my arms and I looked away. "You knew," I said uncertainly. "In the future, in my past, you must have known it was me at the diner. That I would take your sword. That we'd become…"

Wickedness lit his beautiful angular face again. "Siobhán Walkingstick, thou hast *no idea* what we shall become. But I do. I do. Come," he said again as I gaped at him. "Let us change the future that you know, my *gwyld*. Let us defeat death in these backward days of history, and see what new world awaits."

I wanted to. Oh, God, I wanted to. But I had ridden with the Hunt three times already, and I had barely escaped with my soul to call my own. And I *knew* I hadn't ridden with him now, in the past, because I *had* escaped with my soul, and I didn't think for a moment I could ride with him four times and not be his. Part of me wanted to be his. Part of me always would.

But sometime in the distant future I had already made this choice. Chosen a mortal existence with a mortal man, and even then Cernunnos had left me with an offer. A moment at the end of everything, where he and I might ride together one last time.

And he knew what I didn't: what we would become. I had

only had glimpses of it, if that was the future we shared at all, and I still wasn't ready to make that choice.

"I can't," I whispered with genuine regret. "You know I can't, my lord god of the hunt. I can't ride with you again. I never could."

"And yet I try," Cernunnos said playfully. "Time and again throughout time, I try. Until we meet again, my *gwyld*. Until time brings us together again." He swept a bow from the back of his great silver stallion, then looked to Nuada, all his grace turned to sour prissiness. "I would like that sword back, elf king."

"It seems time and this *gwyld* are yours to weave and weft," Nuada said without a hint of remorse. "Make your plea to her, not me. No one else in history has borne two of my blades, horned god. No one else has dared lose one."

I actually expected him to finish the little lecture with "Don't push it," but he managed to avoid the temptation. Cernunnos crooked a smile, acknowledgment of both the scolding and its unspoken end, then reined the stallion up, its hooves punching dents in the soft green hillside. "A pity," he said to all of us. "It would have been good to challenge the Morrígan's master so early in his bid for power, but even I will not ride against death without a force for life at my side."

Gary, diffidently, said, "I could go."

CHAPTER NINE

"What?" At least this time it wasn't just me. Nuada, Cernunnos and I all blurted the word, though Cernunnos looked an awful lot like the cat who stole the cream as he said it. Me, I finished with, "No way. Are you nuts? Are you *crazy?* Ride with the Wild Hunt without me to watch your back? Ride off through *time* on your own? Are you batshit insane? Are you *nuts?*"

"I've done it before," Gary said a bit belligerently.

My hands flew upward and waved in the air like they were trying to escape my wrists. "With Morrison and Suzanne and Billy! You weren't alone! And you weren't thousands of years out of time! And—"

"And I didn't have the Sight," Gary reminded me. "And somebody's gotta go meet Brigid, right? Maybe it ain't you the cauldron spell gets bound to, Jo. Maybe it's me. Besides, Horns here ain't gonna let anything happen to me, are you?" he said to Cernunnos. "Because if you do, you're gonna have Jo to reckon with, and I don't figure that's the kind of reckoning you're lookin' for with her."

The horned god lifted an agreeing eyebrow, which didn't reassure me at all. I gargled in frustration. "Come on, Cernunnos! You're the one who remembers meeting me in the future! You'd remember Gary going gallivanting off with you in the past, too, if it had already happened!"

Cernunnos's other eyebrow rose to match the first. "Would I? Perhaps in the past I remember best he came not to Tara with you. Of all mortals, you should realize that there are paths not taken. Nothing is immutable, Joanne. Not even for a god."

That was *not* the answer I wanted, especially after future-Brigid hadn't particularly seemed to know who Gary was. It lent credence to Cernunnos's argument. I made throttling motions with my fingers, envisioning the horned god's neck between them. "Okay, okay, all right, *fine,* but you just said you needed a force for life—"

"He may not heal," Cernunnos said, "but Master Muldoon is as bright a force of life as I have seen, and I have seen many. More, he carries with him the spirit of tenacity, a creature of great age and soul. He—"

"That's his spirit animal!" I howled. "I helped him *find* that!"

"All the better. It binds him to you and adds some note of your strength to his."

Gary looked triumphant. I stomped my foot, afraid I'd already lost the battle. "I said no! God, just because I got you into this doesn't mean you have to go gallivanting off across time and space to—"

"Save the world?" Gary planted himself in front of me. He made a big wall of a man, especially when he folded his arms across his chest and puffed up a little. "I've told you a hundred times you're the best thing that's happened to me in years, Joanie. You got me all tangled up in this crazy fantastic world of yours and brought me back to life after Annie died. I've watched you fling yourself into things you got no idea what's coming, and you do it all because you're trying to make the world a better place. You keep saying you want to grow up to be like me. Kid, I wish I'd been young like you. Now listen to me. You're my girl, and I'm doing this thing because it's what you would do if you could. 'Sides," he added, gray eyes bright, "this might be my one chance to kick death in the balls. Can't let an old guy miss that dance."

I laughed. I didn't want to, but I laughed. Then I hugged him, muttering, "If you don't come back," which I repeated when I let go of him, except this time I said it to Cernunnos, with a threatening finger added to the phrase.

He inclined his ashy head, temple bones visibly distorted in the fading light. "You have my word, Siobhán Walkingstick, and that is not a thing I give lightly."

"All right. Here." I thrust my rapier into Gary's hands. "You can use this, right? I mean, hell, you can do everything else."

He took it, but not gingerly. "I'm better with a saxophone, doll, but I'll make do. You sure? You might need it."

"I'm not the one proposing to go face down the man himself. You need it more than I do. Gary, are you *sure?* Because this is nuts."

The big man's voice gentled. "You can't do it, Jo. It's time you learn we'll go into battle for you, even if you ain't there."

"I don't want you to."

"Good generals don't." Gary stuck the rapier point down into the ground, took me by the shoulders and kissed my forehead. "I'll see you on the other side, darlin'."

"Of time. Just the other side of time, okay? No stupid hero-
ics, Gary. Not when I'm not there to save you."

"I promise." Gary let me go, took up the rapier again and
turned to Cernunnos. "Mind if I share your ride?"

Cernunnos looked pained and gestured to the boy who
rode beside him. "Share his. The mare is well used to a mortal
rider."

The mare was the boy Rider's human mother, transformed.
A whole pile of unfortunate things, mostly involving crude
comments about riders, immortal and mortal alike, rose to and
were compressed behind my lips. I could be dumb, but not *that*
dumb. Gary took the kid's hand and swung up onto the mare
behind him, then gave me a jaunty salute. "Go get 'em, Jo."

And then my best friend rode off into the sunset.

Nuada remained silent until Gary and Cernunnos vanished
into misty golden skies, which was just as well. I didn't like
Gary going off on his own, and had the sneaking suspicion
hypocrisy was my middle name. After a while I said, "So you
can't marry her," at the same time he said, "I think I have no
choice but to wed the Morrígan."

I was tired of saying "What?" so I just looked at him. He exhaled slowly. I half expected to see silver stream on his breath,
but it was just a puff of air like anyone else's. On it, he said,
"Because as we are bound to her, she is bound to us. I may be
able to temper her actions if I become her groom."

"Or you might end up skewered on the *Lia Fáil*."

Nuada's eyebrows quirked. "Not if I have yet to make that
sword and that necklace. Did you not say the sword comes
from many centuries hence?"

Everybody was smarter than me. I clicked my jaw shot,
looked for an argument and didn't find one. Or not much of

one, anyway: "What if Cernunnos came back in time to have you make it?"

"Then I still live some little ways into the future, for that has yet to happen. She is a goddess, Siobhán. How would you have me escape her?"

"She's only a, a, a small god. An avatar. You, *aos sí,* you're more connected to the earth than humans are. You run way down deep, but the Morrígan's lain down with the devil, which gives her bonus points in the mojo department." I'd used the word *mojo* plenty of times in the past. It had never triggered the mojojojo thing until Gary'd started snickering. I was going to smack him as soon as he got back from galumphing across time and space. "But somebody saddled up with Brigid, too, and it looks like you hang around for centuries making price-less magical artifacts, so stop putting so much stock in gods and…"

He waited a moment while I stared at the earth, dumbstruck by a slowly forming thought. "And forge this necklace," I mumbled eventually. "Close the time loop. Give it to her as a wedding gift. I don't know if the necklace has any power itself." Except it did, because in my personal arsenal it repre-sented shielding my mind. My soul. My garden. However I wanted to look at it, the necklace was definitely invested with some power. I swallowed and kept going. "But it makes it down through the centuries from her all the way to me. That's got to count for something. Maybe I'm not supposed to go up against her back now at all. Maybe this is all just preparation for a throw-down in my era."

In much the same tone Brigid had used, Nuada wondered, "Is this how it is with you, *gwyld?* The connected I have known are not so…"

"Connected?"

He nodded, looking as though he felt a bit foolish. I shook my head, dismissing his embarrassment. "They're probably not. I'm apparently a special case, which is less fun than you might think."

His mouth pursed, almost a smile. "I might remind you that I came to be crowned *ard rí,* and instead have learned I walked to my doom. I may understand "less fun than expected" better than you think I do."

I was too weak to resist. Given the opening, I seized it and nodded toward his silver hand. "You probably do. Gary said one of the other high kings chopped that off. What, um. How did…?"

"The magic that gives it life is beyond any I could command. The horned god invested it with warmth and motion in exchange for the sword I made him." His eyebrows quirked again. "The first sword. I wonder what gift he offers for the second."

"Probably not taking the magic hand away. Really? Cernunnos can do that?" An entire world lived and breathed with Cernunnos's life force. It probably wasn't all that difficult for him to lend a little life to a hunk of metal. I just didn't know why he'd want to.

"He had to, or I could not forge the sword for him."

"Oh." I wondered briefly if Cernunnos lived linearly and remembered anti-linearly, but that was too much for my brain to handle. I put it away for another time, and asked, "Can you make the necklace? I don't know what the timeline is here. Are you supposed to get married this afternoon?"

"You stand out of time already," Nuada said. "Can you not step a day or two away and bid me make it then?"

"If I had the foggiest idea how, maybe, but I obviously haven't because you hadn't seen it until just now. Tara's huge,"

I said with a wave of my hand, trying to encompass it. "Isn't there a forge around here somewhere?" Not that I remembered a Forge of the Kings on the tourist maps. That could be an oversight, but I was pretty sure forges left enough residue that somebody would've noticed and pointed it out.

Nuada looked bemused. "You know little of metal forging. It takes time to build the heat, to—"

"C'mon, it's not like making steel." Incomprehension made Nuada's eyes more silvery still. I dropped my chin to my chest. "Steel. It's a metal from the future. It takes a lot more heat than precious metals do. Maybe I could…" A couple times I'd worked up enough heat for self-immolation, once almost literally. I studied my hands, remembering the burn of a cut across one palm healing, and reached for my magic, hoping I could create fire through my will alone.

Fire rose up, all right, but it was the fire of pain, not actual flames. An itch erupted in the bite, like using my magic excited the cells there, and I hissed at the brief, compelling idea that life would be easier if I was a wolf. I said, "Forget it," as much to the impulse as Nuada, then, more to the silver king, "We'll need a real forge."

"Then the Morrígan shall wait another year for her king." Nuada sounded both resigned and calm. "She should have come by now, as it is. Perhaps your friend holds her attention so we might do our work."

A fist knotted in my gut. "I hate that idea."

"All the more reason to work swiftly and well. Come. The towers will have forges. Does one speak to you?"

Dismay rumbled through me. "I don't want to leave Tara. I'm already in the wrong time. I don't know what happens if I leave this location. If we've got time, why not build a forge?"

Aside from the fact no evidence of one remained in my time, that was.

Nuada gave me a patient look. "I will return you safely to Tara. Now. Does one speak to you?"

I sighed and pointed southwest. "That one. It's still there in my time. Or *a* tower is, anyway. I like the consistency."

"At Troim. They will have what we need."

They did. They also had a village full of curious people—humans, not the *aos sí*—which made me and my short hair and my formerly awesome white leather coat feel considerably more awkward than I had standing more or less alone on a hill in the middle of a sacred circle. Worse, nobody spoke to me. They just watched us, wide-eyed and silent, as if we were wraiths passing unwelcome through time.

Which was unfortunately accurate. Nuada was a dead man walking and I didn't belong there at all. The blacksmith, though, nodded to me when Nuada explained what we needed. That made me feel better until he backed rapidly as soon as he'd shown Nuada where the tools lay. I had a bunch of friends at home who had started reacting the same way after my abrupt shamanic awakening: nominally polite, but eager to get out of my presence. Apparently living sometime in the indeterminable past, alongside elves and small gods, did not make most people any happier or more comfortable with magic being done around them.

"They fear me," Nuada murmured as the blacksmith backed off. I startled, having been so busy taking all the discomfort on myself it hadn't occurred to me he might be a problem, too. He worked as he spoke, bringing the forge's fires up higher and selecting the finest and most delicate tools the blacksmith had to offer. "We live side by side in this place, your people and mine, but we are not friends. We share this site of worship, but never ritual or passion. To them, we are the whispers in the wind and the lightning in the sky. To us, they are the brutal and dangerous things in the night."

"The *Fir Bolg,*" I said, dragging up the name from some bit of reading I'd done. "Weren't they the enemies of the *aos sí?*"

"So they are. Dark men, tied to the earth with their short and ugly lives." He glanced at me, and clarified, "Humans," just in case I hadn't gotten it.

"What a charming sentiment. No wonder you get along so well. Jesus Christ, what are you doing?"

He gave me a look that said volumes about my intellect, which was fair enough, because what he was doing was extremely obvious: he'd stuck his silver hand in the flame and was melting his fingers off. Liquid metal dripped into an iron trough while I watched with horrified fascination. "Doesn't that hurt?"

"Metal feels no pain."

"But—but—!"

"Where did you think the metal for your necklace came from? For the swords? They would be nothing if they were not made of the living silver. Anyone might forge a sword. This is my blood, *gwyld.* My essence. My very life, made metal."

"That's the most awful thing I've seen." I couldn't stop watching. It was like a magical train wreck. Creepy crawlies ran down my spine, up my arms, all over, but I couldn't look away. "It just keeps…bleeding?"

"Melting," he said dourly. "Yes. It has no end, or none I've found. Gift of the god, Siobhán."

I muttered, "Joanne," without any real hope. *Siobhán* obviously sounded more like a name to him, and having heard it from Cernunnos's lips, Nuada wasn't about to let it go. I felt at my hip, not that I ever carried my sword there anyway, and didn't find it. "It really is a magic sword." I hoped like hell that was doing Gary some good.

"And a magic torc. What power will it have?"

"The power to bind. That's what we're doing with the cauldron. Binding the Morrígan to me, so she can do no harm until she faces me again." That sounded pretty good. Some aspect of it would no doubt go terribly wrong, but I was doing my best.

Nuada nodded once. The smell of hot silver baked in my nostrils and the color burned my eyes. Nuada could make the necklace at my request, out of his own very essence, but that wasn't going to be enough. Not to bind the Morrígan to me, not to render her impotent across the centuries. Something else had to lock the time loop in place, and all of a sudden I knew what it was.

Quickly, before my confidence evaporated, I picked up a piece of edged metal from the forge, slashed my palm and let my blood fall into the sizzling metal.

CHAPTER TEN

Silver turned red for the space of a breath. I was certain that with ordinary silver that wouldn't happen, but this wasn't ordinary. Then it all blackened, like the silver had aged a hundred years in an instant. Nuada, unconcerned, worked the metal with a small hammer until black was beaten away and thin sheets of silver remained. He moved quickly, certainly, until I was half hypnotized with the steady flow of his actions and the atonal music of the forge.

He might have worked for an hour or forever, for all I could tell, but suddenly he was finished, stepping back from his work with a critical eye. I hardly dared move, afraid he'd find some flaw, but after long minutes of examination he grunted—not a sound I expected from an elf king—and moved aside so I could see what he had wrought.

And what he had wrought was impossible. I had always assumed my necklace was poured into a mold: the long tubes that curved around its delicate chain, and the two triskelions that separated those tubes, were all much too finely worked to have been done with a hammer and…chisel, or whatever a silversmith called it. There was no roughness to the quartered circle that sat in the hollow of my throat as the necklace's pendant, either, and it was just not possible such crude tools could produce an item of such smooth beauty.

Except they had. I took up the finished piece in astonishment, feeling faint warmth still within the metal. I was sure it had cooled completely, and looked at Nuada in confusion. "It lives, *gwyld*. A part of me. I have told you this already. It will be warm so long as I walk this earth."

The necklace I had been given was warmed by my dying mother's body heat, but hadn't had an inherent warmth like it did now. For once I was smart enough not to say anything and nodded instead. "It's beautiful."

"It is invested with my being and yours, both bent to the single intent of containing the Morrígan. It is a magic of two worlds, and will collar her wretched ambitions for eons." That, apparently, was far more important to Nuada than its beauty, which was fair enough. But then he smiled, suddenly the artist and pleased with the compliment. "Thank you, Joanne." He said my name carefully. "Not only for the making of the necklace, but the warning of what I face with the Morrígan. Now I must return you to Tara before the seasons turn again and my bride comes looking for her groom. You will not want to be there when she finds the trap we've laid for her."

"No, I won't. But I'll throw down with her in my time, Nuada. I'll set this right."

"You cannot set it right, Joanne. You can only end what has been made wrong." A smile twinged his lips. "And I cannot set it right, either, but I can go to my fate knowing I have helped set in motion a thing that will, in time, end the wrongness. There is little else a worthy king might ask for."

My nose got all stuffy with emotion. I hardly knew the guy, but blatant nobility apparently hit me right in the soft spot. "Well, watch yourself, all right? You've got another sword to make, at the very least."

"You, too, watch yourself, Joanne Walker."

We walked back to Tara together without really speaking again. Even when we crossed the moats and passed under the huge wood henges to climb toward the *Lia Fáil,* there was almost nothing to say.

Almost. I reached for the stone, then hesitated just one instant, looking back toward Nuada, and we spoke at the same time: "Good luck."

Smiling, pleased and ready for everything to be back to normal, I put my hands on the Stone of Destiny, and went crashing back through time.

Monday, March 20, 10:52 a.m.

There was a dead woman at my feet.

She sat propped against the *Lia Fáil,* in exactly the same position Brigid had been in last I'd seen her. A dead woman wearing a white cotton eyelet dress and scarves at her hips. The one around her shoulders had slipped away, revealing fiery tattoos around her biceps that hadn't faded in thousands of years.

I stared at her, numb with incomprehension. The Sight slipped on, not because I wanted it, but because I needed it. Tara went thick and gray around me, its power tainted more strongly than before, but of course it was, if Brigid was dead. If she had *been* dead for millennia, and I saw no other possible explanation, then Tara had been missing one of its protectors for most of human history.

A spiderweb of blue and black was buried in Brigid's chest. Deep in it, squeezing her lungs, poisoning her blood: the Morrígan's magic, killing Brigid instead of me. Sick to my stomach, I knelt beside her.

With the Sight, I saw her heart beat once. A slow painful spasm, but a heartbeat. Panicked relief surged and I put my hand over her heart, healing magic already pouring out.

She caught my wrist. I had no idea where she'd gotten the strength to move, but she caught my wrist and she smiled. Shook her head, and whispered, "Not yet, *gwyld*. Not yet."

"What do you mean, not yet? You're going to *die* if I don't act now! Jesus! Gary, talk some sense into this wo—"

Gary wasn't there.

I forgot about Brigid in an instant, stumbling to my feet to look around. Tara, with the exception of Brigid's presence and the heavier grayness to its aura, was the same. Quiet with morning, its power running through the land. The *Lia Fáil* was shrieking again, which I'd barely even noticed. Everything was the same.

But Gary hadn't been returned to this time and place at the end of our adventure. Hands shaking, I fumbled for the cell phone the precinct had assigned me. I'd quit too abruptly to give it back, and no doubt somebody would be outraged at running up international phone bills on it, but that was a problem for another time. I found Gary's listing, swore violently as the out-of-country code told me it didn't know how to call that number and got down on my knees to put my forehead against the grass in supplication toward remembering Ireland's call code. It popped to mind and I punched it and Gary's number in, trembling with anticipation. If the gods—and I meant that rather literally—were kind, he'd pick up from somewhere in the west of Ireland, no worse for wear.

He didn't pick up. After several rings a recorded voice informed me that the number was unavailable. A tiny scared caw broke at the back of my throat and I called again, getting the same message. Then I called Morrison.

He picked up on the second ring, a too-crisp alertness in his voice. "Walker? What's wrong?"

"It's Gary. I lost him. Oh, fuck, it's like three in the morning there. I'm sorry. Shit. I'm sorry, I'll call back—" Not that I had any more idea what Morrison could do six hours from now than he could do now. *He,* after all, had the magical aptitude of a turnip. *He* would not be caught skipping merrily through time, with or without my assistance.

"Joanne. Joanie. What do you mean, you lost him? He caught up with you? Don't hang up. What's going on? Are you okay?"

Like Gary, Morrison never called me Joanie. I had to sound even worse than I felt if he'd gone that route. Either that or he was trying to reassure me, but it didn't work even one little bit at all. "I'm not okay but I'm an idiot and there's nothing you can do about it. Just—just keep trying to call him? Please? Like every hour? And if you get through have him call me right away?"

Morrison made a sound I was familiar with. Strangled frustration, like his tongue was trying to choke him. "He's in Ireland with you?"

"He *was.* Maybe he still is. We went back in time. I came back. He might still be there. Or he might be dead, because he went to fight the Master or the Morrígan and I just don't *know.*"

"You went back in time," Morrison said in a slow deadly

voice. I could imagine his expression, his whole posture. He'd be on his feet, because he wasn't the sort of man who would answer the phone still in bed. He just wasn't. I had no idea what he wore to bed—it was a subject I had some interest in—but maybe a tank top and cotton pants. Something dignified enough to run outside and chase bad guys in, if necessary. Always be prepared. That was Morrison. And he was dragging a hand over his face now, trying to decide where to start with *we went back in time,* because face it, that wasn't the opening gambit you expected your almost-lover to use when she called from the other side of the world. "You went back in time," he repeated, "and you expect his cell phone to work?"

"Well, no, I just, I mean, I came back and he hasn't! Shouldn't he have?"

Morrison, very steadily, said, "Were you together?"

"No! I just said he went to fight the Morrígan!"

"I see." There was a pause. "The man is seventy-four years old, Joanie. He can take care of himself. If you were—" a great and patient pause filled the line before he went on "—time traveling. If you were time traveling and got separated, then I can't think of any reason he would necessarily come back to the present at the same time you did."

"Except I was the focal point, it was my fault, it—!"

"Joanne. Siobhán. Siobhán Grainne MacNamarra Walking-stick."

I didn't think anybody had ever said my name like that before. I gulped down a hysterical sob and whispered, "Yeah?"

Morrison, with gentle emphasis, said, "I love you. Now pull yourself together and go find the bad guy," and hung up.

I stayed kneeling in the grass for a long time, blushing so hard I thought I'd fall over if I got up. Nobody in my adult life had ever said he loved me. Nobody but Gary, who I also loved, but in a whole different way. Morrison's admonishment was the nicest thing anybody'd ever said to me, and I felt like a teenager, so embarrassed and happy I was in danger of crying. He didn't just love me. He loved me *and* expected me to be able to catch the bad guys, even though I'd woken him up in the middle of the night just this side of hysterical.

By God if I wasn't going to prove him right, too. I'd spent an awful lot of time dedicated to proving Morrison wrong, once upon a time. Proving him right sounded a lot nicer. And besides, it would either get Gary back or exact unholy vengeance on the bitch who'd taken him from me, so proving him right had multiple benefits.

I looked back at the *Lia Fáil* and at Brigid. Her eyes were closed, her breathing impossibly shallow. She was not going to be of any help, especially if she wouldn't let me try to heal her. Sighing, I glanced toward the Hall of Kings. It lay off to the right now instead of straight ahead like it had been in Lugh's time. I remembered the shock of power that had come from it being stationed right at Tara's center. If worse came to worst, I would dig the damned stone up and put it back where it belonged in order to throw myself back in time so I could find Gary again.

It was a plan. It wasn't necessarily a good plan, but it was a plan and I was satisfied with it. I crawled back to Brigid and took her hand in mine, whispering, "How about now?"

She said nothing, only slipped deeper into sleep. I didn't want to go against her wishes by healing her, but I needed some answers, or at least some advice. I whispered, "C'mon, c'mon," then, hoping one ancient thing might get the attention of another, put Brigid's hand against the Stone of Destiny, and held it there.

The stone's screaming leapt from inside my ears to outside them, and a woman appeared in my vision.

I knew her. Fair-haired and fair-skinned, I'd seen her work a magic well beyond any I could have imagined. She was the one who'd—centuries ago—lured the first three werewolves to her power circle and then bound them to the cycle of the moon. It had weakened them beyond measure: they had gone from creatures able to shift and kill at will to the traditional monsters as modern mythology knew them, only able to transform three nights out of the month. One of their descendants had tried very hard to make my magic her own in order to break that spell.

She'd failed, but she had managed to leave the bite in my arm. It flared up again, itching like a son of a bitch, and the fair-haired woman's spine stiffened as she looked me over. Then her brow furrowed, confusion in gray-green eyes. "Tainted blood. You must be cleansed before you can survive this battle. Find me, daughter. Together we shall prevail."

"*Daughter?* Wait! Hey! Wa—arghgl!" It was my turn for the tongue-trying-to-strangle-me sound as for the umpteenth time in recent hours, my mysterious visitor up and vanished. Next time somebody showed up like that I was going to cast a mystical net and hold on until I got some answers.

Like why she'd called me daughter. That woman was manifestly not my mother. She *had* been wearing my mother's necklace, which probably meant a connection of some kind. That wasn't good, since Nuada and I had just gone to the trouble of making the necklace for the Morrígan, who wasn't supposed to be able to take it off. Of course, if she couldn't take it off, then Sheila MacNamarra should not have been wearing it or giving it to me fifteen months ago in my own personal timeline. Which meant I shouldn't have had it to show Nuada to commission it from him, which in turn meant that something had already gone horribly wrong.

I swore out loud, and pulled my hands from the standing stone. It went back to shouting only in my skull, which was an improvement.

"It only cries aloud when a scion of the true blood touches it," Brigid whispered.

I knew she was there. I just about jumped out of my skin anyway. "The what? That's ridiculous. I'm not an elf. Where's *Gary?*"

"Not all the high kings of Ireland were *aos sí, gwyld.*"

I slid down the *Lia Fáil* and put my hands in my hair. "Okay. All right, fine, if you want to play it that way, I'll play. Oh, gosh, Brigid, whatever do you mean? Lil' ol' me? The True Heir to Ireland? It cannot be so! I beg of you, tell me more!"

Brigid looked weary and for a moment I felt guilty. Then I remembered Gary hadn't made it home with me. Anything resembling guilt went out the window. I genuinely did not give a rat's ass about what my mystical or ethnic heritage might be. I wanted to fix the werewolf bite and get Gary back, not necessarily in that order, so when Brigid started up again I only half listened. "You already know of Méabh, Queen of Connacht—"

"Meabh," I said under my breath. "That's Maeve, right? You say it a little differently."

As if I hadn't interrupted, Brigid went on, "*Méabh,* Queen of Connacht, said by some to be the Morrígan herself. She was not. She was, though, the Morrígan's first and only child, born to Nuada of the Silver Hand, High King of Ireland, who had gifted her with a necklace—"

My hand closed on the necklace in question and Brigid

smiled faintly. "A necklace which would not come unclasped except by one of the blood of she who had commissioned it made. To be free of Nuada's silver chains, the Morrígan had a daughter, and those daughters had daughters all through time, until it comes to you, Siobhán Walkingstick."

My stomach dropped through the soles of my feet. "No. No, wait. The whole idea was she wasn't supposed to be able to take it off. She was supposed to be bound until she faced me in my time. Blood to bloo—" My stomach would have started digging a hole, if it had the appendages. I stared at Brigid, hoping she would give me a different answer than the conclusion I was rapidly coming to.

Instead she gave my bandaged left arm a tired glance and used the same words the woman in my vision had: "Tainted blood."

I hated cryptic statements. I hated them even more when they illuminated everything. I clutched my arm, teeth bared momentarily at the pain, then whispered a curse. The blood I'd dropped into the silver *had* been tainted. I'd been carrying the werewolf's poison inside me, and I'd known the wolves belonged to the Master. The impulse to stop fighting the ache and the itch swept me again, and I raised my voice to deny it. "It made a window, didn't it. A loophole, one she could get free of the necklace through. Blood to blood," I said again. "Méabh was her way out. Blood of her blood, essence of Nuada's essence. The same magics that bound her could free her. And I should have known that, because I *had* the necklace to show to Nuada, and if it had worked the Morrígan wouldn't have been able to take it off and my mother never would have had it to give to me. *Damn* it."

Somewhere in there I'd come around to accepting that the Morrígan was my great-to-the-umpteenth-grandmother. That

Méabh, who had removed the necklace, basically had to be both the Morrígan's daughter and some distant ancestor of mine. The blood demanded it. I still protested, albeit much less convincingly than I'd have liked. "I can't possibly be the Morrígan's granddaughter. We're on totally opposite sides."

"Like all children of power, Méabh had a choice. She chose the light, as have all her children in turn."

For some reason I thought of Suzanne Quinley again. There was a kid with a whole lot of power. I wondered if she even knew she had a choice in front of her. I might have to talk to her about that someday. Because after all, I was so very, very good at choosing wisely when it came to great cosmic powers. Exasperated, afraid and unable to give in gracefully, I muttered, "Yeah, okay, fine, whatever. Didn't Méabh have like twelve kids all named Finnoula or something? Maybe I'm one of their descendants, sure. I'm probably one of Genghis Khan's, too. Everybody on the damned planet is. Or Charlemagne, or, I don't know, Cleopatra. No, that's reincarnated. Anyway, great, that's dandy, but I'm not the heir to a defunct Irish throne."

"You might be," Brigid murmured, "if you were willing to accept that fate."

I barked laughter, finding bitterness easier than acceptance. "Lady, you have no clue how much fate I've already taken in the teeth. I don't need any more. All I want is to find my friend. And…" An obvious question finally surfaced. I straightened up, frowning. "Brigid, what are you *doing* here? Last I knew you'd…"

She hadn't vanished, per se. Not the way the Morrígan had. Brigid had faded, becoming ephemeral beside the standing stone. "Last I knew you'd saved my life and then time shifted and you were gone. You obviously bound the cauldron, because all that happened to me back in October. So what are you doing here with a fritzed-out aura that looks like it only just now took the Morrígan's best shot?"

"We are sides of a coin, she and I," Brigid said. "My weakness is her strength, and I have been weak since that day. She might have slain me then, had you not been there, pulling time askew. Because of that, I have only touched time, where she has traveled through it."

For a moment I just didn't get it. Then my eyebrows pinched so hard my head hurt. "You mean you, like…you've been bouncing through time? Like a skipping stone?" I mimed throwing one. Brigid nodded and I blurted, *"Why?"*

"So that I might awaken again here, with you, at the place it both begins and ends. I have done less than I might have through the centuries, only acting when the balance was in the measure, rather than fighting to tip the scales toward the light. That, I think, is why the cauldron's bindings failed before you reached it, and for that I apologize."

"Forget it." My voice cracked. "You bound it. That means it was one of the places, one of the times, you splashed down. You were there, Brigid. What happened to Gary?"

"A reckoning is upon us, Siobhán Walkingstick. What strength I have will be yours, but you must rid yourself of the infection or all is lost." She sounded tireder than before, like she was slipping away. It took everything I had not to grab her and rattle the answers out of her. Her eyes closed, and for a moment I thought she'd died. Then she whispered, "He awaits you at Méabh's final resting place."

And then she did die. A rattling exhalation and her eyes half opened, looking sleepily at the world beyond. My heart lurched so hard I nearly threw up. Healing magic jerked through me, spasming toward Brigid, but the reawakened Sight gave it nothing to grasp on to. My hands slid to my sides and hung there uselessly as Brigid grew colder. I could have rushed off to the Dead Zone, trying to catch her spirit, but it seemed unlikely that *aos sí* souls took the same bus that human ones did. I probably could have done about a dozen things, but they all should've been done five minutes earlier, when she wasn't dead yet. When she'd been telling me *not yet*. I bowed my head, eyes closed, and made a promise not to listen next time someone told me *not yet*.

The Morrígan, I thought after a while. The Morrígan had killed Brigid. It had taken her thousands of years to die, but the bleak web of poison within her—the web meant for me— had killed her, and that put me on strangely familiar ground. I'd dealt with a lot of mystical murders in the past year. They pretty much never ended well for the killer.

I got to my feet and straightened my coat. I was going to make damned good and sure this one didn't end well, either.

Calm with anger, I left Brigid's body behind and went to find Méabh's tomb.

Monday, March 20, 1:17 p.m.

That would have been much more dramatic if the tomb in question didn't turn out to be another heritage site. It'd be one thing to traipse the length and breadth of Ireland, seeking out dead life forms and ancient civilizations only to finally come upon the Lost Tomb of the Warrior Queen. It was something else to follow little brown-and-white road signs all the way to County Sligo, where I found a small mountain with a big pile of rocks on top of it.

This was not untraveled territory. There were signs saying "Please don't take the cairn stones," and well-worn paths going up and down the mountainside. I breathed, "Hope you were right, Bridge," and started up one of them. I felt guilty for leaving her body like that. I sort of suspected it would do some kind of magic *aos sí* thing and fade into the earth or something, and it wasn't like I could've stuffed her in the trunk, but I still felt badly.

The guilt faded into breathless wheezing and resentment by about halfway up the hill. She hadn't warned me Méabh's tomb was on top of a mountain. I wished I had a walking stick. The kind to support myself with, not the kind I was named after. Stick bugs would be singularly useless in getting me up a mountain. Unless they could fly me up, but bugs named for sticks weren't really well known for their aviary skills.

That line of thought did nothing to disguise my heart rate's elevation or how its quick beat made my arm itch like the devil. I stopped for a breather and cautiously unwound the bandages to take a peek at the bite.

And wished I hadn't. Whether it was the fresh air against it or seeing how awful it looked, the itching redoubled and became hot red pain. The skin around the punctures emanated heat, shiny tight surface looking and feeling infected. An infected werewolf bite had to be worse than just a regular werewolf bite. I touched it gingerly and hissed at both its warmth and the bright flash of *ow* that pressure sent through it. I muttered, "C'mon, Jo, you're supposed to be a healer," and tried my magic on it again.

Maybe it was the sleep I'd had on the airplane. Maybe it was the soothing drive across the country. But this time when the magic didn't respond, I went a little deeper, and Saw what was going on.

It was already going all-out trying to keep the infection from spreading. Viewed with the Sight, my arm looked like a petri dish swarm of antibodies attacking bacteria. The speed and activity made me dizzy, and watching made it itch even more, until I was about ready to rip my own arm off and beat myself to death with it just to escape the itch. I closed my eyes hard, shutting the Sight down, but it was too late. I knew what was going on. I felt genuinely worse than before, like viewing it had let the heat spread. My lips were parched, and I'd left my water bottle in the car. I swallowed, light-headed, and looked up the insurmountable hill.

Gary had my sword. If he was in Méabh's tomb, he could chop my arm off for me. That would be easier than tearing it off. Buoyed by that unlikely, feverish logic, I staggered to my feet and lurched toward the cairn above.

The view from the top of Knocknaree was magnificent. I could see half of Ireland, even if it was doing a wavy little dance. Everybody needed to dance now and again. I wobbled around the whole cairn, which was a fancy word for "big pile of rocks," for about twenty minutes. There was no entrance anywhere, and when I came around to the front again I noticed a sign I'd missed while admiring the wobbly view. It said Méabh's "tomb," quotation marks theirs, was a Neolithic structure and had never been excavated. Also, it said, please don't take any rocks. I nodded solemnly, spun back to the big piles of rocks and started pitching stones away.

Three minutes later a grinning skeleton toppled out of the cairn and spat its false teeth at me.

CHAPTER ELEVEN

I screamed in genuine horror-movie terror. The skeleton fell apart into about eleventy million pieces, or at least two hundred and six. Seven, counting the teeth. I dropped to my knees and scooped them up, already blinded by tears. Finding Gary's bones might technically qualify as him waiting for me in the tomb, but it was not the answer I was looking for. The teeth were heavy and sharp, a snaggle catching my palm as I turned them over and over. If this was going to be my legacy, I didn't want it. To hell with phenomenal cosmic power, to hell with saving the world, to hell with all the lessons I'd learned clawing my way to where I was now. I'd stepped up. I'd done everything I could to be the hero, and all I'd gotten for it was a view to literally die for.

Somehow I was on my feet, screaming at the distant horizon. "Fuck you! Fuck you *all!* I did not sign up for getting my friends killed, and you can all go fuck yourselves! I am *not playing this game anymore!*" I threw the teeth as hard as I could, the snaggle poking my hand a second time as I clenched and released. A sob wrenched my throat and I fell to my knees again, face buried in my hands. The stupid little poke from the teeth itched. Nothing like the werewolf bite, but enough to be a horrible reminder that I'd just thrown away the last remnant of the best friend I'd ever had. I'd come to grips with my powers because people had died when I hadn't. People dying because I *had* seemed like a justifiable reason to lose that grip. Gary wouldn't want me to, but I didn't have so many friends I was willing to lose them over a power set I hadn't asked for. I reversed my legs, scootching on my butt toward the downward path. I was going home. I was going to ask Morrison for my job back. Or not, because I couldn't be his employee and his girlfriend at the same time. Maybe I'd open that mechanic shop I'd always wanted to. With all the spare cash I'd saved up against quitting my job on no notice. It didn't matter. The Morrígan and the cauldron and Brigid and the Master and whatever the hell else was out there could just sort itself out, and I'd amputate my goddamned arm to avoid becoming a werewolf. I was done.

A stray bolt of sunlight caught the white curve of the teeth I'd thrown down the hill.

Gary's teeth were perfect.

My whole body went so cold the werewolf bite stopped itching. I sat there on my butt, utterly frozen, staring at the teeth as the illuminating sunlight faded away. They had a snaggle, and Gary's teeth were perfect. The collapsed skeleton behind me did not belong to my friend.

For the second time in as many minutes I was on my feet, shrieking at the horizon again as I punched the sky. "Take *that*, motherfuckers! Take that, you ugly sons of bitches! I'm going to find you, you hear me? I'm going to find you and me and Gary are gonna *kick your asses!* Fuck you! Fuck all of you right in the ear!"

I went on like that for quite a while, until I noticed that tears were streaming down my face again. It struck me that I was possibly in need of some therapy. I wondered what the police department shrink, who had told me just three days ago that I was handling having shot somebody pretty well, would think of my current antics. I wondered if she was in any way equipped to therapize somebody like me, whose life really did encompass the impossible. I'd have to ask when I got back, because it had been a rough weekend even by my standards, and there wasn't much standing between me and a total mental breakdown. It seemed like Gary not being quantifiably dead should restore me, not send me over the edge, but I was teetering dangerously close to the edge.

Gary. If that wasn't Gary up there, it was somebody else. Somebody who'd died recently enough to have modern false teeth. Somebody who had been buried shallowly in a national monument, and hadn't yet been discovered.

Somebody who had decomposed into a fragile skeleton instead of a heap of smelly flesh. Maybe it wasn't such a recent death after all. I pulled myself together and went to check.

The skeleton really was in about two hundred and six pieces, and there were no markers—no clothes, no jewelry, no handy wallet—to indicate who it might once have been. I was no forensic anthropologist. I couldn't tell if the splayed hip bones were male or female. And ghosts were not my strong suit, which was to say, I couldn't call one up if my life depended on it. Even Billy wouldn't be much help this time, since he was good with the newly dead, and unless my friend here had been dumped in a vat of acid, he wasn't all that newly dead. So he was probably a murder victim, and I should probably call the local cops.

The question of whether or not to call was abruptly negated by a banshee rising out of the disturbed bones.

I'd met a banshee before. This one was…fresher. Skin drawn less tightly across her bones, black hair still thick and lush instead of scraggly. Clawed fingernails slightly less clawlike, as if she hadn't had centuries to hone them. And I guessed that answered the question of whether the skeleton was male or female. For an instant we stared at one another, me shocked and her—I don't know what she was thinking. It looked like she was assessing me as a potential threat. I started to reach for my sword, remembered it was lost somewhere in time with Gary and with that failure apparently came up lacking in the banshee's estimation. She dove at me, shrieking, and I fell ass over teakettle trying to get out of the way. The bite on my arm flared, itch suddenly all-consuming as the urge to become *other* struck me again.

This time I was tempted. I hadn't come out so well fighting a banshee the first time around. It had taken my dead mother to pull my hiney out of the fire, and I didn't think she would be able to do it again. Being four-legged, furry and with vicious teeth sounded like a better bet than my own raggedy-ass self. The only problem was I wanted to be in control of a change. The raging heat in my forearm assured me I wouldn't be.

The banshee overshot thanks to my display of gymnastic excellence. I scrambled to all fours, crouching on the mountaintop as she swung back around. Her aura shone black against the cloud-spattered skies, making my tight-to-skin shields a bastion of light in comparison. She probably literally had the home field advantage, but I hadn't been in control of my magic when I'd last met a banshee. I repeated that to myself and tried not to look too hard at her nails. They were more than long enough to eviscerate me. Shields or not, I still wanted my tender underbelly well out of her reach. It wasn't killing season as far as ritualistically feeding the Master was concerned, but it also wasn't far off, and besides, I felt relatively certain he'd make a special exception if one of his minions managed to get me served up on a plate.

This particular minion, though, hung there in midair with rage contorting her papery face as she snarled, "Firstborn daughter, blooded child, Master's slave is driven wild!"

Oh, hell. I'd forgotten about that. The damned banshees spoke in terrible poems. Last time I'd faced one I was afraid I'd be rhymed to death. Cryptic was bad enough. Cryptic rhymes were rubbing salt in the wound.

But *slave* was an interesting choice of word. I stayed huddled, trying to remember if the last banshee had responded when I didn't speak in rhyme. I hoped so, because under pressure like this I couldn't come up with even a bad poem to save my life. "I don't mean to go all Spartacus on you, but there's one sure way out of slavery. If you want to come down here and talk it out I'll…" *Rip your head off with my bare hands* was kind of how that sentence ended, but I didn't think that would go over so well. "…help you."

Rather than take me up on my generous offer, she screamed and came at me again. Fingernails on chalkboards and metal tearing and hysterical babies and every other hideous, piercing, reverberating sound in the history of mankind rang through that scream, and it tried to shiver my skin off. It actually *did* get through my shields, not entirely, but enough to crack them. I yelped, as much startled as afraid, then clenched my belly and strengthened the idea of pearlescent shields shimmering around me, *Star Trek*-like.

It was too late. Somehow she was under the shields, her scream seeping through to suck up against my skin and worm its way deeper. My vulnerabilities were exposed, all the spiderweb cracks in my windshield. She went for them like she knew they were there, endless shrieks wresting them apart. Gary's disappearance was the newest crack in my facade, and my fear for him grew with each new banshee cry.

I wondered if that was how banshees killed people when they weren't eviscerating them. Death by screaming. Death by prying at all the cracks that made up a persona until they shattered and the few really unbearable things in a life were exposed and remembered. In that case, they weren't harbingers of death at all, regardless of what the legends said. They were murderers through and through.

She pushed past my worries about Gary and latched onto a deeper concern. An older one: Morrison. The Almighty Morrison, with his silvering hair and ice-blue eyes and his strong, competent hands. Morrison, who had been so utterly gorgeous the first time I'd laid eyes on him I'd gotten all fourth grade and hit him—metaphorically if not physically—to show him how much I liked him. Morrison with his frustrated grace in deciding to use my powers, powers neither of us understood, to solve cases that had no rational explanation. Morrison with his expectations of me, expectations I desperately wanted to live up to without admitting that to either of us. Morrison in the wilderness of a mountain forest, with the shadow of a tattoo on his shoulder. A tattoo that didn't really exist. Yet.

I bristled, fingernails digging into the dirt as I shoved back.

Morrison was *my* territory, and I wasn't about to give him up to a shrieking she-demon from the world beyond. Glee shot through her hideous voice like she'd made a palpable hit, and a vision of Morrison going down under a banshee's attack swept me.

A vision of Morrison unloading his gun into the banshee's belly swept me, too. It wouldn't stop her. Supernatural creatures usually didn't die from mundane weapons. But it would sure as hell slow her down, and once I got done with this jaunt to Ireland it was my goal in life to never be so far from Morrison's side that slowing down a monster wouldn't buy enough time for me to get there and go medieval on its ass.

I snapped my teeth at the banshee in my own sort of savage glee, and somewhere way down at the back of my brain I started worrying that all this snapping and bristling was starting to get very lupine. I had to haul myself back. My arm didn't itch anymore. It felt like it was on fire instead, and the fire was spreading through my whole body. The very cells were crying out to change, and I was just barely staying on this side of self-aware enough to fight it.

The banshee's voice went high and almost sweet, and drove right through my skull down to my most buried and most vulnerable concerns. "What's this, what's this, she remembers a kiss!" Delicious spite brightened her voice, making it sound like swords scraping. "The Master's meal was a little wild, bore herself a wee boy child!"

I whispered, "Oh, come on, that's twice in a row you've used *wild/child*. You can do better than that," but the mockery wasn't enough to keep rage from rising as silver in my gaze. I'd given Aidan up for adoption so he could have a better life than my fifteen-year-old self was prepared to offer him. Letting banshees know about his existence and come hunting him did not in any way qualify as better. Maybe fighting to the death to protect a child was stereotypical, but right there, right then, I was okay with that. I sounded raw and cracked as the banshee as I grated, "You will not touch my son."

I stopped fighting it and let the werewolf take me.

Pure savagery rose in my bones, contorting them with snaps and stretches. The boiling heat within me expanded outward, sudden rush of kinetic energy released. It hurt like scratching a bad itch did: it hurt good. That was wrong, because according to Coyote, shapeshifting was supposed to be a seamless and painless transition, but I'd spent so much time itching and being unable to scratch that it was just a relief. I didn't care if it was wrong.

I was in motion before the shift even finished, four feet grasping the earth more certainly than two could ever do. The animal was angry, not my protective fury, but a deep rage that drove its every move. A banshee was as good a target as any to unleash that anger on, though a whiff of scent told my hind brain that it and I—me the werewolf, not me the shaman— were probably on the same side. It was a familiar scent of decay, of dark magic, a thing I hadn't even known *had* a scent, and it said we were born of the same master. There was another smell, too, one that caught at the back of my throat for just a moment, and which the werewolf couldn't put a name to. I disregarded it, hell-bent on the banshee. *It* was free, and I was bound to the moon—full tonight, last of the three full moons, and it seemed a werewolf didn't change only at night after all—and its freedom was reason enough for it to die whether we served the same master or not. I sprang upward, tooth and claw reaching for the banshee with glorious, furious power.

The whole thing, from beginning to end, lasted about fifteen seconds. Then fresh magic slammed into me so hard I collapsed, and when I woke up I'd been buried alive.

CHAPTER TWELVE

Stone curved so close to my face I began to hyperventilate. I hadn't noticed a dislike of enclosed rocky spaces until just this past weekend, when I'd gone traipsing around an awful lot of caverns that weren't supposed to be beneath Seattle. The weight of the world pressing down turned out to be more than I could handle. Panicked, I rolled sideways in search of escape, and crashed into a woman eight inches taller than I.

She was made of granite, and lay serenely on the tomb we shared. I sat up a few inches, clobbered my head and fell back down with a whimper. My granite friend held an actual sword in her stone hands. She wore an all-too-familiar necklace, too, though it was carved of stone, not made of silver. An effigy, that's what she was. A remarkable amount of curly stone hair lay around her shoulders, and for a second I wondered if she was an effigy of a comic-book character, since real people hardly ever had that much hair.

It slowly dawned on me that for someone who'd been buried alive I could see very clearly. Not the glowy bright world visible through the Sight, but just ordinary ol' Joanne vision, slightly fuzzy because I'd lost my goddamned glasses again when I shapechanged. I was still wearing my clothes, though, including the leather coat, which had apparently fit a wolf well enough not to entangle me while I jumped a banshee. Either that, or someone had thoughtfully dressed me before burying me.

I was clearly not dead if that was my major concern. I exhaled very, very carefully, and lifted my head to look for the source of the light.

It came from somewhere beyond my feet. I dug my heels in, bent my knees until they hit the low ceiling and hitched myself down a few inches. After a few repeats, I edged off the tomb's far end and landed on my ass in a small round room covered in rubble.

"Sure and it's sorry I am for shoving ye in there," said the living embodiment of the granite woman, "but there was nowheres else to put ye so I could sit and wait on ye, too."

I did not say "What?" which I thought took a great deal of restraint. I didn't say anything else, either, not out of restraint but out of gaping astonishment.

She wasn't just the living color version of the effigy. She was the woman in my visions, the one who had bound the werewolves to the moon's cycle. Fair copper hair in as much quantity as the statue possessed, which made me touch my own short-cropped and stick-straight hair self-consciously. Light eyes, a strong build and an aura that sank down into the earth, anchoring her so it looked like nothing could possibly knock her from her feet. After many long seconds I managed what I thought was a pleasantly casual, "Méabh, I presume."

She bowed, which was pretty talented for someone sitting down. Coppery curls fell around her shoulders and she shook them back as she straightened again. I had hair envy. I'd never had hair envy in my life. I was so busy having hair envy I almost forgot to respond to her, "And you'll be Siobhán Walkingstick, I think."

"Yeah. Well, I mean, no. I like Joanne better. Jo." I'd never voluntarily suggested someone call me Jo, before. It had always been Joanie. But aside from being welcome in the midst of the occasional meltdown, Joanie was starting to sound like a little kid's name. I was finally clawing my way out of emotional immaturity, and I'd never been little. Sometime in the past year or so, I'd left Joanie behind. "Where are we?"

As soon as I asked I knew the answer. We were in Méabh's tomb, of course, and the more interesting question was, "How did I get here? What happened? I...was a wolf. And there was a banshee..." Really. Normal people did not find themselves saying things like that. I pinched the bridge of my nose, noticing again that my glasses had gone missing, and muttered, "Don't suppose you found my glasses out there."

To my surprise, she held them up between two fingertips. "You were a wolf," she agreed, "and there was a banshee. And I'll have none of that sort of thing contaminating my bones, not even when she's one of my own. What," she added, pointing my glasses at my forearm, "is *that?*"

I tried to hide the half-bandaged bites with my other arm. The itching was gone, leaving ordinary pain in its place. "It's a..." For a second I thought I could get away with "dog bite," but something in Méabh's expression suggested I would find my ass kicked from here to breakfast if I tried that. I mumbled,

"Werewolf bite. I got bit by a werewolf the other day. I can't heal it. Can you?"

Instead of helping she cast her gaze to the small room's ceiling. "A werewolf bite," she said to it. "Sure and I spend a lifetime building the stone circles, gathering the power, hunting the bitches down, and all for what? For my daughter to come to me poisoned by the very blood I bound."

"I'm not your daughter." I hadn't liked my own mother very much in the short time I'd known her, but I'd be damned if somebody else would go around claiming me as hers. "I'm human, for God's sake. You're *aos sí*."

"And Nuada was the last of the *aos sí* kings so," she said with a shrug. "He wed my mother and broke the cycle of sacrifice, but the cost was the throne. It's men who've come to the seat of Tara since, and all of them my husbands, too. The children I've borne have married men time and again, until it comes to you, Siobhán Walkingstick, Joanne Walker, my child. You are human," she agreed. "There would be no trace of the *sí* in your blood. But you're my child still, and heir to the power and the battle we fight."

I opened my mouth to argue about whether somebody could find traces of the *aos sí* in my DNA if I was in fact genetically related to them, then remembered nobody had yet convincingly found Neanderthal blood in *Homo sapiens* even though I knew people who looked like immediate family had been straight out of that lineage. I shut my mouth again. Méabh cocked an eyebrow and I shook my head, looking for something else to say. I came up with, "How about granddaughter, then," which wasn't brilliant but was a bearable alternative.

"Sure and that's a mouthful." She got a look at my expression and said, as if she'd always meant to, "Granddaughter it is. We've work to do, Grand— "

"Joanne. For God's sake, just call me Joanne. I don't need a damned title. What *happened* out there? Wait." I sat bolt upright, sickness and hope both churning my stomach. "You've been around forever, right? Do you know what happened to Gary? Is he okay? Did he come back home? Did they fight the Master? Where is he?"

She couldn't possibly answer through the barrage of questions, which, as they became more repetitive, I started to think was a deliberate delaying tactic on my part. There was only one answer I wanted, and if I kept asking questions she couldn't give the wrong one. But I had to breathe eventually, and she snapped a hand up to stop me from continuing when I gasped for air. "Your friend is a legend, Gran—Joanne. He rode with the hounds to this very place, and here they fought so long and so hard the mountaintop melted into a smooth and bloody field. The Morrígan and her ravens came to do battle and was met by her sister Brigid, who had never before been seen to make war. A sea of dead men rose from the cauldron and were struck down by Brigid's life magic. They say the necklace the Morrígan wore burned her then, like calling to like, and in that moment her master faltered, and she fell. It was a victory for the ages, Joanne. It set this world back on a path less dark than the one it had known."

"But what happened to *Gary?*"

"No one knows." Méabh's voice dropped with sympathy. "Some say he rides with the Hunt even still, while others claim it's the *aos sí* who have taken him in."

"You're *aos sí*," I snapped. "Did they? You? Whatever?"

"I would not know," Méabh murmured. "He fought before my time, and it's much more part of the mortal world that I am, than part of my father's people."

"Well, *go find out!*"

"I can't." Her implacability silenced me, and when it became clear I'd shut up for a moment, she went on. "I chose the *Fir Bolg,* Joanne. I chose humanity. It's unwelcome I am with my own kind. Every path has its price, does it not? If only the price of recognizing a life unled, but a price it is, and a price must be paid."

I had a startling amount of experience with recognizing lives unled, thanks to Suzanne Quinley. She'd once shown me a whole host of choices I might have made, and I'd seen all the lives I hadn't chosen. I regretted some of them right to the tips of my toes, though at the same time I couldn't say I was willing to give up the life I had in order to live one of the others. Méabh had probably never actually stood at a crossroads of possibilities, watching all her different lives unfold around her, but that didn't mean she wouldn't have an idea of what she'd lost.

And of what she'd gained. I finally spoke, focusing on a detail I'd noticed before but had been too busy envying her hair to comment on. "You're wearing my necklace."

A smile twitched her lips. "More I should say that you're wearing mine."

I closed my fingers over the necklace we both wore. "Well, whatever, but how can that be? Only one of us can have it at a time."

"Only one of us does. You asked what had happened, and here's what I know. Not an hour ago I stood ready to wed the next *ard rí,* and then an offensive magic shook my very bones. I could not leave it be, and in answering, found myself here. A banshee and a wolf fought over my grave, and I would have none of that. I called on the magic. The banshee was banished and you, Joanne, shed the wolf's clothes and lay at my feet an unconscious child. I knew the passage into the cairn's inner sanctum, though sure and I'd never thought to see it alive, and brought you here to waken. And now I stand ready and waiting, Granddaughter, to see what battle you have drawn me forward in time to face."

"What?" I'd done it again. I clenched my teeth and my eyes, a hand held up for silence and patience. Really, if there was a way to excise that word from my vocabulary entirely, I'd do it. "That's the second time today somebody's told me I was screwing around with time. I wouldn't even know how to begin doing that, so color me just a little skeptical, okay? But just for hilarity's sake, let's say you're right. How do you know you came forward in time instead of me going back?"

"If you had come back," Méabh said patiently, and pointed at the effigy behind me, "then *she* would not yet exist. This cairn has stood longer even than I have lived, but it's here I'll be buried should I die. And die I must, for there's no other reason to stand a stone warrior so the world will remember my face."

"This tomb's never been excavated. I'm the only one who's ever seen it." Wow. I had a real skill for saying exactly the wrong thing.

Méabh shrugged. "Time is long. The chance still lies ahead. Tell me what trials lie ahead and offer me a chance to see some of your world so I might know what my daughters have wrought."

"You keep saying daughters. Don't boys count?"

Surprise lit her face. "Of course, but it's through the daughters that the line continues. A child can only be certain of her mother. Is that not so in your time, too?"

My mouth twitched. "Matriarchies have mostly been obliterated in my time. The idea of the king marrying the land for its blessings or power went out a few thousand years ago. It's mostly about might makes right, these days."

Her eyebrows pulled together. "Now, that's a terrible thing to hear. That's my mother's master's way of things, the very thing we're fighting against."

"Yeah, well, the fight's a long way from won, even in my time. Maybe especially in my time." Somehow I had accepted that Méabh was out of time. Part of me even thought she was probably right, that I was the one responsible. I was, after all, the commonality between this morning's historical adventure and the afternoon's time skip.

A handful of disjointed memories floated to the surface: the way time had stretched and snapped back into place when I'd gone into Morrison's house after Barbara Bragg. I'd gone in astrally first, examining the scene before coming in physically, but I still couldn't remember actually entering his house. It had seemed more like my physical body had simply stepped forward through time to catch up with where my spirit had gone.

Something not exactly similar but not exactly different had happened when I'd been hung upside-down over a cauldron. And I'd been in innumerable fights now where time had slowed down to an impossible degree. That was a common enough phrase that I'd never considered the possibility that time had *actually* slowed. And then there were all the damned time loops that even I could recognize, reaching back to take the studies and power my younger self had accumulated; saddling up with my mother to win a fight that had happened months before my birth, and hell, just this morning trying to tidy up the mess Suzanne had set loose.

Nervousness churned my belly. I had a great big talk with Coyote—and with Raven and Rattler—coming on fast, if I was somehow capable of mucking with time. Nobody had even hinted that was on my skills list, and I had no idea why anybody would be granted that kind of power. Especially since, presented with the idea that I potentially *could* step back and forth through time, I could think of about a hundred and sixty things I'd like to go back and change. Oddly enough, arranging to get the winning numbers for the lottery wasn't even high on that list.

It didn't matter. The nice thing about time travel was that if it hadn't already happened presumably it wasn't going to, so I didn't really have to worry about the temptation to go mucking about with my own timeline. With a degree of trepidation— ignoring things often made them worse, in my experience—I put aside the whole question of my ability to alter time so I could focus on what was going on around me right now.

"Okay. All right, let's just assume you're right and it's my fault you're here. There are at least three things you can probably help with. The first is this." I raised my arm to display the werewolf bite. "You bound them. You must be able to…" I waved my arm around, trusting random gesticulation to get the point across.

It obviously did, but Méabh shook her head. "It's a warrior's path I'm on, Joanne. I'm no healer, for all that ye might wish me to be."

Every time the woman opened her mouth she said something flummoxing. Everybody. *Everybody* I had met who had shamanic power was on the healer's path. Granted, there hadn't been that many of them, but thus far I was a survey sample of one in terms of being out there fighting the good fight with a sword and shield instead of just healing hands. To come face-to-face with someone on the other end of the spectrum, so far to the fight that she didn't heal, was completely beyond my scope. "Wow. *Wow.* How do you do it? I mean, you called up a whole countryside's worth of power to bind the werewolves. And I know that wasn't healing. Believe me." Hairs rose on my arms and the bite started to itch again. I'd sanded Tia Carley's ability to transform to her lupine form away just minutes after she'd bitten me. It had probably been the cruelest thing I'd ever done. "Believe me, I *know* that wasn't an act of mercy. You'd have been kinder to kill them. So how do you juggle the power with the fight? Because my magic rebels if I use it offensively, and everybody else I know can't even pick up a sword. Literally or metaphorically."

"Then there's a balance in you," Méabh said with remarkable satisfaction. "There's none in me, Granddaughter. It's a reaction I am, a reaction to the dark path my mother walks. But I'm a warrior, too, just as she is, and there's no escaping that. It's better," she said more quietly. "I would say it's better, to have the balance."

All of a sudden I really, really wished I'd known my mother better, and what path she'd imagined herself to be on. I closed my eyes a moment, remembering her fondness for Altoids, then let it go. "Okay, if you can't help with the bite, maybe with the banshee. I didn't do so well against one on my own last time."

The softness escaped her expression, leaving her looking fully the part of a warrior queen. "Sure and there's trouble to be found there, when she's one of my own. That's a fight I can take on, sure enough."

That was the second or third time she'd said that. I frowned at her, niggling bits of information refusing to come fully to mind. "What do you mean, one of your own?"

"It's a great victory for him," Méabh said grimly. "To dig his claws into one of our lineage so deeply she is his thrall after death. It's her we must stop, Joanne, for so long as she fights for him I think we've no hope of winning."

"There's a jillion generations of this family line. How is it that *one* person is weak enough to fall? You'd think it would be either dozens or none."

She shook her head. "It's bargains made and sacrifices accepted. My daughters are all children of the *aos sí*. Perhaps every banshee that ever wailed is one of us, and perhaps he draws power from that even as we lose it. I only know that this one now is one of ours, and only newly risen as the wailing woman. We must hunt and destroy her, or we stand no hope at all."

"Guess that answers why you're here, then. How do you know she's a recent convert? A new banshee, I mean?"

"Her bones lie outside my cairn." My blank look conveyed incomprehension and Méabh continued like I wasn't the slow kid in the class. "To become a wailing woman, the banshee's bones must lie undisturbed for a year and a day, from one high holy day to another. The first light to fall on them wakens the beast, and it's the Master's they are from that day onward."

I turned my gaze to the unseen sky and said, a bit numbly, "But it's the twentieth. The equinox is tomorrow."

Méabh shook her head once, firmly. "You called me on the quarter day, to be sure. I felt the balance in my bones."

"I thought the equinoxes and solstices were on the twenty-firsts of the months."

I got a peculiar glance, and wondered if they'd numbered the days of the month in Méabh's time. It suddenly seemed not only unnecessary but possibly dangerous. Slow dread climbed in me. Of all the things I should be confident of, equinoxes and the like seemed pretty high on the list. If I'd misjudged by a day, trusting the calendar instead of the actual sun, that meant Tia Carley's attempt to line up the power of the full moon with the equinox had come a lot closer to succeeding than I'd realized.

I rubbed my arm nervously, winced and rubbed it again, feeling vaguely that if I sat to give it a good scratch, doglike, it would improve. Only the need to respond stopped me, and even that was only a half-focused reply. "Look, either way it doesn't matter. If she was buried here on the last spring equinox, a year and a day isn't until tomorrow or even the next day, because the equinox last year *was* on the twenty-first." Way at the back of my mind, pieces were falling into place, and I was afraid to think too hard for fear of jostling them and losing the oncoming epiphany forever.

"Then you've disturbed her early," Méabh said with vicious pleasure. "That makes her weaker, and us all the stronger. We've a day and a night to find her, Granddaughter. A day and a night to fight together and protect this world."

I nodded, but I was hardly listening. A year ago tomorrow I'd fought a banshee myself, a fight that had taken place not just in my own time, but almost thirty years earlier, on another equinox, as well. I'd almost died, but a woman called Sheila MacNamarra had gone to great lengths to keep me alive, both in the womb and as an adult.

And it had been peppermint. That was the smell that had caught at the back of my throat as I'd shifted into a wolf. Curiously strong peppermint.

The banshee was my mother.

CHAPTER THIRTEEN

"We can't just…" My throat hurt. I cleared it and tried again. "We can't just destroy her. We need to free her. To rescue her. 'Master's slave is driven wild,'" I whispered. "That's what that was about. 'Firstborn daughter, blooded child.' She meant me. She knew me. And oh, Jesus Christ, she knows about Aidan now. I never told her. I never told anybody."

Méabh had the look of polite incomprehension people tended to get around me these days. Actually, on reflection, it was more a look of irritated incomprehension. "Sure and we'll destroy her, Granddaughter. There's nothing to be done for it. That's wh—"

"We will not!" I sprang to my feet, narrowly missing cracking my head on the cairn's low roof. No wonder Méabh had remained seated throughout our exchange. She tensed as I leapt up, her fingers closing on a sword held only by her effigy, but she stayed sitting as I snarled, "We will *not* destroy her. We will find another way. I don't give a damn if I have to go back to the beginning of time and rewrite history from day one. We are going to rescue her from slavery to the Master, and then we are going to kick. His. *Ass*."

Rage-induced tears filled my eyes. God, I hated that part of being a girl. It was worse now because I'd only just told Gary to go kick the Master's ass and now I'd lost him for maybe ever. Méabh drew breath to speak and I jammed a finger at her like it was a blade itself. "Don't even *think* about arguing with me, or so help me God I will leave you here in this stone tomb to *rot*."

"You," Méabh said very, very mildly, "wouldn't be knowing the way out, now, would ye, me fine girl."

Logic was puny in the face of my wrath. Logic was puny and magic was mighty: I had just gotten rebirthed, refilled and renewed, and was fast on my way to resentful. The Sight flooded on full bore, showing me the ancient green serenity of the cairn's protective nature as well as the stress points within the stacked stones. My own skin shimmered with rage. I could blast the goddamned cairn away, leave Knocknaree as flat as it had been when Gary's legendary battle here came to an end, and at that shining moment in time I didn't think anything could stop me.

Yeah, sure, it'd be an act of wanton destruction. Yeah, sure, it would probably make the power clam up and refuse to play along as punishment. But just then I was pretty much willing to take the Master on in barehanded combat, because for the second time in half an hour I had had *enough*. First Gary, now my *mother*. It was unbearable, and I had goddamned well had enough of bearing it.

Of course, the magic crackling through me also showed me the tunnel leading into the cairn's heart, so in fact I knew how to get out of there, which took an itty bitty edge off my outrage. The detail that if I obliterated the cairn I would by definition not be leaving Méabh there to rot also came into play, but I ignored it with the fierceness of an ignoring thing. And finally it did work its way through my tiny brain that possibly Méabh would be on my side if she knew what the source of my discontent was.

It took every ounce of focus and willpower I had to grate, "She's my mother. And I woke her up early, so what we have is a day and a goddamned night to *save her,* and *that is what we are going to do.*"

A genuine and terrible pity colored Méabh's green eyes to almost brown. "Oh, my dear wee lass. My dear girl. Sure and that's a terrible thing for ye to face. But she's of the devil himself now, and there'll be only one way to stop her. We must destroy her."

"No." All of a sudden my rage vanished. Not the good kind of cathartic burning out, but the subsumed fury that powered people through the most hideous scenarios and saw them triumphant on the other side. Mentally disturbed, of course, and wrung out til there was nothing left, but triumphant. "Let's get something straight, Méabh. You may be *aos sí* and *ard rí*… ess…of all Ireland. You may be a legendary queen and a hero to the masses. But what you are *not* is in charge here. This is my time, you're here at my invitation, and by your own admission you're a warrior, not a healer. I'm both, and we will do things my way. Either that or you're going home right now and I'm doing this myself."

"And how is it you'll be sending me home when it's no idea you have of how I got here?"

Shit. She was going to make me ante up. Well, that was fair enough, because if I was going to be slinging myself or other people through history, I'd better have a clear idea of what I was doing. I lifted my gaze to the low ceiling once more, looking for cracks in time.

There weren't any.

What there was was a sense of the passage of years. The idea of eons settled into the stones around me. They had been stacked by human hands millennia ago, each touch leaving the faintest impression of the men and women who had put them there. They had built this place and others like it as signals to the future: they had been here.

And if they could touch me from thousands of years in the past, I could touch them from as many centuries in the future. That was the bedrock of shamanism: belief and change, and for one precious instant I absolutely believed I could connect with a people and a place far out of my time just as they had in their way touched me. I reached, and like Tara had, Knocknaree changed around me.

The mountain had never been pointy, of course. Not since the ice ages had faded, anyway, but stories of great battles flattening it were at least as good as sheets of ice. There was no sense of battles being fought, for that matter; it was just the old patient earth and the footsteps of hundreds moving stones from one place to another. Building cairns, but Méabh's tomb was not yet among them. Hers was the last and the greatest, and it dissolved around us as I strained to anchor us in time. Méabh took a sharp breath, and that reminded me of what she'd said. That she'd been pulled away from a wedding, *ard rí* to warrior queen, and so from our tenuous place in ancient history, I searched forward, looking for the moment where time hiccuped and a wedding was disrupted.

It was that simple. It was not *easy*. The effort pulled at my bones, time objecting to being stretched. Time and space, because the wedding had been at Tara, not in the west at Knocknaree. A flash of understanding hit me: I'd timeslipped at Tara in part because of the sheer ancient power built up there. Knocknaree was sacred, but not quite so persistently holy. It didn't stand at the center of a power circle, the one defined by the towers around Tara. Tara was *made* for magic users. Knocknaree was made for the dead. No wonder, then, what had been literally thoughtless at Tara was exhausting here.

But time did shift at my command, speeding awkwardly forward. Méabh's tomb lurched up around us, dozens of smaller kings and chieftains buried there before Méabh was even born, much less before she became a legend. And once her tomb was built, I still saw the world pass by, Sight unhindered by the aging stones around us.

There *was* a battle atop Knocknaree, brief and bloody, and for a heartwrenching moment I laid eyes on Gary.

He rode a horse I recognized, not the golden mare that belonged to the boy Rider, but the solid brown beast that later would carry a sad-eyed king. He looked confident on the animal's back, wielding my rapier like he'd been doing it all his life. The Morrígan was there, blade flashing and hair wild, and as she rode for Gary, Cernunnos intervened.

A cloak of blackness shot up from beneath the earth and swept away all hope of seeing what happened. I cried out and time nearly stopped, but Méabh was suddenly, finally on her feet, and held my lapels gripped in two strong fists. "You were not here," she warned. "You cannot *be* here, Granddaughter. This fight is not yours to fight. Should they fall it cannot be your fall, too."

"You said they won!"

"Legend says they won," Méabh said with great and honest

sorrow, "but sure and legend never lets truth get in the way of a good story."

"I don't *care!* It's *Gary!*" It was also too late. Too much of my energy had been focused on shoving us forward to the moment Méabh left, and she had broken the concentration that had almost stopped us at the battle. We were spinning forward again, rushing headlong toward a spike of familiar silver-blue power: my magic stabbing backward, finding Méabh, the one person my subconscious thought could get me through the werewolf and the banshee alive. Teeth gritted, I put the brakes on, and time lurched to its normal pace around us as I scowled at Méabh. "This is it, sister. Pay up or get off the ride."

To my credit, Méabh looked very slightly impressed. I had the idea that making the *aos sí* look slightly impressed was kind of like calling the Grand Canyon a little ditch, so I was good with that. "It's your rules, then," she said. "It's your time. It's your way we'll do things, but—" and she gave me a gimlet stare "—if we cannot rescue the banshee..."

"Sheila," I said. "Sheila MacNamarra. My *mother.* And yes." The last was through once-more gritted teeth. "If we can't rescue her I'll finish it. *I.* Will finish it. Not you. You understand that?"

Her eyebrows lifted, a mixture of agreement and mild offense. I didn't imagine most people went around using phrases like "You understand me, young lady?" on legendary warrior queens of old. Then again, I wasn't most people. "Okay then. We're going home now, and then we're going to rescue my mother."

Reaching back through time was exhausting. Staggering forward trying to find the moment Méabh had left was uncomfortable. Going home, though, was like a rubber band snapping into place. I cast one miserable look over my shoulder, like I'd be able to see Gary through the annals of history, then lurched back into the modern day with Méabh still standing more or less nose to nose with me.

Nose to nose because we were still in her tomb, and standing up she really was about eight inches taller than I was. There wasn't room for her to straighten, so she hunched uncomfortably and half a breath from my face said, "I'll be leaving this place now." She shouldered past me to uncover the dug-down tunnel that led out of the cairn, and crawled out.

I stood there alone in her tomb for a long minute, a dozen tiny thoughts whirling around my brain. She was so very *tall*. The other *aos sí* had been tall, but not that tall. It was magnificent. I was six feet and a bit in the boots I had on, but I wanted to be tall like her. Except then I would tower over Morrison, and while once upon a time I'd have liked that, now the idea we were exactly the same height was kind of appealing. And I wouldn't want to be that much taller than Gary. Gary, about whom I was trying hard not to think. It wasn't working very well. I kept seeing the Morrígan riding down on him, and ashy-haired Cernunnos blocking the way. In theory, I knew Cernunnos survived because I'd met him for the first time in my past, but he wasn't quite bound by time, so I couldn't be sure. And Gary's linear life was still in effect, so there was no reason I couldn't have met him a year ago and still have gotten him killed in the distant past. And I really needed to sit down and talk with Coyote about this time thing, because it was absolutely beyond me why anybody would be given the power to timeshift.

It struck me that although I'd napped the entire transatlantic flight, I was still very, very tired, and that dragging my ass back and forth through time today hadn't helped that at all. I said, "Miles to go before I sleep," to the empty tomb, took one thing from its inner sanctum and followed Méabh back into the modern world.

She stood watching jet contrails in a fading sky. She didn't seem like a woman out of time right then. Aside from the contrails, there were no particular signs of my world visible from the mountaintop, and her tall, slender, armor-bedecked self fitted in better with the gray cairns than my leather-coated stompy-boot self. The armor—a breastplate, some kind of thigh guard and what I cautiously thought of as greaves—was silver. Of course it was. Probably magic silver, compliments of one Nuada of the Silver Hand, also known as Daddy. Like the Morrígan, Méabh's arms were both bare and tattooed, bands of knotwork around each biceps. I'd noticed all that in the cairn. I just hadn't *noticed* it. Somehow it all made a much more impressive picture out in the open with fiery sunset washing over her than it had in the little fire-lit stone room. I wasn't strictly sure that made sense, as she'd been the most impressive object *in* the cairn, but sense or not, that was how it was.

She'd collected a small round shield and a silver helm on the way out, and stood over my mother's bones with the one on her arm and the other tucked into her elbow. "I would have been thinking the world had changed more, from the way you're dressed, Granddaughter."

"It has. You just can't see it from up here. You forgot this in there." I came forward with her sword, which she glanced at with a spasm crossing her face.

"I would not have taken that. Not from a dead woman."

"You're not dead yet," I said almost cheerfully, and offered it again. Her mouth twisted, but this time she accepted. Once she had, I pointed down the mountain toward my distant car. "There. There's your first hint that the world's changed. Horseless carriages."

She squinted into the light, then raised her hand to block the long gold rays so she could see better. I copied her, then froze. It had been early afternoon when I'd climbed Knocknaree. Sunlight had been sporadic, falling in occasional bolts, not blazing orange on the horizon. I turned around slowly, like I could convince the world to shift on its axis if I looked carefully enough, but the sun was not on the western horizon. It was on the eastern. Sunrise, not sunset. "You said it's the equinox, right?"

"I said you called me on the quarter day," she agreed. I stared at the sunrise another moment, then fumbled my phone out of a pocket to stare at it instead.

Apparently it was half past ten on Monday evening. I glanced at the sky, like it was somehow lying to me, then shook myself. I hadn't changed the phone's time zone. It was six-thirty Tuesday morning, not ten-thirty Monday night. I changed the time, then shoved my phone back in its pocket and started counting on my fingers. I'd left Seattle Sunday morning. It was a ten-hour flight to Dublin, plus eight hours of time zones. I'd gotten in Monday morning. Gary and I had gone to Tara. It had been early Monday afternoon when I'd reached Knocknaree. No matter how I counted it, I couldn't make it morning again without having lost well over twelve hours. "Son of a stone-cold bitch. How long was I out?"

Méabh's eyebrows rose. "Some hours. It's burning with the fever you were, and nothing I could do for it."

"And you didn't think to mention that?" We'd had a kind of busy half hour or so since I'd woken up. It probably wasn't her fault she hadn't brought up the length of my nap. That, however, was reason, and I had no truck with reason. "Look, never mind, forget it. We're about a day shorter on time than we thought, though. We're going to have to find Sheila by tonight, just in case it counts from equinox to equinox and not 365 days of the year. Otherwise…"

Otherwise my mother spent the rest of eternity in thrall to the monster she'd fought against her whole life, and in general the good guys lost a round. I didn't want to say that aloud, so I drifted into, "…banshees usually haunt their families, right? That's their thing when they're not performing ritual murders for the Master?"

"It is." The Irish I'd met never said "Yes" or "No" if two or more words would do, because their English was heavily informed by the Irish language's structure. I kind of liked that Méabh sounded that way, too. It made a nice connection between the island's history and its present, even if I was pretty sure she wasn't speaking English any more than Cernunnos usually did.

"It is," I repeated under my breath, then got to my feet and pointed down the mountain. "Okay. That's the only possible lead we've got, so we're going back to the farm, Junior. My family's in Westport. Let's go."

"Not without the bones." Méabh crouched and began to collect them while I watched in macabre fascination. That was my mother she was picking up. I hadn't even known my mother had false teeth. I wondered if they counted as bones, and decided not. "Have ye a sack?" Méabh wondered, and I looked in dismay toward my distant car. There was a suitcase in there, anyway, but I didn't want to traipse down and up the mountain.

I sighed, shucked my new, expensive, damaged leather coat and made a sack of it. Méabh, approving, started tossing bones in. I couldn't quite bring myself to help. "Why are we doing this?"

"To burn them or bury them in holy ground. To break the link between body and soul. It'll weaken the wailing woman, and her weakness will be our advantage."

Burn or bury. I thought I could handle that. I knelt, but I didn't start picking bones up. "She was buried once already. I was at the funeral. The coffin cost a fortune."

Méabh paused to give me an uncertain look, and I wondered what magic translations did with words like *coffin,* which probably hadn't existed in her time. I imagined something like "black box of death," which sounded a lot more impressive. "Was she in this 'coffin'?" Méabh asked.

"Well, of course she was! People don't go around burying empty co—" The coffin had been closed, actually. There'd been no viewing, apparently at my mother's vehement insistence in her will. The Irish aunts and cousins and things had tutted over it, but nobody had been quite willing to ignore the last wishes of a dead woman. And I, bitter, closed-off, angry adult daughter that I was, had refused to help carry the coffin. I had no idea if a body's weight had been within it. I cleared my throat and, more mildly, said, "Now that you mention it I'm not sure. I assumed so."

Méabh gave me a look that said a lot about people who made assumptions, then loaded the last of my mother's bones into my beleaguered leather coat and stood. "*Now* it's to Westport we'll go."

I hopped to it, and only remembered halfway down the hill that *I* was supposed to be in charge.

CHAPTER FOURTEEN

Tuesday, March 21, 7:56 a.m.

Westport, as advertised, was a western port in the County Mayo. Basically there was nothing between it and Canada except a stray whale or two. That didn't do the town justice, though. It was gorgeous, with a cool little octagonal town, er, square, and wide streets, which meant two cars almost fit past each other on them. A river ran through it, there were charming back alleys that opened into unexpected shopping streets, and one of the town pubs was owned and run by somebody in the Chieftains. On the whole it didn't look like the sort of place to go burn bones and battle banshees. But then, I didn't have a long list of places I thought *did* look like a girl ought to be doing those things there, so Westport was as good a scene as any. I nearly said as much to Méabh, but then like almost everything else I'd been inclined to say during the drive down, I bit it back.

In all fairness, she was handling the modern world very, very well. She'd stared at the car with interest and hardly seized up at all when I turned the engine on. She'd been wide-eyed and delighted as a kid when we hit the open road, or she had been until the first oncoming traffic came on. I was probably grateful the magic hadn't seen fit to translate what she'd said then. She'd craned her neck to gawk at the towns we drove through, especially when we hit a bigger one a few miles outside of Westport and there were several-story buildings towering above us. She'd turned a little gray then, and only when we'd left its outskirts had she said, "How many people live in this land?"

"What, in Ireland? I don't know, I think it's like four million." I'd glanced her way, seen total incomprehension slide over her features and wondered what had constituted a large town in her time. Hundreds or thousands, probably. Not tens of thousands. Millions was beyond her scope, and realistically, beyond mine. A million was pretty abstract, somewhere in the "One, two, many" range as far as my ability to really comprehend it went.

She took a breath, but let it go again after a long few seconds and murmured, "It wouldn't be mattering." I imagined she'd just decided not to pursue a whole litany of questions, trusting that the modern world's fascinating ways required no approval or understanding on her part. If she could accept them on any level at all, she was doing very well. I nodded and kept my mouth shut as I drove us to the graveyard. Méabh didn't need any of my smart-ass side commentary to distract her from coping.

We got out of the car and I said, "Hey, wait up," before we

headed in. She glanced at me and I gestured at her clothes. "You sort of stand out. Maybe you should…"

Wear some of my clothes was the only way that sentence could end, but Méabh was the tallest woman I'd ever met. My shirts would stop halfway down her rib cage. My jeans would look like pedal pushers on her. There was no chance any of my shoes would fit her at all, so she'd have to leave the leather boots and greaves in place anyway. I gave up before I'd really begun, and dug the carry-on suitcase out of the car's backseat as I said, "You should just keep right on standing out."

Méabh, legendary warrior queen of Ireland, gave me a wink and a smile and strode past me into the graveyard.

Past a young woman on her way out, too. The girl lifted her eyes, gawked, tripped over her own feet and kept herself upright with a hand on a gravestone. I winced an apologetic greeting as I scurried by in Méabh's wake.

A few seconds later, the girl called an incredulous, "Joanne?"

Méabh and I both stopped. She turned toward me curiously, and domino-like, I turned toward the girl, though not so much curiously as with a sinking heart. She was probably a decade my junior, had fire-engine-red hair as short as mine and a slightly too-chubby-for-hourglass figure. Probably baby fat. She'd grow out of it in another year or two and be very attractive.

As far as I was concerned I'd never seen her before. Her gaze flickered from Méabh to me, back to Méabh and then, with a Herculean effort, back to me, where it stayed. "You don't remember me, do you?"

"Um. Well, no. Sorry." She almost had to be related. I hadn't met anybody in Ireland I wasn't related to, which was more commentary on my limited social circle than the interconnected families on a tiny island. But I was pretty sure I'd remember that hair, and none of my cousins had worn that style or color.

"Caitríona," she said. "Caitríona O'Reilly? Sheila's oldest niece?"

Caitríona was one of those names a bit like Siobhán. To my English-language eyes, it looked like Cat-ree-OH-nah. It was in fact pronounced Katrina, which was most of why I remembered her at all. I blurted, "Oh! I didn't recognize you! Your hair was—" I waved at the middle of my back. "And you were—"

"Shorter," she supplied, which probably kind of covered the same ground I'd been going to cover with "rounder." "Yeh." She brushed a hand over her shorn locks. "Forgot that, so I did. I liked yours."

I clutched my own hair, as if it had changed colors without warning. "I've never dyed mine."

"Sure and I couldn't have them all sayin' I was trying to be like the American cousin, could I. Especially after—" Her jaw snapped shut, but I could fill in the blanks easily enough. Especially after I'd cold-shouldered everybody. Especially after I'd left on the next flight after the funeral.

Especially after, and this was the part they didn't know, I'd been in large part responsible for my own mother's death. In my limited defense, it had been her decision, but I'd made a lot of bad choices over the years that forced her hand toward that decision. I'd thought at the time that the woman had basically decided she was done living and had willed herself to death, which seemed pretty extreme for someone in her early fifties. I'd discovered later that yeah, she'd done exactly that, all in the name of making sure *I* stayed alive.

And now she was a banshee and I owed her every chance

I could take to free her from that. I wasn't exactly close with my Irish family to begin with, but I seriously doubted I'd win any friends if all of the sordid details about what I was doing there came out.

"What are you *doing* here?" Caitríona demanded. "And who's that?"

That, of course, was Méabh, who required far more explanation than I was prepared to offer. After barely an instant's consideration, I shrugged. "That's Méabh. Méabh, this is my cousin Caitríona."

"Méabh," Caitríona said, and laid the accent on thick. "Av carse it is."

"We've come to lay your auntie's bones to rest," Méabh said as though it was the most obvious thing in the world. "This is grand so, three of our bloodline to do the job. We couldn't ask for better."

Caitríona's expression went peculiar. She said, "I've never heard an accent like that," in English, then said something else to Méabh in Irish. It became instantly clear to me that Méabh had been speaking Irish all along, because Caitríona sounded more or less like Méabh did if I listened hard to the words and not to what my magic told me she was saying. Bizarrely, though, I couldn't understand a word Cat said in Irish.

Worse, I then couldn't understand Méabh when she answered. I made a strangled noise and waved my hands. "English, please, Caitríona. I can't understand Méabh if you speak Irish. I mean, I can't understand you, either, but—English. Please? Just English?"

"I only wanted to know if she'd learned Irish in the Donegal Gaeltachs." Caitríona shrugged, then did something with her face that reminded me of me. It was this little quirk of her mouth, a tightening of the skin around her eyes, a tensing of the nostrils, all of it minute body language I'd felt myself do a thousand times. It indicated that she'd been ignoring the completely outrageous thing Méabh had said until it made some kind of sense in her own head, except the making sense part wasn't happening so she might as well bite the bullet and ask.

I couldn't decide if it was creepy or fascinating to see all of that on somebody else's face. Especially somebody I barely knew. She also looked like she very much wished she could say two things at the same time as she opted for, "Lay me auntie's bones to rest?"

That was the one I probably would have chosen, too. The whole bloodline thing was a little much to take a run at. But before I had a chance to explain, Cat said, "It's just after fifteen months we'll be doing that."

My American-English brain cramped. Caitríona's statement was a perfectly accurate comment on what was about to happen, but what she, the Irish–English speaker, *meant,* was that they'd done that fifteen months ago. I'd forgotten the peculiar direction sentences landed from in Ireland. I vowed to listen harder to what she meant and to focus less on how she said it. "There was a mix-up at the mortuary. I thought if I just came and dealt with it myself it would be less upsetting."

It almost sounded plausible. Almost, except the part where no local undertaker would have called the American daughter instead of the extensive Irish family, which Caitríona's expression indicated clearly. "Look," I said a bit too loudly, and before she could speak, "look, just go with it, okay? And really, Méabh might be right but you'll be happier if you just head on home and forget you saw us. What're you doing here, anyway?" That was not a tactic to make her leave. I wanted to kick myself again.

"Sheila liked the old holidays. The solstices and Beltane and all. I come to put flowers on her grave at each of them, but I was away to Dublin for the Saint Patrick's Day crack so only could come this morning." Caitríona looked hard between me and Méabh, then crossed her arms under her breasts. "I think I'll be staying."

Of course she would be. I looked for a compelling argument and came up fast on, "Crack?" because admitting to larking off to Dublin for a drug fix seemed a little brash.

Both the Irish women said, "Fun," and Caitríona added, "The parties, the parade and all. Me sisters and I went for a bit of crack and now I'm home again and whatever you're doing, I think I'll be part of it."

"Oh. Okay. No, wait. I meant okay, that's what crack is, not, like, cocaine, and not like okay you can come al—oh, to hell with it, fine, come on then." I had better things to do than argue with people who wanted to get in over their heads. She'd scare off soon enough, and in the meantime, "You can show me where the grave is. I don't really remember." I set off the direction she'd come from, hauling the carry-on behind me.

Caitríona ran to catch up, then to pass me, then to eye the suitcase. "What's that?"

"Mom's bones are in it." It hadn't been practical to keep them in the coat, which was not, after all, especially baglike. Caitríona's eyes bugged. "Really, you're happier not knowing. I should probably warn you we're going to burn them, too."

She stopped dead. I almost crashed into her, and she hopped into motion again. A few steps later she said, "She'd like that so, but sure and you'll have the town up in arms if you're setting fire to the cemetery. You should bring her up there, to the Reek. To Croagh Patrick. She'd like that even more."

Magic lit up within me, fishhook tugs that signaled approval of Caitríona's suggestion. I turned to look at the mountain that dominated the western skyline. There was a lingering low fog, but the mountain was clear and the chapel atop it was almost visible if I used my imagination. I so very much did not want to haul a suitcase up a three-thousand-foot mountain.

"We called it Cromm Crúaich. My father fought a battle here when they first came to Ireland," Méabh said. "Who is Patrick?"

"He was..." I didn't really want to give her Saint Patrick's whole story. "A holy man after your time. He did a pilgrimage on that mountain so they named it after him."

"Patrick defeated Cromm on the mountain." Caitríona gave Méabh a good hard stare. "Cromm was an old god and Patrick banished him along with all the snakes in Ireland. Who *are* you?"

"She's Méabh," I said again. "Honestly, are you sure you don't want to go home? It's too early in the day to be climbing mountains, isn't it?"

Caitríona turned her good hard stare on me. "No."

Well. No arguing with that, then. I sighed and turned back to the car, bumping the suitcase along behind me. "You really think she'd like to be burned up there on the mountain?"

"Oh, yes. She wasn't even a pagan, was Auntie Sheila. She was something else all her own. *Connected,* like. Connected to everything. Are ye like her?" she said to me, and I startled guiltily.

"Not very much, but in some ways, yeah." Wow. Prevarication 101, that was me. "Yes."

Caitríona said, "Hnf," which I felt was somehow condemning, and we all went and got in my car and drove to Croagh Patrick.

Sometime on Saturday night I'd sworn I would take up jogging Monday morning. I hadn't, of course, expected to be in

Ireland when I'd made that oath. Nonetheless, Méabh bounded up the damned goat trail leading to Croagh Patrick's summit with the agility and speed of...well. A goat. And Caitríona, full of teenage resiliency, was barely a few steps behind her. I did have the excuse of lugging a suitcase full of bones, but mostly I was just in no condition to be running up mountainsides. I felt this was not unreasonable, as normal people didn't climb mountains anyway.

Of course, I'd left normal behind a long time ago, a fact which Gary should be happily reminding me of right about now. I hitched the suitcase over a rock and threw out the promise to start jogging in favor of a promise to get him back. I'd already made that promise about a thousand times, but once more didn't hurt. Especially if it got me out of jogging.

I walked into a wall and bounced off. The wall said, "You're no fit warrior, Granddaughter."

I sighed and edged my way around Méabh. "I'll start running up and down mountains as a fitness regime next week. Right now I just need to..." She'd been in the way of my view of the path, and now that I could see it, I wished she'd stayed in front of me. "...I just need to get up that horrible, hideous switchback without killing myself. Does anybody have anything to eat?" The last real food I could actually remember eating was a sandwich sometime early Saturday afternoon. There'd been some candy and potato chips since then, but they didn't count.

"You will not want to have eaten, for this." Méabh passed me again, taking long easy strides up the mountainside while I drooped. Ritualized magic apparently went hand in hand with self-denial. Cleansing the body and spirit and all that crap, I guessed, but since no food was forthcoming there wasn't much reason to bitch about it now. I was going to eat half a cow when we got back down to ground level, though.

"I've eaten." Caitríona surged ahead to catch up with Méabh. "Will it be a problem so?"

Méabh gave her a considering look. "Have ye the power?"

Cat glanced back at me, then settled on Méabh. "Like Auntie Sheila? No. Me Gran had it, but then, she was Sheila's mam, too. We all thought one of us cousins might have it." She said that like it was my fault, which in a way I supposed it was. Probably if Mother hadn't had me, the magic would have come to the fore in somebody else. It didn't seem likely it would just die out after several thousand years of coming down the line.

"Then it should be no trouble. It's Joanne we'll be looking to for the circle." Méabh glowered at me over her shoulder. "Should she survive the walk up the hill, at least."

They were starting to piss me off. As a rule, the healing power I commanded didn't think much of me utilizing it for personal gain, but I took a deep breath and tapped into it, searching for the cool rush of strength that would buoy me through the last couple hundred yards up the mountain.

Instead my arm cramped, muscle around the bites twisting as if using the magic within me only encouraged the impulse to transform. I clenched my fist, afraid to look and see it had become a wolf's paw, but it closed normally. Or as normally as it could, when the muscles used to close it had big teeth marks through them. I swallowed down a whimper and dared peek at it.

The bite itself was starting to look hot again. Not quite as bad as before, like my brief shape change had bled off some of the infection, but it was building again. For the first time I thought maybe I should do what other people did, and go see a doctor. Maybe I would. After I got done climbing a mountain and burning my mother's bones.

On the positive side, panic over the idea of turning into a werewolf gave me a plenty-big boost, and I trotted up the rest of the mountain on Méabh's and Caitríona's heels with no problem.

The view was incredible, with the Atlantic spilling off to the west and half of Ireland glimmering through soft mist around and behind me. Not for the first time, the old country steeped me in magic and power, in presence and in continuity. There was a peace to it unlike anything I'd ever encountered in Seattle. I understood why Saint Patrick had stayed up there for forty days, absorbing everything that Ireland had to offer.

So it really was a pity about the residual human sacrifices staining the mountain so deeply it felt like a mallet to the head.

CHAPTER FIFTEEN

I did very well, all things considered. Instead of collapsing, I carefully knelt until my forehead touched the ground and folded my hands at my nape while I took some deep breaths. Being that close to the earth didn't make it any worse. There were mitigating factors at play, which probably helped. Saint Patrick really had been here once upon a time, and whether I approved of going around converting the masses or not, the guy had apparently wielded—welt?—some significant power. The land had been healed to some degree, the deepest of the bloodstains washed away, and several hundred years of ordinary human worship had gone further yet in wiping out the death magic that had been done here. Had gone a long way, in fact, because otherwise I'd have known from Westport's streets that the mountain was a blight on the land. That didn't make it any more pleasant to discover now that I was up here. Muffled, because I was mostly talking into the dirt, I said, "So who was the Crúaich guy your father fought here, Méabh?"

"Cromm," she said. "Crúaich is the mountain itself."

If I wasn't trying so hard not to puke I'd have gotten up and kicked her. "What. *Ever.*"

Sensitive creature that she was, she picked up on my irritation. "He was the Fomorian king. It was his people we drove from this land so we might call it our own."

"Fomorians. I don't know the Fomorians." I'd been doing so well to pull the *Fir Bolg* out of my sketchy memory. Discovering there were still more ancient Irish peoples I'd missed was kind of depressing.

"Dark and cruel monsters," Caitríona said, but she said it with an edge. I turned my head half an inch to peer at her. She clearly didn't know which of us to glare at more fiercely. "Cromm was defeated by Nuada of the Silver Hand when the *Tuatha de Daanan* came to Ireland."

I decided Méabh was getting the hard end of the glower. That was okay with me. I put my head back where it had been and kept breathing deeply. The impact was lessening some. I was reminded of the baseball diamond back in Seattle where three ritual murders had been carried out. It had been a literal black stain on Seattle's psychic energy. Croagh Patrick was both worse and better than that. The deaths here were far more numerous, but also much older, and a lot of effort had gone into cleaning them up. They still made my stomach churn, and the sweat standing out on my body wasn't from hiking up the hill. I snaked an ever-so-tentative thread of power into the earth, torn between hoping to help and terrified at how my magic might respond to being used. Bizarrely, it didn't object at all, and the ground sucked it down greedily, like a drink it was dying for.

While I did that, Méabh, serenely, said, "Yes. My father was Nuada, and he would be your grandfather a thousand times removed."

"Jo*anne!*"

I had never had a younger sister, but I imagined that was exactly what one sounded like when someone older and presumably wiser was giving her a line of bullshit and she wanted Big Sis to make it stop. It was kind of nice. It was equally annoying. I wondered if that defined the relationship between most sisters, and thought maybe I was glad I didn't have one. "I told you she was Méabh."

"Yes, but—em. Em. What are you doing?"

I'd forgotten how many of the Irish said "em" instead of "um." It had driven me crazy when I'd visited the first time. Now it was more of a charming idiosyncrasy. "Trying not to puke."

"No, I mean like everything's glowing so."

I peeled one eye open. Caitríona was right. The ground half an inch away glowed with my magic, silver-blue power pouring into parched earth. I'd done something like that one other time, in Cernunnos's home world of Tir na nOg, but it had taken it out of me then. This was a much more gentle flow, magic seeping down dry cracks and swelling them with revitalization.

All of a sudden I had the distinct feeling it had been one year, and possibly as many as, oh, twenty-eight come May, since someone had been up here to offer anything other than ordinary human worship to the mountain's hungry stone. "You said my mother would like to be burned up here. Did she come up here a lot?"

"All the time. On the holy days when she could, but she'd say there were so many sites that needed tending to that she couldn't always be here on the day itself. So she'd use other holy days instead. There isn't a day in the year that someone doesn't hold high, she'd say. I liked that idea, so I did. It's why I didn't worry about coming to the graveyard on the equinox proper. There's always something special going on in the world. Always a reason to give thanks to God. Always a good day to worship."

This was probably not the time to get in a theological debate with my Irish Catholic cousin. Besides, regardless of who or what thanks might be given to, she was right. It was a nice idea, and it was probably true. "How many holy days? Or not holy, whatever."

"Every six weeks or so. Imbolc, Beltane, Lughnasa, Samhain and the quarterly days. The solstices and equinoxes."

Eight times a year. And she'd missed at least three while we'd traveled Europe together eighteen months earlier. No wonder the ground was parched. I nodded against the stone my forehead rested on. "Just how glowy are we talking?"

"The whole of the mountaintop," Caitríona said in satisfyingly obvious awe. "Even the chapel is alight."

"I thought ye hadn't the power." Méabh sounded one note shy of accusing. I tipped my head sideways again, prepared to leap up and defend my cousin at any moment. As soon as the nausea finished fading. Surely Méabh wouldn't smack her around until then.

"I haven't, but the glow is plain to see." Belligerence met accusation, Caitríona's Irish getting up in fine form.

"Only to one with the power!"

They were going to get in a knock-down drag-out. It was a small mountain compared to the Rockies, but it was plenty big to do Caitríona a lot of harm should she get thrown off. I had no doubt it was she who would lose, since even if Méabh wasn't a trained fighter, she had a good solid foot in height on the O'Reilly girl. "Maybe," I said loudly, into the ground, "*maybe* it's me. I've put on visible fireworks before. Or *maybe* Cat's got the power and just doesn't know it yet. Or *maybe* it's the goddamned stars aligning, but whatever it is, I would like to invite you to *shut the hell up,* because the last thing I need right now is your petty bitching adding to the weight of a few hundred human sacrifices. Capiche?"

"Sacrifices?" Caitríona's voice shot up into a squeak just like mine did when I got alarmed. Then she downshifted into mortally offended historian mode, which I also might have done if I had the right knowledge. "That's just a story they made up to scare people off from being pagan. The druids didn't sacrifice anybody."

"No," Méabh said hollowly, "but my mother did. And today she seeks to again."

A red-capped man with a scythe erupted from the earth and took a swing at Caitríona's head.

I went head over heels, dislodged earth scattering in arcs of still-brilliant power. Metal clanged somewhere above me. I ended up on my back with Méabh standing above me, and between Red Cap and Caitríona. Méabh's sword tangled his scythe, and she looked like she'd finally found her purpose in being here.

Red Cap was the grimmest, nastiest-looking little man I'd ever seen. Barely four feet tall, his scythe was half again his height, but he used it with brutal confidence: a sharp twist dislodged it from Méabh's sword. She blanched with surprise and rolled the hilt in her palm to keep a grip on it. Nasty pleasure warped his deep-set wrinkles into smug superiority. His red cap, shoved far down over furious black eyes, made his ears poke through wild hair of a begrudging filthy gray. He bared his teeth at Méabh in a nasty grin—look, he was just nasty, there was no other word for him—and showed off vicious pointed teeth with the expression.

Caitríona was screaming her fool head off. Red Cap swung at her again and I snaked an arm out, grabbed her ankle and hauled her off her feet. The scythe zipped through the air where her head had been and she hit the ground with a grunt, her screams cut short. I bellowed, "Rumpelstiltskin! Rumpelstiltskin! Rumpelstiltskin!" into the silence, which only had the effect of making Red Cap and Méabh both gape. I slumped, for all I was on the ground. It had been worth a shot.

The reprieve caused by my shouting didn't last nearly long enough. Red Cap swung his scythe high and brought it down at me like a pickax. I threw my arm up, which was a stupid, *stupid* thing to do if I ever wanted to drive a manual clutch again. I almost had time to regret it.

The scythe reverberated off more than just my power. Red Cap hit so hard he wobbled away, and Caitríona screamed again, this time in confusion. Even Méabh took a moment to stare curiously at the small round shield suddenly clamped to my arm.

It was copper embedded with gold and purple. I didn't have to see to know there were stylized animals etched around the shield's edge, because the bracelet my father had given me had those animals on it. Nor did I have to see the gold interior quartered by a purple cross to know they were marked with the weight of honor. I had only ever once brought those things together smoothly, and that had been for a dreamscape battle. I'd carried this very shield then, so it was as familiar as it was totally unexpected. I hadn't called for it the way I'd called for my sword in the past. It had just appeared on its own.

Part of me wondered why it hadn't done that when I was, oh, say, fighting zombies, but I didn't have to look very far for the answer. My damned shields were finally instinctive, and more, my power was finally, *finally,* becoming an integrated whole. I only just now had all those needs and pieces functioning together in the real world. Of course, that flew in the face of being unable to heal the damned werewolf bite, but my burst of enlightenment ended as Red Cap wobbled, snarled and struck at me again.

I had, time and again, tried to use my magic and my sword together as a weapon. Time and again it had backfired. Warrior's path or no, my healing magic was not meant to do damage. But right now I didn't have the sword, and I didn't need the healing power. All I needed was a little *change,* the tenet of shamanism. The shield's edges were relatively dull. I willed them to be sharp, and swung the shield up to catch the scythe.

Its metal haft parted like butter under a hot knife. The blade bounced away, nearly skewering Caitríona, and Red Cap paused long enough for a fatal gawk. I crunched up, swung the shield again and opened the nasty little gnome from hip to collarbone.

By all rights, viscera and goo should have spattered from him. Instead, magic poured out of him. Blood red, to be sure, but magic, not blood, as if it was magic and magic alone that sustained him. I flinched under the onslaught until I realized I wasn't being covered in gunk, and then, as it slowed, had a look at Méabh. Cernunnos bled: I knew that for a fact. I wondered if the *aos sí* were more like him, or more like Red Cap, creatures made entirely of magic. Nuada had a silver arm, after all. Anything could happen. But then, Lugh had done a pretty good job of bleeding. It was possible I would never fully understand magic. Of course, if it could be fully understood it'd be science, and the things I did were entirely comfortable with ignoring scientific probability.

Méabh studied me like I'd become something new and much more interesting. "It's wrong I was, Granddaughter. You're a worthy warrior after all."

"Oh gosh, thanks." The shield faded now that the need was gone, but I could feel its weight now, just like I could feel the sword I didn't exactly carry. I got to my feet, feeling a little grim. "That was not your mother."

"No. But it was her creature, and any one of us dead here today w—"

"That was a bloody Red Cap!" Caitríona bounced to her feet. "A *fear darrig!* A *leprechaun,* for sweet God's sake! They don't exist! They don't—they're not—they—they—!!"

I made a note to go back and apologize profusely to everybody I'd ever said anything like that to, then, inanely, said, "Leprechaun? I thought they wore green. And gave people pots of gold, not razor-close shaves. And lived at the end of rainbows." I gave the still-power-enriched earth a nervous glance as I said that last. I'd triggered an end-times sign once because my newborn power had emitted all the colors of the rainbow. For a horrible moment I thought maybe I'd done it again, making a rainbow's end on top of Croagh Patrick and thus inviting a leprechaun to visit, but the vestiges of power were the silver-blue they were supposed to be.

"Bloody tourist boards," Caitríona muttered. "Turning the Red Caps green and giving them fairy powers. A real Red Cap is—" She gestured at the body, which, released of the magic that had sustained it, was now shriveling into dust. Magic-born things seemed to do that. "But they're not supposed to be real! Will someone please tell me what is going on!"

Méabh and I exchanged glances, and I shrugged. Caitríona'd

asked. I figured she deserved the answer. "This is Méabh, warrior queen of Ireland, daughter of Nuada of the Silver Hand and the Morrígan, who spent a few generations murdering the *aos sí* high kings to gain power for her master, who I refuse to accept is the Devil Himself. Seriously, I don't think he is," I said to Caitríona's widening eyes, "but he's absolutely a death power in this world, maybe *the* death power. My mother, your aunt, spent her whole life fighting against him, and I managed to screw it up not once but twice, and the price for that is she saved me but ended up in thrall to the Master as one of his murderous, blighted banshees. We have…" I turned my wrist up, found the bandages and bracelet there instead of a watch, but it didn't matter because I didn't need the exact time anyway. "Until sunset to burn her bones, find her captured spirit and free her before she becomes the Master's forever. I also probably have just about that much time to find my friend Gary, who went off to fight a major battle with the Morrígan and the Master several thousand years ago, and if I don't find him I'm going back to the beginning of time and rewriting this whole goddamned world's history, which I can do because I'm a shaman, which means I have healing powers and also that I kick ass." I turned to Méabh. "Did I miss anything?"

She nodded at the bandages I'd just re-noticed and I lifted my arm. "Oh yeah, right, yeah. All that and I'm turning into a werewolf. The end."

Caitríona fainted.

CHAPTER SIXTEEN

People fall down fast when they faint. There's not usually time to catch them, and neither Méabh nor I even tried. In fact, we both watched Caitríona collapse with a sort of clinical awfulness, me wincing as her cheek bounced off a sharp stone and a bruise began to blossom under a sudden rivulet of blood.

"You're a healer," Méabh said after a moment, and gentle-hearted me shrugged.

"She already believes some of this, but I might as well wait for her to wake up and notice she's— Hi, are you okay?" Faints didn't usually last very long, either. I crouched beside an exceedingly bewildered Caitríona and patted her shoulder. "You fainted. Perfectly understandable, it's been a rough day. It's going to get worse. Or differently interesting, anyway. How's your cheek?"

"It hurts." Poor Caitríona was too overwhelmed to even whine. At worst her statement qualified as a whimper. I felt around in the pockets of my brand-new coat like I'd find a mirror there—as if I *ever* carried a compact mirror—then waved my hand at Méabh.

"C'mere, let her see herself in your sword. It's the only reflective surface we've got." The polished silver was in fact remarkably reflective, and Caitríona's eyes filled with tears as the visual component added insult to injury.

"It'll scar so it will."

Under normal circumstances, she'd be right. There was a nice little puncture seeping blood at a remarkable rate, and since it had been made by a rock, it was likely dirty. But I was there, so it wasn't normal circumstances by very definition. Fully aware of how much facial wounds hurt, I touched her cheek very gently and said, "Well, no, it probably won't."

Healing, now that I could do it without all the vehicle metaphors, felt fairly awesome. It was like putting the last lug nut onto a wheel, the absolute finishing touch to a restoration. It carried a little click of satisfaction, of a job well done, of something brought back to rightness. It wasn't effortless: the power to make something change had to come from somewhere, and largely it came from me. I'd learned the hard way that big diseases like cancer really needed a power circle to spread the power draw around so I didn't kill myself trying to make somebody else healthy. But Caitríona's cheek wasn't anything like that magnitude, and it took only a moment of envisioning it as whole, complete, *right,* for that change to happen. The bruise faded, round cut at its center disappearing into unblemished skin. Her eyes got bigger and she clapped her hand over her cheek when I released her and sat back. I'd healed Gary yesterday. I'd thrown shields around. I'd just healed Caitríona. The only person I couldn't fix was myself. There was probably a lesson in that, but before I figured out what it was, Cat's eyes narrowed and she pointed at my cheek. "You didn't have that when you were here before."

I touched the thin scar on my right cheek. "Nope."

"So how come you've got it? You shouldn't have any scars."

"I got it the day I became a shaman. It's a reminder. I like it." Not that facial scars were generally high on my list of favorite things, but I did like the little cheekbone scar. It kept me balanced, somehow.

Cat had gone back to prodding her own cheek. "It's healed? I can't feel it at all anymore. Aunt Sheila never did that."

"Did she not?" I was turning Irish with my phrasing. I shook myself and tried again. "Paper cuts and scrapes never went away when she was around? I kind of do that a lot. My precinct's jumped to the head of the class for fewest sick days called in."

"She had—" Caitríona broke off, comprehension dawning. "She had magic plasters. Put them on and don't take them off for three days, three days, d'ye hear me so? Sure and we'd take them off sooner, but the cuts and bruises were always healed. She magicked us!"

I couldn't help grinning. "Yeah, she did. She totally magicked you." A shiver ran over me and I straightened. "And now we're going to magic her in return. Méabh? Um, Méabh?"

The warrior queen stood at the mountain's edge, looking into a rising mist. "Do ye's not see it, Granddaughters? Do ye's not see the coming storm?"

We both crept to where she stood, me trying not to look down. I didn't generally have a problem with heights, but the magic mountain creeped me out. I didn't want to get too close to the two-thousand-foot drop, just in case. "Sure and it's black on the horizon," Méabh whispered. "Coming for my children, hungry as only the dark can be. Do ye's not see it?"

Caitríona and I exchanged glances, then eyed the horizon cautiously. She let me be the one to say, "All I see is mist in the valley. Do you see the future a lot, Méabh?"

Memory swept me as soon as I spoke. Premonitions fed to me by a coyote in a hard white desert, dreams of futures yet to be. A few of them had come to pass. More were no doubt pending. I wasn't especially keen on that, but there wasn't much I could do but man up and take it on the chin. But Méabh shivered and shook her head. "My power's in the heat of battle, not in foresight and forewarning. If it's my sight that sees what's coming, then it's a bloody road indeed. I'll stand at your side to fight it if I may, but there's none so clear as that in the signs I see."

"What *do* you see?"

"Blood of my blood lost to me. Lost to time, sure and so. A people gone. A dying world. It's black as night, Joanne. There's no future for us here."

There were moments I really hated pioneering a new exciting path through the unexplored wildernesses of magic. Warrior and healer, future-tripper, past-visitor, accidental end-times-sign, bearer of bad news. I wanted that Shaman's Handbook, damn it, and nobody was ever going to give me one. I clapped Méabh on the shoulder and put on my best hail men and hearty voice. "The future's mutable, Grandmother. If we can't see one past the storm, then we'll by God make one we *can* see."

She startled, then smiled, which was precisely why I'd chosen to use the nomenclature. "You're a bold one, aren't you, Granddaughter?"

"It's part of my charm." Worry lanced through me, depleting any hope of actual charm rolling off me. Gary used that phrase all the time, and Gary wasn't here. Much more subdued,

I said, "Look, let's get this thing done before the Morrígan notices we axed her go-to guy and sends something scarier. Like herself. Why would she not come herself? It's just past the equinox, the banshees should be at full strength, the Master must be hungry...."

"Sure and you stepped through time to stop her sacrifice, sent a warrior and the Wild Hunt to do battle with her in your name, set a goddess to bind her deathless cauldron and caused the forging of a wedding gift that broke her power and which only a child of her own blood could remove from her throat. It is possible," Méabh said, oh so dryly, "that my mother has learned caution. The *fear darrig* is no idle threat, Joanne Walker. They torture and trick the strongest men, and yet you were slowed not at all."

I wasn't sure which astonished me more, the approval behind her litany or the revelation that Méabh, Warrior Queen of Connacht, considered a Red Cap to be a significant threat. I'd gotten so used to having my ass handed to me that I kind of figured anything I could dispatch without much effort—albeit with the help of an awesome magic shield—probably didn't rate on the scale of nasty monsters. Caitríona gave me a distinct "I told you so" look, although she hadn't actually told me how scary Red Caps were because the attempt had left her spluttering. Still, I kind of wanted to pat myself on the back. In fact, I almost did, which made my arm start itching again, which did a dandy job of deflating me. Nothing like the threat of turning into a werewolf to make a girl reconsider just how swell she thought she was.

"And there's the magic flooding this mountain, too," Méabh said thoughtfully, as if I hadn't been going through mental gymnastics while she took a breath. "Life magic, anathema to the Master and his chosen few. It may be this place is too steeped in white magic for her and her kind to safely come."

"Not likely. There's all that residual death magic here. Black magic stains. I don't know how long it takes for white magic to bleach the really bad stuff away." Back at home, my friend Melinda Holliday had done a fantastic job of cleaning up after some very ugly ritual magic had made a mess around her house, so it was possible. Hundreds of sacrificial murders just evidently took more than Saint Patrick hanging out on the mountain for forty days, or my mother coming up here several times a year to lend a helping hand.

My heart lurched. "This burning Mother's bones thing, that's a purifying ritual, right?"

Méabh nodded and my heart lurched a second time, heartbeat disrupted enough to make nausea rise again. If Melinda could wipe out the results of a suicide in her front yard, I could probably finish cleaning the ancient poison at a sacred site by means of a burning meant to purify. I croaked, "You're right, Cat. Mother would like this to be done up here. It might even be what she always wanted. I just wish we had one more of our bloodline here to help."

"We do," Méabh said gently, and knelt by the suitcase full of Sheila's bones.

The mountaintop was round, if I used my imagination vividly enough. Had I been arranging the universe, the chapel would have sat plunk in the middle of the vague roundness, but since someone else had arranged it, it was more toward the western slope, closer to the distant ocean and the nearby footpath than centered. I wibbled about it a bit, then decided to pretend the chapel wasn't there at all, and built my power circle based on the mountaintop's shape rather than the otherwise-obvious focal point that was the chapel. Besides, the chapel was locked up and I bet it wouldn't go over well with anybody, either the locals or the powers that be, if we broke in to park in the power circle's center.

Mother's bones went at the north compass point of the circle, for the cold of death. I took the south, figuring the mother-daughter connection made as much of a power channel as could be asked for, and that living flesh and blood versus dead bones made a reasonable warmth of life contrast. I put Méabh in the west, for age represented by the setting sun, and Caitríona in the east for youth. I thought that made a nice channel, too: oldest of the bloodline to youngest. Or at least to the youngest available, since I knew there were younger cousins, never mind my own son, about whom I was trying hard not to think. It was too late, of course. Sheila the banshee knew about him now, and there was a good chance that she'd already passed the information on to her new master. But I was going to have to cross that bridge later. I had bones to burn now.

"I know you can call up a power circle, whether you can heal or not," I shouted at Méabh. "I want your help here, okay? I want this circle to belong to both of us."

"What about me?" Caitríona sounded less petulant than I would've in her shoes at her age. In fact, I might even label her tone hopeful, if I was feeling honest. It made me want to give her a meaningful task, whether she had the power or not. After a second I hit on something and answered swiftly enough to seem like I hadn't hesitated at all.

"I want you to concentrate on Sheila. On everything you knew about her. Put that out there, focus it like you could call her up with your imagination. Put energy into it. The circle will pick up on that and your essence and your memories will become part of the power."

"And what will it do?"

"The more people that weave power together the stronger the connection is. I've used other people's energy before, but not for something like this. That's why I want you to think about Sheila. You knew her a lot better than I did. We want to call as much of her spirit here as we can, to give her over to cleansing the mountain and also to breaking the bond between her bones and her soul." I hadn't been previously aware of bonds like that, but then, ghosts weren't my specialty. That was my partner—former partner, which Morrison had probably told him by now, which was going to go down like a lead balloon—my former partner Billy Holliday's forte. I also wasn't absolutely certain my mother qualified as a ghost, but I was pretty sure she fell in the realm of undead, and for all I knew, the undead were deeply tied to their bones.

There was one potential snag in my plan. We might succeed in washing the mountain clean with all the heart and white magic Sheila had to offer, and that might leave nothing but the black-hearted banshee behind. I counted it a risk worth taking. In my judgment, the parts that counted as my mother would have been saved, and the rest, well. Everybody had a dark side, and there was a certain dramatic satisfaction in the idea of lopping the head off that dark side in a very literal fashion.

I decided it probably wasn't necessary to explain the possible flaw in the plan, and instead called Raven to me. It wasn't exactly that I needed his guidance in raising a power circle. More that I was heading into his realm, into the gray territory between life and death, and it was safer to do that with him nearby. He appeared, quarking curiously, and I scratched under his beak as he settled on my shoulder. "We have a big job, Raven. Life and death stuff. I need a circle that runs to the mountain's roots, that's how deep it has to go, and reaches up to where the air's too thin to breathe. Earth and sky. I can be earth, you can be sky, huh?"

He quarked again, this time clearly delighted, and leapt off my shoulder to wheel above our heads, sketching an outline of the circle. For an instant I simply loved the silly animal, loved his enthusiasm and his opinions and his brashness, and I hoped like hell he knew that. He zipped around above us, dipping close to Méabh, then zooming around the top half of the circle to come around to Caitríona. I didn't know if either of them could see him, though I saw Caitríona's hair fliff as he caught a wing tip in it. Then he went back to the north again, this time climbing high before he turned his head to give me a birdy black eye in warning.

He dove, and magic fell down in a curtain with him. I squealed, as thoughtlessly delighted as he was, and yelled, "Now, Méabh!" as I pulled magic up from the earth.

Hers came from within, relying on the connection with the world that the *aos sí* shared. It linked Croagh Patrick with Cromm Crúaich, tying the present to the far-distant past, just as Méabh was currently tied. Even Caitríona reacted, throwing forth a burst of energy more solidly formulated than someone without mystical training had any business offering. Her strength and Méabh's shot toward each other, making another link in the past/present rope, and for an instant their colors glimmered harmoniously.

Then my magic and Raven's crashed together, top to bottom, in a blast of gunmetal blue. Méabh and Caitríona's offerings, sandwiched between them, shone brilliantly for an instant, then exploded in rivulets through the ball of magic now encompassing Croagh Patrick.

It sounded like static, like the aurora was supposed to. It *felt* like laughter, a sheer primal joy in sympathetic magic. This was what wielding vast cosmic power was supposed to feel like: confident, strong, joyous, sharing. I'd thought once I could maybe heal Seattle. Maybe heal the world. All of a sudden I understood I was only part of a huge network of magic users, adepts, *connected,* whatever they wanted to be called, who could change the world if, and only if, they worked together like we were doing now. *This* was how my magic was meant to be used: as one of many. Nothing I could do on my own would ever feel so good.

Caitríona yelped, from which I ascertained she could either see or feel the power flowing. Méabh, far more stoic, stood her ground and mostly didn't let a little smile get out of control. I stretched my power toward my mother's bones, searching for the heat I'd once felt while healing. Fire shouldn't be that difficult to call up; it was only a change of state, and shamanism was about change.

A hint of Mother's red-gold power still clung to her bones. I dug into the marrow, reaching for every last whisper of that, ready to burn it out in a glorious, defiant blaze. Raven helped, settling on the bones with clenched claws, like he could snap and shake the last dregs of power from them. Between us, I felt her remaining magic gather, then lift, though neither Raven nor myself did the lifting. I tried to shutter the Sight on more deeply, and caught a glimpse of a much more fragile raven, so old his wings and beak had turned to white. Sheila's raven: I knew it instantly, though I'd never even imagined she *had* spirit animals. But it made sense. Oh, it made sense, if we were the long-calendar descendants of the Morrígan. Ravens were part of us. They always would be.

And the faded streak that was Mother's spirit raven held the fragments of her power in its claws, wings beating with a desperate, ponderous slowness. Time was so short, so very short, and there was so much to do. I pitched my voice to carry, not wanting to shout within the confines of the power circle. It seemed disrespectful, and if we'd just eked a spirit raven back from beyond to finish this task, the last thing I wanted was to show disrespect. "Give your memories of Sheila everything you've got, Cat. Let's wipe this place clean and give her the send-off she deserves."

Caitríona lowered her chin to her chest, eyes closed in concentration, and all of us held our breath, waiting to see Sheila's ghost break free of the white bones.

A goddess rose up instead.

CHAPTER SEVENTEEN

I had met gods, demigods, semi-gods or whatever the grand-children of gods should be called, archetypes, demons, elves and avatars. There were magnitudes of difference in the power each category blazed with, and I had not one single teeny tiny doubt that I was finally—finally!—in the presence of a genu-ine god*dess*. The utterly irreverent part of me thought it was about damned time. The rest of me tried not to fall down on my knees in gibbering worship.

Cernunnos had that effect on me, too, but their similarities mostly ended there. *He* was a creature of order, for all that I thought of death and its attending miseries to be chaotic. But he helped maintain the flow of life into death, while *she* was the chaos of new life. Power boiled off her incandescent skin, curls of magic licking life into existence with each molecule of air they touched. Chance exploded at every instance, ran-dom and frantic exploration of mutations pursuing survival.

Happenstance and hope guided all the permutations, fractals of magic struggling to create sustainable life in a world already filled with it. My eyes burned from watching her for barely the space of an indrawn breath. Then I howled and clapped my hands over my face, shutting down the Sight.

It faded slowly instead of its usual on-off switch, the goddess's afterimage burning my retinas for a shockingly long time. When I finally dared open my eyes again, she was merely unbelievably, inhumanly, immortally beautiful instead of eye-searingly powerful. Like Cernunnos—who had also nearly burned my eyes out when I looked at him with the Sight—her hair was scattered with light, though hers was molten sunlight instead of his starlight. Also like him, her features were chiseled, delicate, remote, flawless: high round cheekbones, large eyes, a small chin, all like she was just verging on womanhood instead of bearing a godhead.

Unlike Cernunnos, however, she was naked.

I had seen a lot more naked women the past few days than I was accustomed to. I scratched my ear, tried to find somewhere safer to look and discovered Caitríona gaping at either me or our new naked friend. It was hard to tell. I sighed, shrugged my leather coat off and offered it to the goddess. She took it curiously. After a minute I took it back and put it on her, which earned me a lightning-bolt smile of pure delight. She snuggled into it and I decided not to explain about the dead lambs whose skin it was. "Hi. I'm…" There was really only one name that would do here. "Siobhán. Siobhán Walkingstick. Is there a name we would know you by?"

"Áine," she said, and it sounded like goddamned silver bells chiming.

It also meant nothing to me. I glanced at Méabh and Caitríona, both of whom looked impressed. I took it as writ that Áine was somebody important in Irish cosmology, and smiled at the little goddess. She *was* little, now that she wasn't blasting my eyes out: she couldn't have been more than five feet tall. Even Melinda was taller than that.

Melinda, who had a personal relationship with a goddess. I blurted, "Do you know my friend Melinda?"

Áine looked amused. I ducked my head, muttering, "Yeah, right, no reason you'd be her goddess, right, sorry. Hey. Wait. Did you know my *mother?*"

Ineffable sorrow came into her eyes. I couldn't tell what color they were. Not white, because that would be creepy, but they shifted from gray to blue to green and back to gray with the passing of clouds and the ripple of wind. It made her seem that much more elemental, and she really didn't need any help in that department. I got hold of myself, trying to focus on her expression rather than her inhuman gaze. "You did know her. Is that why you came? We're trying to lay her to rest. If you want to help, we'd be…"

Words sort of didn't encompass it. I settled on "Grateful," trusting she'd get the idea despite its utter inadequacy, then cleared my throat and tried again. "I can't, um. I can heal and I can fight, but I guess I can't set things on fire with my mind. Would you…do the honors?"

Áine pursed her lips and wandered from me to Caitríona, who she studied for a long time before putting her hands on Cat's shoulders and drawing her close to kiss her forehead. An imprint of lips shone there for a moment, and Caitríona looked starstruck as Áine wandered away. At Mother's bones, she knelt with an air of regret, and although I couldn't See it, when she lifted her cupped hands, I was sure it was to hold and comfort the ancient spirit raven. She put the raven on her shoulder, then, much more purposefully, went to Méabh, at whom she smiled. Méabh's expression remained solemn, and Áine smiled even more broadly, reaching up—way, way up—to pat the warrior queen's cheek before she came back to me.

"You're Brigid's goddess, aren't you?" I said when she got to me. "The one who elevated her the way the Master elevated the Morrígan. What is he? He must be something more than a god, because he just about wiped Cernunnos out, and I'd think they'd be on a pretty level playing field if they were both gods. If you were all gods. Whatever. So what is he? Is he like Coyote? Big Coyote, I mean, the archetypical Trickster, not my Coyote. Cyrano. My teacher. Is he, like, I don't know, the archetype of death?" God. I was talking and I couldn't shut up. Still, I really wanted to know what I was up against, and Cernunnos hadn't been inclined to talk about it.

Of course, Áine didn't much seem inclined to talk at all, even when I finally managed to shut up. Which lasted only a few seconds, since no answers were forthcoming. "And if he's on a different level from you guys, how come you were able to uplift Brigid the way he did the Morrígan? And why is she *the* Morrígan instead of just Morrígan? Never mind, that doesn't matter. Or maybe you couldn't. Maybe that's why Brigid needed a link with the time the cauldron was destroyed in order to bind it. Maybe she's not as high on the avatar echelon as the Morrígan is. Oh, God, please, somebody make me stop talking."

Áine laughed. It was like a baby's laughter, a sound I wanted to get her to make again. I didn't, however, want to start babbling again, so I pressed my lips together and smiled hopefully.

Instead of speaking, she turned her palms up and stood there patiently. After a handful of uncertain seconds, I put my palms down, against hers.

The werewolf bite on my forearm turned venomous.

★ ★ ★

Shining, blistering red-hot pain rocketed through it, so fierce I went dizzy before I could even take a breath. The blast of gorgeous, ice-cool healing power that followed was even more dizzifying. Little Coyote, my Coyote, had healed me of some bumps and bruises once, but it had been *nothing* like Áine's power coursing through me. Her magic was elemental, sensual, sexual, *profound*. I could bask in it for days, like a lizard under the hot sun. It was absolute reassurance that all would be right with the world, and it was the most comforting, loving embrace I'd ever encountered. It felt like someone giving me a good scrubbing from the DNA on up. I'd just been more or less rewritten from the DNA on up, but that had been a much less pleasant experience.

Or it had been up until Áine's power slammed into the magic that actually *was* trying to rewrite me from the DNA on up, because then things got down to some serious pain. Intellectually I knew there'd probably been barely a second between the first intense burst of agony from the bite when Áine touched me, the cushioning effect of her magic rushing through me and the infection's response, but the moment of respite had seemed wonderfully drawn-out.

At least, it seemed drawn-out in comparison to the railroad spikes now being driven through my arm. I pried one eye open to make sure that wasn't really happening. It wasn't. That was good enough for me. I closed my eyes again and tried not to snivel.

My own power had been going great guns holding the infection in place. I kind of thought Áine's should just smack it aside like a pesky bug, but I could feel her crashing against it, waves against the shore, neither giving way to the other. I didn't dare trigger the Sight, not with a goddess using her power full tilt. I'd go blind, or possibly burn my brain out. Neither would be any fun. So I just held on, teeth gritted against relentless surges of magic battling it out under my skin, until Áine suddenly released me and stepped back.

The bite still hurt like blue blazes, and I didn't really need to look to know it wasn't one bit more healed than it had been. I looked anyway.

It wasn't one bit more healed than it had been. Some of the inflammation that had erupted when Áine touched me was already fading, but the bite itself was just as dark, infected and nasty as it had been since I'd received it. All I could think was, holy crap, the Master was powerful. Or the werewolves were powerful. Somebody, anyway, was powerful, because if a goddess was stymied by the shapechanging magic running through my bloodstream, then I was infected with something so absurdly far out of my league I didn't even know where to begin. I'd thought Méabh had had power in spades when I'd seen her bind the werewolves to the lunar cycle. But she'd just told me that had taken a lifetime of preparation, so while it had been an astounding performance, it didn't seem to be something she was in a position to repeat.

I took a moment—just a moment—to really hate being the go-to girl who *could* pull out the repeat performances, and then I got over myself, because Áine looked genuinely dismayed that my arm still shone with red, superheated infection. Offhand, I guessed she'd never run into something she couldn't heal, either. That was considerably more of a come-uppance for a goddess than it was for snot-nosed little me. "It's okay. I'm gonna figure it out. And I know it means I bear his mark and all, but don't let that stop you from helping my mother, okay? Please? I'll bow out of the circle if I need to, so there's no taint, but man, she really doesn't deserve this."

Áine got an expression I suspected had crossed my own face more than once in the past several months. Petulance was not an emotion I would typically expect to ascribe to a goddess, but if there was a better word for the pouty lower lip, the set jaw and the slightly drawn-down eyebrows, I didn't know what it was. She did something peculiar: scooped her hands at her shoulder, then spread them palms-down over mine in a kind of splashing, throwaway gesture, then whipped away from me. Dramatically, with all that white leather swooping around, even if the coat was much too large for her—and raised her hands like the world's tiniest conductor calling an orchestra to attention.

I'd regret for the rest of my life that I only dared see, and not See, what she did next.

There was a fair amount of magic already flying around the mountaintop. Méabh and I had plenty of power to unleash individually, and together it made for an impressive show, especially when Raven was throwing his whole black-winged little soul into helping out. Sight or no Sight, I heard him shrieking in utter delight, and bet a bird's-eye view of Áine's antics was a delight to see.

I felt her bring my power into line with hers while at the same time excising my heart. Excising the part of me closest to the werewolf bite, and, to be fair, probably the least important part of my power in terms of saving my mother went. I had barely known the woman. I hadn't much liked her, much less loved her. I had learned enough now to regret all three of those things, but it was a little late now. So my intellectual good intent went into Áine's weaving, if not my heart-wrenching loss and sorrow, and I was okay with that.

I felt her gathering up Méabh's magic, too, both the connection to the earth that the *aos sís'* long lives offered, and, as

I'd thought was important, the connection of past and present. Not that a goddess didn't encompass all that time frame herself, but despite Áine coming to lend a hand, this was still a working of power of and for mortals. Méabh might barely qualify as mortal, but elves could and did die, so in my book, that counted.

I knew without having to See that Caitríona lent the heart I lacked. I wanted very badly to view the conjuring she'd dreamed up of who and what my mother had been, but even if this succeeded and we broke the bond of bones and spirit, we still had to hunt down Sheila-the-banshee and rescue her, whatever that took. I couldn't afford to be blinded or burned out no matter how much I wanted to See what was going on. It was a crying shame, because Cat *had* loved my mother, and it would've been nice to see the woman through those eyes. Still, I felt the surge of emotion build up and become part of Áine's working, and that was something.

Then, unexpectedly, I felt one more addition to the circle. Áine reached back to all the days my mother had spent on Croagh Patrick working toward healing it, and wrenched all those years of power forward. I *knew* that was what she was doing: I had mucked with time enough myself, both today and over the past year, to recognize the sensation. Two things became obvious. One, the mountain was so parched because Áine had pulled forty or fifty years of magic away from it so it could be invested here, today, all at once. Yet another closed time loop. I hated them, but they were probably better than open ones.

Two—not that I hadn't already known this, but still—my mother's willpower was *staggering*. Literally. I staggered as Áine yanked all that magic forward, its weight pressing down on me as heavily as if Mother was there herself, guiding a lifetime's worth of power into a healing ritual meant to change the landscape forever. No adept would stand to have her home overlooked by a shadowed magic, not if she could help it, and my mom could by God help it.

It no longer mattered that I wasn't using the Sight. As occasionally happened, the power had taken on real-world visibility, white magic sheeting down around us in waves of extraordinary beauty. I bet half of Ireland could see the mountaintop glowing, and I started thinking we'd better get the show on the road before people came bounding up to find out what was going on. Not that right now I could have the slightest effect on whether the show got on the road or not, so I decided I'd better stand back and enjoy it.

I could almost see my mother stepping through the curtains of magic. Kneeling here and there—always somewhere different—to invest the mountain with magic. Covering so much ground over the decades, so many times a year, that she became multiples of herself, crouched side by side by side, until she had knelt and touched virtually the whole of the mountaintop. There were spaces between handprints—finger-width spaces—but they touched the curve of a different year's thumb or hand, heel or fingertips, so there was a continuous net of power built up, glimmering with her distinctive magic. It sank into the earth in her time, and burst upward in mine.

Áine caught all that magic, more focused will than I thought any human could handle at once, and gave it right back to the Reek. She pushed it down, deeper and deeper, until it went below the mountain's foot. Until it rooted out the blood that had once stained the holy place, and scrubbed it clean.

Pure triumph erupted from the cool green earth as the last of ancient blood faded away. Everywhere for miles, tens of miles, flared with joy. With life exultant, with the thrill of victory after so many eons of defeat. Hot tears sliced trails down my cheeks, and I didn't even have much of a horse in this race, not as far as an abiding love of the countryside went. But this, once more, was what I could be good for: making things a little *better.* At the end of the day I wasn't sure anything else really mattered.

Áine gave a happy trill, bringing all the newly awakened power to high alert. It wanted to dance for her, wanted to celebrate its survival, and if there was anything more suited to the tiny goddess than that jubilant emotion, I couldn't imagine what it was. She brought her hands together, heels touching and fingertips dancing like flames.

Every ounce of celebratory power in the West shot to her, and, guided by her desire, became the fire that burned my mother's bones.

It took no time at all for them to become dust. Áine, with an air of total satisfaction, discarded my leather coat, did a twelve-step dance—I counted—around it, then gave me a blinding smile and disappeared.

This once I didn't hold it against the disappearee. I was okay with gods doing things like that. Disappearing mysteriously should, in fact, be high up in a god's repertoire. Besides, I was too agape to be upset. Áine had taken the power circle down with her when she went, and I sat with a thump, gawking across its remnants at my mother's smoldering remains.

"What... I mean, what the... Who's Áine? Really, seriously, did you *see* that?" Of course they had. They'd been right there, just like me. They'd been right there while a goddess dropped by to immolate a dead woman's bones and sink so much fresh life magic into a mountaintop I was expecting it to spontaneously erupt in flowers. Or possibly in song. Or both. At any moment Julie Andrews would appear, and it would all be over. I wondered if I would rate that kind of exit performance when it was my turn to go.

Caitríona stalked over and hit my shoulder with a solid fist, which put paid to any self-aggrandizing ideas of shuffling off my mortal coil. I clutched my shoulder in astonished injury as she yelled, "'Can't set things on fire with me mind?' Jaysus, the lip on ye! Can't set—!" She stalked off again, but only as far as Méabh, to whom she also said, "Can't set things on fire with her mind so! Sure and it's a pity, isn't it? It's every day I get up and say to meself, no, not today, Cat, today ye can't set things on fire with yer mind, but tomorrow so, tomorrow will be grand and you'll just *set things on fire with your mind*."

The chapel roof exploded into flames.

CHAPTER EIGHTEEN

I burst out laughing. I just couldn't help it. I'd had enough.
More than enough, and the flames dancing merrily over the
chapel roof were the final straw. Although setting things on
fire with my mind was not in my skill set, I was surprisingly
confident of being able to douse them, and extended shields
over the chapel. If I could keep scythes and avalanches and psychic attacks out with my shields, I saw no reason why I couldn't
keep oxygen out, too, and within moments the fire sputtered
out under the increasing pressure of silver-blue magic. There
wasn't even any damage to the roof, possibly thanks to my
hastiness, but more, I thought, thanks to the magical nature
of the flames. They had been set with the power of the mind.
Probably that kind of fire didn't really need fuel at all, but it
did need concentration, and Caitríona's was gone all to hell
and back.

　　When I turned away from the chapel, Méabh was staring

accusingly at Caitríona, who was in turn staring at me accusingly. "Oh, no," I said. "That was you, sister, not me."

"What?"

"But she hasn't the power!"

My eyebrows shot up. "Maybe she hadn't the power, but I'd say she's got it now. Áine kissed her, remember?"

"It doesn't work that way!"

My eyebrows remained elevated. They felt like they might never come down, in fact. "Doesn't it? Because as far as I knew, I didn't have the power, either, not until Cernunnos skewered me. I'm kinda thinking close encounters with the deitific kind trigger all sorts of interesting responses in—" and I dropped my voice dramatically "—the granddaughters of Méabh."

Méabh looked like she would set my head on fire if it was within the power of *her* mind to do so. "There are *rituals,* Granddaughter. There are slow awakenings. There are—"

"Yeah, yeah, I know. Sweat lodges and spirit danc—"

I was vaguely aware Caitríona had been saying, "Sorry, what?" and "Sorry?" and "Excuse me," in increasingly voluble tones, but she broke into my litany with a roared, "What do you mean, *that was me?*" that stopped Méabh and me from snapping at one another's heels I peeked over my shoulder to make sure the chapel wasn't on fire again, then smiled brightly at Caitríona. "I mean I can't set things on fire with my mind, and I'm guessing Méabh can't, either, which leaves you, who was concentrating very hard on the idea of setting things on fire with your mind when the chapel went up. Wow. That's a totally offensive power."

Offense was the right word, all right. Caitríona balled her fist again and came at me. To her huge outrage, I caught the punch in my palm effortlessly. I was a lot bigger than she was, and it was a lousy attack. The verbal one was clearer, if not necessarily more heartfelt. "What do you mean, an offensive power? Sure and you're the one trucking with a dead woman's bones, there's nothing more offensive than that!"

"No, no." I leaned into Cat's fist, holding her in place. "Not offensive bad. Offensive like offense, defense. It's a power you can bring to the attack." She relaxed a little, suddenly less, well, offended. "Which I'm guessing means whatever you are in the cosmic scheme of things, it's not a shaman. Maybe more like Méabh here. She doesn't heal. She just brings the fight to the bad guys."

"I wield shamanic power," Méabh said stiffly.

I wrinkled my nose. "I don't think you do. You wield magic, absolutely, and it's a magic that can shape bodies, but I'm not sure it's shamanic. Healing's a big part of shamanism. You're more of a…" My hand fluttered away from holding Caitríona's fist, waving in the air as if searching for words to pluck from it. I had firsthand experience with sorcerers. They were basically evil shamans. Méabh wasn't one of those. And witches needed a coven and a deity to guide them, so she wasn't a witch, either. I'd never met a wizard, but that had too many fantasy novel connotations for me. I finally settled on, "Mage!" and felt pretty good about it.

Or I did until I remembered that was exactly the word a Seattle speaker-with-the-dead had used to describe my mother. Sheila MacNamarra, the Irish mage, she'd said. Which meant your average mage, if there was such a thing, should be able to heal, since my mother apparently had been able to. Either that or magery came with different skill sets depending on the adept, which seemed fairly likely.

I was going to *write* the goddamned handbook, is what I was going to do. As soon as I was done hunting down a banshee and finding Gary and right after I'd gone home to tie

Morrison to a bed for a week and then taken up jogging with any energy I happened to have left over. I didn't have a job to go to anymore, after all. No doubt I could write a bestselling shamanic handbook in my suddenly copious free time and live off the riches from that.

Méabh and Caitríona, who were not, thankfully, privy to that whole line of thought, had equal looks of satisfaction. Apparently being mages sounded cool. I kind of thought it did, too, and momentarily tried it on for size. Joanne Walker, Mage For Hire. Siobhán Walkingstick, Magistrate. Not that I was certain *magistrate* could be used that way, but on the other hand, who was going to stop me?

I was, really. I'd kind of gotten used to the idea of being a shaman. Maybe if Sheila had raised me, I'd have come up in the idea of being a mage, but I'd had more exposure to my Cherokee side, and the magic had shaped itself in the idea of shamanism. Perhaps an unnaturally broad spectrum of sha-manism, but still, that was the title I was comfortable with. Caitríona could be a mage. *The* mage, presumably. The Irish Mage. I felt guilty. That was a hell of a burden to plant on a nineteen-year-old.

"Am I really like you so? Like Auntie Sheila?" Cat didn't sound burdened. She sounded breathless. Hopeful. Excited. All the things I'd been, now that I reached back for it, when Coyote had approached my thirteen-year-old self in dreams and had started to teach me to be a shaman. Maybe it wasn't so bad after all.

Méabh, grumpily, said, "No," at the same time I said, "Yeah, I think so." We eyed each other, my expression falling into a frown. "What's your problem, Granny? I'd think you'd be pleased."

She looked as though she'd like to throttle us both. "The

power doesn't come on ye in a burst. It's grown up into, day by day, bit by bit. It's madness to be drowned in it all at once."

I could hardly argue the latter point, but the former was manifestly untrue. I started to protest, trailed off before I got going, then tried again, with something totally different than I'd expected to say. "You're *aos sí,* Méabh. We're human. It might work differently for you. You're connected to the world in a way I've never seen. If that all came up and smacked a person at once, yeah, it'd be madness, but I think maybe we mere mortals don't have quite as much oomph to take under our wings."

Méabh's jaw worked. She clearly wanted to be annoyed, but I was honestly a bit agog at the *aos sí* connection to the world, and it had come through in my voice. It's hard to be irritated with someone who's all impressed by you. "Well," she finally said, somewhere between grudging and exasperated, "what are we to do with her, then? Sure and we can't leave a newly awakened power to fumble along on her own."

"Sure and we won't," I said cheerfully. "She's coming with us. I dunno where we're going, but it can't hurt to have new phenomenal cosmic power tagging along."

Caitríona squeaked, "Really?" and I started to nod before she finished with, "Phenomenal cosmic power? Am I that grand?"

I said, "Time will tell," in my very best intonation of wisdom voice, but Cat didn't look impressed. Kids these days, I tell ya. "If you're really going to step into Sheila's shoes, you've probably got some fairly significant power. But it may take a while to access it all. Méabh's right. These things usually do come up in bits and pieces, through lots of training, rather than being all Hammer time."

She stared at me, a firm reminder that people born a decade

later than I'd been were not versed in the same popular lingo. "Never mind. Just try not to set anything else on fire, okay?"

"I wouldn't know how to." Her eyes, though, were big and interested, and I caught her eyeing the chapel again.

"Don't even think about it. I need to do some important stuff." I really wished I'd had specifics to put in there, but I was coming up short on them. "I wish Billy was here. Or Sonata. A medium, anyway. I don't know how to tell if Mother's spirit has been…loosened."

"Can ye not tell?" Méabh asked incredulously. "With all the power here, can ye not tell?"

"Speaking with the dead is way out of my skill set. Cat, did you feel anything from Sheila during that whole…" I waved my hand. "Thing?"

"Joy," she said without missing a beat. "She was here, Joanne. I'm sure of it. She knows what was done here, and it's gladdened her heart."

"Go us." I picked up my coat and mashed it against my mouth while I thought. It smelled faintly of stardust. Don't ask how I knew what stardust smelled like. It just smelled of stardust. Clear and thin and distant and crisp. "Okay. The body is destroyed. That means the spirit's attachment to the world is weaker, but it also means if she was attached to the bones, then the spirit hasn't crossed over. Whatever's on the other side, it ain't there yet." I did my best to sound like Gary, which was a mistake. Fortunately I already had the coat covering half my face and could wipe at tears without being too obvious about it. Not that leather was any good for absorbing tears, but at least they weren't leaking down my face. I had to get him back. I had to do about a million things, all by sunset tonight.

"That's right," Méabh said while I wiped my face and glanced at the sky. Midmorning, if not a little later. We had six or eight hours to stage all the rescues in. I clung to that and turned my attention back to Méabh, who was saying, "He'll have wanted her bound by her bones to this earth for all time. No spirit in his grasp can cross if he holds her bones."

"Okay. Okay. So what do we do next? How do we free her spirit?"

Méabh, font of all knowledge, dried up. I waited, then waited some more, and finally realized she wasn't going to come through with an answer. Desperate, I glanced at Caitríona, but she only shrugged apologetically. I stomped in a small circle, swore, reversed the whole thing, swore again and said, "Okay, fine. Then I'm going to go try to talk to her, because maybe she'll know. I don't know what else to do."

"Talk to who?" Caitríona and Méabh asked with varying degrees of wariness and suspicion.

I spread my hands and sat to sketch a circle around myself. "My mother, who else?"

They exchanged glances, making me feel ganged up on. Méabh was voted spokesperson by silent ballot, and said, in a purely accusational tone, "I thought ye said speaking with the dead wasn't a skill ye had."

"It's not, but apparently her spirit's been tied to her bones all this time, which means if we've shaken her spirit loose at all we've only just done it, so maybe she hasn't gotten that far into the great beyond. If she hasn't, then I've got an inside man for the job."

Raven dove down out of the sky.

Typically, my avian friend was pretty enthusiastic about— well, everything. The slightest opportunity to explore regions unknown was generally greeted by quarking and kloking and an admirable tattoo of wings. This time, though, he landed in a poof of feathers, then tucked his wings around himself and cocked his head to give me an unmistakably concerned look. I didn't think of birds as having a lot of emotive capability, but Raven was happy to prove me wrong. Or unhappy, as the case happened to be.

My shoulders slumped. "What? Do you have a better idea? We've gotten off pretty lucky so far, and any day that includes accidental time travel, losing a friend in the annals of history and setting a mountaintop on fire doesn't exactly rise high on my list of lucky days. If Mom can give us any guidance at all, we need it."

He gave a low, drawn-out "quaa-aaa-aaar-k-k-k" of dismay. I slumped further. "Yeah, I know, but like I said, do you have a better idea?"

How I knew his hopeful hop and perky look around meant "We could go look for shiny food!" I don't know, but I was absolutely certain that was his better idea. I chuckled and put my hands out to him. He hopped in, even though his expression said quite clearly that he knew I was assuaging his dashed hopes. "I meant a better idea with regards to how to find Mom before she becomes a hundred-percent banshee, get Gary back and kick the Morrígan's ass, because I promise I'm not going home until I've gotten a piece of that bitch."

What there was of Raven's shoulders drooped. I kissed his head and said, "Yeah, I thought not. So will you guide me, Raven? Can we go into the Dead Zone and see if we can connect with Sheila MacNamarra before the Master takes her for his own?"

He sighed a heartfelt birdy sigh, hopped back out of my hands and stretched his wings until they touched both sides of the power circle. I twisted and touched it at opposite points, and magic rose with soothing, gentle ease to usher Raven and myself into the Dead Zone.

There was a weight on my shoulder. Slight, not like Raven's heft. I turned my head to find myself nose to beak with the ancient, white-winged raven that had been my mother's spirit companion. Raven, my Raven, still in my palms, made a sound of astonishment and hopped onto my other shoulder to peer around my head at the new arrival. White Wings peered the other way, and in no time at all they were playing a game, trying to catch the other out as they ducked back and forth around my head. I swore they were laughing, their rapid-fire *kloks* sounding like joyful, long-overdue greetings.

Me, I couldn't actually see them. Partly because it was hard to focus on things on my shoulders, but mostly because my eyes prickled with tears. I hardly had a voice to say, "Hey, Wings," to the white raven. "That's what Áine was doing. She gave you to me before she burned the bones. I am so glad to meet you."

Wings stopped playing hide-and-seek in my hair and pressed his head against my cheek. He didn't even seem to mind that doing so spilled the tears from my eyes and made wet spots on top of his white head. Raven, a little jealous, pressed against me from the other side, and I put my hands up to cover both of them in a gentle embrace. "I have never been so glad to see anybody as I am to see you two right now. Wings, we've got to look for my mother. Raven's amazing at guiding me through the Dead Zone, but you know her better than anybody, huh? With both of you helping I can't go wrong, can I?"

I probably could, but there was no need to say that to them. Neither was willing to leave my shoulders, but they both hopped on them, evidently happy with the arrangement. My vision finally cleared enough to see, and for a moment I was too astonished to do anything but look.

I was accustomed to the Dead Zone being a black expanse a hairsbreadth smaller than infinity. It was featureless, unnavigable and generally scary in the sense of being implacably large to my infinitesimal smallness, which smallness I had no doubt the Dead Zone could crush like a bug at its faintest whim. It didn't help that I had occasionally met giant murderous snakes and the occasional ferryman while here, neither of which was reassuring.

Raven's presence made the whole place just slightly less dreadful. Just slightly, but sometimes that was enough. With him on my shoulder, I got a sense of landscape, though it changed with every breath. With him, I could see the rivers that carried the dead, the reapers that collected souls, takers-of-the-dead from different cultures all over the world. None of them saw each other, all traveling through the same idea— space without ever impinging on one another's territory. I was the only one who did that.

Viewed with the help of two ravens, the Dead Zone became navigable. More than that: it became a real landscape, a countryside that misted around the edges but no longer stretched over intimidating distances. No longer threatening, though I had no doubt it remained dangerous. But it had a sense of comfort about it now, a sense of recognition of history that my travails from Seattle hadn't shared. More of a reverence for the dead, less fear and more acceptance, maybe, than I was accustomed to. I still didn't want to wander the green rolling hills, knowing they only tempered the Dead Zone's dangers, but at least I wasn't a mote in a vast nothingness.

I shivered, then exhaled quietly. I had blood ties to the spirit I was looking for this time, and her raven on my shoulder. That ought to help. I hoped. I called up a picture of my mother and said, "You're not the Master's yet," to the darkness. "And God knows you were the most willful woman I've ever met, so I'm guessing if you want to you can break away from whatever hold he's got on you, and come say hi."

Wings *kloked* in dismay and I shrugged. "Look, we didn't get along all that brilliantly, okay? I could be all mushy and squishy and sob story, but I don't think she'd even know who I was if I did that. I might as well call it like I see it."

"That," Sheila MacNamarra said a little wryly, "that you got from me."

CHAPTER NINETEEN

Someday I was going to be cool enough to not shriek and fall over when things like that happened, but today was not that day. My raven dug his claws in, and Wings flew up into the air to go land on Sheila's shoulder as I sat up again clutching my heart. She forgot me for an instant and turned her face against Wings's wing, the small motion replete with joy. They communed a little while, until she finally looked toward me again, the corner of her mouth turning up. "Thank you for bringing him to see me, Siobhán. No," she added without hesitation. "You didn't like that. Joanne, then."

Feeling like I was giving one up for the team, I took a deep breath and said, "Siobhán's all right. I've gotten a little more used to it the past year."

"Is that so." I'd almost never seen my mother smile. It warmed her eyes considerably. I thought she was quite pretty in that clear-complexioned Irish way. It was even clearer now that she was dead, her freckles faded from lack of sunlight, so her dark hair was all the more striking around her pale face. I didn't look like her, but I didn't not, either. That was a revelation, since I'd thought we didn't look anything at all alike.

She'd been studying me while I studied her, and broke the silence. "You'll still prefer Joanne, I think."

"I will. I mean, I do. Yes. But, y'know, whatever works."

"The past year, is it? A year since when, Joanne? Since I died?"

"Since you saved my ass from the Blade." That banshee had had a name. I didn't know why it rated and the others were just nameless banshees, but probably the opportunity to earn a name was not something I wanted for my mother's undead soul. "Look, um, I'm not sure I said thanks for that. Or...a lot of things. So let me just get this out of the way, okay? I understand a lot more than I did then, and I'm really sorry I was such a dick. Although to be fair you could've at least tried to explain why you'd brought me to America." That was not exactly high up there in the ranks of graceful apologies. I cringed.

Sheila, however, looked ever so faintly amused. "Would you have listened?"

"No, but it might have seeped through eventually. Once I started learning about all...this." I gestured to the complete and total emptiness around us, which didn't really go very far in impressing a *this* on me.

"It seems to have seeped through anyway."

I couldn't tell if she was being funny or superior. My lips peeled back from my teeth in one of those telling microexpressions, and she looked away with a sigh. "A warm and loving family we are not, Siobhán MacNamarra. How bad has it gotten, then, that you come seeking me?"

"Did you know?" My voice broke on the three little words

and I cleared my throat, trying to sound stronger. "When you came back from the dead to help me fight the Blade, did you know it was going to put you in thrall to...*him?*"

"For Heaven's sake, Joanne," my mother said crisply, "he's not Voldemort. You can say his name."

"I don't..." I couldn't get past my mother knowing who Voldemort was. It took a minute to finish the sentence. "I don't know his name. All I've got for him is a title. The Master," I said in my best portentous voice. "It gets old. So what's his name?"

Sheila had the grace to look ever so slightly abashed. "I know him by the title, as well. The name itself is a secret well-guarded."

"What, would the Rumpelstiltskin thing work on him? It didn't on Rumpelstiltskin."

"...you met Rumpelstiltskin?"

"A horrible little gnome creature, anyway. Caitríona said he was a frog derek. Something like that. A Red Cap. He was wearing one. Look, that's not the point. Did you know you were going to end up his slave?"

"Rumpelstiltskin's?" Sheila asked archly, and Raven, the betraying little bastard, laughed. So did Wings, which made it worse.

Ravens laughing would usually be awesome enough to undermine my irritation, but I wanted to throttle them both. All. Mostly because I had the sudden dismaying suspicion that I did exactly that same kind of verbal game. I put another bullet point on the endless list of things I really needed to change about myself, and grated, "No. The Master's. I don't know how long we've got here, Mom. Should we really be screwing around with semantics and unclear pronouns?"

Her humor fell away. "I suppose these are bridges that ought to have been crossed while I lived, not now. And I'm not enslaved yet, Joanne. Not yet. You've burned my bones, haven't you? All that's left is to destroy the banshee queen. I'm too small, too far removed from the Master for him to catch me with his own long fingers. He needs her, and so without her I'm free."

"The banshee queen." I pressed my eyes shut. "Great. I'll get right on that. You're not answering the question."

Tension came into Sheila's presence, and when I opened my eyes she spoke through compressed lips. "Very well. Yes. I knew."

A double prong of guilt and horror stabbed me in the gut. If my dead mother was reaching out from beyond the grave, I should probably make some effort to meet her halfway and try building a meaningful emotional relationship. But we *were* on a tight schedule, and really, shock obliterated the guilt pretty fast.

Despite asking, I hadn't in a million years really thought she'd have known what she was getting into. That added a whole new level of guilt to the trip I was busy burying. Voice rising, I demanded, "Then what the hell'd you do it for!" even though the answer was terribly, terribly obvious.

Sheila said, "You," and my world fell down.

The Dead Zone dissolved, which it had never done before. Soft green landscape melted like sugar in rain to reveal the black nothingness I was more familiar with. Then that softened, too, gray bleeding down to bubble against earth that slowly turned green with grass. Rigidly cut grass, millimeter-exact in height, but at least it was no longer so short the earth could be seen between individual blades. Elsewhere the Dead Zone's matter began to burble, the sound of a small waterfall falling into a pool. There were paving stones leading hither and yon through the greening garden, and benches that had softened from concrete to slatted wood. I had a momentary vision of a day when they might just be moss-covered hillocks, cool and prickly to snuggle into, but the idea faded before the reality of my inner sanctuary.

I hadn't been here in a while, truth be told. The tall ivy-covered walls were more fragile than they had been, time wearing away at them so they were lived-in and comfortable rather than imprisoning. A single bird twittered like mad, and I smiled. I couldn't see him, but it was a robin. An American one, because it had twisted my brain inside-out the first time I saw an Irish robin and realized Mary Lennox's key-finding companion had been a completely different kind of bird than I'd always thought. In *my* secret garden, the robins were like the North Carolina birds of my teen years.

"It's not what I'd have expected of you," Sheila said gently, and I closed my eyes. Her garden would have the sparrow-like robins, if it had birds at all. We were creations of completely different cultures, my mother and I.

"It's a lot better than it was. The first time I came here it was almost dead. Not exactly the most spiritually competent kid on the block, me."

"What happened?"

God. There was so much we hadn't talked about. A whole lifetime, neither of us able to breach the chasm of my resentment in the few months we'd had. But I couldn't just answer, oh no. That would be easy. Instead I said, "Don't you know?"

She was silent a long time. So long I'd have thought she'd disappeared, except I had invited her here when I'd left the Dead Zone, and she wouldn't leave without my permission. I wasn't sure she *couldn't,* but she wouldn't, because this was the closest I'd ever come to opening up to my mother. This place was the center of my soul, with all the faults and flaws and strengths and wisdom exposed and on display. She'd have to be a real ass to walk out, and mostly that title belonged to me.

"Mother's daughter was a little wild," she whispered eventually. "Had herself a wee boy child."

"And a girl." I still hadn't looked at her. I wasn't sure I would, as long as we were in here. I already felt naked. Meeting her eyes seemed like it would be too much. "She died, she died right away. I wasn't a healer yet. I'd stolen my own magic away and I couldn't do anything to help. But that was after." I made my voice harsh so I could keep talking. "The twins were the aftermath. That wasn't what went wrong. My life is so screwed up, Mom. Do you reach through time? Because I've been doing it all my life. Right from when you were pregnant with me and we fought the Blade."

Her silence this time was brief but full of the things I didn't want her to say. I was about a hair's breadth from crying on my mommy's shoulder, and that was so far outside my comfort zone I couldn't even begin to express it. I thought she knew it, too, because when she did speak, she said, "No, *alanna*. I suppose that would be from your father's side of the family," rather than offer any kind of sympathy or condolence.

That was okay, because it brought my brain to a full stop. Choked off Emo Jo and made me spin around on a heel to gape at her. "My father's side of the family?"

Sheila MacNamarra got a sly little smile that made her look about nineteen. "Sure and you didn't think I flew all the way to New York just for a pretty face, lovey, though oh my Lord, he was pretty. I could feel his pull from Ireland, Siobhán. The power, the passion for the earth, the…"

I could not have been more astonished if she'd pulled up her skirts and started doing an authentic Can-Can. She trailed off, then said, "You don't know any of this, do you, my girl?"

"Dad...has magic?"

"A shaman's magic, to be sure. Not like my own, oh no. Magery is spells and incantations, Siobhán. I could do most anything with it, but with preparation and study. Your father, though." Mother's eyes were shining. I'd thought she and Dad hardly knew each other, but it suddenly struck me that didn't mean they hadn't been in love. That she wasn't *still* in love with him, a year after she'd been buried. No wonder I didn't have any siblings. "Your father could just will it to be, and it was. He said it could be such a dangerous magic, such an easy path to the dark, but he shone like nothing I'd ever seen. Everywhere he went, the very earth responded to him like a lover, eager for his touch."

Our endless road trips abruptly made more sense. I'd thought Dad just hated being in one place, since the only time he'd settled down for any length of time, an Irish woman had come back from across the ocean and handed him a baby before disappearing forever. I'd just found out a few days earlier that the only other time he'd come close to settling down, his mother had been killed in a horrific car wreck that had sent him away from Qualla Boundary for good.

But maybe we'd been on the road constantly because he was responding to the needs of a weary earth. My vivid memory of visiting Montana and the Battle of Little Bighorn site abruptly seemed a lot like the afternoon's antics on Croagh Patrick. Dad had been disgusted with the white men who'd fought there, which even my eight-year-old self had understood. There were still bullets buried in the tops of the small, sharply rolling hills: it was not a site for modern warfare to take place. But Dad's disgust could have gone much deeper than that...and so could have the time we'd spent there, crawling up and down hills, our hands in the dirt. *I'd* just been playing, but if Dad had power, too, then that wasn't a place he'd be playing at.

An awful, awful lot of the places we'd visited came clear when seen in that light. We'd followed the Trail of Tears. Visited nuclear test sites in Nevada, and I remembered Dad talking with Shoshone tribal elders before we went out into the desert. The Hopewell mound cities in Ohio. Mount Rushmore, which I recalled had almost literally made Dad's head steam. I'd been about twelve then, and wondered now if I'd been Seeing some of his anger at the desecration of ancient Native holy places.

I sat, face hidden in my hands. After a moment I spread my fingers to stare between them at Sheila, who looked discomfited. "You'd no idea, had you."

"Not a clue. Not a single…" I closed my fingers again and sat there a long damned time. Finally, and more to myself than Sheila, I said, "I'd like a do-over. I mean, in the end I'm doing okay with my life, I think. I got the guy, I got the best friend, I got the magic. I'm doing okay. But I want a do-over. I want to go back through my life and knock the giant-ass chip off my shoulder. I want to *hear* what Dad might've been trying to say to me. I want to have the nerve to ask about my mother. I want…" It didn't really matter what I wanted. I pushed my tongue around inside my lower lip, contorting my face before finishing, "I want to know what my life would've been like if I hadn't been such a jackass through most of it. It's too damned late to be sorry, but I am anyway, Mom. You probably deserved a much better kid than me. I'm sure Dad did. So I'm sorry."

"It may be you deserved a better mother, *alanna*. Shall we forgive one another while we still can?"

"Oh, sure. I'm sure I deserved a better mother than the one who chose not to hand the Master a major defeat because it might've risked my unborn self, or the one who gave me up to my father so the Master couldn't keep the bead he'd had on me, or the one who gave me a magic silver necklace to protect my soul from evil, or the one who came back from the dead to lay a smackdown on the Master and kick a banshee's ass because I was too new and feeble in my powers to do it myself. I'm sure I deserved—"

"A mother," Sheila interrupted, and to my horror tears flooded my eyes. "Shall we forgive?" she asked again, even more quietly. I nodded, miserable with embarrassment, and she sighed before a note of playfulness came into her voice. "Now, I know we've little time and much to talk about, Siobhán, but there's two things you've said that have my attention, so they do."

I looked up, snuffling, to see her smile and lift a finger to touch its tip. "One—you got the guy?"

I laughed through snorting snot, which made for a very wet burbly disgusting laugh, but it was heartfelt. "My boss. My former boss. Captain Morrison? Did I mention—"

"The one who can't tell a Corvette from a Mustang," Sheila said, eyes solemn. Then she leaned forward confidentially and admitted, "I'm Irish, lass. I wouldn't know the one from the other if my life depended on it."

"Yes, but you're *Irish*. He's a red-blooded American male, it just shouldn't be possible for him not to know." I snuffled again and wiped my hand under my nose. Six-year-olds had more dignity than I did. "But anyway, yeah. We sort of…yeah. It's not like you and Dad." A thought which bent my brain. "Morrison's not magical at all. But I don't need any more magic in my life. He grounds me. He's…" God. My stupid eyes filled up with tears again, for a whole different reason this time. I was turning into a regular Waterworks Wendy.

"That's grand so," my mother said in delight. "Congratulations, Joanne. Be happy, *alanna*. Be happy."

"I hope so." I cleared my throat. "What was the other thing?"

"Oh!" Her eyes lit up. "A magic necklace?"

"Yeah, my—your—silver choker? It's magic. Didn't you know that? Nuada made it for the Morrígan when he married her and it bound her to this whole fight we're in. Hobbled her, like." I was falling into the Irish idiom of adding "like" or "so" to the end of sentences for no apparent reason. If I stayed here more than a week I'd forget how to speak American English. "I don't know if it's got any other power, but reining in goddesses is a pretty good one-shot to have. And, oh, it's, um, sort of bound to our family line. I was kind of there when it was forged and put some of my blood into the forging. The Morrígan had to bear a child to have it removed, and that child was Méabh, who made a choice to fight against her mother and our whole family has been doing it ever since. I've got Caitríona O'Reilly with me now. She's taking up your mantle, she'll be the new Irish mage, since I'm not cut out for it."

Mother hesitated. "Caitríona? Truly?"

"Oh, yeah. She found us at the graveyard about to burn your bones and made us come up to Croagh Patrick, where Áine triggered her magic. Méabh's having a fit because that's not how it's done in her estimation, but it sure looks like that's what's happened anyway."

I was as unaccustomed to seeing pride on Sheila's face as I was smiles, but there was unmistakable pride now. "Caitríona will be grand so. Oh, but she's got so much study ahead of her, Joanne. The mage's path isn't an easy one. She's a fine lass, though, strong and quick. She'll do well. Tell her I said so, won't you?"

"Yeah." I cleared my throat. "Yeah, of course I will. It'll torque Méabh's jaws, but that'll be fun, too."

It was Sheila's turn to clear her throat, after which she said, "Méabh," cautiously. "We're the daughters of Méabh? Of *the* Méabh? Queen Méabh of Connacht?"

"Yep, that one." Ah, how my life had shifted, that I could say that so casually. "She's kind of hanging around on Croagh Patrick right now while I talk to you. Do you want to meet her?"

Mother's eyes got very nearly as big as saucer plates, which in the garden of the soul was a dangerous kind of phrase to indulge in. "I would so," she whispered, and I sat up straighter, pleased to be able to offer something to my mother that would mean something to her.

If I turned my attention outward, Méabh's presence was easy to distinguish, a roaring flame of connected power. A flame which appeared to be in heated argument with Caitríona. I was going to have to separate those two, but not just yet. I softened my shields ever so slightly, extending an invitation to Méabh. She broke off fighting with Cat and spun to face me, her own shields melding until they fit the shape of doorway I offered. A moment later she stepped through, larger than life and glorious even in the garden of my mind.

Which would have been fine, except the Morrígan stalked into my garden on her heels.

CHAPTER TWENTY

Under any other circumstances I'd have applauded the entrance. The woman was amazing, with her blue-black hair and her blue-banded biceps and the flowing, gorgeous robes that didn't impede her fighting ability at all. Furthermore, my shields glimmered around her as she pushed through, giving her a glowing curtain of power that clung to her skin and shone silver highlights on the curve of strong muscles. Méabh was Amazonian, but fair-haired. The Morrígan seemed more like what I could look like if I was at my absolute peak of awesomeness.

My forearm burned suddenly, the half-forgotten bite awakening again. The Morrígan lay along an unforgiving path, where admiring any part of her made me all the more susceptible to her master's powers. I clenched my right hand over the bite and squeezed hard, half hoping it would pop, pimplelike, and all the poisoned blood would gush out.

Well. That was gross enough to wipe away the folly of admiring the bad guys. I surged to my feet, snapping, "You can't *be* here," but I could See the path she'd taken to get in. There were too many links here: me, Sheila, Méabh and the necklace, all of us tied to the Morrígan in one way or another. That, and although a few hundred generations separated us, we had a trace of magic in common, too. It made my shields just vulnerable enough, when I'd already invited her daughter through them.

Méabh and Sheila both spun to see the interloper, Méabh with her sword drawn before she'd finished turning. I started to reach for my own sword and stopped, remembering with a pang that it and Gary were lost to time. Lost to a battle they'd fought against the woman who'd just walked into my garden as if it were her own. Smart money was on kicking her right out, but I'd never been all that smart. "Tell me what happened to Gary."

Méabh gave me a sharp look, and Sheila a curious one, but neither of them questioned me as the Morrígan laughed, low and warm and friendly. "And why would I do that?"

Every once in a while my shit came together and I knew the right answer to a challenging question. Cool with anger, I straightened to my full height—a height which was more impressive among humans; the Morrígan didn't tower over me the way Méabh did, but she still had me by a couple inches—and did my best to look disdainfully down my nose at a goddess. "Because I'll let you go free from this place if you do, and otherwise I will bind you beneath the stone of this mountain as your master has been bound beneath the earth before, and you will lie with its weight pressing down on you, and its white power will stymie your magics and you will be a prisoner until the end of time."

It was my garden. I could have counted her nose hairs, if I'd wanted to. I didn't, but I *could* see, very clearly, the wave of goose bumps rise and settle on her arms. She held off a full-body shiver through will alone, but her gaze slipped sideways, betraying uncertainty before she thrust her chin out in body language that reminded me of myself. "And how would you do that?"

Méabh took a very shallow breath. She'd thrown a similar gauntlet at me not all that long ago and I'd picked it up and bitch slapped her with it. She pretty clearly expected me to do the same again.

So, frankly, did I. I walked forward, taking point between my mother and Méabh, and spoke softly. "By having three of your blood here, Morrígan, and by having a fourth no more than a shout away. By dint of you being within *my* garden, where the world is shaped as *I* will have it. By the depth of magic lent to me by a raven, who is no less my companion than yours, and of another here who is also raven-bound. Nuada, a *man,* was able to break your power with a circlet and a splash of my blood. What do you think four of your daughters and their ravens and all the magic at their command can do?"

The Morrígan's gaze slipped away again. I had the distinct impression this was not going the way she'd planned. Since virtually nothing in my life went the way I planned, I had no sympathy for her at all. "Tell me," I said again. "Tell me what happened to Gary."

She looked back at me, snake-quick, and hissed her answer: "He is lost to you, *gwyld,* daughter of my daughters. Time is his enemy and you are not its master. He fought well, he fought valiantly, but in the end, what could you expect? He was old when you sent him to fight death, and death conquers us all.

The banshee comes for him, as she comes for all of those you love. It will be her beginning and his end."

I said, "Wrong answer," and lashed a fist out to hit her in the face.

Her head snapped back with the impact, bright blood blossoming over her mouth. I'd gotten lucky and knew it. I would never get another hit like that in. But *damn,* it had been satisfying.

Satisfaction lasted long enough for the Morrígan to crank her head back up and throw a backhanded fist across my cheekbone. Bone shattered and healed in the same instant, a combination of pain and relief so sharp it left me dizzy. Healing myself wasn't working so well outside my garden, not with the bite screwing up my powers, but in here I conformed to my own template. The fact that I was even aware of the werewolf bite in here was testimony to its strength: it *should* have been left in the physical world, rather than tag along into my perception of myself.

In the moment I spent reeling, swords clashed. Méabh had the look of a woman planning to take it to the limit, and I wondered if she and her mother had ever gone mano a mano before. Watching the viciousness with which they struck at one another, I was just as glad Sheila and I were merely estranged, not actually enemies. People of great power generally made bad enemies. When both sides were equally stacked in the mojo department, the resulting altercations were a bit on the earth-shattering side.

Or in this case, garden-shattering. Soft dirt came dislodged under their feet, the sparse green grass losing its hold. I'd put a lot of effort into getting it as lush as it was, and was childishly upset at the mess they were making. "Méabh!"

She hesitated, which would have been fatal if she hadn't been within my garden. Silvery-blue shields bounced the Morrígan's next blow back, leaving both of them surprised. Méabh, however, stepped away from the fight, which was what I wanted.

This place was my heart and soul. The small changes I'd made in improving it had been part and parcel of my own spirit growing up and getting it together. I'd never fought a real battle here, or needed the garden for more than that.

Not until now, anyway. I flexed, feeling the spring's pool respond; feeling the earth under my feet respond. The Morrígan sneered and swung her sword, such a lazy open blow that her contempt for me was clear.

I crouched, catching a bit of torn-up dirt in my fingertips, and when I scooped my open hand upward again, the garden came with it. My hand, replicated at about eight times its own size in earth, rose up and seized the Morrígan. Tossed her with my gesture across the garden into one of the sturdy stone walls. I felt like the driver of one of those giant mechs, the factory machines that let an individual lift multi-ton items. The Morrígan slithered down the wall to land on her butt in the dirt, no longer looking quite so threatening. I was beginning to think she wasn't such a badass after all. Earthen hands ready to capture her again, I growled, "My garden. My rules."

Rage glinted in the Morrígan's eyes and she curled her fingers up, nails suddenly long and deadly looking. "True, so true, but it was never you I was here for, daughter of my daughters. It was never you I wanted."

Surprise held me motionless for a fateful half second. The Morrígan's fist closed and Sheila wailed as power dragged her across the garden. Her cries grew sharper and louder, less human and more deadly, as the Morrígan buried her fingers in her hair, then hauled her, kicking and screaming, out of my garden fair.

★ ★ ★

I came awake on the mountaintop. Raven was nowhere to be seen, but that was probably okay. He'd want to scold me for having left the Dead Zone without his guidance, and in retrospect, that had probably been a stupid thing to do. Caitríona was snapping a hand in front of Méabh's eyes, saying, "Hello? Hello? Are ye in there so?" She yelped when Méabh suddenly came to life again and batted her hand out of the way.

My great-grandmother turned on me in a barely controlled fury. "Have ye found what we needed to know? Is she held by my mother's master? Do ye know where to take the fight to them? Are we—"

I started out saying "No" quietly and graduated to a full-fledged bellow halfway through her last question. Her mouth snapped shut and I muttered, "No," one more time. "We were just…bonding. Well, and she sa—"

"Bonding. *Bonding?* It's your own self who won't sacrifice the woman, Joanne. What are we to do if you cannot find it in you to learn what we must know to win this battle? This is no time for *bonding*."

I looked up, more neutral than I expected to be. "I know it's not, but this is really our last chance. This has to be over by sunset one way or another." I'd chosen sunset because midnight was too arbitrary, too much a function of human time-keeping devices. Sunset was the end of day for older cultures, and I'd rather get it all done early than find myself holding the ball after the game ended. "Sorry I blew it. Sort of."

I didn't even quite know how Sheila and I had gone from sniping to bonding, but I did know I'd have regretted not having those couple minutes far more than I would ever bring myself to regret what might happen because we had. "Caitríona, do you get along with your mom?"

She startled. "What? Yes, of course I do. What kind of question is that?"

I shrugged my eyebrows. "Just hoping somebody here did, that's all. She was glad to hear you were here, was Sheila. She says you'll be an incredible power for good."

Caitríona puffed up like a cardinal. "Did she, now?"

Okay, maybe I was extrapolating from what Mother *had* said, but the sentiment was close enough. "She's proud of you, Cat. You're gonna be amazing. And she says magery is about spells and preparation, so you were mostly right, Méabh. Initial explosions of power or no, Cat's got a lot of studying to do."

"Who'll teach me?"

I looked off the mountain like the answer would come to me. It didn't, so after a moment I shrugged my shoulders as well as my eyebrows. "I don't know. Me, maybe, at least for a little while. I'll have to find you somebody versed in magery, but I can teach you about the safeties and shielding, anyway." Coyote would find that very ironic. Hell, *I* found it ironic. I also rubbed my forearm, the bite a dull itching throb. There'd been no more impulse to change since we got to the top of Croagh Patrick, but I was a little afraid of what would happen when we left. And staying there wasn't an option. "She said we have to defeat the banshee queen."

Méabh rounded on me again, this time in angry astonishment. "Why did ye not say so?"

"You were too busy yelling at me."

She fell abruptly silent, which I thought was a pleasant change. "Cat, any idea where we find a banshee queen?"

My cousin eyed the silent warrior queen, then nervously said, "It's Evil you'd want so."

I sighed. "I'm pretty sure it's evil we're trying to defeat, yes.

If you don't know, that's fine. We'll…" I didn't know what we'd do. I frowned, trying to clear my thoughts.

"No. *Aibhill,* Joanne. A–i–b–h–i–l–l. Aibhill," she said one more time. It still sounded like *evil* to me, or maybe just slightly like "Ae–vil," but I got the point even before she said, "The O'Brien banshee. Queen of the banshees, they say. It's her we'd need to fight."

"We?"

"Sure and I'm not leaving you now, just when it's getting good."

I smiled despite myself. "You sound like my friend Gary. I'll introduce you. I hope." I bit my lip, then bit it harder. "Okay. How do we find Aibhill?" I wasn't sure I liked all the changes I'd gone through, particularly since I was now calmly contemplating hunting somebody down and killing her. Of course, the somebody in question was presumably a monster, but even so.

"The O'Briens were in Munster," Caitríona said cautiously.

I squinted. "What's wrong with Munster?" My sum total knowledge of Munster was that, like Connacht, it was one of the ancient Irish provinces. There was an Ulster and a something else, too. "So?"

"Nothing, save it's as far away as we can get on this island. We'll never make it before sunset." Caitríona sagged. "Not get to the O'Brien lands, call up Aibhill and fight her, however it is we'd do that anyway. Auntie Sheila's doomed."

"Good attitude, good attitude." I looked across the mountaintop at the remains of my mother's bones. They still smoldered, a faint light coming from within. Maybe Wings was in there. I couldn't leave him behind. Still thinking, I made my way toward the mess, aware that Méabh and Caitríona trailed behind me. "We're going to have to try. I mean, I've got nothing else. Méabh, do you know anything about the magic of Munster?"

"It's where I built *an Mhór Chuaird,*" she said after a moment.

Caitríona made an astonished sound of recognition as I sagged. She said, "The Ring of Kerry? But there's no…" She trailed off, obviously suddenly wondering if what she knew was true. "No standing stones defining the ring. You couldn't have built that, it's just a tourist circle and it's the size of the county itself."

Méabh's eyebrows quirked upward. "Large it was, but not so large as that. But at the heart of Kerry a circle once stood. If the stones are gone, then time has taken them. I couldn't risk Tara, you see, and had to go as far from it as I could. All that old power there, even when I was young. What if it had gone wrong? What if my mother's master had wrested control from me? Twisted the magic so the wolves were many instead of few? No." Méabh shook her head. "It had to be a new circle, its power untried. So yes, I built the Ring of Kerry, and it's pleased I am to hear its name still lingers."

"That's grand, we can go there then—" Caitríona stopped, remembering her own original protest.

It was only around eleven in the morning. We might have been able to make it into Munster, but the Ring of Kerry was, in fact, about as far away as a person could get and stay on the island. If Irish roads were broader and less twisty, it might not be an issue, but even I, who had cut my teeth on equally twisty Appalachian mountains, was dubious about my ability to get us into the Ring before sundown. And that didn't even count the difficulty of finding its center in time to be of any use. "It can't be Kerry," I said, mostly to myself. "Brigid said it began and ended at Tara. We're going to have to risk contaminating it. Maybe we can use it as a gauntlet, throw it down to challenge the banshee queen…" I got to Sheila's immolated bones and trailed off.

It was not Wings lighting them up. It was a soft glow from a pit lying beneath the bones in a physically impossible manner. It looked like it went straight to China, or to whatever was opposite Ireland on the globe, and the ashy remains were resting quietly on the air above it, as if it didn't really quite exist. I nudged a stone toward its edge.

The stone rolled in, bounced off the sides a couple times, and fell a long, long way. For a hole that didn't exist, it was a very convincing fall. I cleared my throat and glanced at my companions. "Either of you do this?"

They obviously hadn't. They also looked like I felt, which was to say, they suspected that in a few short minutes we would all be going down the rabbit hole, because rabbit holes did not appear in our lives for absolutely no reason at all. Tentative, I called on the Sight, and gave a rushed laugh of relief.

The pit glowed with white magic, with the power that had so recently scrubbed the mountain clean. It smelled, as my coat did, of stardust, and as a result I found myself trusting it.

"It looks safe," Caitríona said dubiously, which suggested she was feeling the same effect I was. Méabh frowned at us both, but the expression lightened when she looked into the hole. Apparently she thought it looked safe, too.

"Isn't that what Alice thought before she went down the rabbit hole?"

Caitríona, sounding very nineteen, said, "Oh, what the hell," and dove in headfirst.

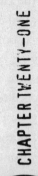

CHAPTER TWENTY-ONE

Tuesday, March 21, 11:00 a.m.

I was not normally blessed with lightning-quick reflexes, but I snagged the back of Cat's shirt just before she disappeared into the hole. Méabh, thank goodness, snagged the back of *mine,* preventing us both from tumbling headlong into its depths. Cat came up flush with disappointment, and I wagged a finger at her without being able to work myself up to a real scolding. Truth was, I wanted to dive right after her. All that stopped me was the dire uncertainty of whether we'd be coming back. That in and of itself didn't bother me so much. I'd kind of gotten used to not knowing if I was coming back. But I'd never had somebody to say goodbye to before, not for real. I stopped wagging a finger at Caitríona, and walked a little distance away to call Morrison.

His phone rang while I tried to subtract time zones. It was

something like four in the morning again, another totally un-civilized time to call, but he picked up fast, with a gruff, "I haven't heard from him. Are you okay?"

I bit my lip, which made speaking clearly difficult, but I managed to say, "Not dead yet, anyway. How's things there?"

"The usual." He sounded very awake for a man I'd presum-ably woken up. "Baxter wonders if you quit because of the shooting, Ray Campbell is stomping around glaring at me like it's all my fault and Holliday is preparing a lecture for when you get home. He's used it on about half of Homicide already. He made one of them cry."

The guys I worked with were generally a bunch of tough mooks. I gawked at the view, trying to imagine which of them might have been brought to tears, then heard Morrison's faint breath of laughter. "Not really, Walker. He is ready to read you the riot act, though."

"You're probably first in line to do that."

"Not as long as you come home safe. Why're you calling?"

Sadly for me, those two sentences were clearly connected. I sighed. "Because I'm off to do something stupid again, and I wanted to say…" My throat swelled up and I had a hard time swallowing.

Three little words. Not that hard to say, except in the sense of never having said them to somebody before, which some-how made them unbearably scary. There was a momentary pause before Morrison said, "Yeah, I know, Walker," like he understood the tongue-tied-ness. "Be careful, okay? I'll talk to you soon."

"No!" Panic sharpened the word and I could all but hear Morrison bring the phone back to his ear. "No," I said again. "I mean it, Morrison. I love you."

"Yeah," he said, and this time I was sure I could hear him

smile. "Yeah, I know, Walker. I love you, too. Talk to you later."

It sounded so *easy* for him to say. I hung up, folded the phone against my chest and turned to find Méabh and Caitríona both standing there with dippy yet knowledgeable smiles. The pit Áine had dug—I assumed she was behind it, since it glowed with her power—glimmered behind them, somehow as dippily pleased as they were. I muttered, "All right, all right, the show's over, let's get this wagon train rolling," and together we all jumped into the rabbit hole.

The world inverted, went black and spat us out the other side into sunlight. It was weirdly familiar: I'd entered my garden that way more than once, and overall it reassured me.

Or it did, anyway, until I recognized where we'd been spat.

Méabh's tomb stood on a near-distant hilltop. Forests lay between us and it, which was not true in my time. Cold rushed me and I turned around slowly, afraid of what I would see.

A bleak black hole lay in the mountainside right behind us. I knew that hole. It wasn't infested with Áine's light. It was much more the other end of the spectrum, dark and scary and dank. Werewolves had come rolling out of that hole once upon a time, mutated monsters made at the Master's bidding. Three of them. Three women, in fact.

Stiff, afraid, barely breathing, I lifted my hands to look at them.

They were my hands, unchanged, including the bite on my forearm, which was picking up in the itching department again. Sick relief soured my stomach. I'd had the ugly idea that we'd been twisted into monsters and regurgitated into Ireland's history. And maybe we had been, but if so, at least we weren't the wolves. I'd seen them when they came out of the earth, mewling black slicks of evil, and all three of us looked perfectly normal. I sat down, looped my arms around my knees and exhaled squeakily. "Not really what I was expecting. Where are we? Or maybe when are we, I know where we are. But—"

"The cairns are as I knew them as a child," Méabh said to the distant hilltops. To the cairn that bore her own name, specifically. I glanced toward it, squinted and decided maybe it was smaller than it was in my day. "There's something about the land, Joanne," she said uncertainly before Caitríona interrupted in delight.

"Are we time traveling?"

"I'm not sure." I leaned forward to take a handful of earth, wishing it could tell me where Áine had sent us.

As it happened, the fact I was leaning forward saved my life.

In my vision, the werewolves had come boiling from the cave at night, black on black, as writhing hideous little beasts that got larger and more dangerous as they rolled and wriggled from the cave mouth. But then, in my vision, Méabh had built her power circle in the northwest of the island, where she'd been born and had reigned as queen, and the Ring of Kerry was in the southwest. Visions, I was learning, were a bit on the symbolic side, and not so much with the accurate details.

Three long-legged, full-grown beasts raced from the cave, two of them leaping over my head to attack Méabh and Caitríona. The third slung itself low, coming for me, and in a moment of grace worthy of my own usual antics, tripped over its own feet and went crashing halfway down the mountain. It yelped as it bounced off rocks and bumps. I had no doubt it would whip around and come back again, but in the instant the fight was met, I was given respite, and it probably saved us all.

Méabh, who I was beginning to think of as an unstoppable

killing machine, managed to draw her sword before her wolf tackled her. She didn't get it up, didn't make a killing blow, but she had it out, and blocked the creature's gnashy teeth with the sword's edge. Silver shot from the blade, leaping to the wolf as if the metal had a life and will of its own. Streaks raced back from the wolf's mouth, etching along its fur until it had racing stripes. Still too close to use the sword, Méabh strong-armed the animal, grabbing its throat and throwing it off her. Half a breath later she was chasing it, but it skittered and leapt away, able to cover far more distance in a step with its four legs than she could with her two.

At the same time, Cat's wolf dragged her to the ground, teeth shredding her sweater. I threw a shield at her, forcing it against her skin so she glimmered with power, and the wolf's next tearing bite scraped off the magic and saved her from the same fate I was currently facing.

That gave me a bright idea, and for the second time in two days I gave myself up to the bite burning my arm.

This was *not* proper shifting. The pain began in the bite and exploded outward relentlessly, twisting my bones, stretching and compressing them, breaking them until I was made anew. The smart thing would've been to call on Rattler and try to push my way to a shape of my own, but my magic wasn't working so well internally. I felt pretty sure it was this or nothing, and right now I needed a something.

Besides, it felt so *good*. Not the shift itself, but the utter abandon that came with success. All of a sudden I didn't *care* anymore. I didn't care who won or who lost, just as long as I came out on top. I didn't care what the price of power was on myself or on my friends. I didn't worry about Gary, about my mother, about Méabh or Caitríona, about anything at all except the hunt. And there were three glorious bitches just *asking* for somebody to take them down. I scrambled free of my pants—the shirt was less constricting—and went after the wolf on Caitríona. It yelped—so did Cat—as I knocked it off her, and we rolled, snarling and snapping, a few yards away.

I was bigger than she was. Whether it was a woman of the modern era versus a person of an older age or whether I'd just gotten lucky, I was bigger, and I felt her struggling for breath beneath my weight. She writhed, paws scrabbling, then heaved a mighty heave that got her out from under me. I crashed into her again, but all of a sudden she had two heads and an awful lot of claws, plus she'd grown some shining silver streaks.

Ah. Méabh's wolf had come to play. I flung myself backward and got out of reach, shoulders hunched within my shirt. I needed to learn to undress before shifting. Especially before a fight: the cloth might give my enemies extra purchase to hold me with. The thought angered me and I snarled, ready for the battle to be on again.

But the small pack scented of confusion. I was one of them, impossible as that was. They were new, fresh-born, and they were three. I was a fourth, larger, by physical definition more dominant, and moreover, unexpected, which made them weak. I snarled and stepped forward one pace, and Streaks, the larger of the two facing me, flinched. My growl was made of triumph.

Except my wolf, the clumsy one, hadn't gotten the memo, and came tearing back up the hill to slam into my side. Smaller or not, she had momentum, and I hit the dirt with a deep grunt.

All three of them were on me in a heartbeat. I twisted, snapping everywhere, and saw flashes of snarling white teeth in response. Fury blinded me. I was bigger, I was dominant, I would *win*. I reached for my power, ready to use it offensively if I had to.

There was no response. No hint of magic waiting to be called on. No healing power, no sense of the earth offering strength for me to lean on, no nothing. I hadn't come up that dry since I'd come half an inch from sacrificing myself on a sorcerer's altar.

A very dim idea of *oh, shit* wafted after that realization, and with bone-wrenching intensity, I shifted back to my own form and waited to die.

Instead the smallest wolf yelped and fell, revealing Caitríona standing over it with a knobbly tree branch. It surged to its feet again, but it did so shaking its head like it was concussed. For a peculiar instant I felt sorry for the beast. Then Méabh's silver-greaved foot lashed out and caught Streaks in the ribs, and I gathered myself to roll onto all fours and snarl just as convincingly as a human as I had as a wolf. I hoped.

They didn't look scared, the wolves. They looked discomfited, and possibly like an idea had been put into their heads. They glanced at one another, then backed away, the dizzy one moving slowly and the other two refusing to abandon it. They got a good distance away—a safe distance—then looked at each other again.

Streaks curled her lips back from her teeth, and I *heard* the popping and grinding of bone as she forced herself from a lupine form into a human one. Horror caught me in the gut as the other two did the same, all of them becoming strong, healthy, naked, scary ladies. Streaks still had silver in her hair, and she gave me an approximation of a smile. Bared her teeth, anyway, and ran her tongue over them before shifting again, back to wolf form, and leading her also-changing sisters away.

I collapsed onto my forearms, panting into the earth as I

tried to count the number of ways in which I'd been phenomenally stupid. I lacked my sword, but there were always nets. I was good at nets, and the werewolves weren't like the wendigo. They were, for lack of a better term, real magic. Solid magic. Corporeal magic. They didn't slip between the Middle and Lower Worlds at a whim, which meant I could have netted them and then delivered them tidily to Méabh for her binding spell. But, oh no, I had to go all Gunga Din and embrace the animal. And even that might have been okay, except I'd *managed to teach werewolves how to shift shape,* which had to be the ugliest damned time loop I'd opened and closed so far. And just to add a cherry on top, I was pretty damned sure of one other thing: "I'm guessing he knows we're here now."

"He does," said a grim and weirdly familiar male voice, "but if we hurry, you might just live."

CHAPTER TWENTY-TWO

Hairs stood up on the back of my neck. I didn't move. I was half-naked and just this side of wolf—crazy, but I couldn't quite make myself move, because there was no way Morrison was standing behind me. It had been unlikely in the extreme that Gary could catch me at Dublin airport, but it was sheerly im-possible that Morrison, to whom I'd just spoken on the phone, had transported himself halfway around the world. I turned my head about three-quarters of an inch, just far enough to see Caitríona. "What does the man behind me look like?"

Her forehead was as wrinkled as mine felt. "Like me da. Only not quite."

My shoulders dropped in a sort of relief. It *wasn't* Morrison. I knew that, and still it was good—and bad—to have it verified. I kinda wished he *had* transported halfway around the world. It would make my life that much stranger, but that much hap-pier, too. I seized my pants—the fight hadn't taken me far away from them—and yanked them on as Méabh said, "Your da? Sure and it's Ailill I see before me," in a surprisingly soft voice.

I did my best side whisper to Caitríona as I finished dressing: "Al-yil?"

"Ailill Mac Mata. The love of Méabh of Connacht's life, so they say. Of course, she killed him in the end."

"He was unfaithful," Méabh said with utmost serenity.

I stopped worrying about the guy behind me and gaped at her. "So you killed him? This from the woman who married every high king in Irish history?"

Just as serenely, she said, "That was duty." Then she smiled, and I remembered that this was also a woman who had by all appearances held half the country together for millennia on end. Mostly I'd been finding her a bit condescending. All of a sudden I found her just a little scary instead. That was the kind of smile it was. I decided not to pursue the matter any further, and very sensibly turned to address the issue of the Man Who Wasn't Morrison.

He looked an awful lot like Morrison. Not exactly like him, but a lot like him. Like somebody had sanded Morrison's rough edges off, maybe, and polished him up a bit. His hair was more gold than silver, but Morrison had apparently been a blond back in the day. His eyes were too green for Morrison, but the height, the breadth, the smile, were all eerily similar. It made me want to trust him, an impulse I didn't trust at all. "I think you'd better show us your true form."

True form. Nobody said things like that. Mucking with magic really did rearrange the speech patterns laid down over a lifetime. I sighed, ready to give it another shot—something like "Show me what you really look like"—but he shrugged before I spoke. "I don't have one, not the way you mean. I'm shaped by desire."

Caitríona, horrified, blurted, "I don't desire me da!"

He gave her Morrison's best reassuring smile, which was pretty damned reassuring. Or would have been, if he'd been Morrison. Even so, I was reassured as he explained, "Not necessarily sexual desire. Safety, reassurance, stability. I answer whatever need is utmost in your mind."

"Gancanagh," Méabh said. I resisted the urge to say "Bless you," and the handsome devil-may-care fellow turned to give Méabh an acknowledging nod. "You're dangerous," she said without sounding like she meant it. "A woman should never trust her heart's desire. He seduces," she told us. Me, perhaps, since presumably Caitríona was in fact not hot for her daddy. "He is one of the fae, like the *fear darrig*. We cannot trust him."

"Of course you can't. But I can lead you to evil's lair."

My voice shot up. "Why would we want you to do that?"

All three of them, Gancanagh, Méabh and Caitríona, said, *"Aibhill,"* which still sounded like "Evil" to me, but this time I recognized they probably meant the O'Brien banshee. "To Aibhill and her host of wailing women," Gancanagh went on. "Four and twenty of them."

"Twenty-five," Cat said obstinately, but Gancanagh clicked his tongue and winked at me. "Twenty-four now. She lost one recently, you know."

I did know, having kind of ripped a banshee's head off a year ago. "Twenty-four isn't really an improvement in the odds."

Gancanagh smiled and shrugged. I caught a scent of Morrison's cologne and ground my teeth together. This was not my boss. It was not the man I'd fallen in love with. It was not even, according to what Méabh had just said, technically a man at all. I could accept that intellectually, but on a gut level I was just relieved as hell to see Morrison here and ready to fight at my side. Fists knotted until my nails stung my palms, I grated, "Never mind the odds. Why would you lead us there?"

"Because I don't want to see the world end, Walker. Aibhill's master doesn't have a place in his lineup for someone like me. I'm about life and love, not death and loathing, so if he wins a major victory I'm left out in the cold." He shivered delicately, which Morrison would never do, and murmured, "I don't like being cold."

Morrison would probably never say that, either, but something about the way he said it made Méabh and me both take a step toward him, ready to warm him up in any way his little heart desired. Only Caitríona's squawk of dismay stopped us, and for a few seconds we glared at each other while Cat said, "Jaysus and they're going to be all over me da if this doesn't end quickly. I can't take it. We're going with you, but don't say a *word* to them, d'ye hear me?"

Gancanagh put a finger over his lips, playful and sensuous, and I thought it was a damned good thing Caitríona wasn't suffering from an egregious schoolgirl crush at this particular time in her life. I didn't know who the most popular Irish heartthrob was, but if she was seeing him instead of her father we would all be—so to speak—screwed. I cringed at my choice of words, even unspoken, and fell obediently into line behind Caitríona and Gancanagh.

Not so much into line, actually, as two by two, them in front and me and Méabh elbow to elbow where we could make sure neither had a better view of Gancanagh's very fine derriere or, more important, make sure one of us had no chance to speak to him without the other. I knew I was being ridiculous, but hints of Old Spice kept wafting back toward me, and it was all I could do to not punch Méabh just for existing. A little desperate, I said, "Tell me about Ailill."

Méabh glowered. "So you can steal him for yourself? I think not."

"For— This is not some kind of perverse Mrs. Robinson thing, Méabh! I'm just trying to distract myself!"

"From eyeing my man!" She rounded on me, but I saw it coming and ducked under the fist she threw.

Caitríona bellowed, "Ah, fer sweet Christ's sake, will ye's stop?" and fell back to put herself between us. "What is *wrong* with you?"

"She thinks I want to steal her boyfriend. I totally don't." In fact, the last thing I wanted to do was get in a bare-knuckles match with somebody who had a thousand years of fighting skills on her side. Besides, if anything, she was trying to horn in on my territory, not the other way around.

I seized my head, trying to stop that line of thought. Gancanagh dropped back to walk beside me, murmuring, "She's a beautiful woman. You're powerful, to be sure, but there's something exotic about her, isn't there?"

"Morrison doesn't like women taller than he is." I had no idea if that was true, but it gave me something to hang my hat on. I forced my way past his flirtation and scowled at the landscape. It was still Ireland, but it seemed like every step we took it got darker. The grass turned jade, not emerald. Leaves deepened to evergreen shades, and thick-barked oaks sucked light in until we meandered through gloom. Morrison's scent caught me off guard every time I took a breath, though Gancanagh himself sidled between me and Méabh while Caitríona tried to herd him back to a lead position. At least *she* didn't want a piece of my man, though Morrison really was too old for her. Hell, at thirty-nine he was almost too old for me. Which would make him a babe in Méabh's arms. The impulse to smack her rose again. Desperate to keep my head on straight, I muttered, "Where are we going?"

"Into the heart of *Thiobraid Árann,* where kings and priests once ruled."

On the positive side, that was definitely not something Morrison would say, which helped me remember it wasn't him. On the less positive side, I still had no idea where we were going. Caitríona volunteered, "*Thiobraid Árann* is Tipperary," which I could sort of see once she'd spoken the Anglicization of it. She went on with, "The O'Brien took his crown at Cashel, where Patrick had converted his ancestors to Christianity," while I compulsively mumbled, "It's a long way to Tipperary."

Cat gave me a dirty look and I spread my hands in self-defense before asking, "*The* O'Brien? Weren't there a lot of them?" and then, "It really *is* a long way to Tipperary, especially if we're walking. We're sort of on a deadline here, folks. How're we gonna—"

Gancanagh started to answer. Caitríona shot a glare his way and he subsided with a smile and a flutter of eyelashes. She, rather ferociously, said, "There may be a hundred O'Briens, but only one is The O'Brien. The leader, the king, the one they all looked to. And The O'Brien of whom I speak is Boru, who was crowned—"

"Oh!" I said gleefully. "I know this one! At the Rock of Cashel! The big awesome castle! Mom and I went there!"

For once I didn't get the look that said I'd crushed a thousand fondly held memories by the way I'd phrased my limited historical knowledge. Caitríona seemed pleased. I was so proud of myself I danced a little jig, which Gancanagh joined in on, catching my arm to swing me around.

Right into Méabh's breastplate. I clanged against it and held very still, as if a rabbit who perhaps would go unnoticed by the bird of prey if I didn't move. Of course, rabbits didn't usually have their noses in the bird's cleavage, not that breastplates made for a lot of cleavage. I held still anyway.

"I'll have your head if I see you talking to my man in such a way again," Méabh growled.

I rolled my eyes up, trying to meet her gaze without moving. "He started it." Ah yes. Very mature, Joanne. "Besides, he's not your man. He's mi-aaaiii!"

"Mi-aaaiii!" was not the possessive pronoun I'd intended it to be. It was the sound of me being strong-armed straight backward, far enough away for Méabh to unsheathe her sword and waver it between Gancanagh and myself.

All my smarts left me and instead of calming her down, I baited her. "He's your lover, remember? You probably don't want to kill him. I sure don't want you to." I didn't really care if she killed her own lover, since she'd apparently done it once already anyway. I just didn't like the idea of this near-Morrison taking it in the teeth.

Méabh, who was apparently even more susceptible to Gancanagh than I was, snarled and moved the sword toward me. In a fit of unusual stupidity, I put both hands on either side of it and held it like I could keep her from skewering me by strength alone. I wasn't an action hero, so there was no chance of that happening, but it looked cool. And I *could* keep her from skewering me by using magic, so maybe it wasn't all that stupid after all.

It certainly got her attention, anyway. As calmly and slowly as I could, I said, "He's not Ailill. He's not Morrison. He's not Cat's dad, either. He's a fairy and he's screwing with us. But he says he's going to lead us to the banshee, so if you can just keep that thing in your pants awhile longer, we'll get there and you can have a nice big juicy fight. But right now Ganesh here has to get us there without us tearing ourselves apart over him. Okay?"

"Gancanagh," he said, offended. I echoed that, too, mostly because I was pretty certain Ganesh was a god and didn't want to offend *it*.

Méabh made him the recipient of a once-over I wouldn't have wanted visited on me. Then she muttered, "Ailill's eyes are blue, not green," and stepped away, her mouth a grim line.

"Ol' green-eyes, eh?" I said to Gancanagh. "Can't change that, can you? Morrison's eyes are blue, too."

"So're me da's," Cat said. She was still the only clearheaded one among us, because it was she who remembered to say, "Tipperary *is* a long way. How will we get there before nightfall, fairy man?"

"How far do you think we've come, my lass?" Gancanagh opened his hand to indicate the gloom we'd been marching through, and I finally looked beyond his glorious self to see that the landscape had changed.

Mountains had given way to trees quickly enough, but we'd left the forests behind, too, and were tromping through bogland. Stretches of low hills rolled out before us, and I could see we'd crested one, but I hadn't particularly noticed the incline. Startled, I turned back, but the mountains had been swallowed by mist and darkness. "Hnh."

"Hnh?" That was Caitríona, sounding suspicious.

"Nothing. It's just kind of like the Lower World. Distance isn't what it seems. I have to walk through it the long way, but my friend Coyote can skip and bounce all over the place." I peered at the sun, but the gloom was too significant to tell whether it hung closer to the land than normal.

"It's the fairy realm." Gancanagh stopped beside me, suddenly very close and smelling very good, with his too-green gaze intent on mine. I swallowed and looked away, but that made it worse, because then his scent and body nearness seemed all the more Morrison. I wet my lips and looked back to find him smiling. Devilish, charming smile. The kind of smile that clearly needed either a kiss or a slap. Possibly both. I wet my lips again and he, being no fool, moved in for the kill.

But he had to tilt his chin up to do so. I was a good two inches taller than he was, but *Morrison* was exactly my height. Another mark against the seductive fairy. I got my hand between us just in time, croaked, "Walk," and pushed him away.

In a world that made sense, he would have taken the hint and gone off all dejected. In the world I lived in, however, he looked more like I'd presented an unexpected challenge, and delight glinted in his eyes as he did as he was told.

Méabh stomped by, the weight of her footsteps putting my earlier stomp to shame. I started to protest my innocence, but Caitríona came along behind her, not so much stomping as seeming to propel herself forward by the force of exaggerated eye-rolling. Amusement overcame the feeling of unjust persecution and I tagged along behind them all, grinning. Gan's voice drifted back to me: "This realm's been tainted, it's true, but I'm still part of it. It knows I'm not a threat, and lets me walk as I wish."

His voice was like honey mead and warm chocolate, which I thought was cheating. Morrison's voice was fine, particularly when lowered in intimacy, but Gancanagh had somehow kicked it up a notch. I clung to the content of his words, not the delivery, but it still took quite a lot of walking before I shook off the effects. "Wait, what do you mean, you're part of it. That can't be good, if it's tainted."

Gancanagh looked back at me. By all rights it was too gloomy to see well, and I wasn't using the Sight, but his gaze was vivid and bright anyway. He breathed, "Sure and she doesn't know much, does she," briefly sounding more like an Irish monster than like Morrison, then went back to the more Americanized way of phrasing things. "Nothing's all light and happiness, Walker. Seduction's got its dark side, and so someone like me is susceptible to someone like him. And when you're part of a pantheon that's all magic, it's easy for the corruption to spread. I wasn't his way in, but I would never be able to stop him, either."

I scurried to catch up with Méabh. "Are you two part of the same pantheon? I mean, you're both...not human. You called him fae. You're *aos sí*. I'm pretty sure that qualifies as fae." I wished Gary was there. He'd know for sure.

Méabh scowled. "We're all of us other than human, so we are. *I'd* not say I was of the likes of him."

From her emphasis, I assumed everybody else would. "But you're not gods, either. I mean, that's what I've met so far, gods and monsters. You fae sorts are the first non-human non-monsters I've come across. I didn't know there were things like you out there. I mean, where did you come from? I don't even know if you've got North American counterparts. Not that I've run into, anyway." I sighed. "On the other hand, there are plenty of people who've managed to be corrupted by the Master on my home turf, too, so even if the lineup is different I guess the results aren't. Look, Gan, you're also the first person I've talked to who was willing or maybe able to discuss the Master's influence. So just how badly into this are you?"

He shrugged, which was distractingly attractive. "I'm nothing, really. He gets a lot more power from murders and black magic than from something like me, but if dark impulses are acted upon, he gains strength from them."

"So couldn't you ignore the impulses?"

He looked over his shoulder at me. "Could you ignore the magic that boils in your belly, all hot and ready, Walker?"

He really hadn't needed to add the *hot and ready* part. My throat went dry and other parts of me went a bit hot and ready. "Jesus, Morris—*Gancanagh*."

"And why is it we're trusting him?" Caitríona muttered.

It seemed like a good question, and I was pretty sure "Because he's sexxxay" was the wrong answer. Méabh came up with a better one: "What choice have we? It's this or chase werewolves, and Aili—*Gancanagh*—is finer to look upon."

"He looks like me *da!*"

I took that to mean Cat wished we would stop having palpitations over the guy, which was fair enough. I wished we would, too, but I couldn't stop sneaking glances at his backside. "How long," I said a bit desperately. "How long will it take to get to Evil's lair?"

"Ah, sure," Gancanagh said blithely, "ah sure and we're there."

A three-headed dragon rose out of the dark and spat fire at us.

CHAPTER TWENTY-THREE

If the werewolf hadn't bit me, I wouldn't have learned to keep my shields up at all times and we would have been roasted, so in some small way Tia Carley had done me a favor. But the heat blast still knocked us over backward, and we lay there in the dark for a split second before the beast galumphed toward us. Méabh, always quick with a sword, sprang to her feet and charged the dragon head-on while I mostly just wondered who or what I'd offended in a past life that this one was peopled by dragons. Except I didn't have any past lives, so apparently I'd offended somebody in *this* life and was facing instant karma. That didn't really improve anything, in my ever so humble opinion.

Caitríona sat up beside me, both hands fisted against her mouth. Tiny sounds emitted from behind the fists, but at least she wasn't all-out screaming. Me, I kept lying there, reviewing my list of things to do: heal the werewolf bite. Kill the

Morrígan. Find Gary. Save my mother. I added "string Gancanagh up by his luscious toes and use him for target practice" to the list, and finally sat up.

Gancanagh had disappeared. *Quel surprise.* Méabh's silver sword barely dented the dragon's scales, but on the other hand, neither it nor she nor her armor were melting as the monster spat fire at her again. I knew I should leap up and rush to her side, but I didn't have a damned thing to fight a dragon with. My sword was missing, and besides that, not much use, if Méabh's was any indication. My power never had cottoned on to being used as a weapon, and frankly, I didn't think a dragon would be much impressed if I went after it with tooth and nail.

The damned bite flared up again, suggesting I had more tooth and nail at my disposal than usual. I ground my teeth and reached past both pain and temptation—the goddamned thing didn't *hurt* when I gave in, at least not once the actual transformation was over—and rather pathetically whispered, *Rattler?* at the back of my mind. *Any chance we can push past the poison for a…normal…shapeshifting?*

Perhaps. The magic is there. But the taint is…distracting. My poor snaky spirit guide was really wiped out, if he wasn't getting all sibilant on his esses. *Fix a simple shape in mind, Siobhán Walkingssstick. Something familiar to us both. Something—*

"Something that strikes?" I started shimmying out of my clothes. Caitríona dropped her fists to gape at me and I handed her my glasses. "Don't let them get crunched, okay?"

She took them speechlessly and I interpreted that as agreement. Everything else, including my precious, ruined coat, became a pile on the ground as Rattler coiled himself in my mind. He got stronger the tighter he curled on himself, like he was concentrating his focus so we might shove past the poison trying to turn me into a monster. He balled up smaller and smaller, becoming brighter and brighter, and just at the moment he became incandescent, I snapped the image of what I wanted to become into place.

It was not supposed to feel like the world was being torn apart. Like *I* was being torn apart. Like my left arm, specifically, had gone to war with the rest of me, resisting transformation with a will of its own. I was a mass of twisting bones, trying to find a shape that satisfied me, but the shape I wanted was at odds with the werewolf's curse. I changed partway and gasped for breath, caught in a loop of unending shifts.

A hiss erupted from somewhere near the bottom of Rattler's snaky little soul. He lunged for the wrongness permeating my magic, his jaws gaping in a reminder that snakes could and did eat things three times their own size, and he fastened on to the werewolf's bite from the inside.

Magic pumped through his bite, spirit animal power at war with demonic determination. That flood of strength backed up my own magic, all the power that had for days been frantically trying to keep me from transforming. Then it superseded my power, freeing up a magic that was working overtime, and between one breath and the next the pain of prolonged shifting was gone. I flowed into my new shape, and struck.

Méabh flung herself to the side as I threw myself into the fray. For an instant she looked as though I might be a fresh new enemy, but Caitríona's protest reverberated off my ear bones when Méabh lifted her sword against me. Then I was nose to nose with a more-than-slightly shocked dragon, and much like Rattler had done, I dropped my jaw in my own version of a snaky grin. The dragon backed the hell up, all three heads taking a break from breathing fire to get a good look at me instead.

I was pretty sure I was worth looking at, what with being fifteen feet of rattlesnake. Fifteen feet of raspy muscle and rattling tail and, very importantly, of venom-injecting fangs. The dragon was bulkier, but not a lot longer. It had fire, but I was betting I had speed. It had claws, but I had—

—all right, still with the speed, but that was going to have to be enough. I coiled and struck all at once, relying on my peculiar heat-sensing snaky vision to find the dragon's most vulnerable spots. The throats, in this case: there were heat blooms in all three throats, suggesting the fire it spat was engendered right there. My teeth closed on the nearest throat, quenching the fire a-borning.

Quenching *that* fire a-borning, anyway. The dragon screamed with its other two throats and flame washed over me. It didn't burn, my shields as strong in a shapeshifted form as they were as a human, but my muscles kind of melted anyway. Sunshine melting, the happiness of a snake baking on a desert rock. If I'd had shoulders they would have sagged, and as it was, I dragged the head I'd captured with me toward the ground as comfort sluiced through me.

Clearly I had not thought this whole "fighting as a snake" thing through. I clenched my teeth harder, determined not to let the one throat go even if I had to take a little nap midbattle. The dragon spat flame again, then coiled its other two heads down to gnash at me with multitudinous teeth. I had a much bigger mouth than theirs, and while I could get my teeth around one of their throats, they couldn't exchange the favor. That was good, since although I assumed poison was pumping through its veins by now, I had no idea how much it took to bring down a dragon, nor was I certain that rattlesnakes poisoned their prey rather than suffocating them. It was possible the poison was just a paralytic to make the suffocating easier, which would be less helpful than it could be if I had one mouth and three necks to choke. And Rattler, who presumably might offer some insight into those questions, had gone quiet inside the confines of my skull. I suspected he might still be fighting the infection, and didn't really want to disturb him for fear breaking his concentration might send me back to the spasms of conflicting shapeshifts.

The dragon backed up, dragging my melty self with it. I caught a glimpse of the distant blobs that were Méabh and Caitríona, both of them emitting a kind of cool uncertainty that had to be psychic but still registered in my heat-based vision. I wanted to yell to them, to say, "Come on in, the water's fine!" except I had a mouthful of dragon and the damned thing wasn't suffocating fast enough. Nor would it ever, with two more windpipes to breathe through. I gave up on the hope of suffocating it, let go and hoped the poison would do the trick before the encroaching warmth-induced sleepies did me in.

To my great satisfaction, the head I'd been hanging on to flopped down in a convincing approximation of lifelessness. Possibly it would pull itself back together, but that was a problem for when it happened. No longer stymied by its weight, I slithered and wriggled forward. Dragon teeth slid off my scales and shields, making uncomfortable sparks but not quite managing to hold me.

The ground was warm. Hot, even. Sun-baked-stone hot. I bet dragons liked that as much as snakes, but the dragon had feet and I had a fifteen-foot-long belly pressed against all that cozy warmth. I didn't think snake eyes could cross with pleasure, but mine nearly did anyway. I hissed, more to wake myself up than anything else, and coiled up as tight as I could so less of me was on the nice warm ground. There had to be a hot springs or a lava bubble or something beneath us to make it that warm. Not that Ireland was well-known for either of those things. But then, the bleak hell dimension I'd accidentally visited while trying to fight the wendigo had some lava-bubble-like aspects, and I had the uncomfortable feeling we were closer to that place than I'd like us to be.

My blunt nose hit the ground at the end of all that contemplation, and the dragon jumped on me like the vulnerable prey I was. I flattened and, shields or no, felt cartilage crunching under the monster's weight. The idea that my shields were weakened by my warmth and contentedness swam through my mind. A dragon's head, all glazed eyes and lolling tongue and torn-out throat, flopped into my vision. It was cooler than it had been, details fading, which probably meant I'd managed to kill one-third of the beast. Too bad about napping through the encore.

Caitríona stalked up and hit me in the face with a snow flurry.

Shocking cold ripped me from my stupor. I surged up, shaking my head—my whole upper half, since snake heads weren't hooked on the way human heads were—and spat a forky tongue at my cousin.

She blanched, body heat visibly paling, but she stood her ground, hands lifted in the heart of a tiny snowstorm. I hissed again, ready to have the interfering little human for lunch, but one of the dragon's still-living heads struck at her and I remembered what I was there for.

Lack of ears or not, I certainly *felt* Caitríona's screech as I launched myself over her head to meet the oncoming dragon. The snowstorm stopped, but I was full of vim and vigor again, ready to take the fight to the mat. Caitríona disappeared from my awareness, presumably having ducked under me and sensibly run away. The dragon and I met in midair above where she'd been, and I swallowed its head.

I didn't exactly mean to. It was just a rattlesnake's attack came in the form of gaping jaws, and none of the dragon's heads were very big. It was like the mass of a normal one-headed dragon's head had been split into three, which meant my head was bigger than its, and my mouth opened a whole lot farther. It all made for an unfortunately literal head-on collision.

For an instant there we both froze, the dragon mid-fiery-belch, me as bug-eyed and freaked out as a snake could get. Then the dragon finished its burp and fire shot down my throat. I had no voice to scream with, and even if I did, I had a mouthful of dragon stifling the sound. Pain and outrage were expressed by my rattle suddenly sounding like a buzz saw preparing to cut the world apart. I thought swallowing fire like that should probably kill me. I also kind of thought, *well, insides are wet, probably it'll just quench the fire,* and by some faint grace, my power responded accordingly. Possibly being shapeshifted gave me access to my internal magics, since I was no longer fighting the good fight against the werewolf bite. There was an argument, then, for staying shifted until we got out of Gancanagh's territory alive.

Which was a questionable outcome, just then. I had no incisors, just two great long fangs, so biting the thing's head off wasn't an option. I was grateful for that, really. Swallowing fire was bad enough. I could not imagine the grossitude of a gullet filled with dragon blood.

The dragon, not at all happy with having one of its two remaining heads swallowed, began thrashing and bellowing. It had feet. I didn't. It could get purchase on the ground. I couldn't.

I went whipping around, hanging on to a dragon's neck for dear life. My rattle was going full bore thanks to the dragon's ministrations: I, certainly, wasn't the one shaking it. The peat-bog earth was softer than I expected, my body whacking divots out of it as I was slammed up and down. The remaining head kept lashing at me, trying to break through my shields and scales with teeth or fire, it didn't care. I wanted to bite it, too, but I was afraid to let go of the head I had. It'd taken a couple minutes to suffocate the other one. I didn't want to release this one too soon and earn only a reprieve, not a victory, against the beast.

Power tingled along the entire length of my spine. I opened my eyes—I hadn't even known they were closed—and saw absolutely nothing of where it was coming from. Magic didn't have a visible component most of the time, even if I wasn't relying on a snake's heat vision. I could See power in a sort of uninteresting grayscale when snakeshifted, but I was more than a little concerned about what triggering the Sight might do when I was eyeball deep in dragon and Rattler was somewhere in the dark of my mind making sure I didn't lose control over the shape I currently held. I got bashed into the ground again, bit down harder and decided unless something actively attacked I would assume the upsurge in magic use was from somebody on my team.

Méabh justified that decision by sweeping in and decapitating the head I'd captured. The headless neck fell away and the remaining living dragon head screamed while the rattlesnake part of my brain automatically swallowed. The human part gagged and choked, but it was too late. I had eaten a dragon head. Whole. That was going to cause some serious, serious problems when I turned back into a human, which idea was horrible enough that I gagged again.

Snakes, it turned out, could regurgitate. I'd had no idea. I had also never been so grateful to learn something so disgusting. I spat out a dragon's head, stared at it and shuddered all the way down the considerable length of my body. I could've stayed there the rest of the day, gagging and being grossed out, but Méabh yelled. The sound reverberated off my skin and I glanced up to see her charging the last dragon head with all the enthusiasm in the world. I sprang after her, foregoing the whole biting scenario to wind myself around the beast's body and haul its head back to expose what I hoped was a vulnerable throat. I was no boa constrictor, but snakes were all muscle, and the dragon was in sorry shape. Méabh, still yelling, struck off the remaining head, and the entire monster collapsed into waves of deep red, almost black, magic. Dissolved, just like the Red Cap had done. I landed in the dirt and magic with a crash while Méabh staggered a few steps back, her body heat peaking and fading as adrenaline crested, then drained away.

Rattler whispered *Sssuccesss* at the back of my mind, then nudged me. I clung to the idea of my own shape, and slid toward it, shedding the rattlesnake shape as I became myself again. Pain flared in my arm again and I clutched it. *I thought you said success?*

We defeated the dragon, did we not? he asked irritably, which was fair enough. I sent a wave of apology at him, and he slipped away, leaving a sense of weariness behind. I'd been asking too much of him the past few days. We needed a break, he and I.

A break we weren't likely to get. Caitríona said, "You took off all your clothes and turned into a *snake*."

"Yes. Yes, I did. And you…" I didn't even know what she'd done. I peered at her through the gloom, hoping for an answer.

She came toward me cautiously, her arms full of my clothes

as she mumbled, "Sure and I'll just *set it on fire with me mind*," in embarrassment, and dropped my clothes. I scrambled into them, trying hard not to wonder if Gancanagh was still around and watching.

"You said Auntie Sheila'd said magery was about spell casting and preparation," Cat said. "I got to thinking the way I'd said it, set it on fire with me mind, so many times, and I thought maybe that was an enchantment in itself. And it was so warm, like the peat was roasting, and I started thinking heat into snow, that's the way it should go, and then it was on me lips and—and—"

"And then she went without shield or sword to draw you back from stupor," Méabh finished with great satisfaction. A far cry from the woman who'd been annoyed at Caitríona's sudden maturity into adepthood a few hours ago, she now all but overflowed with pride. "My granddaughters are warriors indeed."

"We are, but Cat's wiped out." I was only half-dressed, but I managed to half catch my cousin just as her eyes crossed. She didn't faint, but she thumped down with a woozy groan, and I called another pulse of healing power up for her.

It responded as well as it had done earlier—external magics were still okay, apparently—but it enflamed the werewolf bite again, too. I bared my teeth at it. I wanted the itch to go away. More, I didn't want to give in again to the bone-deep nagging impulse to transform, and the deeper we went into the Master-tainted land, the harder I thought it would be to stay on the straight and narrow.

Caitríona looked healthier when she lifted her gaze. "Why does that keep happening to me?"

"Magic comes from two places. Within, which is what you're using now, and which is exhausting, and without, which is what we did with the power circle. You totally saved my bacon, but try not to do that again until I've shown you how to build a circle. I'm thinking maybe mages need one even more than shamans." Or at least more than this particular shaman, but I wasn't going to get into that. "Méabh, what did *you* do? The sword wasn't working against the drag—"

"The *Aillén Trechend*," Cat said before I'd even finished the word. Apparently she didn't want dragons to exist any more than I wanted, say, vampires to. I paused obligingly, waiting for her explanation, and she gave a stiff shrug. "It's the beast that beleaguers Tara. It rises from the…" She trailed off to give first me, then the dank, warm peat bog a wide-eyed look. "From the bowels of the earth to savage the sacred circle every twenty-three years. Or it did do, in times gone by. Auntie Sheila always told me the old stories about it and all the other monsters. Was she…?"

"Preparing you? Yeah, I think maybe she was." A pang struck me. I might've been the one Mom told all the stories to, if things had been very different. Caitríona saw the regret in my expression and looked uncomfortable, obviously searching for something to say. I shook my head. "No grudges, Cat. It's played out this way. We'll go with it. I'm just glad you were there for her to teach."

Her shy smile was worth letting that regret go. I smiled back, then exhaled and looked toward Méabh. "So what'd you do? The sword couldn't touch the…Aileen Treygent…at first." Irish pronunciation was not my strong suit, but neither of my family members chose to correct me.

"I called on the power of the land, as I did to bind the wolves. A power circle, Joanne, to guide the sword's strength. Against mortal enemies the blade is true, but when the taint it fights is older than its forging…" Méabh shook her head.

I finished getting dressed as she spoke, and asked a question I didn't much want the answer to: "How much older?"

"You already know." Gancanagh spoke from beside me, nearly earning himself a punch in the nose by doing so. He gave me a wink, a once-over and a sly smile, and I did punch him, because Morrison, who he still reminded me of, wouldn't have been so crass. He clutched his upper arm where I'd hit him, looking crestfallen, and as if hoping to get back in my good graces, said, "The *Aillén Trechend* has risen from the depths since the *ard rí* Bres was stolen from time. This is a blow, *gwyld*. This is a blow against the dark one."

Morrison wouldn't have called me *gwyld,* either. I almost started to like Gancanagh for that. For differentiating himself. Then I remembered he'd led us smack into the dragon's jaws, and again lifted a fist to hit him. "You said evil's lair!" he blurted before I could. "Not Aibhill's! And we'd reached evil's lair, had we not? Even the mistress of banshees places guards between herself and the world, and her domain lies just beyond. You don't want to be without me, not yet."

I didn't lower my fist. I did look beyond my erstwhile boss at Caitríona and Méabh, to see what they thought. They both looked like I should go back to my original plan of stringing him up by his toes, but Méabh, rolling her jaw, said, "He may still be useful."

"As cannon fodder," Caitríona suggested darkly.

I turned back to Gancanagh with the fist still cocked. "One false move, buster. One false move."

Green glinted in his gaze as he lowered his eyes, then led us once more into the darkness.

CHAPTER TWENTY—FOUR

Caitríona sidled up to me as we left the dragon's dusted remains. "You turned into a snake."

She'd said that once before. On the other hand, by all reasonable expectation she should be gibbering like a madman
about now, so probably a little repetition wasn't that big a deal.
"I have a peculiar repertoire of talents."

"Will I turn into a snake?"

"I seriously doubt it. Even if mages can accomplish shapeshifting, Ireland doesn't have snakes. It probably wouldn't be
high on your list of things to turn into." I thought of beached
flounders and Coyote's warning about how a shifter should
always have a clear idea of their target animal, and amended,
"But if it's something you want to change into, then yeah,
probably you could. Assuming it's in the skill set."

"What about an elk? One of the big ones, the Irish elk?"

Hopeful, she extended her hands to approximate the rack on an Irish elk, which was about twice as long as her armspan.

"You'd make a really tiny elk. You saw how big a snake I was? That's because as far as I can tell, mass doesn't change. I bet one of those baby Irish elk weighs as much as you do, so that's about as big as you'd be. A hundred and sixty-five pounds of rattlesnake is awe-inspiring. A hundred and sixty-five pounds of baby elk wouldn't be so much so."

I saw her do the conversion in her head before offense flew across her face. "I do not weigh twelve stone!"

"No, not you, me. You probably weigh, what, one…fifteen?" I figured it was more like one-thirty, but no one in their right mind ever guessed a woman's weight at what they thought it really was.

She eyed me, doing the conversion again, then resentfully allowed, "A bit more, maybe."

"Okay, so you'd be a…" I was pretty sure a stone equaled fourteen pounds. I did the conversion myself and came up with, "An eight-and-a-half-stone elk. Not exactly the six-foot-tall behemoth you're imagining, right? But I could be wrong, maybe there's a spell that lets you change mass. You're handling this pretty well."

"I half think I'm dreaming," she admitted. "That it's some wild story Auntie Sheila's telling me, and I'll wake up snug and sound in me own bed. But it's not, is it. Why did ye tell us none of this at the funeral?"

"My life wasn't like this then. It only started after I got home. Besides, I'd have never dreamed anyone would believe me. I didn't know my mother very well. I had no idea she might have softened you up for accepting this kind of weirdness. Do you watch *Star Trek?*"

Caitríona blinked, rightfully bewildered by the segue. "Sure, who hasn't seen an episode or two?"

"Good. You know the ship's shields? You're going to need something like that to protect yourself with."

"Like you've been using on us, all blue and shimmery?"

"Except yours won't be blue. That's a reflection of my power. Of my aura, really. Mine's blue and silver. Yours is more red and green."

"Ah sure," she said in disgust, "sure and I'm a tartan so."

I laughed, which made Gancanagh look back at me with a full-court-press smile. I bared my teeth at him and he deflated, which somehow made the light dim even further. I checked the impulse to catch up to him and say it was all okay, and instead focused hard on Caitríona. "Do the Irish even have tartans? I thought it was all about the sweaters, here."

"The Aran clan sweaters? That was a marketing ploy." She took no notice of my dismayed gawk as she went on. "We've a few tartans, but not like the Scots. I wouldn't know the O'Reilly tartan if it bit me," she admitted. "How do I build shields?"

"It's a really internal thing, and probably hiking through the heart of the Master's realm isn't the best place to learn. I'd hate for him to get a thread inside your shields, because it's a bitch to root those out."

"You sound like you know what you're talking about."

"In the case of letting unfortunate people inside my shields, yeah, I do. This would be a good time to learn from my mistakes." We'd covered a lot of distance while chatting, but I was starting to get worried. The clock was running out, and I had no way to tell, down beneath the earth, just how close we were pushing it. "Gancanagh?"

"What do you want, Walker?"

I tripped over my own feet, bit my tongue and righted myself with a curse. "Stop that. Don't use my name. Not like that. You are not Morrison. How much farther do we have to go?"

He turned with a finger against his lips: *shh*. "Do you not hear it?"

I hadn't, of course, because Cat and I had been talking. As soon as we went silent, though, I *did* hear it: wailing, not unlike the *Lia Fáil*. Only that had been one voice, the voice of the land, whereas this was many. Twenty-five, at a guess, assuming Aibhill was not only mistress of the banshees but a banshee herself. Hairs stood up on my neck and arms and I dragged to a halt.

Truth was, I didn't want to go into banshee stomping grounds. I'd *been* stomped the one time I'd really gone up against one of Aibhill's blades, and having a touchy *aos sí* and a newborn mage along with me this time didn't seem like it evened the odds enough. "A battle plan might be a good idea here."

"Have ye the lay of the land?" Méabh asked Gancanagh with a note of doubt.

"She'll be in her tower on the hill." Whether it was due to my objection to him sounding like Morrison or because he was talking to Méabh, he sounded more Irish again, for which I was grateful. Morrison didn't put his sentences together the way the Irish did, which made it easier to remember the handsome fellow in front of me wasn't my captain.

Méabh, however, wasn't concerned with his linguistic choices. She grimaced and loosened her sword in its sheath. "And will there be an easy route up that hill, or will it be a battle every step of the way?"

"It can't be." This time the grim note was in my voice.

"We can't take on four and twenty banshees, not unless they're already baked in a pie. Even if they were pushovers, which they're not, the odds are too bad. We're going to have to sneak." I prodded at the edges of my power, wondering if I dared call up the invisibility cloak. Of course, we'd already pulled off shapeshifting and weather witchery, so probably I was being too cautious. And if I thought about it, the time for caution was long past. Caution would have been good just before I'd triggered the Sight at Tara and sent us tumbling through history. Caution would have been good when I dragged Gary home with me instead of letting him go off and get himself killed fighting the Master at Knocknaree. Caution would have been good time and again, but right now we were eyeball deep in the bad guy's territory, so caution had clearly been thrown to the wind a while ago and I should now seize the day.

"Joanne," Caitríona said nervously, "you're glowing again."

I didn't even look. I just extended the power that had built up with my silent rant and wrapped everybody, even Gancanagh, in it. My arm itched, but my cohorts all faded from my vision instantly.

That was great, except totally useless in terms of sneaking around as a unit. Muttering, I started reeling power back in to try again—I did not want to have us wandering around visually separated from one another—but a thrill shot through Gancanagh and I felt it. I mean, really *felt* it, like he, a creature of magic himself, had a visceral, connected reaction to being swathed in more magic. It was baby oil and massages and a promise of getting down to the good stuff, for him, and it hit me with a heart-knocking thump of desire at a level usually reserved for hormone-addled teenagers. Then, despite us all being invisible, he found his way to me and pressed up against me smelling all Morrison-y and delicious and absolutely full of wicked intentions.

My mouth went dry. His, soft against my throat, did not. I swallowed and he purred, warm comforting sound that vibrated my skin, which was just about already vibrating on its own. I couldn't get so much as a squeak or a whimper out, mostly because my brain was busy betraying me by thinking there was something kinda dangerous and sexy about an invisible tryst, and making any sort of sound would notify Caitríona and Méabh as to what we were up to.

Méabh said, "Granddaughter," in a tone that suggested she already knew exactly what we were up to. Then, even more coldly, she said, *"Ailill,"* and I remembered she'd already killed her lover once for screwing around on her. Cat hadn't said what she'd done to Ailill's girlfriend. I shoved Gancanagh away, gasped for breath and croaked, "We're going now."

His disappointment roiled through me and I staggered away, hoping distance would alleviate some of the one-two punch of psychic desire. It didn't help at all. Swearing under my breath, I forged onward, following the sounds of the banshee cries until Cat, in a small voice, said, "Should we be moving?" from somewhere behind me. "I can't see ye's."

I stopped. Dropped my chin to my chest. Turned back, and went back to concentrating on the idea of an invisibility bubble surrounding all of us, not each of us. My shields, which that particular trick rode on, slowly slithered away from each individual and met up with themselves so we were all encompassed within them. "Sorry. I got distracted."

Méabh gave Gancanagh a black look and me an even blacker one, but Caitríona just ran to catch up. I marched along beside her, feeling increasingly crabby. I wanted my magic to be nice and comprehensible like it had been a week ago. I wanted the damned bite, which now that it had started itching again, was beginning to drive me to distraction, to be *healed*. I wanted lots of things, most of which I wasn't going to get, though I would probably get this one: "We should probably be quiet. I have no idea how well banshees hear."

"Not so well, over all that shrieking. The poison's growing worse, isn't it, Granddaughter?" Méabh inserted herself between me and Gancanagh, who was already several body spaces away from me.

I clutched my arm, trying not to wince at the wave of pain that induced. "How can you tell?"

"You're flushed." We shared a moment of not looking at Gancanagh, but really, I was afraid he wasn't the reason for the heat building up in me anyway.

Rattler had gotten me through the fight with the dragon, but I'd lost ground during the transformations. My arm was inflamed, not just the forearm but all the way to the shoulder. The joint hurt, and my collarbone was starting to feel fragile. I didn't want to think about what would happen when the poison got to my heart. I entertained the idea that freeing Sheila and getting Gary back would be my heroic last stand, but then I caught another whiff of Morrison's scent off Gancanagh and snapped, "I'll be fine," because there was no way I was giving up my reunion with the Almighty Morrison.

Méabh took a breath to argue, but just then we stepped out of the darkness into blinding afternoon sunlight. All four of us lurched to a stop, me and Caitríona turning to look at the gloom we'd left. There'd been no warning at all of the transition between light and dark, which was impossible, except we were traveling through fairy realms and the rules apparently didn't apply. We glanced at each other, then shrugged and looked back at the monstrous hill in front of us.

"The Rock," Caitríona said after a moment, grimly.

I had to agree with the grim. The hill rose at a steep but climbable angle, green grass patched with massive stones and stretches of bare earth. If it was anything like the real-world Rock of Cashel—and it wasn't the real one, I was sure of that, because we'd been walking a few hours at the most, and Tipperary really was a long way—if it was like the real one, there was a much less steep approach on the other side. Of course, getting to it meant hiking around the hill's foot, during which time it was always possible something would breach the shields and we'd be discovered. Going up the back side would probably be faster. A short gray wall cordoned off the hill's peak, and behind the wall a tower shot toward the sky. A big blocky tower, square and impregnable-looking. "Well," I said half under my breath, "it's our job to pregnate it. Let's go."

About forty feet up the hill I revised my opinion of its climbability and whether it was faster to go this way than hike around. It wasn't, thank God, as tall as Croagh Patrick, but it was steeper and rougher underfoot, reminding me of the Midwestern badlands for the second time in a day. No one in their right mind would take this route to attack the castle above. A single individual could hold off dozens of men with nothing more than a bow and arrow or some hot pitch. My left arm burned every time I used it, so it became more of an aching dead weight than help climbing, and by the time we reached the wall, I was wheezing.

The wall, of course, wasn't as short as it had seemed from below. It was taller than I was. Taller than Méabh, even. We stared at it, then at each other, and she made stirrups with her hands to offer me a lift. I shook my head and made my own stirrups. "You first. I'm not going to be so good for hauling people up."

She pursed her lips, but nodded and stepped into my hands. I moved as fast as I could, not letting myself think about the roar of agony from my left side as I boosted her upward. Gratifyingly, she all but flew to the wall's top, partly because she was lighter than she looked and partly because I was damned strong, thanks to all the years I'd spent working on cars. She had no idea how much of an admission it was to have sent her up first, because normally I'd have been able to swing any of the three up to the top of the wall without a problem.

"I could go last," Cat volunteered, but I shook my head again.

"I'm tallest with the most reach. It'll be easier for Méabh to grab me than you." I started to make stirrups again, but Gancanagh, to my surprise, intervened and tossed Cat up instead. Then he made a stirrup for me, and when I began the same protest again, shook *his* head. "Trust me."

"On a cold day in hell." But I stepped into the stirrup anyway, and he flung me toward Méabh with far more grace and strength than I expected. I didn't know why: Morrison, whose build he appeared to share, was certainly strong enough to lift me. But I had this idea that under the Morrison image Gancanagh was a slight little thing, and therefore shouldn't be able to fling me around.

Nor should he be able to fling himself around, by that logic, but he leapt up the wall with the insouciance of a cat, which made him seem really truly not human for the first time. He caught me gawking and winked, and I bit back another schoolgirl giggle. Not even Cernunnos made me want to lick him quite so much. Fairy magic, I decided, was dangerous.

Well, on a good day, so was mine. We all thumped down on the other side of the wall—a longer drop than I expected, as the hill ran down against it—and peered up at Aibhill's castle.

There was a front door on the side facing us. That made perverse sense, particularly since the other side of the hill was a less treacherous climb than the side we'd come up. No reason to invite enemies in through the easiest access point. "I don't suppose we just go knock."

"Sure and she'd invite us right in," Caitríona breathed. "What's the worst a banshee can do?"

"Flay your soul from your skin with its voice."

Her eyes bugged. I shrugged stiffly. My left arm didn't want to move at all. I didn't look at it for fear I'd see a wolf's paw dangling from the shredded remains of my coat sleeve. Realistically I didn't think I had a lot of choice coming up: I was afraid I'd have to go all lupine again to have even the slightest chance of us coming out ahead when we fought Aibhill.

The very thought just about talked myself into turning tail and running. Instead I made a dash for the castle's front door.

There were two doors, actually, once I got close enough to see clearly. One was massive, large enough to let half an army out at once. The other was set inside the big one and was normal-size. It had one of those little barred windows for checking out incomers before they came in, but no one was standing guard. Instead a big hoary-looking lock made a promise that we wouldn't be getting in anytime soon. I sagged as the other three caught up to me, but Caitríona glanced at the lock, sniffed and pulled a jackknife out of her jeans pocket.

Less than sixty seconds later the lock popped open and Cat folded the knife up, eminently satisfied with herself. "What?" she said to our wide-eyed admiration. "Me brothers used to try to keep me out of the shed they stored girly mags in. I thought they were hiding chocolates."

Breathless with astonished laughter, I shoved through the door and the others spilled after me. Gancanagh whisked it shut behind him. We all pushed ourselves up against the big doors as if we were hidden by pressing against them, though in fact we stood inside a grassy courtyard with not a hint of cover in sight. Still, every one of us was bright with triumph at getting in. All we had to do now was find Aibhill, kill her and rescue my mother.

Right about then, the banshees came for us.

CHAPTER TWENTY–FIVE

We all gasped right from our very toes, not one of us remembering that I was maintaining a magic that rendered us unseeable. That collective gasp should have been our undoing.

But nothing short of a freight train whistle could have been audible over the banshees' keening, and even that would probably just blend in. They knew the door had opened and closed again: that was clear from how they dove at it time and again while the four of us scattered. Bleak-faced women zoomed by close enough to touch, scraggly hair streaming behind them and their skeletal faces contorted in rage. They scraped long nails through the grass, tufts flying everywhere as we all rolled frantically in different directions, trying to avoid their touch. It would take only one to let them know it hadn't been the wind banging the locked door around.

By the time they began to settle we were spread across the entire courtyard. Caitríona had found a doorway to press into, but she kept giving it worried looks, as if it might open behind her. Méabh had curled up into a space next to what I thought of as a buttress, although I also kind of thought those belonged on castle roofs, not in their courtyards. Either way, the *aos sí* woman's face was twisted, presumably with anger at being forced to hide instead of fight. Gancanagh had gone to ground in an oddly literal way, becoming a lump of earth that hadn't been there before. I could see him if I tried, but his chameleon performance reminded me that this fairy realm was his as well as the Master's.

That idea floated in my mind for an instant, then solidified on the thought I'd had earlier: that we'd crossed into the Lower World when we'd taken the tunnel beneath Sheila's bones.

I was far more familiar with Native American cosmology than Irish. There were three easily accessible levels of reality in Native cosmology—the Middle World, which was the one everybody lived in day to day, the Upper World, a rarified place of spirits and souls, and the Lower World, which was very much like the Middle World except the colors were wrong, distances were peculiar and it was littered with all sorts of astonishing creatures, many of which were dangerous. Dangerous was still the name of the game, and although the landscape was different, Gancanagh's sudden melding with the earth looked so much like something that would easily happen in the Lower World that I was pretty certain I was just viewing it through another mythology's eyes. On one hand, that was *great*: I had a reasonable amount of experience in the Lower World.

On the other, it was very, very bad, because the Native American version of the Lower World wasn't so permeated by the Master's touch that its denizens regarded it as essentially his territory. I didn't know if all of Europe—and if all of Europe then I would think all of what had been Mesopotamia and never mind the vast Chinese empire that stretched back far beyond European civilization—I didn't know if Ireland's corruption meant all those places also had versions of the Lower World that were saturated by the Master's influence.

Which might mean the Americas, with their comparatively recent settlements—the Americas and maybe Australia—were the last holdouts in a world already deeply affected by the Master's life-destroying ways.

I stood there squished into a corner while a host of thwarted banshees gathered in the center of the courtyard, their keening much quieter now, as if they'd lowered their voices to discuss what to do next. They chatted, and I glared futilely at the sky. At the makers of the world, if they lived up there. At Grandfather Sky, whom Coyote had once named specifically as someone responsible for my arrival on this little blue ball floating in space.

I didn't want to buy into the whole "peaceful natives save the world" storyline. I might not have known a lot about the mythology of the Native peoples of America, but I knew a fair amount about their history. The modern implication of "peaceful natives save the earth" was "backward savages don't recognize the benefits of progress," a violently prejudiced viewpoint of what had been some truly astounding cultures. I wanted to scream with outrage at anything that lent itself toward perpetuating it, including myself. There were plenty of examples where American native settlements and cities had gone beyond their resources and collapsed the system.

None of which negated the fact that a great number of them had lived harmoniously within the system for a long time, and perhaps in doing so had given the Master just a little less room for a toehold in their territories. So by all rights maybe I should have been full-blooded Cherokee, one hundred percent about reversing wrongs and saving the world, but oh no. No, I was goddamned Luke Skywalker, bringing balance to the Force. Product of two cultures, both steeped in magic, one that had been fighting contamination since way back when and the other comparatively fresh and clean.

I scowled at the shredded arm of my coat and promised myself that was as close as I'd come to getting my damned hand chopped off.

Méabh sneezed.

Gunfire couldn't have been louder. The banshees went utterly, unnervingly silent, and everybody in the whole courtyard looked toward Méabh's corner.

Her face was still contorted, another sneeze threatening. I'd never tried healing somebody when I couldn't lay hands on them, and besides, I wasn't sure sneezes were things to heal anyway. By the time I'd thought that through, it was too late: she sneezed again, even more explosively, and two dozen banshees converged on her.

Unholy delight filled her face as she bared her sword to take on Aibhill's host. I would never, not in a million years, show that kind of glee going into battle. My many-times-to-the-great-grandmother *lived* for this shit, and right now she had one huge honking advantage: they couldn't see her.

Magic silver swords forged by Nuada might not have been much against dragons, but it turned out they took on banshees just fine. She waited until they were on her before she stood, and she came up swinging with all the strength of a six-foot-eight warrior woman whose life had been spent in the pursuit of bloodshed. Banshees, the old ones at least, were papery, and her cleave shredded three of them before the sword caught in the fourth's juicier ribs. Not as juicy as Sheila: dust, not blood, fell from the wound, but still, that one was fresher than some of the others. The first three didn't have time to scream. The fourth one did, and mortar fell from between the courtyard bricks at the sound.

Méabh didn't so much as flinch. She wrenched the sword sideways, moving it deeper into the banshee. Juicier or not, it didn't weigh all that much, and with a roar I could hear over the screams, she heaved the wailing woman to the ground and came down on it with all her weight.

Its spine severed just like the three before it had, and by that time the rest of us were in the fray.

As crews went, we were a motley one. Caitríona and Gancanagh had no weapons at all, making them more liabilities than fighters, and I had only my psychic nets. On the positive side, I'd caught a banshee with my nets before. On the less positive side, it had taken Sheila's help to hold it in place. But on another positive side, I was a lot more confident in my powers than I'd been then. Of course, on the negative side, that confidence was currently stymied by a werewolf bite and a general uncertainty about using my skills at full bore. Then again, back on the positive side—apparently I was an octagon—if things were going to explode, they might take a banshee or two along with them. And on yet another negative side, I wasn't confident of my ability to cast the nets and keep us all hidden from sight, either. I'd gone into battle plenty of times, but never while invisible.

Exasperated, I stopped worrying about what might happen and just cast a damned net.

I was right: as the net flew out, my light-bending trick wobbled and failed. Probably my own fault for not having faith I could manage it all, but then, fighting banshees was a ferocious test of my faith, period. So I was content that the net spun out, silver and blue interconnected in flowing lines, and caught the nearest banshee like she was a tuna. She shrieked and whirled toward me, entangling herself further. Clawlike nails extended from her fingertips, sawing at the net. I felt the reverberations rattling all the way back to my soul, but unlike the first time I'd fought one of these things, the net held. Her jaw dropped and she screamed again, this time like she really meant it. For a hair-raising moment I thought she was going to pull off the trick Sheila had done, breaking through my shields and getting under my skin.

Except Sheila was my *mother,* and on some level I'd known that even when we'd had the little throw-down outside Méabh's cairn. *She* had a lot more connection to me, a lot more reason and ability to break through my shields. Random banshees from Aibhill's host didn't so much. I dropped my own jaw, shouting back in defiance. My shields strengthened with the yell, and the banshee's cry faltered. Buoyed, I pounced forward to dig my fingers through the net and throttle her.

Net or no, her dead skeletal arms were longer than mine, and her nails infinitely sharper and more dangerous. I barely escaped with both my eyes, and wouldn't have if my glasses hadn't still been precariously balanced on my nose. For things I rarely noticed, they certainly could alter between annoying and lifesaving.

The banshee looked like she was counting what I called lifesaving under the "annoying" banner. She opened her mouth to scream again and I slung a power-swollen strand of net into it. She gagged and I chortled, which was probably not good warrior etiquette and which I paid for with her fist in my gut. Apparently thickening one strand of net thinned some others. I doubled over, wheezing, and when I felt her come for me again decided against the whole mano a mano thing. I had a net, after all. I seized the ends nearest to me, wrapped it around my right wrist—my left arm was still all but useless, though the pain had disappeared thanks to the excitement—and spun to slam the banshee into the nearest wall as hard as I could.

It wasn't hard enough. She didn't quite bounce off, but she wasn't out for the count, either. I grunted and did it again, then felt nails score marks along my shields at my spine. I'd gotten so busy with my banshee I'd forgotten there were about nineteen more to deal with. Méabh, however, had not, and while the banshee at my back was busy *with* my back, she shoved her sword through it and crumbled her to dust. Instinct told me to duck and she leapt over my head, gazellelike, to take out my netted screamer, too.

For the space of a breath we were back to back, ready to take all comers. Caitríona was a few yards away, wailing like one of the banshees herself, a weird wobbly tune with familiar notes I couldn't quite place. Whatever she was singing obviously took a lot of concentration but put it to great effect: the darling girl had shields glimmering around her. Not very steady ones, as they rose and fell with the intensity of her humming, but they were enough to rebound the worst of clawed attacks. I wanted to applaud, but Gancanagh sauntered in front of me to face an oncoming banshee.

I saw Morrison, or someone very like him, walking into the face of danger. *She,* the banshee, saw…something else entirely. She stopped, horror and hope written on a face that might have at one time been lovely. For the first time I heard a banshee speak not in rhyme, but then, it was only a single word: *"Aidan?"*

My heart stopped. My *blood* stopped. Everything in me went cold, just for a split second. Then I knew she was seeing an old lover in Gancanagh, not my son—my son, whose name probably wasn't actually Aidan, since somebody had adopted him and probably given him a new name—but for that hideous instant I thought it was going to all be about me and her and keeping a little boy I didn't even know safe from devils he didn't need to dance with.

"Sure and it's me, *alanna*," Gancanagh whispered. "I've missed ye so, me love. Come to me, my girl, for all our troubles are behind us now." He extended a hand, and although he was in front of me, talking to someone else, I wanted to run to him myself.

Banshees weren't immune to his charm, either. Some of the film cleared from her eyes, like tears were rising to moisten paper, and she stepped forward, reaching out to him as she did.

He took her hands tenderly and drew her close, the whole of his attitude warm with welcome. He lifted a hand to her jaw, the other tracing her collarbone. She smiled, terrible expression of joy in a face too long dead to show emotion as other than a skeletal grin.

Gancanagh, who looked like Morrison, ripped her head off and threw it away.

The air went out of my lungs. He glanced back at me and smiled that come-hither smile, and even with a dead woman's dusty blood staining his hands, even with sickness in the pit of my stomach, I still wanted to go to him. *Dangerous*, Méabh had said. *Gancanagh is dangerous.* "Fight," he said, and I felt a compulsion in my bones to do just that. To do anything he asked, in hopes of winning his love.

This was going to be a problem, later. But now I only nodded once and turned away, heart beating too fast, to do as he'd asked me. To fight, because the odds were still about fifteen to four, and we had yet to meet Aibhill. I flung another net, wishing I dared to catch more than one banshee at a time in it, but the first one had put up enough of a struggle. I didn't want to find out two was more than I could handle. I wished I had a *weapon,* and then with bell-like clarity, an idea came to me. Hoping everybody else would continue to keep up their end of the bargain, I ducked out of the fight for a second time, and fell into my garden.

I'd never been in such a hurry before when I crossed into the gardens. I tore through my own territory to fling open the ivy-hidden door, and raced out into the crater that I'd always found my garden at the bottom of. I scrambled up the sides, heading for the greater gestalt of souls and bellowing, "Coyote! *Coyote!* Wake up, wake up, I need your help! *Get the spear!*"

A few ginormously long strides later I rushed into the arid, beautiful desertscape that was Coyote's garden. He wasn't there. I started picking up stones, desperately trying to find some kind of access point that would let me deeper into his soul, and shouting all the time. I finally hauled a rock nearly as big as I was aside, revealing a cool little cave, but before I could dash into it, Coyote emerged in his coyote form. He looked sleepy and bewildered, his ears at half-mast, but he was carrying the spear I'd asked for, his teeth full of it. I dropped to my knees, hugged him one-armed and blurted, "*Bless* you," with a fervency largely unfamiliar to me.

He shifted mid-hug, and though logically he'd have still held the spear in his mouth, it was instead in one hand as he hugged me with the other arm and said, "What's going on?" in confusion. "Take this, I can't stand it."

I seized the spear, wood cool in my fingers, even where he'd been holding it. It was a piece of art, a weapon grown, not made. The haft was polished white birch, and the head black ironwood, and though they were nominally bound together by leather strips and feathers at the neck, I had no doubt the entire weapon was a seamless single piece of wood. That was what happened when demigods of the forest offered gifts: magic. The demigod in question, Herne, had given it to Coyote as custodian, but my mentor was a healer. Even carrying the weapon gave him the creeps, so I'd been the one to use it. "I need this. We're in a fight. I lost my sword." And Gary, but this was not the time to go into that, even if the reminder made me swallow a sob.

"What—where are you?" He wasn't going to stop me from taking it, but I could see him gathering himself, waking up, preparing to jump on the next flight to Seattle to help pick up the pieces.

"I think I'm in the Irish version of the Lower World. Ireland, anyway, look, I can't talk, but the sword, Coyote, I can pull the sword from anywhere in the world, and you've just given the spear to me here, that means you've relinquished custodianship again, right? So I should be able to pull it to me, too. And even if it doesn't work in the Middle World I'm in the Lower so *it should work*. Right?"

He interjected, "Ire—Low—lost—cust—?" through my panicked response, but gave up halfway through, golden eyes growing increasingly round as I reached the end of the rushed explanation. Then he said, "Yes," with utter certainty, which was all I needed. I *wanted* my idea to work, but I wasn't quite sure I believed it would. *He* did, though. He believed, and shamanism was belief, and I believed him, so I believed me and whispered, *"Thank you,"* with all the heartfelt gratitude I could manage, and surged back to the fight.

Almost nothing had changed. Another banshee was down, a second was failing to fall to Gancanagh's wiles the way the first had—a woman scorned, I thought—and as I steadied myself Caitríona went down under two of the screaming monsters.

She was the only one of us who was genuinely defenseless, though her warbling song kept shields flickering in and out around her. It wasn't enough. I was not going to go to her mother in the Middle World and explain how I'd lost her daughter, my cousin, to a host of banshees in the Lower. I took two running steps, planted the spear's butt in the earth and managed a clumsy, one-armed vault over a low-flying banshee to crash onto one of the two that had toppled Caitríona. The other I seized with a net, and for a minute we were a tumbling, screaming, rolling mass of furious women.

I had no leverage to use the spear and roared, "Caitríona!" as I flung the thing sideways, hoping she would catch it. Then I had my fingers in a banshee's pointy mouth and was trying to pull the top of her head off while another one scrabbled and spat at the net winding ever tighter around her. I'd never fought such a physical battle with as focused a mental aspect. Either I was getting better at this, or fighting in the Lower World helped integrate my talents at a level I despaired of reaching in the real world. The banshee I was fighting exploded into magic-filled dust, and for the second time that day, Caitríona O'Reilly stood over me with a weapon and the remains of a fallen enemy at her feet.

The spear had hit my shields, or it might have gone straight through me, too. A good shot, too: right over my heart. I had a sick lurch of appreciation for Laurie Corvallis's sheer nerve after I'd done the same thing to her with exactly the same weapon, and then Cat was offering her hand and pulling me to my feet. I came up ready to fight, or as ready as I could be with one arm dangling uselessly.

Evidently it was enough. The remaining banshees took a look at the four of us, turned tail and fled.

CHAPTER TWENTY-SIX

A much more ferocious warrior than I probably would have given chase. Méabh started to, in fact, though to my eyes it looked less like she planned to catch them than as if she was giving them an all-out "Yeah, take *that!* Run, you scared little girls! *Run!*" boost on their way. She stopped after a few yards and turned back to the rest of us. Gancanagh was dusting off his Morrison-like suit and slacks, having taken out the woman scorned after all. Caitríona held the spear like she'd never let it go. She was banged up worse than the rest of us, but she looked like she'd just come to life, color high and eyes bright. I was equal parts envious and proud of her.

"What," I said to her, "were you singing?"

A blush of laugher crept up her cheeks. "The old *Star Trek* theme song. You said *Trek* shields…"

"You're a genius." I totally meant it, and gave her a sloppy hug. "Holy crap. We kicked their asses. Damn, we're good."

"I would like to learn that magic," Méabh said. "The power to be unseen. It might change the flow of history."

I'd gotten the idea from comic books and wanted to suggest she go read some. Instead I said, "Except it hasn't, so either you didn't learn it or it didn't matter. Besides, we have enough screwed-up history to fix, or haul back toward center. Let's not add another loop to the timeline." Between losing Gary and my mother's captivity it was hard to remember that taking the Morrígan out to restore some balance was how my day had gotten started. Lugh's scarlet blood splashed over the *Lia Fáil* was visceral, but not as personal as losing Gary. I looked up at the castle towering over us. "If we take the O'Brien banshee down, is that going to get your mother's attention, Méabh? Because I'm tired of pussyfooting around. I'm feeling ready for a showdown."

Méabh, guarded, said, "It will, but it's your mother we're here to save, not mine we're here to defeat."

"It's all the same." I kept expecting the banshees to converge again, but instead I got glimpses of white faces and flowing hair as they rushed from one castle window to another. All that was left of their sisters was dust, so I wasn't sure how many we'd killed, but I thought it was at least half—half of which, in turn, Méabh alone had been responsible for. "The banshees perform ritual murders to strengthen the Master, but there's obviously a hierarchy here. He probably doesn't give the orders to them himself, you know? It goes to the Morrígan to Aibhill to the blades." It wasn't that the one I'd met was the Blade. It was all of them, voices like blades, nails like blades, faces like blades. Maybe a grouping of banshees was a blade of banshees, like a group of crows was a murder. It didn't matter. What did matter was, "I'll work my way up to the top one by one if I have to."

"You would face him?" Gancanagh sounded impressed, and I found myself stalking toward the nearest castle doors as I answered.

"You know what, a week ago I'd have said no, but a lot's changed since then. I wasn't ready then, and maybe I'm still not, but we're getting one step closer to a throw-down every day, and if that means it's on right here and right now, then fine. I've got too much riding on this one to run away, so I'll take it. We'll do our best. I. Will do my best." Since I couldn't really drag the others into my fight just on a say-so.

"You have a warrior's spirit after all," Méabh said in approval. Caitríona, spear still in hand, ran to catch up with us, and Gancanagh, when I looked back, was sauntering along behind like he wasn't really part of the group but didn't want to miss any of the action, either. Morrison wouldn't have been so coy, which made me feel better about the resemblance I saw. Armed with that knowledge, I shoved the doors open and walked into a great hall.

Stone arched dozens of feet above the floor, supported by oak beams and the grace of God. I had one of those moments where it seemed more likely aliens had built the pyramids than humans had been able to create such soaring masterpieces without the help of modern technology. Stained glass found sunlight somewhere and spilled a riot of color onto the gray stone floors, but they weren't the religious figures I was used to seeing depicted in stained glass. A whole different history of the world unfolded up above us, and before I had even the slightest chance to begin appreciating it, a woman came gracefully down a stairway I hadn't noticed.

She was beautiful.

I simply hadn't expected that, not after the banshees I'd encountered, up to and including my mother, who'd been pretty in life. I'd expected skeletal and clawed and papery, not fair and blue-eyed and curvaceous. Aibhill—because it had to be Aibhill—wore white, lots and lots of flowing white. So flowing I couldn't really call it a style or name an era it might have come from. It was like she'd been dressed in breezes dipped in white to make them visible, the way the light fabric flowed and folded and wove around her. That seemed almost likely, given that we were inside and there was no actual wind to give the cloth motion. Her hair wove the same way, tangling delicate hands and soft white arms, then releasing them again. Somehow her face was never obscured. Even I, who had had a crop cut since I was fifteen, might wear my hair long if I could make it never fall in my face.

She came down the stairs toward us, her hands extended in greeting. Prudently, and without discussing it, we all took a step back. Even Gancanagh, whose gaze was a mix between starstruck and avaricious, retreated. I wondered if Aibhill was like him, a seducer, and I wondered what happened if two of them started working their wiles on each other. I bet it would either lead to instant all-out warfare or fantasmagorically good sex. "You," she said to all of us in what could be legitimately called dulcet tones, "you have all been very naughty. Which of you is the child of Sheila MacNamarra?"

Quite certain I would regret it, but also not entirely able to help myself, I reversed the step I'd taken and put myself forward. "That would be me."

Aibhill pursed her lips. Fine full lips of a perfect pearly pink. Women spent vast amounts of money on lipstick trying to achieve that shade, but as she came closer it became clear it was her natural coloring, as was the milky pale skin and the honestly blond hair. No honey-colored roots saying the blond came from sun bleaching: she was one of those rare adults who made it to adulthood and remained towheaded. Why, I wondered, were the banshees so impossibly ugly, if Aibhill was so lovely, and at the back of my mind the suggestion of a penny dropped. I scrabbled after it, lost the thought and tried to focus on the unearthly beauty in front of me. "I'm Joanne Walker. Sheila's daughter."

"And you'll be wanting her back," Aibhill said with gentle amusement. Gancanagh took a step toward her, drawn like a cat to cream, and she smiled at him so sweetly that jealousy spiked in me. I didn't want anybody smiling at Morrison like that except me.

He wasn't Morrison. And my mother wasn't Aibhill's yet, not even halfway, because we'd burned her bones. "She doesn't belong to you."

"No." Aibhill looked Gancanagh up and down, still smiling, then turned her attention back to me in a way that suggested I was a trifle to be dealt with and Morrison—*Gancanagh*—was far, far more interesting. "No," she repeated, idly, "I suppose she doesn't quite, not yet, but I can hardly afford to let her go, can I? Not when you've struck down so many of my blades. Did you not think to ask? Ask, rather than come as warriors?"

I wet my lips and glanced at my companions. Gancanagh paid me no mind, his very breathing in tandem with Aibhill's. I wanted to slap him. So, from Méabh's expression, did she. I cleared my throat, trying to shake off caring how the banshee queen affected a fairy man, and said, "Well, no." There was a reason I hadn't come asking, either. I was sure of it. I was just having a hard time remembering, what with Morrison salivating over the white-gowned woman.

"It's hard work," Aibhill explained rather earnestly. Morrison cast me a condemnatory look, like I should be ashamed for not believing her. "Making the blades. Shaping their grief and anger into weapons. I give them revenge, you understand."

I knotted my hand into a fist and stared at Aibhill's hem so I couldn't see Gancanagh-Morrison. "You mean revenge on innocent people they've never met, all so a horrible death monster can grow stronger."

"Revenge on the lovers who scorned them," Aibhill corrected. "As you would no doubt like revenge on Lucas, mmm? Or you on Ailill," she said to Méabh while my stomach went heavy. Méabh made a sound like what I felt, and Aibhill's smile broadened. "Shall we go to him together, Morrígan's daughter? Shall we give him a taste of your anger?"

"He's tasted my revenge already, and will again soon enough," Méabh said thickly. I could hear the temptation in her voice, but really, she'd killed him once. That was probably enough for most people. Except she probably thought my captain, standing there mesmerized by Aibhill, was her Ailill, which meant she was not only deluded but that Morrison was potentially in trouble. I edged half a step forward.

Aibhill, unconcerned by me or by Méabh, turned her smile back to me. "Then think of the sweetness of your revenge, Sheila's daughter. Served cold, all unexpected, all rich and savory. Would it not be a delicious dish?"

There was nothing even slightly cold about the revenge I was plotting on Méabh just then. My fist worked itself open and closed again. I might be able to take her, if I surprised her enough. Failing all else, I could turn to the wolf.

Heat flared in my left arm like excitement had taken up residence there. It would hurt for a second or two, but then I'd have Méabh's long throat in my teeth and Gancanagh would be *mine*. I might have to rip Aibhill's throat out, too, but I distantly thought that was what I was there for anyway. My voice had an awful lot of growl to it as I asked, "How do you even know what I want, anyway?"

Surprise filtered across her lovely face. "I see into women's hearts, of course. Every score, every mark, every bleeding place a man has left, I see, and offer succor."

Gancanagh drifted even closer to Aibhill, all moth-to-flame. Jealousy flared toward rage. He needed to stay away from the banshee queen. I didn't like his expression of adoration. I didn't like how she turned to him with a welcoming smile, or how their gazes met with a profound understanding. They were too much alike to be happy. I bet he could also see into the hearts of men—or women. I bet that was how he was so shiveringly appealing. Aibhill's smile grew wider still, and she offered him a hand. Smitten, he extended his own.

Méabh, with a barbaric shriek, chopped it off.

Everybody in the room started screaming. Gancanagh, because he was holding the—not bloody, but dusty—stump of his arm in his remaining hand. Aibhill, for no reason that I could see except she was a banshee, which was reason enough. Caitríona, out of shock. Méabh, because she was going after Gancanagh again, sword whicking through the air.

And me, because my great-grandmother had just chopped off Morrison's hand. Utterly ignoring my lack of weapons, I launched myself at her, knocking her aside just before another blow would've severed Gancanagh's pretty head from his shoulders. Her hand hit the stone floor hard enough to loosen her grip on her sword. I batted it away, then punched her in the mouth.

She bit me, slammed an elbow up, caught me in the windpipe, then kicked me as I rolled around on the floor gasping and she jumped to her feet. Her sword wasn't very far away. I didn't have my breath back by the time she got it. Nothing to fight with. No chance against the warrior queen.

Not unless I gave in to the thickness in my arm, the poison running through my blood. Gançanagh's screams, thin and high and furious with pain, reverberated against my skin. Méabh had hurt *my* Gancanagh, and a little lupine vengeance sounded just the thing.

Agony crackled in my arm as I relaxed my fight against the wolf. I rolled to all fours, struggling out of my coat, and lowered my head as the itch became unbearable, then delicious—

—and then stopped. Stopped cold, stopped entirely, stopped beneath the vicious cut of Aibhill's harpy voice. "Both betrayed by Gancanagh's love. I could ask for no more, with my host so depleted."

Beautiful, gentle, sweet Aibhill stepped into my line of vision, unleashed a handful of claws and drove them into Méabh's stomach.

I should have seen it coming. We *all* should have seen it coming, except the part of me that could still think about something besides Gancanagh had expected her to go for me. Méabh made a horrible soft sound of pain and wrapped her hands around Aibhill's wrist, but moved no farther. Caitríona had never stopped screaming. I crawled one tiny jerky step toward the entangled pair, but Aibhill clenched her fist and Méabh went whiter and I held still again.

Only Gancanagh responded quickly. I didn't *see* him move. He simply landed on Aibhill with all fours—all fours, his hand had *grown back*—and he slammed her to the ground. She shrieked, an ordinary woman's scream, but the longer it went on, the more banshee cries I heard in it. They piled in, one on top of another, until her voice could peel paint from the walls, separate solderings, hell, split atoms. It was unbearable, blasting out my eardrums and making my nose bleed. Horrible, itchy, painful blood, except I had it easy, because Méabh was bleeding from everywhere.

From her nose, from her ears, from her belly. She fell to the floor in slow stages: knees, hip, hand, collapse. I forgot the rivalry that had driven me to tackle her in the first place, and crawled another inch toward her. She lay barely three feet away, but Aibhill's screams were a physical barrier. I focused, trying to make my shields pointy so they would slide through the sound more easily, but there was nothing easy about it. Méabh was dying, and I wasn't going to be able to save her. I was afraid to even look at Caitríona for fear her head would have exploded from Aibhill's cries.

I didn't know how the banshee queen could keep screaming while she and Gancanagh fought. They'd rolled several feet away, weight changing from one to the other, but she didn't seem to need to draw breath in order to scream. I wasn't even sure she needed to open her mouth. The screams came off her in relentless waves, and somehow Gancanagh still held on. I could all but see his fury rolling off him, fury that he, of all creatures, had been caught in Aibhill's net. He wasn't fighting for me or Méabh or against the Master. He was fighting for his own lost dignity, for having been the seduced instead of the seducer. He was fighting to restore his sense of self, and he would do anything to achieve that.

Anything. Even die. And he was about to, because he was a thing of small magics, and Aibhill was fed not only by the Master but by the banshees she reigned over. The thought finally came all the way clear: youth and beauty retained by draining the vitality from others. It was classic, in a fairy-tale sense. With half of her host already obliterated, Aibhill was at the weakest she'd ever be.

And it wasn't weak enough. Not for Gancanagh to take her out. But he could distract her, hurt her, give me time to get Méabh back on her feet and maybe, just maybe, give the Morrígan's daughters a fighting chance.

I bellowed from the bottom of my lungs and surged the foot or two to Méabh's side. Collapsed beside her and called for the healing power as triumph entered Aibhill's scream and dust filled the air. Fairy dust, I thought inanely, and wondered if it could make me fly.

What it could not do, it seemed, was make me heal. The power stuttered and ended at my fingertips, as it had done in the past when I'd been making bad choices. I whimpered in shock, which wasn't very grown-up, but at least it was heart-felt. I tried again. No magic, no healing, though since I hadn't turned completely into a werewolf I assumed the power was still running rampant in my veins.

"It's my territory, lass," Aibhill said, and the mockery in her voice was so sweet it could have been sympathy. "There are things I cannot stop you from doing, perhaps, but there are others that I can. Be grateful, little shaman. If I release your power now, the wolf will take you."

I smiled, vicious invitation, and she blanched, backing off as if I had already become the wolf. Then a sneer marred her lovely features and she lifted her voice in another scream.

The walls crumbled, mortar shuddering from between enormous squares of stone. The tall roof I'd admired so much was collapsing, and I could barely focus enough to keep huge chunks from flattening us. It wasn't fair. Whether Mom wanted it to be or not, until the banshee queen was dead, her scream was part of Aibhill's. That let Aibhill get under my shields. They shivered and broke apart, hairline fractures reappearing as quickly as I repaired them. The weight of stone crashing down didn't help. I flinched again and again, feeling impacts against my flesh, though none of them broke through to crush bone and body. Not yet, anyway. I rolled my jaw, fingers dug against the gray stone floor.

Incongruous golden sunlight spilled over my hands, sunset revealed by the falling walls. I took a little heart from that: it seemed like a tether back to the Middle World, and although I wasn't at all sure I could get myself home, I thought I could at least shove Cat back into reality. I wished I dared call Coyote and ask for his help, but I lacked the concentration and was afraid that if I succeeded, it would open a channel straight from Aibhill to him, and that would be unacceptable. I had to do it on my own. Just this once, and I'd apologize to him later.

Easy enough to say, when I doubted there would be a later. My laugh broke and Caitríona seized my arm. I said, "It's okay. We're going home. I'm going to open a path back home. As soon as you see it, run. I'll cover you and be right on your heels."

"We won't save Sheila if we run! The fight will be over, we'll—"

"The fight's already over. Do as I say, Cat. Just do as I say." I had nothing left for words. Coyote was so good at opening passageways between the Middle and Lower Worlds. I tried to remember how he did it, calling yellow roads and low red sunlight. The light tinted more toward crimson, either the oncoming night or a successful path. I decided it was the path and envisioned it more fully, remembering what it had looked like when Coyote sent me into the Lower World to fight the wendigo. Caitríona gasped, signal that she saw it, too, and I said, "Run."

She ran, and I shut the road down behind her.

★ ★ ★

Surprise changed Aibhill's voice for a moment. Deepened it enough that I could shake off the very, very worst of the effects and raise my head to look at her. She stared at the space where Caitríona had been, then turned an enraged gaze on me. She was still beautiful. Even with her wild white robes stained with Méabh's blood and the glittering dust that had once been Gancanagh, even with the voice that tore me apart and held my mother captive, she was beautiful. I wanted evil to be ugly, or to wear black hats. That, after all, was why I'd bought my dramatic white leather coat.

For some reason, thinking about the coat gave me the wherewithal to get on my feet. I wasn't kidding myself. I wasn't going to be able to fight that voice, not with it cracking bigger and bigger pieces off my shield, but I wasn't by God going to go out on my knees. I wished like hell I had my sword, even reached for it, then bit back a sob when it didn't appear. When it, like Gary, was lost to me. My left arm was completely useless, but I shook my right hand until silver-blue power shone through it. Maybe I could take her out with me, one last explosive release of magic that would no doubt shut down my ability to call it forever, but that was okay, since it wasn't looking good for the home team anyway.

Aibhill recognized what I was doing, and gave me a stunning smile. We circled each other, me surprised I could move at all, and stopped when we'd reversed positions. She had the setting sun to her back, golden glow making her all the more angelic, and it felt like the sun had lent her every ounce of its nuclear power when she opened her mouth and screamed again.

My shields flaked away, leaving every weary aspect of me on display. Leaving my despair over Gary and my love for Mor-

rison and my concerns for Aidan all right there for the taking.
Leaving Petite, my Mustang, the one lifelong love affair I'd
had, out in the open. Leaving my perception of Petite reflecting the state of my soul there for her to see. Leaving Billy and
Melinda and their kids and my coworkers and my fondness for
Cernunnos and my protective streak over Suzanne Quinley
and my foolish pride in learning swordplay and my regret over
my fencing teacher's discomfort with my shamanism and on
and on and on, all of it raw and exposed and coming apart
beneath the sounds of her never-ending screams.

I was saying my last prayers when Gary rode out of the
sunset and shoved my sword through the bitch's back.

CHAPTER TWENTY-SEVEN

Aibhill's scream turned to a squeak. She slid forward off the rapier, blood bright over her white gown and astonishment vivid on her pretty face.

Her astonishment had *nothing* on mine. I stood where I was, shock still, with the vestiges of screams faltering around me. With my shields shivering themselves back together, now that they were no longer under assault. With my heart holding still in my chest and my lungs empty of air, because I was afraid if I breathed again, if my heart beat again, that the vision of Gary would disappear once and for all and he would be gone from my life forever.

Forget Aibhill. Forget Lugh and Nuada and Cernunnos and all the other inhumanly gorgeous people I had ever encountered. I had never seen anything as beautiful as Garrison Matthew Muldoon, seventy-four years old, white-haired, broad-shouldered like a linebacker and with a smile to break the hearts of girls young enough to be his granddaughter. Not that he was smiling now. He sat straight in his saddle, expression solemn as he looked at the woman he'd just killed. Aibhill, whose body slowly degraded from beauty to age as I watched. It would get worse, I thought, and I didn't want to see the transition from age to extreme age, then to dust as the life force lent to her by the banshees bled away. I wondered what was happening to them, and whether we'd saved Sheila, and then Gary looked up and did give me that movie-star grin, and said, "H'lo, darlin'. Did I miss anything?"

What air was left in my lungs rushed out and I ran forward on willpower alone, no oxygen, no thought, just the need to crash into my best friend's arms and hug him as hard as I possibly could. He even slid off the horse quickly enough for me to do that, and we both thumped against the animal as I flung myself into his arms. He bent his head over mine and we stayed there until I could draw breath again, which only happened after black dots and stars started dancing in my vision. "Do you have false teeth?"

Gary guffawed. "What kinda question is that, doll?"

"It's just your teeth are so perfect and I know you used to smoke and I always thought they had to be false and then she said you'd be at Méabh's tomb and a skeleton *was* and it had false teeth but they weren't perfect that was how I knew it wasn't you but I was so scared and I was sure at first it was and *do* you?"

Gary set me back and beamed at me. "'Course I do. Got in a fight just after Korea and two of 'em got knocked out. I had the doc pull 'em all. He was furious 'cause I had good teeth, but everybody loses their teeth eventually, so I figured no point in waiting. So what's this about Méabh's tomb? Never been there."

"No, you have to have been, she said you'd be waiting at her final restin—" The breath went out of me again and I got cold. "Her final resting place."

I did not want to turn around. Did not want to look toward Méabh, who I'd forgotten about in the past minutes. But I couldn't not, either, not after the day we'd spent together. I grabbed Gary's hand, both unwilling to ever let him go and reluctant to look at Méabh without support. He gave me a reassuring nod, and I clenched my fingers harder around his and made myself look.

She was horribly still. Eyes open, staring toward the exposed sky. I made a sound, but it didn't get past my throat. Gary very gently tugged me into motion, and then we were running toward her and collapsing on our knees at her side. Her chest rose and fell, minute motions, but it was something. It was *enough,* with Aibhill no longer mistress of this domain. I shot a glance at the banshee queen's body: shriveling now, falling bit by slow bit into white dust. Another minute and she would be nothing. Relieved, I reached for the healing power, and instead was taken aback by another voice I hadn't expected to hear again.

"I might make you an offer." Cernunnos rode out of the sunset as well, ash and silver cutting a mark against gold. He wasn't, though, speaking to me: his gaze was for the woman dying at my side.

Being a master of discretion, I gave a bleat of protest and managed to turn it into words as he dismounted and glanced at me. "She's not exactly up to a bargain, Cernunnos!"

"There is no bargain to be made. No cost for what I will ask, because it is to my benefit as well as hers." He knelt on Méabh's other side, head heavy with horns as he lowered it toward hers. "Do not die here, Queen of Connacht. Instead give up this land, this world and become a creature of my earth instead. It will sustain you and all your kind for as long as I exist, and I am not an easy thing to end." He glanced at me as he spoke, emerald eyes fiery. Not easy, but not impossible: I had almost seen his end, and that was a deep bond between us. That acknowledgment made, he looked back to Méabh, voice softer still. "You know already that the *aos sí* do not exist in Joanne's world, in Joanne's time. The choice is yours, for all your kin: fade away under the hills, or come beyond the sunset—"

"'And all the western stars,'" I whispered. "'Until I die.'"

Méabh's gaze sharpened on me and she laughed. Breathless ugly sound, but a laugh. "A poet and a warrior. Write my song, then, Granddaughter. Write my song, as I go. I'll miss you."

"I'll miss you, too. I'm glad I got to meet you. And the poem's not mine." And I'd mangled it anyway, but it was close enough for the moment. I struggled for the right thing to say, finally blurting, "I'll say it for you, though. On the old holy days, darkest night and brightest day."

"Then I'll go." She looked at Cernunnos, and for the first time I saw the woman soften. I sympathized, even as my heart wrenched. We'd gone through a lot of adventure together in the past day. I didn't want to have yanked her out of time only to have gotten her killed. The thought made me give Gary a look of guilty relief. He beetled his bushy eyebrows at me.

I shook my head. I didn't want to explain that while I didn't *want* to have gotten Méabh killed out of time, I could live with it, whereas I couldn't have forgiven myself for doing the same to him. A jolt of bewilderment finally hit me: I didn't even know how he and Cernunnos had gotten here. Especially since I was still pretty sure "here" was the Lower World, where I doubted Cernunnos belonged at all.

"My people," Méabh said to Cernunnos, "my people aren't mine to call. I wouldn't be one of them, not in my heart, not in my soul."

"But you are in the blood," said the god of the hunt, and then, to me, "Give her strength enough to survive the ride across the stars. That alone, and no more. Tir na nOg will do the rest, and she will be better for it. More, the land will come to know her people through her blood, and they will leave this world for mine. It has long been lonesome," he murmured, and I couldn't meet his eyes. I only nodded, reaching for my magic.

Half to my surprise, power responded promptly, leaping awake with a rush of enthusiasm. It poured through me, starting in my fingertips and sizzling up my arms. I had about a nanosecond to recognize that usually it went the other direction.

Then I turned into a werewolf.

It happened so fast I didn't know what *had* happened. A bolt of pain, but not the drawn-out agony from before. Just a clear pure explosion of it and then the world was a simpler place. Bright sharp smells overwhelmed me: blood and dying magic and surprise and dust and grass and stone and sky. I sneezed once, sending some of the scent away, and focused on the important things.

Like getting out of the itchy human clothes. That was the work of a moment, while I growled over the nice warm lump of bleeding flesh right in front of me. It would sate the hunger in my belly. I'd been so long without food as a human I'd temporarily forgotten the need to eat. Shifting awakened the need, and the bloody, barely breathing body on the floor looked like lunch.

Gary put his hand on my ruff and pulled me back as I dipped my head toward Méabh's gut wound. I snarled and turned on him, teeth snapping a whisker from his nose.

He didn't even flinch, just scruffed my spine and then my furry cheeks. My angry wolf brain went blank for just a moment. This was not how prey was supposed to act. I lost some of my aggression, and inside that moment of confusion, Gary said, "You ain't gonna bite me, darlin'."

No. No, I wasn't. That was Gary. My friend Gary. Gary, who'd come back. I kept to short ideas, important thoughts. Gary was my friend. I wouldn't bite him. I would never bite him. I would never make him a monster. *I* wasn't a monster. Not if I could keep from biting Gary. Over and over, the same litany of promises: I had Gary back. I would never risk him again.

Inch by itching inch, my hackles flattened. I edged my front feet forward centimeters at a time until they, too, lay flat, and I had my chin on the floor. Gary kept hold of my face, just like I was still a real girl. He even smiled, all calm and natural, as if holding off a crazed werewolf was all in the line of duty. "There you go," he said in approval. "That's better. Now, what's goin' on, Jo? You said shapeshifting. Didn't think that meant eating your buddies."

I didn't think much at all, but his voice was soothing. I listened to it, an easy rising and falling cadence, and began to fall asleep. A hint of danger flared as I recognized the oncoming nap, but it was too late: the wolf's thoughts became stronger than my own, more focused. Food would come later. The old human would weaken. He could be taken then. The Master would be pleased. The Master knew this old man. His scent was familiar. Familiar to all the Master's creatures. The old man had fought the Master once, long ago. Before my ancestors had come from the earth to do the Master's bidding. Killing this man would be the Master's desire. If I brought this man to the Master, he would forgive me and all my kind for their weakness in being captured by Méabh.

Familiar scent flared again and my eyes opened wide. Méabh. The Master knew the dying woman's scent, too. My kind would be elevated above all others if I brought him the dying woman *and* the old man. My tail hit the floor once, hard. I gathered my feet under me and sprang away, out of the old man's reach. Out of reach of the food/dying/Méabh-woman, too, but that wouldn't matter soon. I made my throat long, gathering breath for a triumphant howl to the sky.

Something I couldn't see kicked me in the head.

I wobbled, too surprised to howl or whimper. Nothing nothing *nothing:* my senses were afire, searching for what had attacked me. No scent. No body. No footstep on the floor. I backed away, shoulders hunched, head lowered, teeth bared. Growling at the nothing. Willing it to go away. Willing it to be seen, so I could fight it.

Its scent came first. Heavy, earthen, animal. Prey animal: deer. But not weak, not a doe, not a fawn. A stag. In his prime, musky scent growing stronger. Not easy prey. Not wise prey for a single wolf. A pack could take him, but I had no pack. My kind scattered from each other after the change was forced on us. We hunted alone now. We did not hunt the healthy, the strong. We did not hunt the stag.

But there was the old man and the dying woman, and the promise of the Master's forgiveness. I was young. Strong. Perhaps I could take the stag. It would fill my belly. I crouched lower, growling.

Something *wrong* came into the scent. A not-prey smell:

dominance. So strong I almost lay down, almost rolled to expose my hungry belly. Maybe it would think me a puppy. Forgive my mistakes.

No. I had to remember. Master. Old man. Dying woman. I sprang up again, snarling.

The scent became a shape. Like a man, but not. Too thick in the torso, the neck, the head. Antlers there, like the stag. Green eyes, not like the stag. Relentless gaze. No prey animal would lock eyes with me, the wolf, the quick and strong one. I made myself larger, ruff standing on end, and the stag-man said a word: "Enough."

It made me small, that word. Made me quiver. Made my bladder tighten and made me lie down with only the tip of my tail moving. Pleading for forgiveness. I did not *understand*. The stag-man should be prey. Should be afraid. Should be *careful*.

I rolled onto my back and stretched my throat long for the second time, but this time in submission, and didn't know why.

The stag-man knelt beside me and took my fur in his hand. Over my throat, squeezing, pressing, warning as he whispered, "Foolish shifter. Do you think you frighten me? I am Cernunnos, god of the hunt, and you, foolish beast, are a hunter. You are mine, first and so long before you belonged to that thing they call the Master. You have made your allegiances, but never dream that I cannot still master you. Now release my shaman, foolish shifter, or I will destroy you here, in this place so close to your birth space that you will be called back and will never again see sunlight."

He could. He would. I knew it in my bowels, in the way my tail curled between my legs in terror. But he couldn't. Couldn't destroy me without destroying *her,* the one who wasn't wolf. My tail uncoiled a little, and the stag-god smiled. Sharp teeth in that smile. As sharp as mine. "It would be a shame," he said, "but do not imagine her life is so unimportant that I would let a monster live in her place."

The wolf whimpered and flowed away. Pain shot through me again and I lay there, Joanne-shaped, naked and with Cernunnos's mouth half an inch from mine. Had his hand not also been crushing my windpipe quite so thoroughly, it would have been a supremely erotically charged moment. Good thing Morrison wasn't here, which wasn't something I often found myself thinking. "...thanks."

Cernunnos raked a glance over me, ending with a smile so repressed that it obviously said, "Oh, anytime!" Without looking, and with consummate grace, he caught my coat in his free hand as Gary tossed it our way, and covered me with it in some semblance of modesty. I sat up to shove my arms in the sleeves, somewhere between dismayed and relieved that my left arm responded properly. It didn't hurt anymore, either, but it was still shiny and infected-looking. Amputation was starting to sound like a viable option.

"You are damaged, my *gwyld,*" Cernunnos said, too softly for Gary to hear. I shot a "no duh" look between my arm and him, but he shook his star-filled hair. "More deeply than that wound can say. Pain remains in your soul, and until that pain is excised you will be susceptible to magics like this one. Shall I offer again?" He sounded almost lonely. "I offered once, Siobhán Walkingstick. Shall I offer again, to take away that pain?"

I closed the coat at my throat and shook my head. "I'd still say no. I have to. I'm sorry."

"Then see to the wounds that scar you," he advised. "Face them, Joanne. You cannot go on this way."

I thought of my mother, of the few things we'd managed

to say and all the ones left unsaid, and nodded. "I'm working on it."

Without condemnation, he said, "Work harder," and drew me to my feet. "She is yours to watch over now," he told Gary, and my big buddy lumbered over to hand me my shirt and hug me.

"Thank you," Cernunnos went on, still to Gary. "Had she not called you—"

"But I didn't." It was a terrible time to interrupt, but I honestly had no idea how Gary had arrived in the nick of time. "I needed the sword, I tried to call it, but..."

Cernunnos paused, looking at me, then waited on Gary, who spread his hands. "The fight was over, doll. Had been for a while. I was ridin' with the Hunt when the sword went all blue and started fadin'. I held on as hard as I could, an' next thing I know I was here and you looked like you could use some rescuin'."

"All I had to do to get you back was call the sword?" I had *not* called the sword at least twice in the past day, thinking it out of reach. All that worry over Gary for nothing. I clicked my heels together a couple times and muttered, "There's no place like home," then exhaled and gestured to Cernunnos, giving the floor back to him.

He inclined his crown of horns toward me, then addressed Gary again. "Had she not called you, I could not have followed. This is not my place, this world below the world. I belong elsewhere." He left us to crouch and collect Méabh's lanky form. She didn't move, didn't even groan, which scared me, but I wasn't about to risk another healing. Maybe Cernunnos could tell me someday if she'd made it. If he'd succeeded in bringing her to his world, and all the rest of her people with her.

As if he'd heard the thoughts, he said, "The *sí* are a gift to me, Joanne Walker. I could not have made this offer to them anywhere, anytime, else," and I remembered that his memory worked in both directions.

I cracked a grimace meant to be a smile of relief. "You just kept me from howling down the roof and bringing the Master here. Let's call it even."

He nodded and gave me the brief, wicked look that made my heart go pitter-pat, then, Méabh in his arms, mounted his silver stallion and rode away again, sunset swallowing them whole.

CHAPTER TWENTY-EIGHT

I knelt by the smear of Méabh's blood on the stones, fingertips just above it, not quite touching. There were ridges of dust in it already: some white, some black. I hadn't even seen Gancanagh die. It was probably just as well. I didn't think I'd have handled seeing Morrison fall very well. Still, it seemed like I'd owed him that much, even if Méabh and I had been trying to kill each other over him.

Gary came to stand beside me, a hand on my shoulder. "Pyrrhic victory, doll?"

I looked up, uncomprehending, and he said, "Me in exchange for her?"

"No. Jesus, no, don't ever think that. They—she, but they, somebody else died, too—they were gone before you showed up. And you saved my life. No. I just…" I glanced back down at the blood, thinking I ought to have tears. I ought to be able to cry. Somehow I was just too tired, right then. "What happened to you? I lost you. I thought I wasn't going to get you back. Did you win the fight?"

He said, "We won," with an odd note. I looked up again and he shook his head. "I'll tell you about it later. Point is, the cauldron got bound, and that was the whole reason for doin' it, right? Now, look, Jo," he went on before I could answer. His hand slid off my shoulder, an accusing finger pointed at my arm. "I know you said you could shapeshift now, but that ain't good. What's goin' on with you?"

I sighed. "I got bit by a werewolf."

His voice went suspiciously neutral. "When?"

I sighed again. "Saturday night. Sunday morning. Right before I got on the plane, anyway."

"Mike know 'bout this?"

Never in a thousand years was I going to get used to Morrison being referred to as Mike. "No."

"Joanne Grace Wa—" Gary's register went up like an outraged parent's, and almost idly, beneath the scold, I said, "Siobhán."

"She—what?"

It didn't seem quite possible that Gary, to whom I usually confessed all, was the last of my close friends to learn my proper name. People had been using it all day, in front of him even, but I kind of suspected it had been a lot more than one day for Gary, and that he'd probably had other things to worry about than what names people were calling me by. So I said, "Siobhán Grainne MacNamarra Walkingstick," mostly to the sparkling mess on the floor. "My name's not Joanne Grace, it's Siobhán Grainne, which is more or less the Irish version of Joanne Grace. I just figure if you're going to read me the riot act you might as well do it with all guns at your disposal."

"Your name ain't Joanne?" Gary sounded thunderstruck. I was afraid to look at him, for fear of seeing injury in his eyes.

"It *is*. It's what I've used my whole life. It's just not what's actually on the birth certificate. You know everything else about me. I thought you should know that, too."

"...does *Mike?*"

This was not the time to ask him to stop calling Morrison that. My shoulders slumped. "Yeah, he has for months. It came up a while ago."

"Jo." Gary touched my shoulder again, then knelt beside me, bushy eyebrows furrowed. "Jo, does he know about...?"

Grace under pressure, that was my Gary. Not willing to spell out the details of something I'd clearly been uncomfortable talking about. I hadn't been able to look at him while I told him about Aidan and Ayita, and he wasn't making me look at him now, either. I could have kissed him for that, though mostly I just wanted to curl up in his arms and rest. "That came up then, too. He's known longer than anybody else. Not the details, but he knows."

Gary exhaled noisily and let his hands fall into his lap. I dared a glance at him and found his gray gaze serious on mine. "That's about the most important thing, then, I figure. Even if I *oughta* read you the riot act. A werewolf, Jo? You got bit by a werewolf?"

"It was a rough weekend." I couldn't find anything else to say, except, eventually, "Méabh was trying to help me save my mother. Sheila was being turned into a banshee. I had to..." I made a small, almost helpless gesture. "I had to save her." I wondered if I had. We'd burned her bones and killed the banshee queen, but none of the banshees had come flooding down to thank us for our work and then gone off to that

happy banshee heaven in the sky. I had no idea where to look
for Sheila MacNamarra anymore.

"'Scuze me for sayin' so, but I think we gotta save *you*. What
woulda happened if Horns hadn't been here, Jo?"

I shuddered all the way from the bottom of my soul. "We'd
all be toast. I was about to hand you over to my—*the*—Master.
He made the werewolves. Méabh bound them to the moon. I
figured if I gave you and her up to him, he'd break the binding. It seemed like a good idea at the time." I'd cut holes in
jeans and shirts as a small child for that same reason. My father
had nearly exploded with frustration over not understanding
why I would do such a thing. I'd never been able to get across
that *it seemed like a good idea at the time* was all the reason I could
possibly need. It wasn't a *good* reason, I was willing to grant
that, but it was the only one I had. And handing my best friend
over to a murderous dark lord had seemed like a good idea at
the time.

Gary was right. We needed to save *me*. Because Mom, rest
her soul or not, was already dead, and could do only a limited amount of harm. I was alive, kicking and infected with a
poison that made me think selling my friends to the devil was
a good idea. "I don't even know where to go, Gary. We lost
our guide. Aibhill eviscerated him, too. She was the banshee
queen." There was so much he'd missed, in such a short time.
My head spun as I tried to figure out what was most important.
"Taking her out was supposed to free Mom, but..."

But the banshees had gone silent since Aibhill's screams had
faded. Not that I'd seen my mother among them, but it wasn't
like I'd gotten a really good look at the dozen or so left after
Méabh had finished razing her way through them. I'd have
thought they'd come down to wreak unholy vengeance on us

by now. I got to my feet, looking around the fallen castle first with ordinary sight, and then the Sight.

Evidently banshees could hide behind a sort of psychic shield, too, because they were clearly visible with the Sight. Eleven of them hung about in the rafters like right-side-up bats, and they were all staring at Gary with consternation. I looked at him, too, but didn't see anything to worry about. He was just himself, albeit armed with my shiny silver sword.

The sword with which he'd killed Aibhill. A rock dropped into the pit of my stomach. "Oh, dear."

"Oh, dear? Oh, *dear?* Jo, darlin', you don't say things like 'oh, dear.' What the hell does 'oh, dear' mean?" His aura got all trembly and bright, like an engine revving up.

"I think there's a new sheriff in town. Do you still have the Sight?"

"Nah, it wore off bef— What? What? Oh no. Waitaminnit." Gary stepped over the puddle of blood and shoved the sword into my hands. "I'm just the sidekick. You're the boss."

"Yeah, but you're the one who killed the O'Br—"

He clapped his hand over my mouth. "You're. The. Boss." He looked at the rafters and repeated that one more time, even more loudly.

One by one, eleven heads turned my way, gazes fixing on me with far more comprehension and acceptance than they'd shown in looking at Gary. I scowled accusingly at him, but not for very long. These were women scorned, after all. That was how they'd ended up as banshees. Probably leaving a man, any man, even a good man, in charge of them was not the world's best idea. Maybe even especially a good man, because they'd shred him while he was being decent-hearted. "All right," I said, resigned. "All right. I'm sure you're all wondering why

I've called you here. Can anybody tell me how to find my mother?"

As one, their attention turned from me to the ruined castle floors. I looked, too, but my mother wasn't imprisoned within the stone, or any other of the Poe-like dramatics that first leapt to mind. I was about to give them an earful when something moved.

The whole floor started coming alive, swirling, misting, rising up. No, not the floor: the silver-white dust that had recently been Aibhill. I gripped my sword harder and came up with a few choice words for however the hell magic-born beings were germinated. Shoving a blade through *anybody* should be enough to take them down permanently, although it wasn't, of course, enough to take *me* down permanently. That seemed like a bad line of thought to pursue, so I just gritted my teeth and got ready for another damned fight. Gary edged nearer to me, and I wished that Cat hadn't taken the spear with her when she ran. But then, I'd been supposed to be on her heels, so there'd have been no actual reason for her to leave it behind. Oh, well.

By the time I got through those sets of regrets and repudiations, Aibhill's mesmerizing gown had come together again. I wanted to stick the sword in her immediately, but there didn't seem to be any *body* there, just the amorphous dress. Rebuilding her lovely flesh took longer, and she remained wraithlike— I knew, because I poked her a couple times—until in one last sudden instant she coalesced as a whole, features suddenly back in place, long hair suddenly flowing, white hands reaching out. Only it wasn't Aibhill.

It was Sheila MacNamarra.

I had promised. I had *promised* Méabh that if it came to it, I would be the one to finish my mother off. And now Méabh was dead, or mostly dead, and there was nobody on hand to make me keep that promise except myself.

My newly risen mother was as beautiful as Aibhill had been, but dark-haired. Green-eyed. Those things were right; the beauty was not. Mom had been prettier than I was, but not beautiful. That made it easier to breathe, "I don't freaking *think* so," and launch myself at her.

The last thing I expected was a cage of magic bars to slam up around me and hold me in place. I bounced off them, sword clanging, and gaped in astonishment for a second or two. Aibhill had not demonstrated any ability to throw magic around. Then again, Aibhill probably hadn't been known as the Mage of Ireland while she'd lived. And on the third hand, now I *really* didn't understand how creatures of pure magic were birthed, because Mom had been a hundred percent human—well, minus the touch of *aos sí* blood, apparently—and now she patently was not.

On the fourth hand, I forgot my stupid magic wasn't working properly and retaliated.

Luckily, for some value of luck, I threw a net rather than trying any internal magics, and the external ones were mostly still working okay. Iron bars may a cage make, but magic nets weren't particularly stymied by them. My silver-and-blue net whisked through the narrow spaces between her gold-and-red cage and spun large, wrapping her as thoroughly as I'd been trapped. Her concentration broke for an instant and I surged through the dissolving cage bars.

Exasperation flitted across her features. She flung a hand up, palm toward me, and I hit another wall, bouncing onto my butt this time. Mages might be about spells and preparation, but from what I knew of my mother she would have a list of spells as long as her arm prepared. Probably longer. I was going to get knocked around a lot before she worked her way through all of them. Instead of getting up, I tightened my net, and that same mild exasperation showed before concussive power exploded the net all over the place.

I slithered down a distant wall with no real idea of how I'd gotten there. My head hurt. Worse, it rang like Notre Dame's bells, and the fragments of my magic were raw and sharp-edged as I tried pulling them back together. It felt like someone had gotten right inside my power and set off a grenade.

Which, of course, was basically what had happened. Sheila had, after all, been wrapped up nice and tight in a net of my magic. Moreover, she was my mother. She couldn't have been much more inside my magic than that, both literally and emotionally. It was just dawning on me that none of this fight was likely to go the way I wanted it to when she spoke. "I'll scream if I have to, *cuisle mo chroí*."

Cushla mahcree. I knew that phrase. Some of my aunts had used it with their children. It meant something like "my heart," and seemed a little peculiar to add onto the end of a threat.

Because it *was* a threat. I'd barely stood up to Aibhill's scream when it had brought my mother's voice into it. I'd shatter with Sheila's voice as the lead. So for once in my life I tried to do the smart thing, and didn't throw another net.

Well, mostly the smart thing, anyway. I did say, "I have to kill you, you know that, right?"

She came down to earth—I'd hardly noticed she'd been floating, but now that I thought about it, Aibhill had been, too—and knelt next to me. I scooted along the wall, trying to get far enough away to avoid sudden evisceration. She started to follow, then put her palms on the floor as if to say, "Look, no danger!" and otherwise held still. "I'm dead already, *alanna*. There's nothing left to kill."

"You're awfully damned mobile for a dead woman. And I don't do ghosts, so you're something else, and that just can't be good, so I've got to finish it. I promised Méabh."

Disappointment flashed across my mother's too-pale face. "I did so want to meet her. Joanne, Siobhán, *alanna* my dear. Would I be speaking to you this way if I belonged to them?"

I dared a glance at the them in question, the banshees who still hung about the rafters, all hungry haunted eyes and silent voices. "Aibhill was very reasonable, too. Right up until she gutted Méabh. So forgive me if I don't quite trust reasonable and polite."

"Aibhill," my mother said softly, "did not have the bond of bone and blood broken before her soul became the Master's. More, she did not have it done by her daughter, nor with the help of a goddess she had long since loved."

That whole ritual on the mountaintop seemed very distant just then. I looked at her for a long time, trying to understand what she meant, and finally said, "You mean it worked? You're free?"

"Free to choose, *cuisle mo chroí,* and I've chosen this cloak to wear."

I couldn't have heard her correctly. My expression indicated as much, and after a moment she smiled. Not Aibhill's sweet, syrupy smile, but a smile with points. With fangs. A smile that reminded me how my mother had chosen to die through willpower alone, and therefore a smile that I found peculiarly reassuring. I still had to say it. "Why on God's little green earth would you do that? This is… I mean, Mom. Doesn't this kind of cut you out of the circle of life? Of reincarnation? You've got to be an old soul, even if I'm not. Why would you do that?"

"There's not a one of them with power, my girl," Sheila said as if it explained everything. It didn't. She pursed her lips to hide another smile and went on. "Aibhill had power in her mortal life, *alanna*. The magic of her voice, to warn men of their deaths, but the magic to strike vengeance was the Master's alone. The rest are vassals only, creatures of Aibhill's making and of his. Without me, they remain his, but I have power, Joanne. I have the strength they do not. I can guide them. I can draw them away from *him,* and make them what they once were meant to be. Harbingers, not bringers, of death. There's no harm in knowing death comes," she added even more quietly. "It gives those that know how to take it a chance to say goodbye."

There were worlds of meaning in that, things we really probably should discuss, but sitting on the floor of a ruined castle in the Irish version of the Lower World, with banshees and my best friend overlooking us, was not the time or place to discuss them. I pulled my scattered brain cells together and said, "You've done an end-route," blankly. "You pulled a Hail Mary on the big bad. *Jesus,* Mom, that could have gone all wrong."

She smiled again. "I trusted you."

"Me?" Man, and I thought I wasn't too bright sometimes.

"That you would find your magic. That you would come back to Ireland to take up the mantle I discarded too early. That you would stop the ritual from being completed, and that I would be free to make the choices I had to make."

My throat was dry. "You took a hell of a risk."

"But I was right." Sheila MacNamarra stood and offered me a hand. "Now, my daughter, shall we end this fight we began together eight and twenty years ago?"

CHAPTER TWENTY—NINE

"Eight and twenty, Mom? Really?" Still, I got up and offered her my hand. Right hand. The left continued to be a dead weight. Sheila frowned and instead of taking the one I offered, reached for the useless other. I pulled about half an inch away, realized there was nowhere to hide and slumped as she caught the bitten flesh in her hands.

Her eyebrows drew down. "What's this magic you're working, my heart?"

"Magic I'm wo— I'm not working any magic! I got bit by a damned werewolf a couple days ago!"

She gave me a puzzled look. "So?"

"So my magic's screwed up because I'm trying to keep from going all furry!"

Silence met my outburst. After a long moment, my mother said, as gently as she could, "Sure and you don't think a bite transforms you into a werewolf, do you, *cuisle mo chroí?*"

"Of course it does. Everybody knows tha…" I swallowed. "Everybody knows that."

The queen of the banshees looked like she was trying not to laugh. "You've watched too many movies, Joanne. Where does magic come from?"

"Within." I actually knew that one, and as soon as I said it started to feel uncomfortable. "I mean… Well, yeah. It comes from within."

"And so how," she wondered, "could a bite, an external wound, change you from one thing to another?"

My face heated up and I grabbed my arm defensively. A wave of pain washed over me, which helped my righteousness as I snapped, "It's an infection. It gets into the blood. That's the whole idea of how werewolves work."

"Magic is bloodlines, my girl. It can't be forced on you from without. At most it can suggest, but the mind must be willing."

"Bullshit. I turned Morrison into a wolf last week. You can't tell me he was willing for that to happen."

Gary cleared his throat. "Didn't you say that whole spirit dance thing was softenin' people up for transformation, Jo?"

I gave him a gimlet stare. "Yeah. Spiritual transformation, though, not physical."

He shrugged one big shoulder. "Maybe, but you can't tell me Mike ain't willin' to take on you and your magic, sweetheart."

My jaw worked. Gary widened his eyes in an approximation of innocence. I spluttered, then muttered, "Okay, fine, you may have a point. But it's not like I'm lining up to *turn into a werewolf!*"

"You have the shifting power within you," Sheila said, and my stomach turned to lead. "If the thought is buried in your mind, Joanne, that this is what happens, then the magic within you may well grasp the magic without and bend toward its will. The wolf blood is borne from mother to daughter, but if an adept embraces the change, why should the blood not accept her?"

"So you're saying I'm turning myself into a werewolf?"

Way at the back of my mind, that obnoxious little voice I hadn't heard for a while said, "Ding!"

Its long silence did not make its return any more welcome. It was the voice of reason, the one I'd only started noticing around the time my shamanic gifts woke up. I hadn't thought about it, but if I had, I'd have thought I'd incorporated the voice of reason into my everyday thoughts, thus muffling its irritating commentary. Apparently I hadn't quite managed it.

If I was my own worst enemy, that explained why Áine had failed in cleansing the werewolf venom out of me. It also explained why Rattler had come closer to succeeding, but had still ultimately failed. I stared at my enflamed arm like I could set it on fire with the power of my mind, then despite myself, grinned. Good thing Caitríona had gone home, or she'd no doubt be glad to do it for me.

Humor faded, though, leaving me staring at my arm. "Can you heal it, Mom? Caitríona said you used to give them magic Band-Aids."

She shook her head as I glanced up. "Mage I may be, but healing lies within the realm of the living, *alanna*. It's your own self who'll have to do the job."

I'd been afraid she would say that. "You realize this is not a good time. I mean, we're hanging out in the Irish underworld, which the Master has corrupted half of, we've killed one of his dragons and his head banshee, and the new banshee boss in town is the twentieth-century version of his arch-enemy. And you think I should go have a nice communion with myself and get the werewolf bite all sorted out *now?*"

My mother, who had no particular right to use a Mother Knows Best expression on me, assumed one. "Do *you* think going into battle against the Master with his poison running in your veins is wise?"

It was just not fair that she actually did know best. I'd gotten this far with the infection—it had even been helpful in some ways—but I didn't really like to think about just how badly I might get twisted around if he could use the bite against me.

What I *did* like to think about was how much my odds of survival improved with Sheila MacNamarra on my side. I'd sworn up and down I'd take it to the mat this time if I had to, and I meant it. I was almost looking forward to it. The Master and I had had a date looming for over a year now and I'd grown eager to get it over with. And Mom had held him off more than once in the past, so maybe between the two of us we actually had a shot at—

—well. Who was I kidding. We weren't going to eliminate death and illness and horror. But maybe we could haul it back in line to some degree. Push for a world where as much money was spent on peace efforts year in and year out as was spent on war efforts. Fully funded schools while the Air Force held a bake sale to build their next bomber. That kind of thing. If we could drive the Master far enough underground, I could easily spend the rest of my life working to clean up the mess he'd made of the European Lower Worlds, and that could be considered a life well spent. I had other things I was planning to spend my life well doing, too—like one Captain Michael Morrison of the Seattle Police Department—but that wasn't at the top of my priorities just now. I said, "Okay," mostly to myself, then arched my eyebrows at Gary and Sheila. "Don't do anything fun while I'm gone, okay?"

"You mean like learn ta shapeshift?" Gary asked with a not-very-credible glower.

"Hey, you're the one who went off on shore leave with the guys for three days. You could've stayed home and been there for the fireworks."

Gary got a look that said he'd had some fireworks of his own over the weekend, and I realized I'd barely even asked him how the party had gone. There was a laundry list of catching up to do, never mind his adventures through time about which I'd not yet heard a peep. I pointed at him, said, "We gotta talk," then marched back to where Aibhill had fallen and gathered handsful of Gancanagh's dusty remains. It didn't take much to draw a small power circle around myself, and when I was done I sat in its center, black dust glittering in the failing light. Macabre, maybe, but it seemed suitable: he was of this land, and I could use all the friendly surrounds I could get. And Gan had certainly been friendly.

Circle in place, I was as safe from the Master's minions as I could get. I waved at Mom and Gary, then let my heartbeat be the drum that carried me to my garden.

For a rarity I came up through the water when I entered the garden, and strode out feeling a bit Diana at the hunt. That lasted right up until I saw an agitated Coyote pacing the stubbly grass. Technically he shouldn't have been able to wander into my garden uninvited, but that concern came secondary to why he was there at all. "Are you okay?"

He spun around on his heel, changing from animal form to man as he did so. He was breathtaking, as always. Brick-red skin, not a human color at all, and flawless black hair that fell loose to his hips. *That,* he had in real life, but not the skin tones or the golden eyes, which were currently shining with worry. He ran the few steps across the grass to catch me in something that wasn't exactly a hug and wasn't quite a shake, but fell somewhere in between. Then, as Gary often did, he set me back so he could see me, but with him there was a definite rattling of my teeth involved in the motion. "Me? Are *you* okay?"

I put my hands over his wrists and squeezed, not gently. Red-brick beauty or not, Coyote was two inches shorter than me both in real life and in his garden perception of himself, and I was, if not his equal in strength, pretty damned near. I was certainly strong enough to grind his wrist bones together, even if we hadn't been in my garden, where my will reigned supreme. He frowned, then let go of my shoulders as my grip grew increasingly clamplike. "Ow!"

"If you ever shake me again it's going to be a whole lot more than a little ow." I only released him after childish hurt turned to comprehension in his eyes. His "Sorry" was the grudging apology of a man embarrassed to have been caught out. I nodded and exhaled my own anger away. "What're you doing here, Cyrano?"

Maybe not *all* my anger, then. I'd spent a long time thinking Coyote was a spirit animal. After discovering he was a real live human boy—and learning his name—I'd started using the latter occasionally. Generally when I was annoyed with him. He noted it now, and his grudgingness melted away in a thin, acknowledging smile that turned slightly incredulous. "You came tearing into my garden, demanded the spear, went rushing off again with no explanation and you wonder why I'm here?"

Oh. "Oh. Everything's okay. I was just in a tight spot."

Coyote, with wonderful neutrality, said, "In Ireland's underworld."

"Right. Hey, look, since you're here, you want to gi—"

"JOANNE WALKER!"

I sat down hard and nearly swallowed my tongue as I looked up at him, all innocent eyes. "What? *What?*"

Coyote thrust a finger out. Not quite at me. Not after I'd squashed his wrists for shaking me. Just an imperious thrust, piercing the air. "What are you doing in Ireland, in the underworld, asking for the spear, which I see you no longer have, and *what* is wrong with your *arm!*"

Between him and my mother I was getting about all the outraged-parent scenario I could handle. I took a moment to be grateful Dad had raised me on his own so my parents couldn't double-team me, then said, as pleasantly as I could, "I'm in Ireland's underworld trying to find a cure for a werewolf bite," which was succinct and, in its way, accurate.

Coyote's long smooth hair took on a life of its own, strands rising like static pulled them hither and yon. It was a rather appealing show of magic and concern, and regret sluiced through me. It probably always would, when it came to Coyote. Some things couldn't help leave a mark. He, unaware of my thoughts, demanded, "And the spear?"

"I gave it to the Irish Mage."

His mouth opened and shut, but evidently he couldn't find fault with that particular answer. After a minute he, too, sat, rubbing his hands over his face. "Werewolf bite, Jo?"

"It was," I said for the hundredth time, "a rough weekend. Look, I've left my dead mother and Gary hanging around in the underworld while I've come here to try to heal this thing, so while there's an awful damned lot I need to talk to you about, right now is probably not the time to do it. You've known me longer than anybody else. Do you think you can help?"

"Jo, a werewolf—a shapechanger, a skinwalker of any kind—a skinwalker shouldn't be able to…" He struggled for a word and settled on, "Infect. Shouldn't be able to infect you. The healing magic should keep it away, and you can't shape-shift yet, so—"

I said, "Actually," into my elbow, and he fell into a voluminous silence. Poor Coyote. For the past week I'd been doing variations on rushing into his consciousness, screeching for help and rushing out again with nary a word of explanation. I ran through the details of the past several days mentally, then summarized it all with, "The shapeshifting lesson this weekend went fine. No flounders. I did what you told me, I kept an animal in mind to shift into and so far I've done a snake and a coyote and a werewolf, but according to my mother the whole wolf thing is me embracing the shapeshifting in a totally screwed-up way."

Coyote, with what struck me as remarkable restraint, said, "Isn't your mother dead?"

"Yeah."

"I see." He sat there waiting for more for a full thirty seconds before concluding I wasn't going to delve any deeper into that particular well, then sighed from the depths of his soul. "Of course I'll help."

He didn't even put a caveat on, which I thought was very gentlemanly of him. I leaned forward and caught his hand with mine. "I swear I'll call you and tell you the whole story, all of it, no holds barred—" except maybe the part about Morrison kissing me "—and then I'm going to beg you for mentorly advice, because, holy crap, am I in over my head."

"Call," he said, making a phone with his fingers, "or call?" he said, gesturing around the garden.

"Call," I said, repeating the garden motion, and he smiled.

"All right. If I may, then?" He nodded toward my over-heated left arm and I flopped it toward him. A hiss escaped between his teeth as he touched it and almost withdrew. "Sorry if that hurt."

"Actually, it didn't." I knew perfectly well that was worse than it hurting. It suggested somewhere within me I'd started accepting the changes, and that was bad. "I'm fighting myself," I said quietly. "My hind brain is running with the 'werewolf bites mean turning into werewolves!' thing and the healing magic, which I guess is smarter than I am—"

Coyote gave me a look that suggested tree frogs were smarter than I was, but didn't say it. I half smiled and con-tinued. "Anyway, I guess it's going great guns holding the infection in place, not letting it spread. Or not spread quickly, anyway. Nobody else has been able to get a foothold against it."

"Who's tried?"

"A goddess and a spirit animal."

Coyote's eyes popped like Sylvester the Cat's, but he got his expression back under control. "Were either of them invited?"

"Not per se." I knew a cue when I heard one, though, and straightened my spine so my lungs could be properly filled and my "Coyote, will you heal me?" could come out as a nice solid request.

For some reason it made him laugh. I huffed and he laughed again, then, trying for ritual solemnity, replied, "I will," before cracking up a third time. "Sorry. I just expected something a lot more formal. Magic makes people talk funny, have you noticed?"

"Have I ever. But I couldn't figure out a way to dress it up any more than that."

"No, asking for a healing is really pretty straightforward.

All right, listen, Jo. Two things. One, this is probably going to hurt, and two…" He hesitated, regret creasing lines around his mouth. "It's going to require not holding anything back. That shouldn't be hard…."

It shouldn't be, because we'd had a handful of amazing days together only a few months earlier. We'd gotten under each other's skins, into each other's magics and seen each other's souls in a way that only a couple of magic users could ever do. It had been the safest, most comfortable, most erotic intimacy I'd ever imagined.

And then Coyote had gone home to Arizona, and I'd stayed in Seattle, and the truth was, neither of us was going to give up our lives for the other.

More than that, though, was Morrison's presence in my life. I'd been half in love with Coyote since I was a teenager. He was home to me in a way nobody else could ever be. But Morrison was the one who made me dizzy and weak-kneed and splendidly angry and passionately happy. Coyote's magic was breathtaking. Morrison's solidity was my world. Coyote and I both knew it. It hurt him more than it hurt me, but I didn't want to rub salt in the wound.

On the other hand, I didn't want to turn into a werewolf, either. I sighed. "No holds barred, 'Yote. I said that already."

"Okay." He kept my left hand in his right and put his left over my heart. Nice circle, I thought: heart magic. Without thinking I put my right hand over his heart, too. Not as intimate as the left hand, heart-to-heart, but since my left hand was a festering lump of burning infection, that was probably okay. Coyote nodded once, and I Saw his power light up, blocking the poison magic from the rest of my body with the circle he'd created.

Then desert heat exploded in my veins, and everything went white for a while.

CHAPTER THIRTY

A coyote and a wolf fought on a desert mesa. Eggshell-blue sky, hard white earth, a too-large sun pounding relentlessly on the combatants. The wolf was larger, black-furred, green-eyed and looked hot. The coyote, rangier, golden-eyed and quick, was more comfortable in the heat, but outgunned in terms of body weight. I was too far away to help either of them. I was, in fact, trussed and dangling upside-down from a dead white tree for the second, and I fervently hoped the final, time in my life.

The air this time wasn't so hot as to be unbreathable. Not quite. I could just barely manage small sips, enough to keep me from gasping at the lack of oxygen. The sounds of battle carried through it: snarls, growls, bites, yips, howls and less obvious noises like claws scrabbling for purchase against hard dirt. Furthermore, heat waves played with the distance, so at some moments the fight seemed very far away and, others, startlingly near. Discomfort fluctuated in my own body as the fight changed distances, sometimes rocketing past pain into blinding agony, other times rolling back to nothing more than a vague nuisance. I kind of thought the waves should reflect which animal seemed to have the upper hand, but there didn't appear to be a correlation. Or if there was, it hurt more when Coyote was winning. That didn't seem quite fair.

Of course, I was hanging upside-down from a bleached-out desert tree, so I probably wasn't in much position to be dictating what was and wasn't fair. The wolf left black oily footprints behind as it fought, reminiscent of the black shapeless horrors that had formed themselves into the werewolves back at the dawn of time. Once in a while Coyote stepped in some of the goo. My heart rate accelerated every time, in half-rational conviction he would be contaminated by it.

I didn't quite see it coming when the two animals locked on each other's throats. I felt it, though. Felt it in my bloodstream: the blue-gold desert power Coyote brought to the game firing all cylinders against the wolf's slick black magic. My whole body shuddered, contorting into a shape not meant to have arms tied behind its back. I tried for a scream, managed a croak and realized a little belatedly that I was letting Coyote do all the work for me.

My experiences in the desert had mostly been getting pummeled by somebody else's magic. I didn't really know what would happen if I called on my own. On the other hand, I had a fairly clear idea of what would happen if I *didn't,* and it involved my mentor and one-time lover getting his ass handed to him. I bit my tongue until saliva flooded my mouth, and with that one tiny wet swallow, nerved myself to face the healing power again.

It was losing ground, even with Coyote shoring it up. Silver-blue was being eaten alive, mutated, corrupted, by the buzz-

ing spill of black oil. I pushed back, tentatively, and my flesh
wracked again, a modicum of ground regained. I was going to
have to regain a lot more than that, and fast, or my extremities
were going to be pulled from their sockets as I became more
and more wolflike. Healer or no, that was not something I
was eager to experience. I shoved again, this time whispering,
"Your own worst enemy," to myself.

It was true. I had been since the beginning. I'd been some
other people's worst enemy, too, often people I'd meant to be
a friend to, but mostly I'd been in my own way. There were a
million faces to my impediments: my mother, my father, my
children, my job prospects, my romantic prospects—basically
I'd thrown everything I could think of in the way. Excuses
or reasons, regardless of what I called them, they stood there
like trenchermen, my own personality determined to hold me
back.

But so much had gotten cleared away recently. I had to go
back to North Carolina, that was increasingly obvious, but
beyond my dad and Aidan, I'd done so well lately. Like I'd told
my mother, I'd gotten the magic, the guy, the job. I didn't have
much left to be afraid of, and no sense at all of why I should
be so afraid that turning into a werewolf seemed like a better
option.

"You're afraid of success," my own voice said to me. I bobbled around to see myself, aged fifteen, standing a few yards
beyond the deadwood tree. It was the angry version of me, the
one that had lost all contact with the shamanic heritage she'd
been learning about. She'd chopped her hair off in defiance,
and if she wasn't already, she'd be pregnant within a few weeks,
in her timeline. I thought she was a brat.

She was also painfully clear-sighted about some things. She,
who had fought the whole damned world tooth and nail, had

gotten me through a confrontation with a Navajo Maker god by demanding to know why it was *I,* the person she'd become, thought everything *had* to be a fight. It didn't, it turned out. Some things needed acceptance, not railing against. I had no idea how she'd figured that out, when I, a dozen years older and presumably wiser, certainly hadn't. So if she was turning up to let me know new and obvious ways in which she thought I sucked, I should probably listen.

"Who the hell," I demanded, "is afraid of *success?*"

"You are." She walked around me, eyeing the ropes and the dead tree with a sort of scathing respect. Respect for the bindings, scathing for me. "Seriously, look at you. You've spent my entire life running from responsibility and pretending all you're good for is fixing cars. Only, oh, no! It turns out that if you're, like, forced to be, you're pretty good at some other stuff, too. And now you've finally tapped into the real power I was working toward before you screwed me over, and you're all 'Oh, my God! More responsibility!'" She made spooky wavy hands and put a tremble in her voice with the last bit. "'Oh, no! I've gotten this far but I can't handle *even more responsibility!* What if I screw up with it? Worse! What if I don't! What if it turns out I can actually, like, be *really* good at saving the world and helping people? No, no, Brer Rabbit, we can't risk that, better get turned into a horrible monster instead! Oh, my God, Morrison really likes me! We can't have that! I better run off and get myself killed fighting banshees instead! Oh, no! Mom didn't hate me after all! I better—'"

"ALL RIGHT ALREADY." *Jesus* but I didn't like that kid. I bobbled around in another circle and glared when she came back into view. "What're you doing here, anyway? I didn't go stealing power from you this time, there's no time loop to cl—"

Scathing respect had faded into the rant, but now scathing pity rose to replace it. "Are you kidding? We're almost at the end of the time loop now. Not just ours, but the big one, the one the Master and the Morrígan set in place when they made the cauldron. I always would've been here, in Ireland, fighting this fight, because of what happened with us and Mom and the banshee before we were born. This is it," she said a lot more softly. "This is the end of me. Tie us up with a bow. Tell Coyote goodbye, because from here on out it's all you, *Siobhán.*"

Desert heat or not, the idea that my younger self was facing her last moments was a bucket of cold water in the face. I didn't like her, but she appeared to have her shit together in a way I hadn't for a long time, and she had, frankly, deserved better than me. I tried to wet my lips, had nothing to do it with and croaked, "Sorry."

"Don't be *sorry*. Be *good*. Be right. Be a hero." She'd demanded that of me once before, and I supposed if anybody did, she had the right. She pointed at my arm, at the shiny red-hot infection, said, "Man up, Joanne," and vanished.

Right there in that instant, she healed me. Not because she was throwing power around, but because she'd hit me so hard I had to see the world a different way, and that was all it took for a shaman. Just a moment's change of viewpoint. I'd been so proud of myself for doing increasingly well it had never occurred to me I might be afraid of doing better yet. Of succeeding. But my younger self, brat or not, was nobody's fool, either, and all of a sudden I could see success for the huge, scary beastie that it was.

I'd never had ambitions toward greatness. I genuinely believed I'd have been happy running a mechanic shop, tinkering with Petite and drinking beer with the guys on days off. But that wasn't in the cards, and I'd gotten good at the hand I'd been dealt. I'd been pleased with that and hadn't wanted more. It never crossed my mind that being dealt an even better hand would scare me, but Joanne The Younger was right.

It terrified me. And terror, George Lucas forgive me, was the way to the dark. Realistically I should've been scared spit-less back when this began, but I hadn't known enough. I'd just resented it. Now, when I knew a lot more, I didn't have nearly as much to be afraid of, even if the potential power load had increased. Now I had Billy and Melinda. Now I had Gary. I had Coyote. I had Morrison, and it was all his damned fault I'd gotten better at things anyway, because not only had he been more willing to use my esoteric skill set, but because I, foolish creature that I was, hadn't wanted to disappoint him.

He was going to be very disappointed if I came home from Ireland a werewolf.

Coyote nominally had the healing gig in hand. I didn't try to usurp it. I just ripped down all the shells and shields and protective barriers and finally, finally let my fresh new topped-up Siobhán Walkingstick magic flow in behind his, his robin's-egg-blue flooding forward on a tide of steely-blue, his hot-desert-gold cooled by a rush of my silver.

For just an instant there I was raw to him. Exposed, open, vulnerable. It was mostly about Morrison, between us. My former boss, silver-haired, blue-eyed, solid as the earth. My laughter, my tears, my safety and my future. My everything, these days.

For the space of a breath, his presence between us cut too deep. Coyote retreated, leaving me all alone against the black magic running through my veins. I staggered, shocked at its strength. I thought I could beat it, but not easily. I couldn't do everything alone, after all. I'd found that out the hard way. But I'd do this alone, if I had to, because I was not going to go home to Morrison all furry and toothy.

Then the breath was gone and Coyote's power surged back to the fore, leading mine in a ferocious battle against the wolf. Two coyotes on the mesa now, and the black wolf dwindled simply because of my attention, my presence, in the battle. I sensed its rage as the infection grew less profound, sensed the threads that had slowly bound me closer to the Master shriveling and sensed *his* fury that one of my lineage had once more slipped through his fingers.

But not all of us. Crystal-clear thought in the midst of his anger. *Master's meal was a little wild, bore herself a wee boy child.* The one precious piece of information Sheila had garnered while still in his thrall. The one thing she'd shared with the Master, before her bones were burned and he lost most of his hold on her.

I could all but feel his promise: that he would find and destroy Aidan not for the sake of damaging the family line, but sheerly for revenge against *me*. Me, the one who had helped Sheila MacNamarra get away thirty years ago and just last night. The one who had thrown down a gauntlet a few months ago, a gauntlet the Master had declined—or been unable—to take up.

I whispered, "Like hell. I'm coming for your witch Morrígan and then I'm coming for you."

Raucous laughter answered me. Raven's laughter, harsh and unkind. Heard a challenge in that laughter, a dare: if I met the Morrígan, he would come to me himself. Right here, right now. We could finally go mano a mano, and if I won, well, then. He would leave Aidan be.

"You'd have to, you stupid bastard. I'm gonna kick your ass

so far back into the caves even the cavemen won't be able to find you. I'll see you at Tara, you son of a bitch."

The Master cackled again and the threads along which we communicated were suddenly gone. So was the ache, the infection, the terrible redness in my arm. The black magic receded, and in the planescape of psychic battle, the wolf simply disappeared. I snapped back to the hanging tree, still dangling upside-down, and Coyote, limping, disheveled, his hair in tangles, came across the mesa and sat at the foot of the tree with a thud.

Big Coyote, who hadn't been there before, but who was also always here in this desert, meandered up and shoved his nose into Coyote's hand, which made him chuckle and drag the gleaming animal into a hug. They were astonishing together, Big Coyote's every strand of fur a bristling wire of gold or copper or brass, and his eyes full of stars, while my Coyote was a sweat-stained red-skinned tangle-haired dirty mess. Or he was at first. All of it washed away under Big Coyote's lean, and my Coyote looked refreshed when he let the archetype go. "Seriously," he said as I rotated in another slow circle: tree, desertscape, blinding sky, more desert, tree and coyotes again. "Seriously," my Coyote repeated, "you thought I was *him?*"

They wobbled out of my view as I spun again. Twisting my head toward them only made an impending headache worse, so I stopped trying and mumbled, "Well, yeah. Back in the day. I didn't know better."

Big Coyote snorted. So did Little. I tried shrugging, but that made my head hurt, too. Hanging upside-down was not my favorite place to be. "Look, I'm sorry, okay? But we won, right? Does that mean someone's going to let me down now?"

The two coyotes exchanged glances in a way that didn't bode well for the home team. But then Coyote, my Coyote, got up and did something I couldn't see to the ropes. They went elastic-y and dropped me on my skull, which was moderately better than hanging upside-down. It wasn't good, though, and I spent a minute with my arms curled around my head, trying to get past the starbursts in my vision. When I finally looked up, both coyotes looked like I was their idea of a great afternoon's entertainment. I started to say something caustic, then thought better of it. "You guys saved my bacon. Thank you."

Big Coyote's tongue slurped halfway around his head, like not even amazing animistic representations of archetypes were immune to the power of bacon. I had another dizzy moment of wondering when, exactly, I'd last eaten something worth calling food, and hoped all this not-eating would have knocked off the five or so pounds I'd put back on recently. If it had, I promised I wouldn't eat so many doughnuts once I got home. And that I would take up jogging. And follow through on whatever other rash promises I'd made over the past several days. "Coyote?"

One pricked his ears and the other sat up a little straighter. I chuckled, but it was the second one I spoke to, humor fading fast. "I'm supposed to say goodbye to you f—"

"*What?* Joanne, no, you—"

Okay, that hadn't been the best way to launch into the goodbye. I sat up, grateful my head had stopped throbbing, and waved my hands in the face of his protests. "Listen! Stop freaking out! I'm supposed to say goodbye from…me. From me fifteen years ago, from me you started teaching when I was a kid. She's…"

Little Coyote looked uncomprehending while I searched for the right way to explain, but Big Coyote's star-filled eyes were sad and acknowledging and maybe a little proud. He, at least, understood what had gone on between my younger and current self. Probably understood better than I did, for that matter. And he was certainly in a position to be watching over time loops, so he must have known this one was coming to an end.

"She's been this annoying little voice of reason at the back of my skull for ages now," I said after a while. "My dream self, the part of me that remembered your teachings even after I went and ripped them away from myself mid-lessons. But she says no matter what, she would have ended up here, fighting this fight in Ireland, and that means we're coming to the end of her. I'm…integrating. Siobhán and Joanne and magic and…all of it. So she—" In the middle of the sentence I understood. She, the younger Joanne, the one who'd been in love with Coyote, was the one saying goodbye. Another loop closed. I faltered, then swallowed and, helpless, said, "She loved you. She loves you. And she's…"

"Gone." One rough low word from my mentor, and suddenly even Big Coyote's brilliance wasn't enough to make Little Coyote reflect shining glory. He turned his face away, giving me a profile shot: strong nose, strong jaw, restless black hair, brick-red skin against the bleached desert whiteness. Beautiful. Perfect. Very literally the man of my childhood dreams.

And then, because this was a landscape of the mind, and because magic let us do things that we couldn't otherwise, because of those things, and because I'd finally and for the last time broken his heart…

…he was gone.

CHAPTER THIRTY-ONE

I opened my eyes to find Gary and my mother sitting cross-legged up against a half-fallen wall, both of them laughing so hard they had tears running down their faces. My mother had Gary's forearm in one hand as she wheezed, "She didn't, she didn't!" and wiped tears away with the other, and Gary nodded so merrily it appeared his head would go bobbling off.

It was so completely incongruous with the farewell I'd just experienced I just sat there, offended on general principles, and waited for them to notice I'd woken up. Instead my mother threw her head back and shrieked like a delighted banshee, laughter bouncing off the crumbling walls.

I looked upward. The surviving banshees still sat in the oak rafters, many of them with expressions of accusation. This was not how things were done, and it was clearly all my fault. I shrugged a protestation of innocence, and when Gary started in with, "That's nothing, you should've seen her when—" I decided I'd better take matters into my own hands before I found out for sure they were in hysterics over me.

I cleared my throat. Loudly. Gary, without the slightest hint of guilt, looked up, beamed and said, "There you are, darlin'. You never told me your old lady was so much fun," which made my solemn, reserved, Altoids-loving mother whack his shoulder.

"Auld me foot," said she, "sure and you're old enough to be me own father, so let's hear none of this auld lady nonsense. How's your arm, Joanne?"

I couldn't think of anything I'd done half so funny as to bring people to such gales of laughter, but I couldn't shake the feeling they were laughing at me, so I extended my arm petulantly without speaking. The action sounded like wings whispering together, which made my skin crawl, but there was no sign of bite or infection under the shredded remains of my coat sleeve.

"There's me lass!" my mother said in delight. "I knew it couldn't keep ye down. Now to—" Now to notice my expression, apparently, because her gaiety fell away into concern. "Joanne?"

"I'm fine. What's so funny?"

Gary lumbered to his feet and came to offer me a hand up. "I was just tellin' her some stories about me and Annie back in the day. I wish you coulda met her, Jo. You'da liked her."

Annie, Gary's wife, who had died on their forty-eighth wedding anniversary, three years before I'd met Gary. Annie, who'd been a nurse and whose bout of illness had left her unable to bear children. Annie, who had largely kept them together financially for years, allowing Gary to pursue a love of saxophone playing that had never quite turned professional. Annie, who would have, according to Gary, approved of me.

I wished I'd known her, too, and I felt like a complete jerk for assuming they'd been laughing at me. I took Gary's hand and let him pull me up, then stepped out of my dust circle to hug him. He grunted, surprised, but returned the embrace, and when I let go, my mother looked suspiciously misty-eyed. "He's a charmer," she said to me. "I might want to steal this one away from you."

Great. Even my dead mother, who had been told better, thought I possibly had something going on with Gary. I said, "You can't. You're dead," which wasn't very charming or even daughterly, and given what little I knew of my mother, also might not have been true. If anybody could come back from the grave to steal a guy, it would probably be her. The idea sent another whisper of wings over me, a shiver up and down my spine. It wasn't that I lusted after Gary, but the idea of my mother going after him was creepy.

Sheila MacNamarra gave a cheerful shrug and finally, as far as I could tell, turned her attention to the banshees she'd in-herited. She didn't say anything, but they came floating down from the rafters like recalcitrant schoolgirls, all eyeing one another to see who'd caused the trouble.

"There'll be no more of the murderin' and sacrificin'," Sheila announced. "This is your chance, lasses. Your chance to lay down arms and an eternity of lament, if that's what you want. Too much was asked of you already, and I'll not ask more if it's ready to rest you are."

Half—more than half—of the wailing women faded almost instantly, like just the offer was such a relief they could now let go of whatever held them to the afterlife. I was sure it couldn't be that simple, not after all the hoopla we'd gone through to make sure Sheila got free of the Master's clutches, but it was probably a start.

Sheila smiled and stepped toward the ones who'd faded. Lifted her hands, as if in benediction, and all of them came forward eagerly. I wasn't using the Sight, but just then I didn't need to be: power suddenly roared in my mother, flame erupting from her palms. Papery banshees barely had time to burn, mostly turning from wraiths to ash inside an instant.

But the fire still burned, and I triggered the Sight half knowing what I'd see.

Lifelines, if that's what they could be called. Lifelines alight with flames that rushed their length, growing ever-hotter as they spread from the Lower World into the Middle, all the way to Knocknaree and its many cairns, only the largest of which was Méabh's. Flames burst from half a dozen or more of the smaller cairns, abrupt explosions that faded as quickly as they'd begun. Old bones immolated, releasing the women who'd lived in them to a gentler sort of death than the one they'd known so far. I reeled the Sight in, not yet prepared to follow it back to the Middle World, and heard a familiar *klok klok klok!* I smiled, comforted by the idea that the banshees would be guided into the great beyond, and looked at those who were left.

Six of them. Six out of twenty-four, which seemed like both a lot and not many at all to me. My mother looked pleased. "Spoiling for a fight, are the rest of you? That's grand so, for I've one waiting. All these years you were meant to be harbingers, not bringers, of death. What say you we warn a witch of her coming demise? The Morrígan awaits us, lasses, and after her, her master. I've been preparing for this fight a lifetime and longer. Will ye's join me?"

I wondered briefly what she would do if they said no, but before I really had time to worry about it, the five of them spun together in a gleeful shrieking whirlwind, then broke apart, seized Gary and me and carried us into the night.

★ ★ ★

It struck me a little late that perhaps this had all gone terribly wrong. That I had trusted my dead banshee mother because she was my mother, and had foolishly overlooked the dead and banshee parts. In retrospect, it almost certainly wasn't a good thing that she'd risen from Aibhill's silvery-white ashes. I hoped, as we got whisked across the Lower World's Irish landscape, that I would have a chance to rectify my increasingly obvious error.

Sheila was nowhere to be seen, no matter how I twisted and turned in my banshees' grasps. I didn't want to writhe too much, as I had no idea how high we were or how, exactly, a fall to earth in the Lower World might affect me. Or worse, how it might affect Gary, since I, as a shaman, might get a free pass on being dropped from unknowable heights in magic realms.

The banshees apparently couldn't fly without screaming bloody murder. I raised my voice, then raised it again, and ended up shouting futilely into the wall of sound they made: "Gary? Gary, can you hear me? Are you okay? *Gary?*"

Of course he couldn't hear me, and it was too damned dark to see him. As soon as we landed somewhere I was going to get positively medieval on somebody's ass. I thought about taking a quick trip to my garden and once more shrieking for Coyote's help, but having just broken his heart into a zillion pieces I wasn't sure that was such a great idea. Especially when I couldn't think of anything he could do: battles were not his strong suit, and we weren't in a good position to distract our captors anyway.

Around about that thought, I noticed a distant light in the east. My stomach, which had plenty of height to do it from, plummeted. Maybe there'd been a chance to save my mother, but if dawn was coming on, we'd blown it. It was without a doubt past the year-and-a-day marker, if the sun was rising.

For a hazy minute I wondered why the Master had used the equinoxes instead of the solstices to bind Sheila. She'd died the evening of the winter solstice. Maybe the Master had been concerned about the niceties of stealing her body from a mortuary slab, but probably not. Maybe he just hadn't gotten the memo about her death in time. Or maybe he'd realized even I, the prodigal daughter, would have been upset about Sheila's body disappearing from the mortuary. Fifteen months ago he'd known more about my potential than I had. Possibly wisdom had been the better part of valor, even for the high and mighty bad guy.

The high and mighty bad guy who had won one, this time around. I sagged in my banshees' grips, then bared my teeth at the white dawn. To hell with that. I'd give him half a victory at most. I still had the Morrígan to deal with, and I had every intention of taking her out. Lugh deserved as much. Lugh and all the kings who had come before him, right up to Eochaidh, the first of the cauldron born. Born and borne: borne across time and oceans and continents, all the way to Seattle, where Suzanne Quinley could unmake a zombie and change the course of history. That girl and I had a serious talk coming, as soon as I got home.

Sunrise, I thought idly, wasn't usually white.

A few seconds later I straightened in my banshees' grasps, gaping at the distant earth. Sunrise *wasn't* white. *Tara* was white, a bastion of power glowing so brilliantly I didn't need the Sight to see it. Like the spotlights after the twin towers fell, its circle of light shot straight up into the darkness, only gradually dissipating into mist and soft stars.

My shout of glee silenced even the banshees. Gary's voice

came suddenly clear: "Joanne? Jo? Jo! What's goin' on? Where are we? Are you arright?"

I bellowed, "I'm fine! I dunno what's happening, but we're not out of time yet!" and only belatedly realized that might not make a whole lot of sense. I started to explain, but the banshees got over their surprise and began wailing again, which left me effectively voiceless. But at least I knew Gary was still with me, and relatively safe. For the value of safe that meant "being hauled through the air by banshees," of course, but it was better than, say, being dashed to the ground by banshees.

Tara grew more impressive as we flew closer. I'd seen it in its ancient glory, but an aerial view gave me a whole new appreciation for just how much territory the age-old holy site encompassed. It had to be half a mile or more across, and its Lower World replica had never been desecrated or destroyed. In fact, I suspected the Lower World version was in all ways more impressive than the Middle World's original.

This one had a moat between the double row of oak henges that marked the site's boundaries, just like the Middle World one had had thousands of years ago. But this moat had the smooth look of a deadly undercurrent, and I had the impression it ran much deeper than the Middle World's moat had. This one was a captured—or coaxed—river, cutting Tara away from the rest of the world.

Inside the moat's borders, ancient buildings still stood. The Hall of Kings, the Mound of Hostages, which in my time was a lumpy hill, and here, now, was a cairn with a narrow birthing canal that I bet looked out at a rising or setting sun on some important day of the year. Forts sprang up within the site's boundaries, forts and temples and food halls and forges, the last of which made me smile. Maybe there'd been no forge in the Middle World, but the idea of it had stamped itself onto the Lower World's copy of Tara. I glanced south, finding the distant tower at Troim, and saw it, too, glimmered with power. The other three towers, marking the outermost sphere of Tara's influence, also stood squat and strong in the Lower World.

And at the heart of it all, at the center of the light, was the *Lia Fáil.* I wondered if it had ever glowed so brilliantly in the Middle World. It should not, I thought, be so pure here, where the Master's power had reigned for so long. But so many little things had gone wrong for him: the Morrígan had sacrificed only a dozen or so *aos sí* kings to their cauldron before she and it were bound; the banshees had failed repeatedly to offer him sustenance over the past few decades. Moreover, the Tara of the Middle World had remained a place of human worship for generations after the *sí* had slipped away. Maybe that, too, had made it less the Master's ground than mine. Something had, certainly, because at the heart of the Irish Lower World, Tara had held off corruption and its centerpiece, the *Lia Fáil,* was a bastion of hope and light. Elation stung me for about half a moment. If Tara could hold its own against the dark, maybe I could hold *my* own against the Morrígan.

The banshees dropped suddenly, bringing us closer to the power circle. I shrieked and tried to duck as we rushed the double row of oak henges. I'd passed under them with Nuada in his era, and they'd been easily twice my height, unquestionably impressive.

These ones, though, were *massive. Twice my height* ceased to be a useful term of measurement. They stood *stories* in height, two modern-building stories, pushing twenty-five or thirty feet. Every henge post was a tree unto itself, so large Gary and I wouldn't be able to reach around and touch hands. The adjoining slabs were equally huge, six or eight feet thick. Different-colored wood blended together in the top slabs, and

I had the impression that each of them was made from the two trees upon which they rested. It was beautifully sympathetic magic.

The banshees bounced off its sympathy like ping-pong balls. Gary and I didn't.

Momentum kept us going, but not nearly far enough. We hit the swiftly flowing moat—which probably wasn't a moat if it had a current—about two-thirds of the way across its twenty-foot breadth, and the current whisked us away. I caught a glimpse of the banshees all but rubbing their noses in offense at having hit a wall, and then I was too busy trying to keep my head above water and worrying about Gary to think about the banshees.

The current was impossibly strong. I wondered if there was a river beneath Tara in the Middle World, one ready to suck down unwary travelers, but I wondered it with my head underwater and panic building in my chest. I was an okay swimmer, but not in stompy boots and a leather coat and besides, I'd need to be a damned dolphin to keep ahead of the current, and I was forty-seven years younger than Gary, which meant he was probably in twice as bad trouble as me. I couldn't lose him. Not again. I kicked up, broke the surface and went down again without a whimper. All that splashing and screaming that went on in films when people were drowning was bullshit. Real drownings happened silently and fast, the body too concerned with surviving to flail or shout. I knew that. I didn't think I'd ever experience it firsthand. My lungs already hurt, and any second I was going to gasp for air where there wasn't any. I couldn't even see Gary.

I would need to be a dolphin to survive the current.

The last thing I remembered clearly was screaming *Rattler!* inside my head. After that it turned into impressions, the way being a wolf had been, except there was no burst of excruciating pain as I gave in to the change. I lost my clothes, suddenly free and comfortable with my skin naked, to the water. The current was exciting, fast, throwing me around. I leapt into the air, chattering with delight. Hit the water again and my squeaks bounced off a familiar shape. A man. A man in trouble. Dolphins rather liked humans, a shared affinity between big-brained mammals. Darting against the current was easy.

The man was cold, clumsy. I slipped away from him and returned, trying to get his useless long flippers over my back. Failed. The man was like a drowning baby. It took many to keep a baby afloat, but there was only me. I pushed him up with my nose. He broke the surface. I rolled, putting a flipper under him while I breathed. Dove again, nose poking his back. Push push push. Toward the shore, where men were supposed to be.

He came to life with a surge. I clicked with pleasure and flipped over. He grabbed my fin. We went to shore. No beach, just deep water and then land. He grabbed for land and missed. I dove. Came up under him, between his lower fins. Rose all the way out of the water on my tail. Flung us both forward—

—Gary hit the earth and I smashed down beside him, landing on my belly with my arms sprawled wide and Rattler hissing horrified amusement at the back of my skull. Dolphins weren't desert animals. Not, in his opinion, the sort of thing I should be turning into. I was just grateful I hadn't turned into a flounder, and flopped onto my back, heaving for breath.

My stomach cramped, not with the need to pursue magic, but with simple hunger. I caught a sob between my teeth and Gary, gasping for air himself, sat up in a panic. "Jo? You okay?"

"I'm so hungry I could cry." It was such a pathetic complaint in the face of almost drowning I laughed, except it turned into another sob. I was a child of the first world. I used the phrase "I'm starving" lightly, because I could. But right then I swore I could feel my body turning on its own resources to fuel itself. My extra five pounds had to be history. My muscles felt like they were going that way, too, shriveling under a healing magic's desperate need to find something to survive on.

"Joanie, you look bad. Where's your clothes?" Gary started patting his pockets, like he'd find a stash of airport candy in one of them.

I croaked laughter. "Guess so, if you're calling me Joanie. Look, I'll be fine." In a show of bravado, I pushed up.

My arms collapsed and I fell down again. Gary pulled his shirt off—he was wearing a T-shirt beneath it, as perhaps only a man of his age would be—and covered me with it. It, like him and me, was wet, but it was very slightly better than being naked and starving. Then he put a hand on my shoulder, eyebrows beetled with real concern. "Seriously, Jo, you look bad."

I lifted a shaking hand to examine it. I did look bad. My skin was drawn over ropy muscles, like I'd been exercising too much and not eating enough. "Shapeshifting," I said after a groggy minute. "I've done it four or five times today. I guess it takes it out of me. Literally. I'm *starving*." I struggled to sit up and struggled just as hard to get into Gary's shirt—plaid cotton, long enough to come to my thighs—and sat there shivering. I'd have been shivering after a dip in the cold water anyway, never mind burning my own body up with magic.

Gary said, "Hah!" triumphantly and withdrew a mashed bag of peanut M&M's from his jeans pocket. I ate them so fast I barely tasted them, and they made no dent in my hunger, but somehow they helped restore my equilibrium. I crawled to the water, hoping my clothes would come zooming by on the current, but they didn't. Instead the sound of rushing water faded beneath what I thought was blood in my ears, then sounded more like wings in the air. Gary scootched over to me and put an arm around my shoulders. Shared body heat was definitely better than freezing on the moat bank by myself. Probably I could warm us both up with healing magic, if I could only focus, but even my glasses had been swept away on the current, so focusing was hard.

The stupid joke made me giggle, and although it remained uncomfortably close to tears, it also made me feel a little better. "Well, look at us. Half-naked and wet on a riverbank. Nobody's going to believe you're not my sugar daddy now."

"Don't tell Mike." There was a grin in Gary's voice, but I thought it might be a sound suggestion anyway.

"I won't. Gary, can you hear them?" I turned my head against his shoulder, then without looking put one hand on top of his head and tucked the other below his feet and whispered, *"See."*

He started with, "Can I see wha—" and drew in a sharp breath that ended the question as power whispered out of me.

I wasn't even using the Sight, and didn't much know what he might be Seeing now, but whatever was coming our way, I wanted us both to be as prepared as we could be. My eyes remained closed, but by then I was certain of what I'd been hearing for a long time now: the beat of a thousand wings. "Can you hear them?" I asked again, but now I was sure he could.

I knew them. I knew all the ravens, all of them in their glossy blue-black feathers, in their wise and wicked eyes, in their prattling beaks and bouncing steps. Mine was foremost, my beloved spirit animal, half again the size of his brethren. But I knew them all: I knew the ancient bird whose wings had turned to white and whose black eyes were patient where all the others were anticipatory. That was Sheila's friend, and I could see in him—See in him—the long stretch of Irish mages he had served over the millennia.

There were the Morrígan's ravens, three of them again, as if the fight at the *Lia Fáil* had never occurred. There was another pair I recognized instinctively as Huginn and Muninn, and then there were dozens, hundreds, thousands of others: Tower Ravens and Quoth The Ravens and trickster ravens and battlefield ravens, and they all, all, all, spun into a madness of birds in the sky, blocking out the misty stars themselves.

The Morrígan came from their darkness.

CHAPTER THIRTY-TWO

She was crystal-hard, vivid against the black mist of birds. Her blue robes were crisp and the tattoos encircling her biceps were sharp and clear, as if new. Her hair was bound in a thick black braid woven with blue, and the sword she carried was so sharp it looked as though it could cut the very air in slices. She stopped about a dozen feet away and sneered, not that I could blame her. I mean, there I sat on the river's edge, weaponless, barefoot, trembling with hunger and wearing a wet plaid cotton shirt. My hair, far from being so thick and long it could be a weapon of its own, was plastered against my skull. I was not exactly the most terrifying sight of the ages, and the Morrígan had seen plenty of ages to be terrified in.

"A Red Cap," I said without getting up. "Sorry, *fear darrig,* right? Werewolves, and the Aileen Trechard." I knew I'd bungled the pronunciation on that one, but it was the best I could do. "The banshee queen, and maybe even Gancanagh, although that one kind of backfired, eh? You sent them all after me, or put them between me and you in one way or another. So it doesn't really matter if I don't look like much, does it? You're already afraid I've got it all over you, and a lot of what's left is posturing. It's okay if you just want to give up now. I'm not going to tell on you, and it might save your life."

I knew there was no real chance she'd agree, but I had to try. My younger self had reminded me that not everything had to end in a fight. Also, while Lugh and Brigid needed avenging, I wasn't a cold-blooded killer. I didn't know how well I would handle facing the Morrígan in a battle to the death when I had to enter that battle not already in a panic for my life.

A third and much more immediate reason was I was freezing my ass off, half-naked, and shaking with hunger. Not, in other words, at the top of my fighting form. Even if I had been, I would still be toast. But none of that mattered, because from where she was standing, it was face down me or face down her master. I was the far easier target.

She came at me in a cloud of black birds. Rushed me, sword a shining line across the ravens, and she swung with all her considerable strength.

Swung, and instead of parting my head from my neck, crashed into my shields. Gary drew in a breath so sharp it sounded like an attack all by itself, but I didn't even move. They were magic shields, solid as my confidence in them, and today, that was legendary.

But it was also a magic sword, and she was, in some distant way, my grandmother.

My shields dented. More than dented: gave way, so her sword's edge bent my skin. But it didn't prick, and I didn't bleed. I did say, "Okay. If that's how it's going to be," and for all that I was cold, wet and probably about to die, my blood started running hotter.

The Morrígan fell back, silent with fury at both her failure to chop off my head and, I suspected, at my blasé response. Nice that being obnoxious was good for something. I got to my feet, wriggled my toes in the grass and tried something I hadn't tried before: asking the Lower World for a boost.

I'd blown out all the lights in Seattle asking for the same in the Middle World, but I was a lot better at this game now. I still didn't expect the warmth that surged from the earth, drying me from toes to head. I certainly didn't expect my clothes to come back, but they did, stompy boots and jeans and T-shirt and sweater and even my leather coat, which still had a ruined sleeve. The Morrígan looked startled, but I figured the Lower World could be affected by perception just like inner gardens. My self-perception was not of someone who went into a fight wearing a plaid shirt and no skivvies.

I shot a glance at Gary, whose shirt had returned to him, and who looked a whole lot warmer and drier, too. I said, "Stay out of it," and he said, "Like hell," and I laughed and turned to face the Morrígan in battle for the second time.

Brigid stood before me instead.

For the space of a breath I was flummoxed, and then I laughed. "If you strike me down I'll become more powerful than you could possibly imagine?"

Brigid looked utterly blank. Humor rolled out of me and I ducked my head in apology. "What are you doing here?" I asked instead. "You were dead."

"The *aos sí* are of the Otherworld, Joanne," Brigid said. "We came from below the human world and we can, if we wish, return to this place in death."

I remembered my fleeting speculation that the body I'd left at Tara would just sink into the earth or otherwise disappear, and blushed. I'd been being a smart-ass, trying to convince myself I hadn't done something reprehensible. It had never occurred to me that I might be right. "You're really from the Lower World," I heard myself say. "You're really not human. I mean, I knew that, I just…wow. I thought it was all demons and monsters down here."

"Nowhere, Siobhán Walkingstick, is all of one thing and nothing of another."

I smiled a little. "Yeah, no, I guess not. I knew that. But you haven't been coming back here when you die, have you?"

"Those of us who could have chosen nothingness over the corruption that has filled our home. Now we have another choice, offered by the Horned God."

"But you're not going with him." That one wasn't a question.

Brigid gave me a small smile in return. "No. Not I. My sister is bound to her master, and cannot take that path. I have served my mistress, and so neither shall I. I am dead, Joanne, and she and I are sides of a coin."

I opened my mouth and shut it again, a chill sweeping me before I could speak. "Are you saying what I think you are?"

"Her strength is my strength," Brigid answered softly. "My weakness is her weakness. She cannot survive without me, and she has killed me even so."

"She was trying to kill *me!*"

"She never could, not in that moment, not in that time. But by trying, by seeking your death on a day that I could accept it instead, she bound me to you, Joanne Walker. You pulled me through time so I might die at your side, in the moment you would most need my strength. I might have done much more," she said, as she'd said earlier. "I might have brought the world toward the light, instead of skipping through, touching down only when fate lay in the balance. But today we bring light together, you and I."

"I have to fight her," I said blankly. "You're the healer, the peacemaker. The hearth and home, not the warrior."

"Just because I do not fight does not mean I cannot fight, Siobhán. I have had so long, in and out of time, to learn. Do they not say what is so fierce as a mother defending her young?"

Brigid had fought at the battle of Knocknaree, Méabh had said. It was the only time she'd been known to fight at all.

Gary had been at Knocknaree.

I never had the chance to ask. Brigid came toward me, and with every step shed her *aos sí* figure, until the mother's fire burned within me, and I once more faced the Morrígan.

She knew. I was sure she *knew,* when she looked at me, what had happened. But there was no sign of it as she roared anger and came at me with lifted blade.

I sidestepped neatly, astonishing us both, and slapped her on the ass with my own magic sword, which surprised her a lot more than it did me. It shouldn't have. She'd seen me draw the sword from nowhere before. Still, apparently it wasn't a trick she expected a second time, because she swung again like my blade didn't even exist.

I flung it up and caught hers against it, reverberations rattling both our arms. There were no sparks: silver didn't spark the way steel did, and we both fought with Nuada's swords. My strength matched hers; I'd expected that back at the beginning, thanks to all my years of working on cars. But my skills had stepped up. I shoved her away, kicked her in the stomach and launched a flurry of attacks that sent her retreating several feet over Tara's soft rolling hills. She broke away and ran several more feet, coming around at me on the left side. Ravens exploded from the air around her, a black flurry to help her attack. I turned toward them, toward her, but I couldn't see a damned thing. Even the Sight was only an eruption of wings and feathers.

It didn't matter. There were shields, and then there was The Shield. The Morrígan's sword slammed into it before she'd even seen it, ravens doing her as much damage as they did me. She bounced back, just like the banshees had done at Tara's border, and gaped at the small round bracer-style shield on my left arm. "C'mon," I said, just a little smug. "Give it another go."

She did. Rage and power and the fear of her master drove her, and I ducked and parried and hit back and swore when she scored blood and felt vicious triumph when I did. We were *fast,* much faster than I could usually move; that was Rattler's gift, maybe, but he hadn't given me the fighting knowledge to go toe to toe with a warrior born. I almost felt sorry for the Morrígan, not because I might win, but because she couldn't imagine that happening.

When she broke away the next time it was to pant, "*How?* You were no match for me, *gwyld*. No match at all."

"Well," I said brightly, "that *was* thousands of years ago." She snarled and I grinned, but my flippancy faded fast. "Your gentler half gave me the gift of her fire, Morrígan."

A sneer marred the Morrígan's features. "Brigid is weak, a healer, a coward. She hasn't the strength to face me."

"Or she did, and she was storing it up against when it counts. She's dead, Morrígan. You killed her, and she's sent the one you were aiming for to finish the fight. I'm the vessel, that's all."

Her bravado faltered for an instant. She was *aos sí,* not a human magic user. I didn't know if she could See, but I knew what fire burned inside me. If the Morrígan's colors were blue and black, colors of cold and dark, then Brigid's were gold and white, shades of heat and light. My own mother had carried some of that gold within her, and if I'd inherited any of it at all, Brigid's burning spirit brought it to the fore. "This is it, you know," I said quietly. "This is pretty much the last chance. You've got a lot to answer for, but you could answer by forsaking your master."

"That would spell my doom."

"Yeah, but I'm going to do that anyway. The cauldron's been destroyed, Morrígan. The time loop is closing. All the hours and days that were bent wrongly to make a shape for you are coming to an end. You're going to die," I said flatly, "but how you die is up to you."

She snarled, "In battle, if I must."

"If that's what you want."

By all rights she should have charged me then. She might even have gotten lucky, because for the first time since the fight began I stopped paying attention to her, and turned all my focus on the magic within me.

Healer's magic. Warrior's magic. Two sides of a coin that couldn't even see the other. I'd been running around the outer edge of that coin for over a year, falling one direction or the other depending on which kind of power I needed.

I reached into that mental image and plucked out the coin.

The sword had always been magic. It had always been able to accept *more* magic, lighting up with my power when I poured it in. It had been my own healing that had struggled against that amalgamation, but not anymore. Power fused, warrior and healer no longer at odds. Ravens settled on my shoulder: Raven on my left, above my heart, and Wings on my right. Something snapped into place behind my heart, a thick pinch. For an instant I thought of my younger self, and bid her a farewell.

Then I lifted my gaze, feeling as though it blazed.

The Morrígan flinched.

I banished the shield made by my talismans and instead came at her with a blade in one hand and a fist full of glowing power in the other. For the first time she retreated in full, almost running, and then running in fact. Running for the *Lia Fáil,* the source of power and the source of taint within Tara. I followed more sedately, confident of Tara's ability to keep the Morrígan within its boundaries. Not that she intended to flee: she got to the screaming stone and gashed her arm open, letting blood splash over the white rock.

"Come! Come now! Your enemy stands at the heart of Tara! Her blood will bind it to you forever! *Come now, my love!*"

I got there before her Master did. Maybe he would never have come at all. I didn't know, nor did I much care. She stood at the stone, wounded forearm pressed against it, even as I walked up to her and whispered, "I really am sorry about this," and thrust my hand *into* her chest, searching for the power I knew lay there.

It burned cold when I found it. Cold like the space between stars, cold like the blizzard I'd struggled through in hunting the wendigo. Cold like something beyond death, because even dead things eventually responded to ambient temperatures. Cold like a power that could lift an extraordinary mortal into something nearly—*nearly*—immortal, and hold it there for millennia on end. Cold so immutable it seemed nothing could affect it.

But I had warmth. The persistence of life, the outrageous chaotic excitement that Áine, Brigid's mistress, embodied. The burn of possibilities, all of the things that Brigid had offered me. Two sides of a coin, the one unable to survive without the other. The Morrígan had been doomed before we even began to fight.

Fire's sources might be frozen and quench the flame, but a thaw always came, in the end.

I made a fist and lifted the ice from within the Morrígan, and it shattered into black dust as I removed it from her chest.

She screamed, and she died, and the *Lia Fáil's* light went out.

CHAPTER THIRTY-THREE

The darkness was tremendous. Even with my sword still lit blue and bright and full of magic, there was nothing in the world but dark. I was a matchstick, not even a candle, just a firecracker popping sparks in the night. Even that light sputtered, my outrageous confidence suddenly cut down to size by the sheer intensity of black.

The silence was even worse. The stone's scream had ended, hacked off as brutally as its light. If the fast-moving moat had whispered with water, it did no longer. My heartbeat echoed in my ears, each thump crisp and clear and clean, the only sound in the world.

Gary, somewhere in the near distance, inhaled to speak. My hand made a hatchet, cutting him off. I did *not* want whatever was out there in the dark—because something was out there, cold and malignant and so very, very angry—I did *not* want that thing's attention brought to my friend. Bad enough to have caught its attention myself. I would not let it notice Gary. So we stood there, he and I, waiting in the failing light of my courage.

Ravens began to call.

A few of them at first, and from far away. Then more, closer, and more again. I'd thought the Morrígan had come on raven wings, but the blackness was filled with them now, their voices shrieking and their scent that of carrion. My blade's blue light glittered on their feathers and reflected in shining black eyes, but could not distinguish between where they ended and the darkness began. My heartbeat was no longer loud enough to be heard over their screams of laughter and rage, and for a hollow moment I wondered if it was even still beating. I had been afraid dozens of times in the past year, but I had never been so cold with it. An hour ago I'd been ready to face the Master, but my confidence and resolution were bottled inside me, frozen by dark and raven calls. He was *in* there, my enemy. Somewhere in the blackness, and I was the only point of light. He could see me, and I could not see him.

The reckless impulse to extinguish the sword flickered through me and almost made me laugh. "Right," I whispered beneath the ravens, "right. Turn off the light so I can't see him coming. Good idea, Jo. Very smart." Mocking myself made me feel ever so slightly better, which in comparison to numb, motion-stealing fear, was a huge improvement.

Claws tightened on my shoulders. A hard squeeze, neither warning nor teasing, but seeking comfort instead. *My* Raven, scared, which I'd never imagined he could be. And on my other shoulder, Wings, his aged feet flexing and loosening. *He* leaned forward, wings spread a few inches, and though when his mouth opened he made no sound, I had the impression he was—not laughing, but spitting. Spitting in the eye of the dark.

Because he had been here before, I realized. He had done this. *He* had faced the Master, even if Raven and I had not, and he'd lived to tell about it. "Yeah," I said, very softly. "Yeah, okay, let's do this thing." I took a step past the *Lia Fáil*. Just one step, but it meant I could move, and that was enough to shore up my faltering confidence. Healing magic started to flow through me more freely, warming the chill, steadying the sick patter of my heart. "Your go-to girl is dead," I whispered to the Master. "It's finally just you and me. How 'bout I get a chance to see your ugly face?"

The thunder of wings ended, and I went cold again. I thought I should be braver, not running hot and cold with passions and panic, but maybe keeping going into the dark when I was terrified was what bravery *was*. My steps drifted left. Heart-side of the body, where the Master had always called to me from. Rattler, still weary, coiled at the base of my skull, waiting for me to need the speed he could offer. I didn't know how to fight amorphous blackness, but hell, I hadn't known how to fight most of what I'd faced. Learning on the job, that's what they called it. I just needed to learn this one last lesson. Rattler's speed wouldn't hurt, nor the ravens on shoulders, nor the touch of Brigid's fire still burning within me. I had my shields, my sword, my magic and I had Gary at my back. I knew I would die to protect him, and that was when my fear fell away.

The Master came to me as an old man, stepping free of the night all bent and broken with age. Thin hair drifted over his shoulders, white against a cloak of raven feathers, and his gaze was mild and blue. Tattoos banded the wasting flesh of his upper arms. He carried a walking stick and wore a shapeless white tunic and no shoes beneath the feathered cloak.

For one stupid moment I thought, *that's it?*

And for that, I had hell to pay.

Power lanced toward me without warning. I mean, he did *nothing,* didn't blink, didn't nod, didn't point his walking stick at me. Blackness just exploded from him, hit me in the sternum and knocked me halfway across Tara. I landed on my back, skidding, and came to rest with my head against a standing stone. My sword was somewhere else. Possibly back next to the *Lia Fáil,* since I thought my hand had opened when I'd been hit. I was going to have to do something about that, because without a weapon I was toast.

This was not a good time to admit, even to myself, that I was toast anyway. I had been stabbed in the gut more than once. The Master's opening shot felt like that, only worse. Like this time I'd been stabbed with a barbed weapon and it was sawing back and forth inside me, black magic leaking ichor into my system. I couldn't cry. I couldn't even breathe. All the air had left me and showed no inclination to come back in. I lifted my head about a quarter of an inch and looked down my body.

There was a gaping hole in my shields, a shattered, magic-oozing mess where cold raw death power had punched through. I tried wheezing out any last air inside me, knowing there was no other way to inhale again, but I couldn't. Not around the ruins of my magic. I had the hideous idea that I had been broken in half, that even if I could inhale again I would find only my shoulders and head could still move. The fear was supported by excruciating pain that stopped somewhere around my sternum. I just couldn't feel anything below that. Luckily, I hurt so much where I *could* feel that I had almost nothing left to be scared with about the rest of it.

One hit. He'd torn me in half with one hit, and I'd thought I'd been ready for him. He was coming my way now, his cold rage in no particular hurry. Gary was back there somewhere and I hoped like hell he was staying out of it like I'd told him to. Not following the death-making beast approaching me.

Oh, God, the Master was angry. I'd thwarted him in the past and now I'd pulled the heart from his favorite creation. His fury rolled through the dark, a palpable thing, and when it reached me again, it grabbed the bleeding wretched wreck of my magic and squeezed. I still couldn't even scream, and the magic, trying frantically to make things better, wouldn't let me pass out. I tried anyway.

The pain disappeared. As quickly as it had come, as profound as it had been, it was gone without a trace. I finally wheezed in a new breath. I could move again, hands and feet and legs and all, everything where it should be and working as well as it was meant to. I clutched my chest and sat up, hardening my shields against what I figured was the inevitable next blow.

It came just as fast as I expected it to, liquid nitrogen cold, freezing the air in my lungs, freezing my brain, my magic, everything. Pain erupted all over again, throbbing through me and leaving me scrambling for any kind of weapon against it. Nothing, I had *nothing,* and a bit late I realized the Master wasn't trying to kill me. I was pretty sure I'd already be dead if he wanted me that way. He was playing with his food, punishing me for being a pain in his ass the past fifteen months.

I took one very brief moment to thank all the makers of the world for a bad guy who liked to get even instead of just getting it over with, and the next time the pain abated, I reached through the distance for my sword.

It jammed, refusing to come to my call. Incoherent with confusion, I screamed. The Master cackled, a proper wicked old man's cackle, and hit me again. I waited it out, which sounds stoic but wasn't, and in the instant's respite between that attack and the next, I looked up.

By the light of my sword, way up there by the *Lia Fáil,* I saw Gary. Gary *with* my sword, finishing burying it hilt-down at an angle, so the Stone of Destiny helped prop it in place. I could not for the life of me imagine what he was doing.

He took a deep breath, visible even at the distance, and glanced my way. Flicked a salute and mouthed, "I love you, doll," and all of a sudden I understood what was happening.

Gary took half a dozen quick steps back, then ran for the sword. *Dove* at it, swan dive, chest open and broad and ready to be impaled.

A banshee's scream cut the world apart.

They came from everywhere, from all directions around Tara. Streaks of white against the dark, disrupting ravens and drowning out their calls with shrieks of their own. They converged on the *Lia Fáil,* diving into it and restoring its light while one, and one alone, came on across the hills and smashed into the Master's spine.

He tumbled as easily as any frail old man might, shock written large across his face in the moment before he hit the earth. The banshee queen continued on, ignoring him in favor of me. She stopped in front of me, between her daughter and the devil, and whispered, "Joanne."

My heart broke into a thousand pieces. We had no time. There were hundreds of things I wanted to say, and I had no time. Sheila MacNamarra, tall and wraithlike in Aibhill's flowing white robes, smiled at me. Sad proud smile, before she nodded once and turned away.

"Girls," my mother said, and the banshees rose from the earth to join her.

Not just join her like fall into ranks, but *join* her. One by one, but inside the space of an instant, they rushed toward her and were absorbed. Her strength visibly increased with each impact, taking her from the death-softened red and gold that was her own aura to a white so brilliant my eyes watered to see her. The Master came to his feet in that light, his aged features raging in harsh relief. He cast away his walking stick, and brought his hands together, gathering power against Sheila in a way he hadn't needed to with me.

And then for the third time, my mother went up against the Master for no other reason than to save my life.

I had never really witnessed a battle of magics before. I couldn't do the things my mother could, not in life or in death. She carried lightning in one hand and fire in the other, and wielded the banshee cry as a weapon of its own. The Master met her with black ice and dampening thunder, but her song, their song, crept under his skin and flailed him just as it might any man. I had been vulnerable to the banshee magic because my mother was part of its voice.

I thought the Master was vulnerable because he had for so long been their master. The magic to strip a man's soul from his body was his, not Aibhill's. He had given it to her to foster her vengeance against a betraying lover, and in exchange had used her for eternity, never imagining a day when a mage in her own right might rip that power away and use it against him.

It took seven lives to defeat him: six times Sheila Mac-Namarra fell, a banshee ghost extinguished, and the seventh was Sheila herself. There were no nets, no magic swords, no spears or cages of any sort. He was weakened by then, and the banshees belonged to the Lower World in a way he and I did not. Sheila dove into him, *into* him, a thread of magic within his chest, and she screamed one last time. Brought his own power to bear against him, and shattered the shell he had made to come here with. Here, the Lower World, a place between my home and his.

He should have stopped me here, I thought as my mother died again, and forever. He should have stopped me here, because if he came through to the Middle World—and he would, he would have to now—he would be one step further removed from his own place of power, and I would be fully at home in mine. He wouldn't wait. He would recoup from today's losses and then come for me. Come for Aidan, and come for Coyote and Billy and Morrison and Gary. For all my friends and the people I loved, and when he did, I would be ready.

Come for Gary. Gary, who had flung himself on my sword and of whom I hadn't thought since. All the cold calm rushed out of me and I scrambled to hands and knees, already running before I had my feet under me. Up and over low rolling hills, nails digging in the earth to give me purchase when I lost balance, all the way to the *Lia Fáil,* where Gary lay like Christ on the cross, arms flung wide and face to the sky.

Unbloodied, breathing and chortling. I tripped over my own feet, collapsed on top of him and started hitting his shoulders as tears streamed down my face. I honestly couldn't talk, my rage and fear and relief so tangled together that even hiccuping sobs were almost more than I could manage. My gut roiled so hard I thought I'd throw up, and almost wished I would. Something had to give, and puking up bile sounded like a necessary release after the ten minutes I'd just had. My body spasmed with shivers, and the fists I thumped against Gary's shoulders were pathetic in their lack of strength.

Gary sat up, pushed me upright, too, and caught my wrists at his shoulders so I'd stop hitting him. I had nothing left to fight him with. I fell forward bonelessly, the top of my head against his chest, and heaved sobs. He stayed quiet a minute or two, waiting for me to pull it together, but I couldn't.

Eventually he murmured, "I know you told me not to do anything like that again, darlin', but you were gettin' your ass kicked. I could see yer ma and the others out there, stuck on the other side of the power circle, and I thought, hey, banshees, they gotta come warn you when you're about to die, right? An' take away the body, maybe, I forget if they do that. So I figured their raison d'être might overrule the power circle and that would get 'em in here. I knew Sheila'd help you then, if she could. So I threw myself on the sword." He chuckled. "Never thought I'd say that and mean it literally. Your mom knocked me sideways before goin' after you. Made sure I didn't impale myself. Woman's got a tackle like a linebacker, doll. Must run in the family."

I'd stopped sobbing somewhere during the explanation, and had lifted my head to stare at him with hollow-feeling eyes. His hopeful smile with the last words made me feel like I should smile in return, but I couldn't make it there. I'd run past the end of my resources and then had what was left dragged out and kicked across the lawn. Nothing was left. Gary's expression gentled even further and he stood without letting me go, hugging me against his broad chest. "S'okay, darlin'. It's all gonna be okay. I got a lot to tell you, y'know? A big ol' adventure, and also that fight at Knocknaree."

A laugh burst out and died again just as fast. "If your St. Patrick's Day weekend was a bigger adventure than fighting at Knocknaree…" I had no idea how to finish that, but at least he'd made me smile.

"There's my girl." Gary kissed the top of my head, took my hand in his and put them both atop the *Lia Fáil*.

We shot up through the top of the world.

CHAPTER THIRTY-FOUR

Wednesday, March 22, 3:14 p.m.

The switchback on Croagh Patrick was every bit as bad the second time as it had been the first. This time, however, I was wearing lightweight tennies, not heavy stompy boots, which helped. It was too warm for the long leather coat I had on, but it had—bizarrely—been whole again when Gary and I returned from the Lower World. I didn't know if killing the Morrígan had undone her most recent magics, or if I'd somehow brought the idea of the coat whole and well back with me and imposed that on the real thing. Whatever the reason, I was so pleased I pretty much hadn't taken the coat off since discovering its wholeness.

I also pretty much hadn't stopped eating since we left the Lower World. I stopped halfway up the switchback and defiantly ate two breakfast bars and the half pint of milk I'd been lugging just for that purpose. Defiantly, because Méabh had forbidden me to eat, last time I'd climbed this mountain. Then I went the rest of the way up, and wasn't surprised to find the mountaintop deserted save one person.

My cousin Caitríona O'Reilly, the Irish Mage. She stood where Méabh had once stood, both hands wrapped loosely around a spear two feet taller than she was. She looked like some odd new version of a Native warrior: pale-skinned, fire-engine-red-haired, wearing a hand-knitted cream sweater two sizes too large and a short black skirt over black leggings and boots as stompy as the ones I often wore. It worked: she exuded a certain confident power as she gazed toward the distant western waters. Her voice, clear and certain, carried back to me: "She was right, you know."

"Was she? About what?" I joined her and offered a breakfast bar. I had two boxes of them with me, and it was nice to share.

Cat took the bar but didn't open it. "About the darkness on the horizon. About the things coming for the daughters of Méabh."

My appetite vanished. I studied the ocean, then shook my head. "I don't see the future unless someone else makes me, I guess. I believe you, but I'm just as happy to not see it looming."

"I hope it stays looming long enough for me to learn my duties." Caitríona sat and I joined her. She opened her breakfast bar and took a bite before saying, "You lied to me, down there."

"Yeah."

She snorted, amused. "You're supposed to apologize."

"Like hell. Gary and I barely made it out. I'm glad I didn't have to worry about you, too. I'm not gonna apologize for that."

She made another sound, less derisive, and we sat together, eating breakfast bars and contemplating the view. "So what happened?" she asked after a while, and although I had no desire at all to revisit the last few minutes in the Lower World—the Otherworld, Brigid had called it—I did, ending with, "You'll need to go to Tara soon, Cat. It's down there, you know."

Caitríona gave me a curious glance and I pulled my knees up, chin resting on them. "Old Tara. The way it was. It's down there in the Lower World, waiting for somebody to lift it up again. It tried following us when we left." I shivered at the recollection. Tara's power was immense, and the Otherworld had been shaken free of the Master's grip. All that power, essentially lost to humanity for eons, was awake again, and ready for a fight.

"You could have done it," Cat said after a judicious pause.

I shook my head. "I think we might be lucky I couldn't have even lifted a finger right then, Cat. I'd been put through the wringer, and I think if I'd been using any kind of active power it might have latched on and followed us back up. This isn't my territory. That's not my decision to make, especially through an exhausted screw-up. It's your decision and job, not mine."

"Should I?"

"Mmm. I dunno. I want to say yes, just because it was so awesome. But it would literally rearrange the landscape. It would raise a river that went underground centuries ago. It would obliterate a chunk of highway. And it would force people to accept that something extraordinary had happened." I thought about that last, then amended, "At least it would for a while. Probably pretty soon they'd mostly think Tara had always been restored. We're good at forgetting, especially awkward things like magic. So don't do anything hasty." Me, advising someone not to be hasty. I laughed, and Cat lifted an eyebrow. I shook my head and repeated, "Just don't be hasty."

"I'm nineteen so I've time." She hesitated, then asked what we'd both been half avoiding. "Will ye stay?"

My phone rang as I started to answer, startling us both into laughter. I patted my pockets until I found it, saying, "I forgot I was even carrying it. Good reception up here," and glanced at the ID as I answered. Unknown caller, so it wasn't Morrison. I had to talk to him before I decided about staying in Ireland, but I'd already as much as promised Caitríona that I would. "Hello?"

"Joanne?"

A woman's voice, stiff with discomfort. It took me a few seconds to place it. Then I got to my feet, staring westward, suddenly feeling like I, too, could see the dark mythic clouds on the horizon. *"Sarah?"*

Sarah Isaac, née Buchanan, my high school best friend and worst enemy, now married to the man who'd fathered my children, exhaled so sharply I moved the phone from my ear for an instant. Caitríona, alerted by my tone, got up while I brought the phone back to my ear, afraid to miss whatever could possibly be forcing Sarah to call. "I got your number from a Captain Morrison at the police department," she said, still stiffly. "I told him I was the FBI agent from the cannibal case in December."

"Sarah, what the hell is wrong? Are you okay? Is Lucas okay?"

"I'm fine. We're fine. We're in North Carolina."

I suddenly felt like a tower of building blocks, like the game where blocks are removed until the tower tumbles. One of my blocks, way down at the base, had just been removed, and it was only a matter of time until I fell.

I didn't say anything. I couldn't say anything. Sarah waited five whole seconds, then said, "It's your Dad, Joanne. He's missing. You need to come home."

★ ★ ★ ★ ★

To be continued in
MOUNTAIN ECHOES
Book Eight of the WALKER PAPERS

Acknowledgments

I dedicated this book to my mom because she was the first person who wanted to know Sheila MacNamarra's story, but the acknowledgments for this book are all about her because I would not have gotten it *written* if she had not been there to rely on as a babysitter. I am utterly and completely in her debt for the hours she put in watching her new grandson, and my readers should appreciate her for it, too.

Also, hats off to my dad, who did the first edit pass on this particular book, and who, as always, caught stuff that nobody else notices. Seriously, have I mentioned how completely awesome my family is? Because they are. Totally awesome. Especially Ted, who keeps right on being the best husband any writer could ask for.

While we're fiddling with the hat, a hat-tip to my other usual suspects: Trent, agent Jenn, editor Matrice and especially the Word Warriors, whose unflagging war room presence makes sitting down at the keyboard every day so much easier. Laura Anne, Mikaela, Robin, you guys in particular: *hearts*.

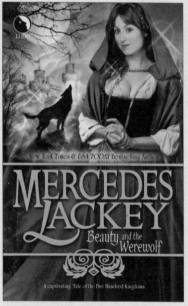

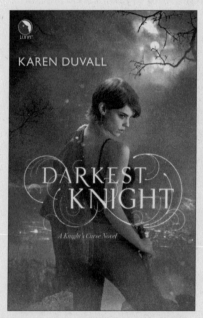

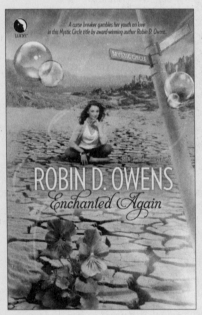